Dark Secrets

Edge Of Evil

Other Books by Shea Berkley

YA Fantasy

The Keepers of Life Trilogy
The Marked Son
The Fallen Prince
The Rising King

Once Upon a Time: The Villains
Queen of All & Enemy Inside
Candy Lane & Sliver of a Soul
Hag & Giant's Way

Adult Paranormal

Dark Secrets: Stone Cold Series
Stone Cold Dead
Stone Cold Past

Dark Secrets: Edge Series
Edge of Evil

Dark Secrets

Edge Of Evil

Shea Berkley

ISBN: 1-942373-02-3
ISBN-13: 978-1-942373-02-5

Cover art and design by Clarissa Yeo

Copyediting by Robin Perini

For Mama.

You've always understood I had a vivid imagination, and you didn't see anything wrong with that.

Maya

CHAPTER ONE

Boston

I wasn't just a left-brained control freak. I was a left-brained control freak sitting in her sad little office on a Monday after the billionth dateless weekend. My life had deteriorated, slipping lower than an ostracized, late-night coroner student. Creepy doesn't even begin to describe their personality structure. I had now sunk to the degrading level of not just undateable, but invisible to the male sex. Humiliating myself now could only take me up a notch. Staring at the website, Heart2Soul, I recognized a certain level of self disgust was necessary to kick-start myself toward change.

Change was good. It's what I told my client, Faith Jennings. She thought breathing someone else's exhaled air would cause her to die from lack of oxygen. When I logically took her through the absurdity of the notion—every elevator would be littered with dead bodies if it were true—and then suggested she use our normally crowded building elevator at the end of our session instead of the stairs, she punctured my leather couch with her nails. Sometimes logic alone isn't enough.

Thinking of Faith made me shiver. I didn't want to be like her, or any of my other clients who had people issues. I gritted my teeth and hit enter.

With one click, I went from lonely to a world that offered instant companionship, and heart2soul.com promised companionship on a *deep* level.

Deep. The opposite of shallow. My teeth tugged on my bottom lip. I was after deep in *sooo* many ways.

Successful at twenty-eight, my psyche should be kicking its feet up and enjoying a sinful serving of chocolate mousse. It wasn't. Somewhere between 10:00 Friday night and 5:00 Monday evening my loneliness had morphed into full-out panic with a side of desperation. I had to castrate that bad boy or I'd be dating a guy who thought farting into his friend's pillow was socially acceptable. And worse? I'd be grateful for the opportunity to date him.

That got my heart seizing. I typed in the required information.

Name: Maya Kelbeck

Education: Ph.D. in Clinical Psychology

Job: Psychotherapist

Interests:

I stared at the blank. Did I have any interests? Everyone has interests.

"Reading." I latched onto that and typed it in.

My fingers stilled. Doubts slapped my brain. Oh my God. Seeing my name and information in black and white…even I didn't want to date me.

I didn't want to do this. I remembered the last time I put my love life in someone else's hands.

My face puckered.

It had been on the night I graduated from Harvard to welcome me into adulthood. My sister had hooked me up with a blind date who was sweet, fit and very attractive, and I made it clear he would get lucky that night. At the end of a lovely evening, he walked me to my door, gave me a lingering kiss, and then handed me a business card.

A business card? How sweet. He wanted to give me his phone number before he forgot. I read the card. It said in delicate black script:

"It's so hard to find the words to say,
It's been fun, but no pay no play."

I thought it was a joke. I had an exceptional ability to judge character. When someone was mentally off, I knew it. This guy had a wacky sense of humor, but he gave off a normal vibe. But then I flipped the card over and there on the back he'd listed his rate by the hour, and a discounted group rate. My humor evaporated. He gave me an innocent smile and tapped his watch. Apparently, my fun meter had just run out.

I couldn't believe it. I was primed for a good time and he wanted me to pay for it? It was humiliating. His defense? Apparently my sister found him at a club serving drinks and paid him to take me out. Well screw that. She deserved her money back.

I totally lost it. I chased him halfway down the block, swinging my purse at his perfect body and cursing him for the idiot he was. If there was justice in this world, every small appendage he owned would rot off, from his nose to his toes, plus the one that, God willing, would give him an STD.

To my sister's dismay, because of that fiasco, from then on I gave men the stink eye and put my energies into building a top-notch client base. On reflection, it hadn't been the wisest move, but it explains why, at seven o'clock at night, I was meeting with yet another new client. Some big shot businessman named Alden Caldwell.

As if thinking about him made him magically appear, he strode in.

I quickly snapped my laptop closed and overheard him

growl into his cell phone. "Don't disappoint me again, Stoval. I won't tolerate any more mistakes."

He ended the call with a swift tap to the screen. Our eyes met and a muscle in his jaw tightened, causing a weird skip in my heartbeat. I'd been walking in a *no man* desert for so long, seeing a perfect specimen put my senses on full alert. The sheen of absolute authority emitting from him brought forth the memory of every classic romantic hero I'd ever read about—successful, articulate, expensively attired and drop-dead gorgeous. A shiver of desire ran through me, catching me off guard.

"I apologize." He tossed his designer coat on the back of a nearby chair and sat across from me. Refined wealth pulsed off him. I couldn't look away if I'd wanted to. I'd never understood what they meant by the *It* factor, but now I did. His presence filled the room.

"That's fine." Why did I sound like a grape was wedged in my windpipe? I cleared my throat. What was wrong with me? He was just a man. A good-looking one, but so what? I was a trained professional. I'd known plenty of handsome men in my life…and I'd never felt anything like this.

I tried to shake off the passionate hum rippling through me, but no amount of logic eased my body's building tension. As I wrestled with my emotions, I felt my cheeks blossom with heat.

The corners of his mouth tipped up ever-so-slightly. Oh God. He knew the sexual appeal he welded.

I looked away and shuffled my paper work. *Get a grip.*

A hint of his earthy cologne wafted near, and my insides swirled as if he'd actually touched me. I was in serious trouble if I didn't find my equilibrium and fast. I took a cleansing breath.

Wow. That was really nice cologne.

I finished straightening the papers and looked up into the most intense brown eyes I'd ever seen. And then I saw it. The bravado hiding a secret truth, a personal pain he could no longer bare alone. Finally. Something I could focus on. It was enough to bring out my usual professional persona. "Mr. Caldwell, how can I help you?"

"It's embarrassing, really." His voice slipped out in deep honeyed tones, nothing like the hard edge he'd used earlier. Yet, as he laced his fingers together, his tightly controlled emotions briefly emerged in a movement here, a throat clearing there.

"I've heard it all," I reassured him. "There is nothing you can say that would shock me."

His eye contact waivered. "I-I have…well, I have a relationship problem."

No wedding ring, so that meant he probably had a girlfriend. Or a boyfriend. Well, of course. A man like him couldn't be single. Not even for a day. "That isn't anything to be embarrassed about. Most couples go through rough times."

His gaze suddenly collided with mine. "We're *not* a couple. I have no interest in her in that way."

I blinked at the ferociousness of his claim. "Oh."

When a client used the word "relationship" it usually meant romantic. I had let his good looks throw me off my game. Now *I* was embarrassed. "I'm sorry. I didn't mean to jump to conclusions." I picked up my pencil and slid my notepad closer. I looked at him attentively. "Please, tell me about your relationship."

He actually blushed. "There's this woman. I guess you'd call her a colleague."

I began my notations—simple sentences that would hopefully root out the problem.

I waited for him to continue. He didn't. I looked up.

His face had transformed into a death mask, stifling all emotion. He'd detached himself from the moment. I waited. Deep-seated issues caused road blocks and here, sitting before me was a man trying desperately to push through that barrier. I knew the moment he'd succeeded. It showed in his eyes. It was chilling.

"I obey her."

It clicked. This was about control. I hid my shock and

scribbled:

Passive issue—submissive toward female colleague.

I placed a question mark beside the comment. My instincts couldn't reconcile the notation with the man in front of me. From what I'd seen, submissiveness was *not* his problem.

I wasn't about to jump to another conclusion. "And you want to stop obeying her?"

"I *have* to stop."

Wants to change unhealthy relationship.

I looked up from my notepad and smiled. "I know it sounds cliché, but admitting there's a problem is a step in the right direction."

He shook his head. "I can't wait for steps. I need to run. I have to stop it. Now!"

Overly strong emotions.

Too strong for what he'd relayed so far, which wasn't much. I had to dig a little deeper to find the root of the problem. "Stop what?"

"Everything."

I leaned forward and said as gently as possible, "If you want my help, you're going to have to be a bit more specific."

Fear. Anxiety. Helplessness. All flowed across his handsome features. All struggled to hide from me. "This isn't easy. It's…"

I waited. Acceptance was a gift I gave my clients. "A step at a time, Mr. Caldwell."

That seemed to shift him into the next gear.

"Whatever she wants, I supply it."

Better, but not good enough. "And what does she want?"

I lowered my gaze to the notepaper. Many people opened up more if they didn't have a pair of eyes boring into theirs. A confessional is a great example. You know the priest is lurking behind that screen, but you can't quite make him out. It frees you to spill it all. Every last sinful deed.

"Food," he snapped. "I bring it to her. I do her laundry.

Take care of her bills. Clean her apartment. I fetch and carry whatever she wants. I *do* whatever she wants."

She sounded like a kept woman. And spoiled. But something in that last sentence held a world of meaning, of disgust. He was holding something back. "Is that all?"

His gaze, so bright and heated with self-loathing, lowered. "Sex. I'm no better than a gigolo to her."

I leaned back, my mind clicking onto every angle of his problem. This sounded more like a romantic relationship gone sour to me. "Do you want to be more?"

His eyes clouded, as if he were somewhere else. "I want to be left alone. I want to be free."

With a woman as demanding as his supposed colleague, this could just be a case of wanting recognition. Of feeling important.

"Everyone wants to feel loved. Appreciated." If that were the case, I'd have to speak with them as a couple. But he'd insisted earlier they weren't involved in a romantic way.

A fierce frown tore at his good looks, making him seem darker, even dangerous. "No," the word exploded from his lips. He took a deep breath and calmed himself. "No," he repeated. "I don't even like her."

My eyebrows arched high. Didn't even like her? What kind of hold did this woman have on him? "Where did you meet?"

"In Europe. A long time ago."

He couldn't be much more than thirty. How long ago could it have been?

"I followed her. I was young and foolish. I left family, friends…everything to be near her. From the beginning, I had to be where she was."

Obsessive tendencies.

"And now?" I asked.

"I don't want anything to do with her. This can't continue. It's killing people."

He was right in that. Unhealthy relationships had a ripple effect. More than the two involved felt its negative energy. His whole office environment was probably a mess.

"I even moved across town, but it hasn't helped. She's in my head, and I just want her to leave me alone."

That he had willingly moved away from the woman was a good sign. It made my job a little easier.

He leaned forward and grabbed the edge of my desk. His knuckles turned white, and I heard the wood crack. "Please. You have to help me. I can't keep living like this."

Alarmed, I stood and rounded my desk. Gently, I pulled his hands off the wood and held them. His skin was warm, almost hot. The appealing scent of his spicy cologne enveloped me. "I'll try, but I can't wave a magic stick and erase the habits of a lifetime. I can give you the tools to make the transition easier, but only you can find the source within yourself to fight these urges."

"I'll do whatever you tell me."

A small prickle of unease slipped under my skin. Something wasn't right. He was a successful man. Used to control, of getting what he wanted. The puzzle wasn't fitting into a recognizable picture. Too many contradictions were present. My jaw tightened, and I forcibly relaxed. "We're a team, Mr. Caldwell. You aren't alone anymore."

A slight shiver ran through him, and he shook his head. "You don't know how strong she is. It's taken me years…" His gaze met mine. "She's unlike anyone. Unforgiving. Cruel. If she knew I was trying to fight her…"

"Together, we're stronger. I promise I will devote whatever resources I have to helping you. Do you believe me?"

A moment passed, as if he were sizing his chances with me. Finally, he nodded and a long ragged sigh escaped. "You have no idea how long I've kept this to myself."

"I'm glad you came to see me today." I glanced at the clock on my desk. "Our time is almost up."

He stood. Tall, dark and sophisticated. Even though he'd told me himself, it was hard to believe he would submit unwillingly to anyone. Under my gaze, he collected his coat from the back of his seat and turned. "When do I see you again?"

"Next week. On your way out, stop by the front desk and make an appointment."

His gaze slammed into mine. "Next week? What do I do if she calls? She will. She does nearly every day." Real panic sliced through his voice.

Time to test the waters. "Tell her no."

His face drained of all color. "I-I can't…"

Too much too soon. I drew near and place my hand on his sleeve. "How about delaying your answer. Count to twenty before you say anything, and then wait a half an hour before you leave on your task."

His body relaxed just a bit. "I can do that."

"Good. Next week, I want you to tell me how it went. Don't give me a false report. Breaking this cycle will only happen if we tell each other the truth."

Color returned to his face. He shrugged on the coat—a black, perfectly tailored wool overcoat by Burberry—and he instantly became the confident man who had walked into my office. He faced me, his eyes piercing. He looked like every woman's dream come true. A real prince of a man, and he turned that façade onto me. "Tell me this, and no lying. Can you help me?"

No matter our appearance, we are all insecure, faulty creatures on the inside. I cocked my head. "I'll push you beyond your comfort zone every week. If you keep up, I have every faith that you can achieve a complete separation from this woman…if that's truly what you want."

"It is. You have no idea how much I want that."

I held out my hand. "Then I'll see you next week."

He cupped my hand in his and squeezed. My heart warmed instantly to him. I predicted he would be free of the woman in less than two months. By then I'd have either embarrassed myself by entering into a wholly unprofessional relationship with him, or I'd be patting myself on the back and going home alone.

I tucked a stray unruly curl back into my professional updo.

Neither thought made me feel good.

After escorting him to the front, I turned back to my office, but Cal, my mentor, motioned me into the break room. "Is that who I think it is?" he whispered.

"I don't know. Who do you think it is?" I whispered back.

Raising one eyebrow, he folded his arms across his chest. "Alden Caldwell, one of the wealthiest men under thirty-five. That's who he is."

So Mr. Caldwell was rich. Whoop-tee-do. Even I knew that. I turned to get an orange and a bottle of water from the fridge. "How nice for him."

"Nice? Your little buckaroo is wiping up the competition with his financial brilliance. He's philanthropic enough. *More* than enough. Maybe he's got something to atone for with all that money he's throwing around."

Cal's gaze honed in on mine. I unscrewed the water bottle cap and took a swig, all the while staring him down. After a moment of arched looks, I said, "Don't ask."

"I didn't."

"You looked."

"I look all the time. What I'm saying is, if he's happy with our work then he'll tell his friends and soon we'll be on the move up."

This from the man who stayed in the university system because money couldn't touch the reward of teaching? I had to laugh. "Do I see dollar signs in your eyes?"

"Multiple," he confessed. "So don't mess this up."

"Mess what up?" Mike Eden, one of the three psychiatrists in our group, asked as he came into the room for a fresh cup of coffee.

"Alden Caldwell. He's seeing Maya."

Mike stopped dead in his tracks. "I don't believe it. He's a billionaire with supermodel tastes. You can't be dating him."

He made that sound so impossible. I'd always thought my mother's Spanish ancestry coincided with my father's Irish slash Czechoslovakian heritage in a pleasing manner. Maybe I was the one deluding myself. My bruised self-confidence naturally took offense. "I can date a billionaire if I want."

"Wait." Mike flashed a cocky smile. "He's a new client, isn't he?"

Now I had to come clean. "Today was our first session. And I'm not dating him. That would be wrong." It would. I had come to terms with that, but that didn't mean I had to be happy about it.

"Damn straight it would. Don't you dare tarnish our perfect record with sloppy work. If we make a good impression, he'll—"

"I don't need a lesson on the domino effect, and don't you ever accuse me of sloppy work. I bust my—"

"Settle down," Cal said, waving his hand in the air. He turned to Mike. "He's Maya's, buddy. He chose her, and I have every confidence she'll set him straight."

"Fine." Mike shrugged his shoulders as if he didn't care. But he did. He had a huge ego. In an attempt to throw me off guard, he lazily swirled a spoon around in his cup. "Listen, Maya. If he displays any serious sociopathic behavior—"

"I know the protocol," I snapped. Playing the helpful colleague role didn't camouflage his greed.

"Okay, okay." He gave my shoulder an awkward squeeze. "Just send him over when you need a second opinion. Alden Caldwell is a once-in-a-lifetime opportunity."

Oh yeah. He was nearly salivating with envy. I shoved his hand from my shoulder and headed for the door. "Thanks for the vote of confidence."

"Relax, Maya," Mike said on the cusp of a smile. "As of now, I'm hands off."

I threw him a departing glare. "I'd like that in writing."

When I entered the safety of my office, I closed the door and a flood of doubt rushed in. Could I handle Alden Caldwell? He was a billionaire who juggled dating supermodels while supposedly being controlled by a jealous, kept woman. Why didn't he mention that? It rankled me that Mike knew more personal information about my client than I did. Apparently scouring the society pages proved helpful. I definitely needed to get my nose out of textbooks and into local gossip columns once in a while.

I checked the clock. Ten minutes before my next appointment. Just enough time to scour the Internet on Mr. Alden Caldwell before I settled in with Alex Quintos and his mother issues.

Maya

CHAPTER TWO

The clock struck nine when I finally walked through my front door. The apartment complex I lived in wasn't high end. It was old in that quaint, drafty, reeks-of-history sort of way, but the architecture was fabulous. It pre-dated the civil war. I would huddle near my hissing, popping radiator during the winter, and wrestle open the windows for a chance breeze in the summer just for the pleasure of living in the old girl. The secrets this building must know. It gave me chills—in a good way.

The polished hardwood floors creaked as I made my way through the apartment, big compared to most with a bedroom, kitchen, bath, living room and office space. It had all the earmarks of a home—sofa, TV, stereo and bookshelves—without actually being one. Though it was where I lived, there were no stains on the Turkish rug, or creases in the designer couch cushions or water spots on the only dishcloth I owned. The place looked brand new—a domestic mask of my life, such as the rational masks my patients portrayed to the world. My home reflected the life I wanted, but didn't have. The truth? My office was my life. This was where I slept.

Only when I entered my bedroom did the scene change. I instantly felt a sense of relief. It was a reflection of me in a house fit for someone else. It was my oasis and tonight was no exception. Yet, if I were truly honest with myself, even in here the illusion lingered.

The bed took up the bulk of the room—an Austrian bed of deep mahogany and heavily ornate. Its regal bearing made me feel like Sleeping Beauty awaiting her prince. An innocent fantasy, except the silk bedding was pure sinful and challenged my need to go beyond the fairy tale I'd created.

Lately, I had become disillusioned by the length of my wait for the man of my dreams. Had my dream man gotten impatient and found another princess to satisfy his needs? Did I now wait expectantly for nothing?

How sad. I looked longingly at my bed. Rich and downy soft, my mattress was the closest I might ever come to a lover's embrace this year. It cradled me to sleep at night and gently woke me in the morning. Richly-colored silks covered its expanse, top to bottom, edge to edge. I sighed as I kicked off my shoes. The bed's decadent looks belied its innocent activity.

My association with Alden Caldwell had shown a light on the lie I was living. I wanted the dream. Man, home and child. And I wanted it badly.

"Oh, that is so pathetic." I would not allow a handsome man to make me feel incomplete. There had to be a whole bunch of women who envied me. Well…at least half a dozen. I could even live with the thought of two. Even one.

Surely there was *one* woman who envied me?

As I slipped into a nightgown—a satin and lace confection from Victoria Secrets—I listened to my answering service; telemarketers, my sister with news of my niece's first visit to the dentist and a hang up. Pretty par for my life. Nothing exciting. I washed my face, brushed my teeth and jumped into bed. The book on personality disorders lay on the bedside table. I should look up dependent personality disorder, but I just couldn't. Not tonight. I'd done an internet search on Alden Caldwell, and I couldn't find a visible problem that tagged him with any definite disorder. That didn't surprise me. Most people with entrenched psychoses were good at hiding their problems. In Mr. Caldwell's case, showing any kind of weakness had the potential to scare off even the most spirited investor.

The clock slid silently past ten o'clock. I reached to turn out the light when the phone rang. I didn't even bother glancing at the caller ID. It had to be family. No one else would call me this late. I picked up the phone. "Hey. What's up?"

"Maya Kelbeck?"

The caller said my name in deep masculine tones. I sat up straight. This wasn't anyone from *my* family. "Yes. Who is this?"

"It's Alden Caldwell."

I yanked my sheet to my chin. "Mr. Caldwell." Sometimes my new patients got a little antsy—it was to be expected—but none of them had ever tracked me to my home. "How did you get my home phone number?" My unlisted number.

"I called your office and it put me in touch with your answering service which put me in touch with one of your associates who's on call tonight and he gave me your number. I know it's irregular, that I shouldn't have called, but I…"

They gave him my home phone number? Great. They wouldn't have done that for any other patient. It was totally unacceptable. A gross slip in professionalism.

Thick silence grew on the other end of the line. I waited for him to finish his sentence. I listened, but the air had gone completely still. I shouldn't encourage him, I should tell him I didn't accept calls at home, but he'd teased my curiosity. "Mr. Caldwell? Are you still there? Is everything okay?"

"She called."

Oh. *Her*. I could feel the anxiety level in those two words—mine and his. "We knew she would."

"I counted."

"That's good."

"I couldn't wait."

This was a major revelation for him. He must have suddenly recognized just how much control he'd given away to this woman. It could either drive him into a deep depression or fuel his desire for freedom.

A harsh bark of male laughter broke the silence. "I failed. I never fail."

My job was to direct him toward freedom. "You counted. That's a success."

"There has to be something more you can do. I can't wait a week. It'll kill me to wait."

Oh great. He was exaggerating his dilemma. He didn't strike me as histrionic when we'd met, but it was still early on in our therapy. "You won't die. I recognize the agony associated with waiting, but—"

"Then please. See me tomorrow."

Finally, I had a handsome, successful, interesting man begging to see me…and he had to be a mental case. The cruel irony did not escape me. I bit my lip. But, if I fixed him, then he'd be a *former* mental case and then… no, I couldn't get involved with a patient.

"I'll pay double your rate. Triple."

A tiny gasp escaped me. It wasn't protocol, but he did sound desperate, and I hated to aggravate his emotional state so soon.

Yeah, right. Suddenly, I felt like a hooker on the corner of 4th and Central weighing the options of a demand for some kinky sex act. And to my disgust, I was actually interested. Money talks. It always does. I sighed, signaling my acceptance of his proposal. "Call my office first thing tomorrow. Somehow, I'll squeeze you in."

"Thank you. Thank you. You have no idea…I…thank you."

I blushed under his effuse gratitude. But this was no time to lose focus. As much as my hormones were thrilled with his attention, I couldn't allow such intimacy. "Mr. Caldwell?"

"Yes?"

I had to be firm—with him and me. "This is my home. I hope you won't make a habit of calling me every evening."

"No. Of course not, but I now have hope because of you." His voice grew soft and I detected a slight quavering. "It's been too long since I've felt that emotion."

How sad. I couldn't stay angry at a man with such a profound sense of gratitude toward me. And wasn't this exactly why I'd entered the hands-on sector of psychology? "You're welcome. Good night, Mr. Caldwell."

"Sweet dreams, Maya." He hung up.

I stared at my phone, a bit bewildered before I hung up. Had he just called me by my first name? That couldn't be good. Maybe he didn't know yet how to address me. I wasn't one to parade my Ph.D. in front or behind my name, but it was clearly stated on the door to the office. Maybe he hadn't noticed. That was ridiculous. Everyone noticed. I shook off the odd feeling. I was being too sensitive, too eager to find fault.

Lying down, I snuggled under my covers and flipped on my side. The phone filled my vision. He just hadn't noticed. It was as simple as that. All would be fine tomorrow.

I pressed another tissue into Adriana Lowry's hand as I walked her out. She wanted so much to be loved, but she had an anger problem, and at times it manifested itself irrationally. Right now, it was directed at her husband and his once beautiful but now mangled car. I firmly guided her toward the reception area. "No more late-night car bashing, okay?"

She blinked back her tears. "I'll try to do better. I promise." She stopped and gave me a big hug. I returned it. "Thank you," she murmured near my ear. "I do love him."

That emotion had a wacky way of expressing itself in some people. "I know you do."

While Adriana proceeded to the front desk, I spied Alden Caldwell lounging in the front room. He looked so out of place in the waiting area. Most new patients were nervous, or embarrassed, but he seemed right at home. He commanded attention, and everyone willingly gave it to him. Even my receptionist couldn't stop staring at him. When Adriana pulled away from the desk, Alden saw me and rose to his feet. He wore jeans, a button down shirt and a brown woolen sports jacket. He had the body of an athlete. Strong and lean.

I motioned him over. He strode past Adriana without a look her way, stopped in front of me and smiled. I smiled back, and way too big for my own good.

Uh-oh. Maybe I *should* pass him onto one of my colleagues.

He was the center of everyone's attention, but he didn't notice. "Are you ready?" he asked.

Absolutely not. I wasn't used to his presence, the sheer maleness of him. I guided him away from the others. "You know, I've been thinking. Maybe you'd be more comfortable with my partner, Dr. Cal Rostik. He's an amazing therapist, multi-published in his field, and has taught me everything I know."

"What?" He truly looked shocked. "You're ditching me? Wait. You can't. I need you. I did my research and your name came up consistently at the top of my list. I'm sure he's good, but you have true talent. You're the best. I want the best. I *need* the best."

Well, then. How could I argue that? "You're sure?" I felt compelled to ask for modesty's sake.

"Since the moment we met. I've never felt so comfortable with another person."

Another blush of pleasure rose to my cheeks. I had to stop that. It was highly unprofessional. I cleared my throat. "All right, then. Let's get started." I motioned him into my office. It was early afternoon and he looked just as good now as he did last night. If I were a lesser woman, I'd melt at his feet.

"If you'll have a seat in the chair by the window." I'd decided we'd try Eye Movement Desensitization Reprocessing, better known as EMDR. It was a therapy designed for people with high levels of anxiety, and after last night's phone call, Mr.

Caldwell certainly fell into that category, I reminded myself.

"What is this?" he asked, seeing the 30" strip of tiny lights sitting on a tripod. "Are you going to interrogate me?" He didn't sound nervous, but something in the way he looked at the set-up made me pause.

"Last night's phone call gave me the impression you wanted to kick start your therapy. Am I wrong?"

"No. You're absolutely not wrong. I want this resolved as soon as possible."

I nodded. "Good. We're going to desensitize your anxiety, your very behavior when you're with…um…" I hesitated. "What is the woman's name?"

"Juliana," he said, genuine nervousness cracking his voice.

"It's a perfectly safe technique used for behavior modification. When I turn it on, the lights will blink, one after the other, to the end and then back again. It'll do that for several minutes and all you have to do is follow the lights with your eyes."

"Just follow the lights with my eyes?" He sounded doubtful.

"That's it." The treatment was deceptively simple. The lights would help focus the patient as he relived the moment he first entered the anxiety. Repeating the moment over and over helped patients take back control.

"Sounds too good to be true, but I trust you." He sat in the heavy wooden chair, placed his arms along the armrests and looked up at me. An unexpected grin revealed a dimple slashed deeply into his left cheek. "I'm ready. Let's do it."

God, he was gorgeous. It was hard not to smile back. I blinked a few times before I caught myself staring. What was it about him that made it hard to look away?

I forced myself to turn my attention to the pulse monitor. "Before we begin, close your eyes and visualize a place where you feel safe and happy. It can be anywhere—an island paradise or even your grandmother's kitchen when you were a little boy." I slipped the pulse monitor onto his index finger. The low, soft beep of his heart rate sounded in the room.

He raised an eyebrow at the sound of his pulse, but said

nothing.

I plugged in the lights and set the tripod height at a comfortable eye level. When I was done, I asked, "Do you have something picked out?"

"Yes. My *grand'mère's* cottage."

Grand'mère's Cottage? How very European. "Good. Now when I turn on the lights, I want you to follow them with your eyes. At anytime, if you get nervous or scared, retreat to your safe place."

At the mention of becoming scared, his eyes popped open, and his pulse rose slightly.

"It's just a precaution," I assured him and his pulse slowed.

Going to my desk, I picked up a remote control and pressed a button. The curtains automatically closed. Another button muted the lights. When I was done, the room was awash in a faint golden glow. I returned and noticed his grip on the chair had tightened and his heart rate had picked up. "Relax. Close your eyes and go to your safe place right now."

I knew when he did. Even if I didn't have the monitor on him, I could see it in the drop of his shoulders and the loosening of his fingers on the chair.

"Good." I flicked on the little lights and they flashed along at a sedate speed. "Okay, let's begin. Open your eyes and follow the lights. Back and forth. Back and forth."

From now until it was over, I wouldn't take my eyes off him. I was going to slowly help him focus on the past. This wasn't hypnosis, but a desensitization process, and I knew the first time would be the roughest. Some patients cried uncontrollably. Others became furious. Still others became so afraid they couldn't vocalize what was happening.

"Now I want you to think about your relationship with Juliana. Think about the first time you gave her power over you."

I followed his eye movement, studied his facial features. I stayed alert for stress. I saw time slip away from him, and I saw his encounter with the woman change his features from acceptance to fear. "Alden? Tell me what you see."

He didn't respond. As he went deeper into the memory, his body tensed. The beep of the heart rate monitor rose. His knuckles whitened. His eyes never blinked as they followed the light.

The beep quickened, faster than with anyone I'd ever worked with. I touched his arm. "Alden? Go to your safe place."

He didn't seem to hear me. Suddenly, a low, angry growl rumbled in his chest. His lips curled back in a frightening sneer and the arms of the chair groaned. His muscles bulged. The vein in his neck protruded. Before I could react, the wood snapped and splintered into a dozen pieces beneath him.

Alden

CHAPTER THREE

1150 AD

I awoke in a dark place. The smell of wet earth and urine made me gag. I knew that smell. It held the misery of countless men trapped in a dungeon. I stretched my arms and felt the heaviness of manacles on my wrists and ankles and the cuts and bruises of a well-fought battle. My left shoulder was a mangled mess, and even the cool air that stroked my naked skin couldn't ease its painful heat. What had happened? How had my enemy captured me? And why? They would soon find I was worth nothing to anyone.

Somewhere beyond my line of sight, a door creaked open. Footsteps sounded, breaking the deep silence. A flickering promise of light danced along the entrance to where a flight of stairs had been hiding in the dark. The footsteps grew even louder. The light brighter. I searched for anything I could use as a weapon. I was not afraid to die, but if that were to be my fate, I would gladly take one of my captors with me.

Voices murmured, hushed and tense. After a moment, the

words became clear. "This is a dangerous venture," said a deep masculine voice. "The decision has not been made. He has not turned yet."

Turn? They would find no traitor here. I was loyal to my lord.

"I wish to see him. That is all," a silky female voice pushed against the stale air.

A woman?

"You will be disappointed," the man warned.

"I won't. Do you think he is the first I've seen in bare flesh?"

"Nay," the man sounded subdued, almost ashamed. "I know you have seen many."

"I watched when Father trained you, and you were perfect. This one will be, too."

"Your father is most brave to allow you to train him. It is no simple act, and especially now. He is unpredictable."

They wished to train me to betray my lord? Never. Anger flushed my skin. My arms bulged against the chains holding me in place. I could feel a bestial growl grow in my throat.

Their footsteps faltered. "Listen, Jakubek." A note of thrill laced her voice. "He is awake."

"Please," the man begged. "Let me take you back. Wait until the decision is made."

"My father trusts me and my ability." There was no mistaking the authority in her voice. She would have her way. "Not another word from you unless it is to accept my bidding."

"Yes, my lady."

The pair appeared at the base of the stairs. The torch held them in a pool of light. She was dressed in a midnight blue gown fitted to every curve of her body; sweet beauty descending into hell to tease the wretched. The hue emphasized the darkness of her hair and the paleness of her skin. She was perfect. In every way an exquisite jewel. I found my anger subsiding.

"There now. See, Jakubek? He recognizes me. There is

nothing to fear."

I turned my gaze onto the man. The hair on the back of my neck spiked and the aggression I had felt only a moment before sprang back to life. My muscles seemed to grow thicker, stronger. I pulled against the bonds that held me, and one of the pins securing the chain to its base sprang from its mooring.

My sudden aggression pleased her. "He is as I thought. Better than I thought." She approached me, but my eyes were only on the man.

"Look at me."

I felt compelled to do so, but I fought her request.

"Look at me," she insisted.

My eyes slipped to hers. I pulled against my constraints. I had a deep desire to protect her from the man.

She lifted her hand, hesitantly at first, and then with more purpose. Her fingers swept back my hair, filthy and greasy as it was. I sank into her touch, longing for more. "There," she purred. "See? He is sweet, but fierce. I chose well."

Reason fought against this new instinct. What was I doing allowing this woman to command me like a beaten slave? I pulled back, inch by slow inch, luring her closer to me. And when I was sure of my success, I engulfed her in my arms.

She cried out and the man leapt forward.

"Stop," I growled roughly, not even recognizing my own voice. "I'll squeeze the life from her."

He hesitated. The woman placed her hands on either side of my face, and with an amazing amount of strength, she pulled my head to hers. Eyes glowing silver bright, she hissed in my face, long fangs glittering in the faint light. "Release me."

Startled by the sight, I instantly obeyed and backed away. What manner of woman was she?

The man pulled her to safety and threw a hateful look my way while asking her, "Are you all right?"

"Perfectly fine." Though her eyes told a different story.

"I warned you of his unpredictability. He has not yet turned, therefore, his obedience isn't guaranteed."

The woman's scare turned to anger before my eyes. She

clutched the man's arm and pushed him forward. "Show him, Jakubek. Show him how that bite on his shoulder has determined what he will become."

My fingers slid along my left shoulder to the ridges of the jagged, flesh-ripping marks. What torture had they inflicted on me while I was unconscious?

"My lady," the man murmured, "it is not wise to—"

"Show him," she snapped.

The man turned from her and faced me. I backed away as he stripped to his bare flesh. I didn't understand. He had no marks of horror on him. No future sign of torture I could look forward to. Then, as I watched, his body began to morph into a grotesque shape. I heard muscles stretch and tear and grow, the sound more terrifying than the vision. When he was done, a huge wolf stood by her side.

She raked her hands through his thick fur and smiled at my horrified face. "This is your future. You will obey me. And if you don't, I'll castrate you and give you to the wardens as a guard dog."

My eyes flickered from the beast before me to my shoulder. A hot ache filled my mind, pressing the horrible truth to light.

"No!" It couldn't be. The legends of the man/wolf were just that…legends.

She stepped beyond the wolf, her eyes piercing mine. "Come here," she commanded.

I crossed myself and fought the urge to obey. I didn't want to become anything as unholy as that man.

"I will give you one more chance. Come here."

Though I fought it, an instinct to obey pulled me forward, even as I silently cursed her.

"Get down and beg my forgiveness." Her pale finger pointed to the ground at her feet.

My face must have belied my rebellious thoughts. She caressed my cheek like a mother does a child and smiled. "Why do you fight the inevitable? Do it now or my threat will become fact."

No matter how much I didn't want to, I dropped to the

ground. My eyes slanted toward the wolf, and even the creature looked away. The acidic smell of old urine burned my nostrils, staining the skin of my palms and knees.

Through a thick, scratchy throat, I begged, "Please forgive me."

Her leg swung out and caught me under my ribs, hurtling me backwards until I slammed into the wall. I crumpled to the floor and grabbed my ribs, staring up at her in horror. She had the strength of ten men. What manner of monster had I fallen prey to?

Her cold, silver eyes glared at me. "Forgiveness not granted. But maybe soon…if it pleases me"

The beautiful devil turned and walked proudly to the stairs. "Come, Jakubek. Let my new pet recover from his first lesson."

Maya

CHAPTER FOUR

Alden Caldwell, wood splinters stuck to his jeans and very expensive jacket, lay sprawled on my couch, out cold as if a boxer had planted a right hook to his head. I turned to Cal. "I've never seen anything like it. One minute he was fine and the next, he broke the chair and just passed out."

"Strange." Cal took Alden's dangling arm and gently placed it on the couch. He looked so helpless.

Mike burst into my office, followed by my coworkers Eduardo and Sean. "What did I miss?" He came up short when he saw the man on my couch. His face grew pale. "Oh, my God. Is that Alden Caldwell?" He turned accusing eyes on me. "What did you do?"

No way was he going to make me seem like an idiot. "I did my job."

Sean went to the heart monitor as Eduardo shook his head. His dark, curly hair brushed the back of his jacket, and his swarthy skin held a hint of distress. "Maybe you should have let Mike take this case."

They all thought I was incompetent. Each of them saw their careers tumbling when the news of Alden Caldwell's disastrous counseling session hit the news. It wouldn't. It couldn't. God, I hoped not.

"It could have happened to any of us," Sean said, joining our group and holding up the ticket with Alden's heart rate scratched into it. "I've never seen anyone react so strongly to this treatment."

Mike grabbed the paper from him and he and Eduardo plotted out the time. Eduardo whistled. "Impressive."

"I know." My gaze swept my colleagues. Worry etched deep lines into their foreheads, aging them ten years. This wasn't my fault. I was sure of it. I did everything by the book. I wasn't like Mike. I always followed the rules, but this was something totally unexpected. "I've had some odd reactions before, but never anyone passing out."

"Huh," Cal grunted.

We all looked at him. With his hand kneading the back of his neck, he stared at Alden, his lips pursed in thought. "This is the most excitement I've had in years."

His deadpan comment surprised us all into an odd moment of silence. I couldn't believe he was taking this so well. Maybe he didn't understand the ramifications of what just happened. Me being me, I had to seek clarification. "You don't sound very worried, Cal."

He looked straight at me, and smiled, then headed for the door. I blinked. He really was taking this well.

"Cal?" Mike called, finding his voice. He never did lose it for long. "Where're you going?"

"I have a patient in five minutes."

"I have one waiting right now, one with severe social displacement issues that manifest themselves in self mutilation, but he can wait." He jabbed a finger at Alden. "What about him?"

Cal stopped at the door and lifted a graying eyebrow sprouting helter-skelter toward his receding hairline. "What about him?"

"We just can't leave him like this. Maya's negligence could bring on questions as to our expertise. What are we going to do?"

I tossed a heated glare at Mike before turning to Cal. Surely he wouldn't agree.

The older man took a deep breath and then shrugged. "That is a good question, Michael. Ask Maya. He's her patient."

I blinked. Had I heard him correctly?

"You can't be serious!" Mike's cheeks flared pink and a trickle of sweat rolled past his sideburns. He pointed to Alden as if to draw the aging therapist's attention to something he'd obviously missed. "H-he passed out. Under her care."

The three psychiatrists looked at Cal, disbelief worn on their usually unreadable faces. I hadn't done anything wrong, but even I was a bit shocked by Cal's attitude. This situation was a potential time bomb waiting to explode. Everything we'd built now rode on Alden Caldwell's good graces. What if he was no longer amicable to my presence? What if he called me before the American Psychotherapy Association Advisory Board?

Nausea gripped my stomach. I placed my hand over my belly, praying I wouldn't embarrass myself further.

"When he wakes, if he doesn't have a problem with Maya continuing his care, then neither do we. Let's not borrow trouble, shall we? It's just a typical day at the office for us." He opened the door and stepped aside. "Gentlemen. I suggest we leave the doctor with her patient."

Mike's feet did a little dance of hesitance. He looked at me. "Did Mr. Caldwell hit his head?"

"No," I huffed indignantly. "I caught him before he collapsed."

"Cool water. That should wake him." He still hesitated, clearly reluctant to leave. "I don't know, Maya. He's acting more like my kind of patient than yours."

"I won't keep him just to spite you." That was Mike's MO,

not mine. "If I can't help him, I'll send him over."

"Good."

I closed the door behind them and whispered, "Or to Sean. At least he cares more about the man than the money."

"And what about you?"

I whirled around. Alden Caldwell had pushed himself to his elbows. Good Lord, how long had he been awake? Relief at his apparent ability to function rushed through me. "Are you okay?"

His stare was intense. "Do you care more for the man or the money?"

I could understand where he was coming from. Was I just playing with him or could I really help? "I'm so sorry. You had a very bad reaction to the treatment."

He swept his hand through his disheveled hair. "I'm exhausted."

I sent a quick glance toward the destroyed chair. "You're incredibly strong."

"Physically. But mentally?" His face softened and the vulnerability he felt showed. "I fainted. That can't be a good sign."

I had to know what had preceded his blackout. "Can you tell me what happened?"

"I don't remember much."

He didn't want to remember, and I couldn't blame him. Whatever he'd experienced had not been pleasant. But it was my job to find out what and rid him of this demon. "Alden, something in your past has made you the man you are. I can't help you if you aren't willing to confront it."

"Say it again."

He had an oddly longing, almost Byronic look on his face. I took a step closer. "I can't help you—"

"No," he interrupted me. "My name. I like the way you say it."

My feet stilled. A pain stabbed against my temples. Was he coming on to me? I could hear it in his voice. See it in his body language. But I had to be imagining it. Once again, I found it nearly impossible to look away. My breath grew shallow, wispy even. A longing so intense washed over me that I had to steady myself against the desk. "You've had a harrowing experience. You're not thinking straight. Let me get you something to drink. I'll be right back."

Like a coward, I ran to the kitchen. Honestly? I was confused. A powerful urge to throw myself at him had overcome me. I couldn't compromise my ethics like that. He had formed an intense attachment to me in a startlingly short period of time, and I couldn't allow it to continue.

Cal entered. "My patient cancelled." He poured himself a cup of coffee and looked over at me. His face crumpled into a caring frown. "You don't look so good."

"I had a patient collapse on me. Of course I look like hell." I filled a glass with water and sighed. "Mr. Caldwell is awake."

"That's great."

I wished I shared his enthusiasm.

"Listen, Maya," he said in that annoying *Father Knows Best* voice he'd developed from watching too much 1950's TV as a child. I was pretty sure I wasn't going to like whatever he was about to say.

"I didn't want to say anything in front of the others, but in our litigious society I feel compelled to warn you that Mr. Caldwell has every right to sue us. We need to avoid that at all costs. Whatever will keep him happy, do it. Okay? At least until I talk to our attorney."

My heart started to pound against my ribs. "Such as?"

"I don't care. Take him home. Fix him a mug of warm milk with a sprinkle of cinnamon on top and tuck him in bed if that's what he wants. Do whatever will keep him from dialing his lawyers."

"Whatever" was a fairly broad word. "How about I just sleep with him, take pictures and then blame his injury on rough sex?" My hand went to my mouth. I hadn't just said that.

He punched my arm playfully. "That's the sacrificial gal I know and love."

Shock pulsed against my ears, deafening me to everything else. "Cal! You aren't seriously suggesting I—"

I saw the teasing glint in his eyes too late. I let out a huge sigh. "Oh. You aren't."

"I don't mean to scare you. I'm just saying, go beyond the usual. Treat him like a VIP. Until we're clear of this, he's like Christ incarnate. All right?"

For Cal to be so benevolent in regards to a patient had warning bells sounding in my head. It was bad enough I might get my license revoked, but I hadn't considered Alden could sue me—and in suing me, the others would suffer. I couldn't let that happen. "Okay."

"That's my gal. Don't worry. I don't think he'll want this in the papers anymore than we do. Something tells me he doesn't want anyone to know he's seeing a nut cracker."

I had to agree with him. A successful businessman couldn't afford that kind of publicity. It would send his stocks tumbling with the rumors of leadership instability.

I returned to my office with the glass of ice water and a new sense of focus. I found Alden examining the remnants of the chair. He stood. "I'll be happy to replace it."

The chair was irreplaceable, and I had to tell him before he set out on the impossible venture. "It's an original—from Africa. It was a present from my father."

"I'm game for the challenge."

I could well imagine. He'd been game for what I'd thrown at him today and it had been a disaster. I should be the one apologizing. "You don't need to. This was all my fault. Something went wrong, and trust me, I have every intention of finding out exactly what." I held out the glass, eager for him to see my sincerity.

He took a healthy swallow, his gaze studying me the whole time. When he gave the glass back, his hand shook, and he gave me a grim smile. "I guess it shook me up worse than I thought. I'm exhausted *and* starving."

"What you need is something to eat."

He laughed. "I do. A steak sounds really good."

"A big, rare steak."

He looked taken aback. "Yeah."

I rounded my desk and punched the button for the front desk. "Tessa, would you please cancel all my appointments for this afternoon."

"Sure thing," she chirped.

With that out of the way, I smiled at Alden. "Whichever steak house is hawking the rarest, juiciest bits of meat today, it's on me."

"Are you sure?"

I was completely out of my element, and I wouldn't dwell on how unethical it felt. Cal had pushed me, suggesting without saying that a little sacrifice on my part could go a long way. It did sound noble, plus I had every intention of letting Cal foot the bill. "Of course I'm sure. I'd feel I'd done you a disservice by not feeding you." I turned away and grimaced. That made absolutely no sense. But who cared just so long as he accepted.

"Okay, if you're sure. I usually go to Jake's."

Jake's, the most expensive, BBQ/steakhouse and backdoor concert club in Boston. You wouldn't know by looking at the place, but the owner poured a lot of money into it to get the authentic look of trailer-park-trash chic. Apparently, the upper crust loved to go slumming.

Alden held the door open for me and smiled. "We'll take my car."

"Great." Yeah, great. Alone in a car with this man. I was insane. No, this was Cal's doing. He was insane. Couldn't the old guy see how incredibly sexy this man was? Shoving him in front of me was like shoving a pound of expensive chocolates in my lap and telling me not to sample one.

I cast a quick glance at Alden. I was developing a serious sweet tooth looking at him. I closed my eyes. "No nibbling," I muttered under my breath.

We took the elevator to street level. Not a word passed between us. Every time I attempted to start a conversation, I took one look at him and felt sick.

Once outside, his car sat waiting at the curb. A Mercedes Benz. SLR McLaren. They ran over $450,000, and that covered only the basic package. I should know. Mike had a picture of a sleek, custom-painted McLaren on his desk that he cast lustful eyes on whenever he thought no one was looking. Alden Caldwell wasn't just rich, he was filthy, obscenely, insanely rich. When he asked, he received. A sudden panic seized me. I stopped him at the curb.

"Alden, I have to make this clear. This isn't a date. I think we need to get…well, if this were a date, then I couldn't help you. I mean, I really want to help you. Your case is one of the most interesting ones I've come across in a while…I don't mean interesting as in you're crazy, just interesting. Oh God. I need to shut up, don't I?"

A quick smile stretch across his face. "It's okay. I understand. I completely agree with the ethics of your profession."

"You do?'

"Absolutely. One must feel comfortable—yet not threatened—by one's therapist." He looked at me with those amazing eyes and said, "I feel *very* comfortable with you, Maya."

"Good." I'd just made a complete ass out of myself. He didn't feel this weird attraction at all. Well, that was dandy. Yep. Just plain dandy.

Maya

CHAPTER FIVE

Money sure did move a body up the line. We were seated less than ten minutes after we arrived at Jake's, and in a prime spot overlooking the harbor. The way the waiter brought out a bottle of wine without Alden even ordering it caused my eyebrows to rise.

I placed my fingers over my wine glass. I didn't need any more stimuli when it came to Alden Caldwell. "Come here often?" I asked.

He shrugged. "More often than I should. I have a cook, but Carlos doesn't like to barbecue and sometimes a guy just wants a thick piece of grilled meat to sink his teeth into."

"Sounds…manly."

His deep laugh filled my head. He was the picture of male confidence and my heart constricted with a mixture of pleasure and sadness. I hated not getting to touch what I really wanted. In the car, I'd resigned myself to that fact. Mr. Caldwell had other aspects that were appealing. Namely his wide circle of acquaintances who may need my guidance to help them deal with their stress. Let him stretch out and get cozy. I could handle it.

And he did just that. He extended his legs and laid his arm across the back of the booth, the epitome of a man at home in his surroundings. "If you don't see something on the menu, just ask and they'll get it for you."

That statement was telling. This guy was used to getting exactly what he wanted. How could I not be fascinated by him? I was totally hooked. He was wealthy, confident, assured of his place in his world, yet riddled with self disgust, and haunted by a painful past. My mind just couldn't wrap itself around his dilemma. How could this man be forced to submit? to do anything he didn't want to do? It just didn't make sense.

I must have been frowning because he leaned forward and whispered, "What gives?"

I blinked away my frown. "Pardon me?"

"You're thinking and it doesn't look pleasant."

"Do you want honesty or small talk?"

His demeanor froze into a mask that appeared too fragile for his surroundings. "I thought we agreed on honesty."

"We did, but sometimes the timing isn't optimal."

"You're worried about my mental state?" A note of genuine surprise touched his voice. "I'm fine now. I need you to be honest with me."

In my experience, men usually said that, but never meant it.

"O-kay." Time to find out just how much truth he could handle. "I'm looking at you and wondering how this Juliana woman fits in with the smart, sexy, successful man sitting in front of me."

He visibly relaxed, took a sip of wine and stared warmly at me over the rim. "We all have our foibles. Even you."

"True." I did *not* want to go there, and thankfully, the waiter saved me from having to expound on what were my own unbecoming quirks.

Alden ordered his usual, and I ordered bacon wrapped filet mignon, a side of Cajun grilled shrimp and a baked sweet potato smothered in butter, brown sugar and cinnamon. If I was going to eat at Jake's, I was going to wade gleefully toward a coronary overkill.

When the waiter left, Alden leaned back and assaulted me with a gorgeous smile. "So, you think I'm sexy?"

I nearly choked on a sip of water. Had I really said that? Oh God, I'd become a living test subject for Freud's theories. "I think I read that in some article. Something about Boston's sexiest and most eligible bachelors."

A big, mischievous grin deepened his dimple. "Checking me out, are you?"

"I-um…" I fumbled for an answer.

His smile softened, became more intimate, and I wanted to sigh, right there, like some teenage girl hormoning over the latest heartthrob. He was gorgeous and he knew it. He tilted his head back and squinted up at the ceiling. "Let me see…that article came out a couple of years ago. When I first moved here."

I swatted down my desire and concentrated on acting like an adult. "How long have you been in Boston?"

He dropped his gaze and reached for his wine. "Over five years now."

"You've made a big name for yourself in a short time."

"Some might think so." His gaze shifted to the harbor and a shadow of pain flashed across his face. "In truth, it's been a long battle."

I instinctively touched his hand. "We don't have to talk about it. This isn't a session. I have no business intruding on your past right now."

"It's not that. My life is complicated."

He turned those lost and hurt eyes on me; the pain arched and then evaporated as a plate loaded with a bloody piece of meat landed in front of him and my smaller plate slid in front of me. I was entranced by the way Alden shoved his pain into a compartment and locked the door in the blink of an eye. Entranced and worried. That wasn't normal, or healthy.

He sunk his knife into his meat and brought the bloody cut to his lips, licking the fork with a moan. "I didn't know I was so hungry."

I've never understood the penchant some people had with eating meat that looked like it fell straight off the cow, bypassing even the semblance of cooking. I looked away. When the waiter left, a tiny barb of guilt prodded me to reiterate, "Like I said, you don't have to tell me anything. Not now. Not ever."

He hesitated. The need to share and the need to suppress unpleasant memories warred within him. All I could do was wait for the outcome. As I cut small bites from my very civilized portion of meat, he came to a decision. "Old money is usually quiet, and very proud. I got tired of being labeled privileged. I know it sounds odd, but I felt like a marble statue in a private garden. People would come and stare and comment on my presence, my looks, even my family bloodline, but they weren't seeing me. They only saw the shadows of the past.

"I love the American work ethic. The way you can start with nothing and end up on the cover of *Forbes*. Europe isn't so easily impressed."

"I thought Europeans find us Americans silly—the instant celebrity of our culture."

"It's refreshing. A man should be measured by what he gives back to the world, not what some relative did twelve generations back.

"That's why, when Juliana decided to move here, I eagerly followed her. I saw my chance for a new beginning. A chance to fight free from the constricting, bloody uptight legacy of my ancestors. I never imagined that in doing so, my longing for freedom would seep into Juliana's and my relationship. But I'm not sorry it happened. I don't want to be her puppet anymore."

I had to ask. "How did it happen?"

"I was young and afraid. I needed someone to show me my place in the world. She was more than willing to teach me, and her methods were like a drug. My whole being rested on her good opinion. It still does. And that terrifies me as much as it angers me."

His eyes pierced me to the bone with their intensity. "If you can't help me, then I'm truly lost. Forever. And frankly, I'd rather be dead than continue living this way."

"Don't say that, Alden. Those are dangerous feelings." Suicidal pronouncements always put me on high alert. My training took over. "Life is a journey with ups and downs. We all face difficulty. Some challenges are harder than others, but they are all temporary, in a constant state of flux. It is apparent you have the skills to—"

"Caldwell."

We jumped apart at the intrusion.

A man in his late twenties, average looking with a scar between his eyebrows, and another crescent shaped one on his left cheek, slapped Alden on the back…but his gaze stayed firmly on me. "What are you doing here?"

Alden's jaw muscles tightened, but his manner was smooth as he placed his napkin neatly by his plate and stood. "Hello, Stovall. I didn't expect to see you here."

"Obviously."

The man's eyes remained latched on me, like that of an inmate who'd just climbed out of solitary confinement. They held a deep, unnatural hunger. Charles Manson had the same look, and the instinct to run rippled through me.

Alden took hold of Stovall's arm and forced him to step away, whispering in his ear like a father would to a disobedient child. Stovall listened, but his gaze never broke from mine. His eyes raked me from head to toe in a languid, disrespectful manner. I quickly looked away and stared out over the water, yet my ears pricked to the nuances in Alden's voice; he sounded irritated, though I couldn't detect any particular word to substantiate the feeling.

Stovall suddenly laughed. "Well, won't she be…pleased. You're definitely moving up in your tastes."

"This is none of your business." The threat in Alden's voice sounded clear even to me, and I whipped my gaze back to the pair.

Alden cast a dark shadow over Stovall. The man's smile became strained as his hand clutched at Alden's fingers gripping his arm. His eyes grew darker, his air less aggressive. Suddenly let free, he winced. "Whatever you say, *Capitaine*." He nodded toward me and left.

I had to suppress a shiver. I got the distinct impression he didn't like Alden and that the feeling was mutual.

Alden sat, and when it became evident he wasn't going to say anything, I realized he didn't have a clue about psychotherapists. We're nosier than a mole grubbing for food. "What was that all about?"

He didn't so much as a blink. "He's an ass. Don't worry about him."

He couldn't be serious. The encounter only made me more curious. "You scared him."

"Then I did it right."

I picked at my food, peeking over at him. "Or wrong, depending on the person."

He threw me a tense glare.

"I'm just saying, the instinct of fight or flight is strong...but sometimes the fight mechanism only waits for the right opportunity. Have you never heard about the Judas affect? You know, give a kiss, then stab 'em in the back? Your *friend* gives off that kind of vibe."

His gaze reluctantly slanted toward where Stovall had disappeared. Hopefully I'd made my point.

We spent the next few minutes eating—me delicately chewing on my filet and he ravaging his blood-soaked steak. He downed a glass of wine in one long, impressive gulp, placed his napkin on the table and glanced at me expectantly. "Ready to go?"

I had half my filet to eat, but I'd lost my appetite. Something in his manner disturbed me. Not the feeling I get when the crazy attitude of Mr. Smith's third personality appeared, but the feeling that I'm not safe. "I…can I go powder my nose?"

"Seriously?"

"No, but would you rather hear me say I have to pee?"

"Can't it wait?"

It couldn't get more embarrassing. "I don't think so."

He looked around as if he were expecting to be attacked at any moment. I wasn't sorry I shared my impressions concerning Stovall, but I didn't mean to make him paranoid.

His eyes snapped back to mine and he frowned. "Fine, but be quick about it."

My jaw tightened at the command. No one talks to me in such a superior voice and gets away with it…but dangit, I really had to go. Frowning, I stood and threw my pristine white napkin on the table. An edge of the cloth dipped onto his plate where the red juices of his steak seeped into the threads. He flicked the napkin off and stood, his manners impeccable despite my show of annoyance. I bit my tongue and muttered, "I'll be just a minute."

I've never peed so fast in my life. His desire to leave infected me. When I reappeared from the bathroom, Alden stood waiting by the entrance. He'd adopted an aggressive stance, shoulders squared, legs apart, arms crossed over his broad chest. He eyed a table where Stovall sat across from a beautiful woman with honey blonde hair, tanned skin and perfectly manicured nails. She reminded me of one of those long legged, spoiled Afghan dogs. I shook my head. It was such a weird image. I didn't even like dogs.

Stovall tried engaging the woman in conversation, but she only had eyes for Alden. Her glossy red lips parted and her long fingers slipped up her arm in a provocative way I'd never witnessed before. Her demeanor oozed, "I'm yours. Come take me, now."

When Alden saw me, he blocked my view of the woman. His warm hand encompassed my upper arm in a firm grip as he steered me to the door. Once outside, he gave a sigh of relief and quickly led me to the car.

"Who was that?" I asked after we'd both buckled our seatbelts.

Ignoring my question, he pulled into traffic. I don't like

being ignored. I stared at him until he answered me with a tight, "Who was who?"

No one was allowed to play that game with me. I was a therapist used to dealing with secretive clients. "Who was that woman you were staring at?"

"No one worth mentioning."

I highly doubted that. "She looked mighty happy to see you."

"When she's in heat, she's happy to see anyone."

My, my but he was testy. "That isn't a very kind thing to say."

"She isn't a very kind woman." He glanced at me, his eyebrows low over his eyes, his jaw held tight. "If you ever meet her, walk away. Hell, run. She's bad news in the biggest way."

The intense timbre of his voice caught my attention. "Was that Juliana?"

"No."

"Then who is she?"

A bitter laugh rushed from his throat. "It's a long story."

As we zipped in and out of traffic, I thought he was done talking, but then he surprised me. What am I saying? He shocked me.

"We had a child. A son."

"You were married?"

"Nothing so respectable. I provided the sperm. She provided the egg. The baby died. Neither of us knows where he's buried. But Juliana does."

"What?" I couldn't have been more shocked.

"Like I said, it's a long story. Maybe one of these days we'll split open that wound and dig around. Sounds fun, huh?"

His whole body had begun to shake. Hard.

I placed a hand on his arm. "It'll be all right."

He laughed, but it sounded more like a sob. "Promise?"

I squeezed his arm. The heat of his emotions and the ridges of his tense muscles filtered through the fabric. The more I delved into Alden Caldwell's history, the more bizarre became his life story.

He was a father without a son. What kind of hole ate into his soul from that experience?

He wanted a promise that everything would turn out right. No one could offer that kind of guarantee. Life had a way of throwing garbage in our path and laughing when we fall face first in the muck. The best I could offer him was hope, and I firmly intended to do so.

Wouldn't you know, my mouth had a voice of its own?

"You bet."

The promise was out. My commitment of a few weeks had suddenly grown into years of therapy. Years of Alden sitting across from me. Great.

My hand still rested on his arm, my fingers starkly pale against the earthy tones of his jacket. I felt connected to him in a way I hadn't expected. I wanted to be near him, couldn't wait to see him again.

A shiver of caution ran through me. What was happening to my staunch code of cool detachment? Where was my iron self control? I had all the warning signs that an unethical relationship was rapidly developing.

I let my hand slide back to my lap. That's better. No problem. I could detach. I could easily handle these odd feelings Alden caused. I was sure of it.

I slid a quick glance at his very masculine profile. My stomach did a weird, little flip.

Uh-oh.

He couldn't drop me off at the office fast enough.

Alden

CHAPTER SIX

After Maya and I parted, a wave of exhaustion swept over me. Would the living nightmare my life had become never end? I went home, sat on my bed and waited for darkness to fall. Something terrible was about to happen. The threat rippled in the air. I needed all my wits to cope, but ever since I had decided to resist Juliana, I'd been afraid to sleep.

The inevitable was happening. My body was shutting down. The darker it grew, the heavier my eyelids became, and without conscious thought, I fell backward, the mattress cosseting me where I landed.

It's my experience that sleep comes to a troubled mind in increments where there's always the hope of pleasant dreams, or at the least, no dreams at all. Those are the two I usually choose between.

But no more.

Maya's therapy awakened a portion of my brain I'd closed off. For good or ill, my memories were determined to replay for my eyes alone. As I sank deeper into sleep, my options grew, or narrowed, depending on one's point of view. No pleasant dreams existed for me; the peace of blank sleep eluded me. Only nightmares surfaced, and the demon that was my past roamed at will within my mind.

The rank odors of the dungeon had burrowed into my skin, my hair, my very breath until I no longer notice the stench. It had happened in an amazingly short time. I crouched, huddled against the corner of my prison like a scared animal. I was indeed frightened. Frightened of the woman who came to visit me every evening; frightened of the humiliation I willingly endured; and frightened of the unholy beast she told me I would become.

My fingers searched my flesh for the mark of the wolf that had ripped into me. I found only the scars of the battles I had fought; an inch wide cut on my back where I'd been skewered by a cowardly enemy; a long puckered slash across my chest given by a rival lord; a puncture wound from an arrow that hit my calf; and multiple, tiny abrasions that marked my hands and forearms due to the life of a soldier. In none of these marks did I find the evidence of ripped flesh. The bite had healed…miraculously so.

The sound of quick footsteps on the stairs caused me to flinch. It was her.

The light from the torch invaded my dark corner. The beauty slowed upon seeing me and smiled. She stopped short of the length of my chains and held out her hand. "Come here, my precious."

I turned my face away. My muscles quivered as I fought to still them. I would not go. I would not obey.

"Don't be so headstrong," she berated. Her voice turned to honey. "Come here. I won't hurt you."

I had heard such promises before. She was a liar. Wicked. Truly evil, but as my mind fought to keep my hate for the woman strong, my body reacted. First one foot slipped forward, and then the other.

"That's my good boy. Come to me."

Hunched, a whimper slipped from my throat as I neared.

"Oh, my sweet one. I'll not hurt you. I promise."

She thought I was afraid of her. I was not. I was afraid of what I had become. Ashamed of this weakness I couldn't fight. I came to the end of my tether and strained to get near her. The iron manacles rubbed against my skin, breaking the capillaries just beneath. Warm blood seeped down my neck, wrists and ankles.

She laughed. "Why do you stay so far away? Come here. Come on," she urged.

I strained harder. I can't explain why I had to do as she commanded, but I did. I needed to fulfill her demand or die trying. I grunted and growled. The cords on my neck rose. My muscles roped and pulled against my bonds. Iron cut into my skin. Blood oozed.

Her laughter rose. Humiliation seeped into my soul and burned. I strained harder. The chains groaned. Suddenly, a series of pops sounded and I was free. Her eyes widened as I rushed forward. I threw my arms outward and crushed her to me as we fell to the stone floor.

I stared down at her, wanting more than anything to rip into her beautiful face. To tear apart the visage that had torn my dignity from me. I lay sprawled atop her, breathing heavily, triumphant in my ability to break free of my bonds.

Her chest rose and fell against mine in deep gasps. Her eyes grew dark. She placed cold hands on either side of my face and drew my head to her chest where my cheek pressed to her soft breasts. With a strong hand, she stroked my hair. "Well done."

My rage vanished. A low, ache rose within me. I didn't understand. I hated her. But I needed her. From someplace I didn't recognize, my voice said, "Whatever you desire, I desire."

"Yes." My vow thrilled her, and it infected me. She brought her hand to my face. Her touch was cool and somehow comforting. "It will be all right. Tonight will see you truly mine."

All my attention centered on her—her voice, her touch, her very being—so when rough hands grabbed me and pulled me to my feet, I yelped in surprise.

Jakubek's harsh features appeared before me. "Go back to your corner, you filthy beast." He pushed me away.

I stumbled back, though I quickly regained my balance. I watched as he touched her. Helped her rise. Whispered into her delicate ear. A low growl crept from me. She smiled over Jakubek's shoulder. "Easy, my pet. You must get ready for your debut. Jakubek will take you to a room and clean you up.

"No fighting," she admonished with a tiny wiggle of her finger. "If you do, I'll be very displeased."

Jakubek and I watched her leave. The sway of her hips and the swish of her skirts, a siren's song to us both. As soon as the door close, I turned on the man. "What is going on?"

He circled me, measuring my skills. "Tonight the beast will be unleashed."

"What beast?"

"You know what I mean. You can feel it pulsing in you, clawing to be free."

Bile rose into my throat. "I am nothing like you."

"You're right. I am far better than you. You may have the lineage she desires, but I never whimpered in the corner like a wounded dog."

We stood toe-to-toe, our breaths mingling with the threat of violence. His eyes burned into mine. I returned his glare. Minutes passed as we studied the other. I could hear his heartbeat; smell the worry that lay just beneath his anger.

I threatened him.

I didn't know why; I didn't care, but his weakness pleased me. Finally, I brought my hands to the manacle resting against my collarbone. "Free me."

He unlocked the irons around my throat, wrists and ankles and stepped back. Looking down his nose at me, he sneered, "You are a passing passion. Her plaything. I have nothing but pity for you."

I looked up from examining my raw flesh. "Then you have nothing to fear. She will be yours again."

"You have it wrong. The only thing I want from her is my freedom. What do I care if she chooses a nobleman's bastard as my replacement?" He turned and growled, "Follow me."

As dutifully as if I had been ordered by my lord, I followed, but not before I kicked the chains toward the wall. The sharp echo of their clang chased me up the stairs.

I jolted from my sleep, my skin damp and my body shaking. The phone rang, again. I stared at it, still fighting the sensations that clung to my dream-clogged mind. I fumbled for the receiver. "Hello?"

The sultry, familiar voice slithered into my ear. "Come to me."

The line went dead. I slowly placed the receiver back on its base. I'd been commanded. I could feel the need rise within me. The want sliced down my nerves as I forced myself to stay still. "One. Two. Three..."

My eyes whipped to the phone. "Four. Five. Six..."

I reached for the receiver and punched in her number. "Seven. Eight. Nine. Ten. Eleven…"

Her voice echoed down the line, pure and perfect. My voice quavered. "Maya? I need you. Now."

Maya

CHAPTER SEVEN

What I wouldn't have done to hear those words from Alden in the heat of passion. But, oh no, that wasn't my lot in life. The man was on a major meltdown. I cared deeply for the welfare of my patients, but Alden was different. I found myself making excuses to go over his case. And truth be told, I was secretly delighted by the order to keep him happy. Cal had made my role in Alden's therapy clear. Do whatever it takes. And that was why I found myself rushing to his side in the dead of night to hold his hand.

Not that I was complaining.

The elevator took me to the top floor of the apartment complex. I couldn't get lost. There was only one door in the long stretch of hallway, and it stood out bright red, with eye-piercing hardware. No chance of me knocking on the wrong door here. He must have been waiting on the other side, because he jerked the panel open in the middle of my second knock and literally yanked me inside.

Being pressed to his naked chest had been another thing I

had visualized in a moment of weakness, though I had refused to let myself dream about it. But here I was, pressed and not particularly eager to pull away.

He was shaking.

That cured my narcissistic desire for a good romp. I disengaged his arms from around me and pulled him to the couch. It was a nice couch, one I'd seen in *House Beautiful* in their issue of things us average people want but will never be able to afford. We sank onto the down-filled cushions, and I studied his face. Dark crescents cupped his eyes, and his pallor had grown sallow. He looked horrible—still better than most men, but not his usual sexy self.

"What's wrong?"

"She called." His fingers contracted and relaxed repeatedly until he clenched them into a tight, white-knuckled fist.

I stroked his arm from elbow to knuckles again and again, willing him to relax. "So you said."

"I have to go. I *need* to go."

His admission pulled at me like a lament. The sorrow in those words nearly killed me. That was it. No more silly fantasies. My empathic nature took hold.

I had to think of a way to calm him. My eyes collided with his chest and I saw a massive scar running from his shoulder to his opposite hip. Other, tinier scars marked him all over. He'd been through some major trauma. The more time I spent with this man, the more I realized I knew nothing about him.

I looked to his eyes. His gaze bounced around the room like a rubber ball gone mad. I took his face between my hands and forced him to look at me. "Alden, you're here. With me. You haven't left. You could have, but you didn't. You stayed until I got here."

His eyes bore into mine, desperate for firm ground in a jungle of quicksand. "I'm here."

"Yes. You're still here."

His gaze brightened, then darkened. "I'm here."

"With me."

I didn't see it coming. I can't even say that if I had I would have stopped him. One moment, we were looking into each other's eyes, and the next, he pressed me into the couch, his lips seared to mine in the most amazing kiss I'd ever had. I should have stopped him. Somewhere in my head, I told myself to push him off, but I couldn't. My body wouldn't obey. It was too intent on feeling. One moment my shirt was on, the next it was flung to the floor. A sweet rush of energy raced under my skin when our torsos touched. My heart nearly burst. I luxuriated in the feel of him. His arms, his shoulders, the tautness of his back. I couldn't get close enough. He stole my very being and I let him. I felt…ravaged and all from one kiss. It lasted a moment…forever. I couldn't think. I just wanted to feel. I wanted him like I had never wanted anyone else.

And then he was gone. I lay seduced on his couch, the apartment door flung wide, and he was gone.

I had no idea what just happened. I lay there stunned. My breathing sounded rough and perverted to my own ears. A cool breeze touched my bare skin. I was sitting in my client's apartment in jeans and a bra and nothing else. What had I just done?

I'd compromised my ethics. I'd kissed my patient. "Oh, God." Snatching my shirt from the floor, I yanked it on. I would have done far more if he hadn't left.

Shaking from head to toe, I pushed myself to my feet and stumbled to the kitchen. I poured myself a glass of water and gargled, desperate to erase the transgression I'd just committed. Water wasn't helping. I could still taste his lips on mine. I opened the refrigerator and pulled out a bottle of white wine. It took me a second to slosh a healthy portion into the glass and repeat the swish, gargle and spit routine a few more times.

It didn't help. I could *still* taste him. Feel him. I closed my eyes and knew exactly where his hands had been. I could feel the kiss deepen, feel my blood rush, my very core flame…

I opened my eyes to find myself panting, bent backward over the counter as if I was actually reliving the kiss. It scared me to death. "Screw this!" I tossed the glass into the sink and heard it shatter. I didn't care.

I ran for the door, but before I got there, I turned, grabbed the bottle of wine and then left without a backward glance. I needed something stronger than the jug of cranberry juice I had in my refrigerator.

I hauled my scared butt into the elevator as fast as I could. Whatever had just happened was well and beyond anything I had ever experienced. It was some kind of weird voodoo thing. Normally I wouldn't believe in that, but right at this moment, I was a believer.

The elevator touched ground level. The doors opened, and there Alden stood, exactly as he had left, shirtless, shoeless, and with his jeans riding low on his hips. He looked amazing. I shook my head. What was wrong with me? The guy was crazy and my body was heating up faster than a fry cook in summer. I backed up.

He dove into the elevator and pounded the close button and then punched the one for his floor. The elevator jumped to life. Turning to me, he asked, "What are you doing here?"

He was acting a little more psychotic than I had expected. "You called me, remember? Listen, I don't get what's going on, but I think you should get a new therapist. Actually, I think you need a psychiatrist."

He took a step closer. "I mean, what are you doing out of the apartment?"

I slowly backed away. Oh crap! I'm stuck on an elevator with an unstable patient. My professors had gone over how to extract oneself from this position without escalating the situation, but my mind was drawing a big, fat blank. "Y-you left."

"I know, but…" He turned and slammed his fist against his floor button again. "Come on. Come on."

He would break the buttons, and then I'd be in serious trouble. I touched his shoulder, gently. Pretend you're in your office, I told myself, safely behind your desk. "What's wrong, Alden? Why are you so upset?"

The elevator came to a stop. Both of us glanced toward the

doors. The light to his floor number pinged off and the doors opened. He grabbed my hand, threw me over his shoulder like a fireman and ran for his apartment. I dropped the wine bottle and watched it roll back into the elevator, the liquid gurgling out onto the carpet. A door crashed in at the end of the corridor near the fire exit just as Alden dashed into his apartment and slammed the door shut. He swung around, grabbed a cross that hung beside the door and pressed it to the lacquered surface. In a husky voice, he quickly whispered something that sounded suspiciously like Latin. When he was done, he tossed the cross to the floor and stared at the door.

"Alden, put me down."

Without taking his eyes off the door, he dropped me to my feet, his fingers digging into my hips. He held me there, staring at the door. I put my hand against his forehead. He felt overly warm. His breath came in deep, ragged gasps. He acted as if he were terrified. "Are you all right?"

He put a finger to my lips, though his eyes remained glued to the door. I looked behind me. The door was firmly closed, but an odd scratching sounded against it. The hair on the back of my neck rose. Something very wrong was going on here. That feeling of danger I'd felt at the restaurant reignited with a vengence.

"Oh, Caldwell?" a playful male voice called from the other side of the door. "I know you're in there. Invite me in."

Alden paled, but his voice rose to penetrate the door. "Not likely."

"Juliana is waiting."

At that pronouncement, Alden's body shuddered. Juliana had sent someone to fetch Alden like a recalcitrant school boy? Unbelievable. I put my hands over his, ready to free myself so I could open the door and kick some sense into the idiot on the other side, but Alden pulled me closer until our bodies touched. He buried his face in my neck, holding onto me as if his life depended on it. I held him, unashamed. It was the right thing to do.

The man on the other side of the door grew angry.

"Caldwell!"

Alden's head snapped up. His jaw muscles jumped, and his nostrils flared.

"She's been patient, but you're pushing her too far. When she calls, you come. That's how it's always been. That's how it'll always be."

What kind of sick game were these people playing? I opened my mouth to tell him off, but Alden covered my mouth with his hand.

His body still shook, but this time it was with anger. "Tell her Stovall is willing, though I doubt he's able. No, wait. He's with Evangeline."

"Really? Juliana won't like that. Evangeline has certainly lowered her standards."

A bitter laugh raked through Alden. "Evangeline has no standards."

"True…"

The voice grew cajoling again. "Come now. You've been summoned. I know you can feel the call. Let go of your stubbornness. Resisting her will only hurt you in the end."

I could feel a deep rumble surge from Alden's chest. "Are you threatening me, Vilmos?"

"Steady, there, big boy. You know I'm not. Juliana won't let anyone touch you but her. You know what? I hope you don't obey. It's been a long time since I've seen her take her pound of flesh from you."

"I'll be sure to get you a front row seat."

"Your kindness almost warms my cold heart. What do you want me to tell her?"

"I have a headache."

The man laughed. "Oh, that'll stir her up. See you soon."

Silence, thick and dark, enveloped the apartment and beyond. Not even the wind dared rattle the windows, or the moon pierce the black sky. After a few moments, Alden let me go. He sighed, and although his muscles were still tense, he stared at me, a quizzical look on his face.

I stared back. "What?"

"I didn't go."

I wasn't exactly sure what had happened here. My brain struggled to fit the events into a logical, reasonable order. Only one thing could I state with a modicum of assurance. One moment he'd been all over me and the next he'd disappeared. I shook my head. "No. You left. Like a teenager late for his curfew, you *ran* out of here."

He pointed at me, a look of pride on his face. "But I came back."

"Why?"

His countenance shadowed. "I saw him. I knew you were up here and I couldn't allow him to see you."

"Why not?"

The question seemed to stump him, and he hesitated. "I had to make sure you were safe."

He swept his hand through his hair, causing the thick waves to shimmer in the dim light of his apartment, and slowly a small smile tugged on his lips. "She called and I didn't go." The smile grew bigger as he stared at me.

I cocked my head. "Why did you answer the phone?"

He looked at me as if I was the one with the problem. "I-I didn't know who it was."

That was absurd. Everyone had caller ID these days. I couldn't help the laugh of disbelief that sounded. "You knew it was her and you answered it anyways. Why?"

His jaw flexed and he looked away, but not before I saw a flash of irritation enter his eyes. "I had to answer it. I just had to do it, okay?"

"Fine. Tomorrow I'm putting your name on every telemarketer's list I can find. That'll keep you from answering your phone."

Disbelief at my comment quickly changed to laughter. "You have a mean streak."

"No I don't. I do what I have to do to create a positive outcome." I sighed and rubbed my forehead. "Honestly, I don't know what to think of all this." The kiss, his run from the apartment, him dragging me back here—and the creepy feeling of danger when that guy showed up. Alden needed to impart a few more details before I could understand any of this. "Who was that guy?"

He obviously didn't want to say, but I wouldn't back down and he saw it. "One of Juliana's men."

That sounded ominous…and archaic. I couldn't control the sarcasm in my voice. "What, does she have an army?"

"I guess you could call it that."

He couldn't be serious. "She has an army."

"Yes." He sounded serious.

Though I wanted to make fun of the idea, his somber look stopped me cold. "I'm being serious."

"So am I. They are people who do what she wants, when she wants."

"Like an entourage."

"No. Like an army, and I'm its *Capitaine*."

I must have looked like an idiot staring at him, my face giving away my thoughts. He'd lost his mind. "You're its leader?"

"Yes." He took hold of my hands and pulled me to the couch—the couch that nearly brought down my career. I didn't want to sit there, but he gave me no choice. I had a moment of deja vu. His chest was still bare and he was still very sexy. He wet his lips and my gaze froze on that spot. His mouth twisted guardedly. "I have to confess something to you."

Why wasn't I surprised? "Confession is good for the soul." I said it automatically, all the while fighting the desire he stirred up in me. I had to stop this. The feelings bombarding me were completely irrational, like my body wasn't my own. If someone told me I was possessed by the spirit of a skanky prostitute, I'd feel relieved. But I was fairly sure I was skank free and acting completely against character. That scared me.

I couldn't help him anymore. I wouldn't compromise my ethics for a quick liplock and hip thrust.

That snapped me out of my covetous thoughts. "Alden. I think it would be best if we stopped seeing—"

"I'm a werewolf."

That got my attention. "A werewolf?"

"Yes. I've lived longer than this country has existed. Juliana is my master. That's why I have to do what she tells me. I don't have a choice. She owns my soul."

I had always insisted on complete honesty with my patients. People placed their trust in me, and to my knowledge, I had never had a patient lie to me. Until now. I stood and faced him, anger and hurt rolling off me. "You're playing me. This is ridiculous. There are no such things as werewolves."

He sat calmly in the face of my anger. "Yes, there are."

I searched his face, his body language, I visually probed him for any speck of a suggestion he was a liar. All I found was a man humiliated by his condition and afraid I would leave.

He was serious.

Perfect. Here sat the sexiest man I'd ever laid eyes on and he suffered from lycanthropy. That was a major psychosis. It manifested itself in bouts of delusions. In a delirious state, many cut themselves and blamed the scars on hunting when in wolf form. My eyes lowered to the multitude of tiny scars on his chest and arms. Yep. That would explain those.

My gaze rose to his face. His eyes were dark, and a shade of deep loneliness throbbed within them. That he believed himself to be a mythical creature with such a violent past tore at my heart. I could almost feel his sorrow, his pain, his need for me to believe him. I couldn't walk away. Not yet.

I sat. "Okay. How long have you been a…werewolf?" I couldn't believe what I was saying, like I was asking him how long he'd attended college.

He let loose a shaky breath. "It was the year 1150. I was a soldier. And a damn good one…one of the best. I'd been sent by my lord to fight a group of rebels on the border between what was then the Duchy of Burgundy and France when Juliana found me. Her pet, Jakubek, killed my horse, and then turned me…into what I am now. I've followed Juliana ever since; I've had no choice. Until now. Until you."

He thought he was over 800 years old? I was speechless.

What did one say to such a confession? After a moment of silence, I used the time-honored phrase all psychotherapists learn, "I see."

I didn't, but hey, it was all I could come up with.

"You believe me, right?" His eagerness to have me on his side wrenched my heart. "You can still help me?"

Oh boy. That was a toughie. I broke eye contact then. I had to. It was hard to stare into his troubled gaze and not say yes. "Let me ask you a question. Has there ever been a…" what did they call themselves? I guessed. "… a lycan who's left his master?"

His tensed. "No. Only by death of one or the other."

"This bond. It sounds metaphysical."

"It appears to be."

It was my turn to let out a shaky breath. I had to be subtle here. "I see. Well, then. That type of obedience might be broken with the right kinds of medications, but the simple techniques I use to break lifelong habits, in your case, multiple centuries of habits, will most likely be ineffectu—"

"Stop it." He got to his feet, frustration etching lines into his handsome face. "You don't believe me. I can tell. You think I'm crazy."

My heart raced at his insistence that he was telling me the truth. "Do you blame me?"

"What will it take to make you believe?"

I could think of only one. "Change into a wolf. Right now."

"That wouldn't be wise."

I snorted. "Oh, that's right. There isn't a full moon."

He squared his shoulders; a look of superiority manifested itself in his mannerism. "I'm a senior lycan. The moon no longer controls my change."

Well, la-de-dah. "Then do it."

"Don't be ridiculous," he said all offended.

"Uh-huh." I couldn't keep the doubt from my voice.

His superior stance crumbled. "I took an oath of allegiance. I can only change when Juliana commands me."

Plainly that had been hard for him to admit. He really

believed he was a werewolf. "Let's say I believe you. What are you like when you're..." I hesitated. That he could be a werewolf was comical. But he looked so sincere.

"Furry?" he supplied. A bitter laugh escaped. "I'm an animal. A predator."

I rose, my face flaming with disbelief. "This *has* to be in your imagination. Look what happened tonight. You left, but you came back. Juliana doesn't have complete control over you. If she did, you wouldn't be here...and you...Can't. Change. Into. A. Werewolf."

He scooped my hands into his. The electricity in his touch pulsed through me. I saw the surprise of it reflected in his eyes. A hunger. Yet unlike the look from Stovall, Alden's had a raw warmth that called to me. He drew me a step closer. "I don't need drugs or a stay in a mental institution. You can help me. I know you can. I'm real. Trust me."

Trust him? Not likely. I was a very practical person. I resisted his pull. "I want to believe you, but there is no scientific data to support your claim. Werewolves aren't real. Only the claim of believing you are a man who can change into a wolf is a scientifically accepted condition."

His eyes reflected the devastation my disbelief caused, and it ripped me up inside. I couldn't leave it at that. My professional attitude softened. "I do believe you feel compelled to obey Juliana. No one can pretend what I saw tonight. You're sick, Alden. And I don't know if I'm the right person to help you."

"You are." His face grew anxious. Desperation filtered into his voice. "When I held you, I felt stronger. I didn't want to go anywhere." He pulled me closer. "And when we kissed? I forgot everything."

Remembering the way I'd abandoned myself to him flashed in my head. I risked a lot in helping this man, but could I refuse him? Our eyes met and held, and I glimpsed the pain lurking behind his.

I placed my hand flat on his stomach, barring any further closeness. "Alden, if I help you, there can't be any more kissing. It's not right."

He pushed a strand of my hair behind my ear. A tender, longing look softened his features. "What about hugging?"

I had to be strong. "Off limits."

He squeezed my fingers. "Hand holding?" The hope in his gaze tore at me. He longed for normal human contact, to connect in a meaningful way. How could I completely reject that need?

A smile pulled at my lips, and I squeezed his fingers back. "Well, maybe in the most dire circumstances, but I'm serious, I won't compromise my ethics. I've already done it once and…"

"You're disappointed in yourself?"

He'd hit the target dead center. "You have no idea."

"Trust me. I know exactly how you feel."

Maya

CHAPTER EIGHT

Three hours. We'd been talking for three hours. It was like watching a dam burst. All the filth and madness from Alden's past poured out of him, and we'd only just started. He had 800 years of unimaginable behavior to acknowledge, confront, and reassess. My brain ached from what he had told me already. I needed a break. I needed advice. He was holding something back, but what worse secret could he have?

I couldn't even hazard a guess.

I stood, stretched and excused myself for a second. I closed the door to Alden's bathroom and locked it. I stared at the door. This whole situation had turned surreal. I was out of my element. Uncertain what to do next, I reached into my pocket, pulled out my cell phone, and pushed Cal's number.

As it rang, I passed the sink and turned on the water before huddling atop the lid of the toilet in Alden's massive bathroom. Marble and high polished exotic wood gleamed everywhere. An exotic brass tub glowed softly in the corner.

This room looked more of a spa than a place to get clean. He even had his own massage table set up with white, fluffy towels and a basket of various oils. You'd think a werewolf would need more specific grooming supplies, like a doggy grooming table and a currier comb. I quickly shut the door, enclosing myself in the toilet area, which was bigger than my kitchen.

"Hello?" answered Cal's groggy voice.

"Cal," I whispered tensely into my phone. "This has gotten totally out of hand."

"Maya? What are you talking about?" He groaned. "What time is it?"

"It's two in the morning. I'm talking about Alden Caldwell. I'm at his apartment and this situation is totally out of control."

"What are you doing in his apartment?" Cal yawned, then asked, "Are you sleeping with him?"

I gasped. "No!"

I wanted to, nearly did, but that wasn't the reason for my call.

"Then I don't see the problem."

Every patient signed a permission statement saying that if we, the doctors, ever feel the need, we can discuss their case with one or more of the other doctors in our clinic. We were a team, and we had been known to approach some cases with that team mentality. It was inescapably clear that Alden needed the team. I didn't decide on this tactic lightly. Cal was my mentor and I trusted him. "You told me to make him happy. I'm making him happy, but then, everything hit the fan. He's completely delusional."

"You called me at 2 am to tell me your client is delusional? Most of our patients are."

"He thinks he's a werewolf."

I heard it. Cal snickered. "All men are wolves now and then."

"This isn't funny. He says he takes people to Juliana, his master, so she can feed. I'm a little concerned with what that implies, but he won't be any more specific."

Heavy silence followed that announcement. I heard him

turn on a light and his bed squeak as if he were sitting up now. "Really? It sounds like he's into some kind of underground society. It isn't unheard of for certain sects of the Gothic movement to delve into blood sharing."

The visual picture he painted gave me the shivers. "Isn't he a little old to participate in that kind of entertainment?"

"Age has nothing to do with this. He'll do anything that supports his delusion. Hold on." He put the phone down. I heard him walk away and a few minutes later, presumably after he had relieved himself, he came back. I could just see him rubbing his bald head, causing the little hair he had left to stand on end. "So, why did you call me?"

Honestly, the man's mind was going. "Alden Caldwell. What should I do?"

"You know what to do. Help him face his delusion. The best way to break that cycle is to take him to the underground society and expose the ruse. Let me warn you, he won't be happy about that, and will go to great lengths to keep you from shaking apart his world. Anything else?"

That was his advice? "You don't sound very concerned about this whole feeding scenario."

"Of course I am. It's a disgusting and dangerous pastime. In the context of behavior, it is about control and submission, though I've seen some who claim it's a mutual expression of their love…the intermingling of blood, taking another's life source into you so that person is a part of you forever. It's rarely violent, but it is a social taboo that certainly appeals to some people." He paused. "None of this is new to you, Maya."

"I know. I guess it's just…"

"Are you afraid you aren't up to the challenge of this case?"

Leave it to Cal to hone in on a person's tone of insecurity. "It's all so odd."

"That it is." He yawned again. "Up until now, all of your cases have dealt more with the allegedly "normal" problems within society, but I think you have grown enough professionally to tackle an unusual one such as this."

"Do you really think so?"

"I wouldn't say it if I didn't believe it. Mr. Caldwell seems like an intelligent man. As soon as he's faced with the impossibility of his condition, I'm sure we'll get to the root of his delusion. Clearly he'll need more therapy. You'll have to address why he slipped into such a bizarre fantasy in the first place, and it wouldn't hurt to schedule an evaluation by one of the boys. With that said, he's all yours, Maya. He's your patient and you need to determine the best course of action to help him. You call the shots."

"My patient. I call the shots." That didn't sound so reassuring.

Cal must have heard my doubt. "You know what? Mr. Caldwell is damn lucky he found you to treat him. If anyone can help him, you can. I'm here for you."

Alden's psychosis was unusual, but not impossible to deal with. Cal certainly didn't think so, and he was the most respected and awarded therapist on the Eastern seaboard. Hearing his quiet confidence in me was exactly what I needed to pull myself together. "Okay. You're right. I can do this." It was as if a huge weight had lifted off me. "Thanks, Cal."

"You're welcome. Don't ever call me this early again," he said and hung up.

I pulled the phone away from my ear and looked at it. So much for being there for me. Cranky old man. I couldn't help but smile.

After turning the phone off, I flushed the toilet out of habit and went to the sink. I splashed my face and cupped my hand for some water. That cleared my head. Glancing into the mirror, I didn't recognize the wide-eyed woman staring back at me. She wasn't neat and professional looking. She looked younger, more hesitant than I had ever seen her. Softer, actually, like all the hard edges had been rubbed away. That couldn't be good.

I finger combed my unruly hair and squared my shoulders. "I *will* find out what's going on, Alden Caldwell. And I will find a way to help you."

That was better. A flash of spirit gleamed from my hazel

eyes, and I gave my image a confident smile. "Your delusion is toast, buddy. And so is Juliana."

Miracles still happened. I was walking around on less than four hours sleep. Usually I racked up nine hours. I know. Pathetic. But I had no life, so I wasn't used to the haze, sort of like an aura, which surrounded everything. The phenomenon was disturbing and frankly, I'd had enough of the bizarre last night.

"Your ten o'clock has been waiting fifteen minutes," Tessa, our efficient office secretary, whispered to me as she handed me a cup of coffee. Her quick gaze took in my riotous hair, partially secured with a hair band, and my body conscious outfit. I'd woken up late and didn't have time to put my hair in the severe style I usually wore. The dress, more pretty than practical with its flared skirt and fitted bodice, was the only thing that didn't need ironing. "Wow, you look different. Wild night?"

If one considered staying up most of the night talking wild…which in Alden's case, I did. We didn't get far. He'd insisted he was a werewolf and I'd insisted—gently—that he wasn't. And every time I'd tried to talk about Juliana, he'd clammed up. Most therapists would have popped two pills and sent him to their rival. Luckily, I wasn't like most therapists. I gave Tessa a faint smile. "It was interesting."

At her quirked brow, I clarified, "Patient crisis."

Her wide mouth twisted wryly, and her petite shoulders encased in a light blue sweater-set took on harder lines. If I didn't think she'd lose her balance in such high heels and tight A-line skirt, I think she would have tapped her foot in annoyance.

"You look positively adorable today," I said, and I meant it. She had style, unlike me. At her continued annoyance, I finally asked, "What's wrong?" As if I didn't know.

"I was hoping you'd found a guy."

Oh, I had found a guy, all right. A big hairy animal of a guy. "Sorry. I'll try not to disappoint you next week."

She went from mother to teenage girl in a second. "If you do, I want details. Meticulous personal details, so file away the memory in the long term portion of your brain. I leave for Maui in," she looked at her watch, "five hours, three minutes and eighteen seconds."

Thoughts of Alden—his hands, his chest, his lips—distracted me and I nodded, absentmindedly. "Good for you." I grabbed my first patient file and headed to my office. "Don't drink too much and have fun."

She threw me a strange look as I passed her, and then I remembered. Tessa was a recovering alcoholic, one of Cal's first patients and a glorious success story.

I waved off my faux pas. "I mean the water." That made it sound as if I thought she were going to some third world country and not America's tropical paradise. I tried again. "You know, too much water, too much sun…just be careful."

Ducking into my office, I closed the door and groaned. I was a complete imbecile. I smacked my forehead against the solid, wood panel twice. "Get a grip, Maya."

"Dr. Kelbeck?"

Today was not starting out well. I slowly turned around to face Courtney Albright's questioning, slightly shocked, expression. My usual, gentle smile turned into an overly-bright one, as if it had been drawn onto my face by a bi-polar clown on a manic day. "Hello, Courtney. If you'll just excuse me for a moment, I've got to refresh my coffee. I'll be right back."

Like a coward, I dashed out of my office and into the break room. I had to pull myself together. I'd known Alden for a total of three days, and I could hardly think of anything or anyone else. My fascination with his psychosis bordered on an obsession. I opened the refrigerator and stared into the yawning, frostbitten compartment.

With a heated sigh, I pushed a cloud of my warm breath all the way to the back. Ice crackled and the smell of two-day-old chicken salad assaulted my nose. I don't know how long I zoned out for as I thought of Alden, but Tessa's snort brought me up straight.

She looked startled to see me, but threw her hand toward the lobby. "I knew this job came with its challenges, but I swear, some of the people you guys attract really creep me out."

Tessa was a trooper and usually didn't let the patients get to her. I closed the fridge. "What are you talking about?"

"This guy. He comes in and asks for an appointment with you for a *friend.* Tonight. It's got to be tonight. I told him you were booked. He says he'll pay extra for a late appointment. I tell him I can get him a late appointment, but not with you. He asks when your last appointment is and that's when I get that feeling you get when you're in an empty parking lot at night, just you, your car and the creepy guy in the shadows." She shivered. "I told him his *friend* could have an appointment with Sean. You were no longer taking new patients. Trust me, you'll thank me later."

How odd. "Did he have a referral?"

"Yeah. But I didn't believe him."

"Why?" I asked, topping off my coffee mug with fresh coffee. "Who was it from?"

"Alden Caldwell."

My breath stilled in my lungs. I knew for a fact Alden hadn't told anyone about seeing a therapist. I forced myself to breathe, to remain calm. "What did this guy look like?"

"Well dressed with average looks, except for the oddest scars. One on his left cheek and another one right b—"

"Between his eyes?"

"Yeah." Tessa blanched. Her calm reserve fell to the wayside. "Oh, no. Do you know him? He wasn't kidding about that whole *friend* thing, was he?"

"Sort of."

"Should I get him back?"

"No." I shook my head as if doing so would shake all the crazy pieces of my disjointed thoughts together. "You did fine."

It took a few more seconds to convince Tessa I meant what I said before I left the break room and headed to my office. What was Stovall doing here? Maybe he'd figured out Alden's secret and was concerned. Surely he knew I couldn't share patient information. But there could be no other explanation. Why else would he want to see me? What really bothered me was putting Stovall in the friend role. From what I saw at lunch the other day, Alden and the guy weren't exactly buddies.

I didn't have time to linger over the mystery. I'd kept my patient waiting far longer than I'd ever allowed in my professional career. Thank God Courtney's problems were passive. She would just smile and laugh, no matter how hurt or upset, and then put down my tardiness as being her fault. I had no idea how she came up with that conclusion, but today I wouldn't argue with her. Shameful, I know.

Lunch slipped by, but since I had started so late, I was pressed to make up time. Dinnertime quickly passed. I did manage to get a mystery meat taco from the supper truck down the street—courtesy of Sean who ordered a tray for the whole team. Sadly, it had become a routine we'd all adopted when staying late.

Dusk, heavy with shadows, filled the sky. If I tilted my chair, I could just make out the last rays of the setting sun. Within a moment it would be night. Another day, another night, and I was still Maya Kelbeck, single woman in the big city. Sure, I had a bead on a guy. He was crazy, but hey, nobody's perfect.

I turned my attention back onto Mr. Brookes. Speaking of imperfection. With this guy, it was always the same. No one treated him right. Every session, he rambled on about his visit with his daughter who hated him—her words, not mine—and how he doesn't understand teenagers—who does?—and how his ex-wife was a vengeful shrew. "I just can't get a decent word out of her. She's poisoned Rosie against me."

He'd had an affair which lasted five years while his wife battled breast cancer, thus the ex-wife's and Rosie's hostility. I leveled a critical eye on him.

He squirmed. "Okay. I made a major misstep. That doesn't mean I didn't love her. I adored my wife. But she turned cold after the chemotherapy and radiation treatments. What's a man supposed to do?"

Was he kidding? His selfishness had ruined not only his life, but his ex-wife's, his daughter's and even the nanny, who he'd eagerly shipped back to the wilds of Peru to be with her family when he found out she was expecting his child.

I fought hard not to lose my trained perspective. Instead of going off on him as he deserved, I calmly suggested, "Why not be sympathetic? Help her through a difficult time? She was scared, and on top of that, adjusting to a new body image. Do you think you could have—"

A rapid, insistent knock came to my door.

That never happened. The rules of the office stated, and I quote, "No one shall disturb a doctor while in a session unless there is a danger to someone losing life or limb," end quote.

Tessa had gone for the day, so it had to be one of the other doctors. All were present, so I could choose from a variety of morons who were most likely to do the offense. The knock sounded again, even more insistent, as if that were possible. I leaned forward and placed my pencil and pad on the desk. "I'm so sorry for the interruption. Let me see what the problem is. I'll be right back."

"You won't charge me for your time away, will you?" Funny how he always begged for more time free of charge.

I smiled, my hand on the doorknob. "Absolutely not."

I opened the door and the face of Cal, wide-eyed and horrified, stared back at me. He leaned close and whispered through pale lips, "A patient. He killed Sean." He looked beyond me to Mr. Brookes and said louder, "There's been a situation. I'm sorry, but everyone needs to evacuate the office. Now."

A rogue patient? That never happened. In all the case studies in all the text books, there were maybe a handful from which we compared warning signs. Violence from patients was always a possibility, though definitely a rarity. It didn't click.

Cal had to be mistaken. "Where is he? Are you sure?"

"Mike sedated him, but not before h-he tore out Sean's throat. With his bare teeth." Cal looked ready to faint and that was saying a lot. He was a Gulf War vet. A Marine.

I put my hand to my own neck. I felt the warmth of my pulse. "Oh God." I swiveled around to Mr. Brookes. He stood, fussing with the line of his jacket as he always did. "Hurry, Mr. Brookes. You have to leave." I turned back to Cal. "Have we called security? The psych ward? 911?"

"Eduardo is doing it now. I think it best if—"

A terrified scream rent the air. Cal and I both turned toward the sound. It came from Sean's office. Suddenly, Mike flew out of the room and hit the opposite wall, cracking the surface from floor to ceiling. His face had frozen in a look of disbelief, his eyes dark and sightless. Blood gushed out of an open neck wound to soak his jacket. Eduardo rushed out of his door still holding the phone, saw Mike and bent over him. It only took a second for his gaze to clash with ours. "He's dead!"

From Sean's room, a man I'd never seen before stumbled out. Handsome, tall, with broad shoulders, unusually pale skin and piercing blue eyes, he glared at Eduardo. "What the hell did he do to me?" He shook his head as if it would shake the tranquilizing affects of the drugs from his system.

Cal's mouth hung agape. "That's impossible. We gave him enough to keep him out for hours."

The sight of Mike's lifeless body galvanized Cal. He yanked me from my room. "Out. Now! Now! NOW!"

The man swung his head toward us, squinting. "Dr. Kelbeck? Is that you?"

I froze at the mention of my name.

The man lurched forward. "What's your hurry, Maya? I came just for you."

Eduardo clutched the man's sleeve. He had a syringe filled with God knew what, ready to jab into the man's arm. One moment Eduardo held the syringe, the next it clattered to the floor as he was lifted by his throat into the air. A loud crack sounded, and the man threw Eduardo to the ground like a forgotten doll.

I screamed. I screamed so loud and so long, I don't remember Mr. Brookes running past me, or Cal holding out his hands and telling the guy everything would be fine. To calm down. Take it easy. It was the sight of the man, his lips red with blood, his shirt rumbled and stained, staggering into Cal; Cal, putting himself between me and danger, forcefully, unmoving; and the man picking him up and tossing him across my office and out the window that finally silenced me. The clash of splintered glass pierced my ears. Cal.

I gasped for air. My pulse raced; my brain had gone numb. This couldn't be happening. This madman couldn't be for real.

The man stumbled toward me. His eyes roamed wildly; his chest heaved with exertion. Or was it excitement at the chaos he had brought?

"Maya." He said my name on a blood tinted tongue. Sean's blood. Mike's blood. Bile rose in my throat at the sight. He reached out a hand, the hand that had killed Eduardo and Cal. "I have a message for you."

Alden

CHAPTER NINE

Four o'clock in the afternoon. I sank gratefully onto the couch. With elbows on my knees, I raked my hands through my hair. How I'd made it this far into the day without falling on my face was a mystery.

I'd stayed awake all night with Maya, listening to her questions—answering some, evading others—and overall trying to convince her I wasn't crazy. Admitting I was a werewolf had been bad enough. No way could I broach the subject of the evilness that was Juliana. Maya would've run from me for sure. And I needed her. More than even she could comprehend.

As we'd sat facing each other on the couch, I strung together innocuous pieces of my life story because I was afraid to go to sleep. I was afraid what memory my dreams would dredge from the dark corners of my mind, those dark secrets I wished to forget. It was with a huge sense of relief when the first blush of dawn tinted the sky. Maya was safe…for now. Without the fear of Vilmos tagging along, I drove her home, and then came straight to work.

Thankfully, my office sprawled across an entire floor consisting of a series of rooms. A conference area, a private office space for me, flanked by several offices for my key employees, an exercise room and a private chamber with all the amenities of home—including a stereo system that, if I so chose to turn it up, would rattle my bones. But not today. After tuning the dial to the classical music station, I stretched out on the couch, exhausted. A body, even one such as mine, can stay awake only so long.

Just a nap. That's all I needed. I set my watch alarm for thirty minutes. Surely I would be safe from deep REM sleep in that allotted time.

I should've known better. No sooner did I close my eyes than my mind instantly tumbled into the abyss of recessed recollections. It brushed away inconsequential, redundant experiences as it searched for the next major event in my long, long life. The memory leapt forward, as if it couldn't wait to be seen in all its painful, humiliating and horrific details.

Cleaned from the stench of the dungeon, I sat in an overstuffed chair in my new clothes, a belted tunic in deep blue—the color of royalty—black braces, and supple leather boots. It felt good to be clean, like I was human again. Even my hair had been trimmed and my nails groomed. When I gazed into the mirror, the horrible wretch that lived in the dungeon, who obeyed like a dog and acted even worse was gone.

Jakubek opened the door and motioned me forward. "It is time."

I sat, staring at him. He had changed into more elaborate dress, making him appear important. If I had to guess, I'd say his age hovered near thirty and seven. He wasn't a handsome man, but his form conveyed an elegance I could not match. I outweighed him by a stone of pure muscle thanks to the rigors of a soldier's life. It wouldn't take much to overpower him.

Then I remembered the beast he had changed into. If I posed a threat, I had no doubt he'd turn into the wolf. Not a pleasant prospect. Yet, if I agreed to this madness, I was damning myself to become just like him. I had to refuse. I would fight against the curse they were thrusting upon me.

As I calculated my next move, he entered and closed the door. He looked uncomfortable. "I know what you're thinking. They all think it. I thought it, and it is pointless to fight. You will turn. No matter where you are or who you are with or what you want, you *will* turn. It is inevitable."

"And if I refuse to go with you?"

"They'll have you killed."

Stubbornly, I stared past his shoulder. Did he think to scare me? I had lived on the edge of death my whole life. My body scarred countless times by the sword. I was a soldier. A man of honor. A good man. I preferred death to being someone's trained hound. "So be it. I sure as hell don't want to be like you."

If pity lived in his body, he quickly snuffed it out. "You don't have a choice." He roughly pulled me to my feet. "I won't let you get in the way of my freedom. As soon as you turn, I will be free. So, get going."

I held my ground. Our eyes locked, and then suddenly his demeanor changed. His voice softened, probing into my head with one simple phrase. "Juliana awaits you."

At the mention of her name, I shivered with longing. My heart sped up; my blood heated at the thought of seeing her. A hollowness only Juliana could fill had grown to an unbearable depth; it overpowered my mind, my conscience and my free will. The terrible wretch from the dungeon resurfaced again, and I hated myself for it.

I fought back. "No."

"She longs to see you. Only you."

Only me. The thought was heady. It grew into an overpowering urge. Despite my mental struggle to resist, I followed Jakubek.

Once out of doors, the cool night air came like a slap to my senses. It seemed like years since I had felt the wind, or heard the creatures of the night snuffle in the undergrowth. I breathed deep, reveling in my last moments of freedom. The soothing scent of jasmine, roses and honeysuckle grew thick, as well as the acrid muskiness of horse dung and hay. I looked around, sniffing the air, but all I could see was an open courtyard.

Jakubek grunted at my bemusement. "Your sense of smell is heightened. So is your ability to run, jump and swim, and once you accept your fate, the power of your body to heal itself will take hold."

The last caught my attention. "I can't be killed?"

He laughed, but it wasn't a pleasant sound. "If only that were true. Silver is deadly to us. Get expertly stabbed with a silver blade and you'll die…slowly and painfully. Lose your head or your heart, and your death will be quicker, but just as final. But, if you manage to avoid those instances, you are indestructible."

Indestructible. Jakubek eyed me, gauging my reaction to the unexpected gift of immortality. Did he think I'd be glad to trade my soul for the hellish existence he was offering? I didn't so much as twitch. I was used to hiding my true feelings from my enemies.

The structure he led me to stood beyond the fortifications of the castle. It sprouted from the earth like a massive molehill. It looked disturbingly like a tomb, an ancient mound of earth where bones rotted and people skirted with respect. Not us. We bent and entered the dark, thin corridor. The smell of mossy soil and sweat and blood grew strong. We made a sharp turn down another, even more cramped, passageway, its gradient easing deeper underground. The muffled sound of voices filtered through the earthen walls. Ahead the corridor brightened and we walked right into the heart of the mound.

Sound exploded in my ears. A bright collision of color assaulted my eyes as I looked up at the various open crypts. Fabric in jewel tones swathed the circular structure, and within each chamber, men and women lounged drinking and eating and laughing with abandon.

The enclosure was overly warm, and at the sound of footsteps, I whipped my head around and saw a small boy trotting after us. Jakubek didn't seem to notice as he led me to the center of the mound.

A pair of manacles lay in the dirt. Though I vowed to stay strong, my heart began to pound. What more would I be subjected to here? Jakubek turned toward me and proceeded to loosen my belt.

I stepped back. "What are you doing?"

"Hold still." Handing my belt to the boy, he proceeded to pull off my tunic. Drops of sweat appeared on my skin. Would he strip me bare? Free of my tunic, my eyes rose to the people, still laughing and drinking, but on the whole, ignoring us.

Jakubek folded the tunic neatly and gave it to the boy. Facing me, he pointed to the ground. "Down."

My gaze collided with his.

His jaw grew tight. "If you do not, I will force you down until your mouth tastes dirt."

"I'd like to see you try."

While he assessed his chances, I surprised him by crouching on my heels. I was no fool. Escape would come. I need only wait for the right opportunity, and I would strike. They would order my release to secure Juliana's safety.

Without a word, Jakubek picked up the manacles and slapped them onto my wrists. The clank of cold, hard iron reverberated within the mound, causing the people to finally take notice. Conversations grew hushed. Bodies pressed forward as Jakubek and the boy backed away.

From across the expanse, Juliana appeared. I'd never seen her look so beautiful. Her pale diaphanous gown floated over a tightly fitted crimson shift, the look innocent and sexual at the same time. I thought I could actually hear the fabric rub against her skin as she walked, touching her in places I would not dare to touch. I yearned to be near her, to hear her voice murmur in my ear, to feel her hands on my skin, her lips on my neck.

How could I want someone I knew to be so cruel? I forced myself to look away and gather the iron chains holding me in place. Something within her gaze imprisoned me. I would not look at her again.

She stood before me, inspecting me like a breeder would a fine stud. My scalp tingled as she swept her hand through my hair. Stopping at my nape, she circled my ear with a slender, cool finger before sliding it over my cheek, past my jaw and down along the pulsing vein in my neck. With only a finger, she guided me to my feet. I could smell the essence of her, that individual scent she carried that I had come to know the moment the dungeon door opened.

She leaned forward, a silky pout on her lips. "Am I so hideous that you cannot look at me?"

It was all I could do to force my eyes away. I couldn't answer. My throat had grown dry. The manacles bit into my flesh and I strained against the iron as a desperate battle for my soul was took place within me. "Am I so dangerous you can only approach me if I am bound?"

"You don't scare me," she said as she circled me, her fingers trailing over my bare torso as she went. "This is for your own protection. Those who fight the change have been known to go crazy. Sadly, they do not survive. You will not be so foolish."

I could only pray for the strength to resist. When she stepped into my view, I quickly looked away. "Release me." It was the first command I had dared to give in a long time.

"Not yet." Her hand skidded down my arm, traversing every dip and hard plane. Suddenly, she stood in front of me. It happened so quickly, I didn't have the chance to look away. Our eyes collided. Her gaze glowed with silver fire while mine became lost in the promise she related. She stepped close and my body quivered with need. "Soon you'll be free, and we will delight ourselves in each other. I promise."

The chains in my hands fell to the ground. I hated myself for what she did to me. Digging deep, I revived the anger, the resentment, I felt for her and gritted my teeth. "I want no part of you."

Her rich throaty laughter enfolded me in a sensual haze. "Is that so? Methinks you are lying." To prove her point, her hand slithered down past my waist and stopped. Triumph blazed in her eyes and she smiled. "Definitely lying."

I pulled away; face red, heart pounding in shame as the crowd above laughed. How had I forgotten their existence? It was as if once she entered, I saw nothing but Juliana. Searing frustration blurred my vision. I bit the inside of my cheek to keep focused. I would not show one ounce of weakness.

Juliana glanced behind her and I followed her gaze high up the dome. A small hole had been carved into the mound. She looked back at me. "It's almost time."

Glancing at Jakubek, she nodded, and backed away, saying, "Take off your shoes and your braces, my pet. I want the world to see what is mine."

I looked away and grit my teeth. My back grew rigid as I fought her command.

Jakubek came up behind me, the boy at his heels. "Do it or she will have you beaten like a dog in front of everyone."

The pain of refusal nearly had me gasping for breath. I began to pant with the exertion of fighting her will. Jakubek snarled in my ear. "Do it or I'll do it for you."

I would not suffer such humiliation. I obeyed, and all too soon, I was bare and handing the remainder of my clothes to Jakubek. As he and the boy backed away, a ripple of ooohs and aahhs floated through the crowd.

"A fine specimen," one man called out.

"More a guard than a pet in my eyes," another man replied.

From the other side of the mound another spoke up. "That only depends on if he lives through the turning."

"Did I not hear he was a soldier?" a woman said. "More than strong enough to survive, I would think, but hardly the type to be submissive. She may end up killing him in the end."

As their voices appraised me, my soul quivered in shame. How had this happened to me? What had I done wrong that I should be subjected to such evil?

A debate as to what type of human made the best pet swelled to full voice when the circle above lit up and a moonbeam struck me full in the face. I cried out as if I'd been burned.

Immediate silence fell.

My skin felt hot. Too tight, as if my muscles had grown too big to fit within its shell. My legs buckled underneath me, bringing me to my hands and knees. When I hit the ground, a small cloud of dirt rose and engulfed my aching body.

Above my pounding heart, I heard Juliana. "Don't fight, my pet. Take hold of it. Feel the power rushing over you, through you. Don't deny yourself what you want."

I would not listen. I would not be subjected to this life, become this creature they wanted me to be. Anger, deep and hot rolled out of my mouth. It felt good on my tongue. As my skin rippled and split, I fought harder.

"Oh ho!" a man's voice called. "He already fights the effects of the moon over him."

A woman's mocking voice cried, "You have your hands full with this one, Juliana, my sweet."

"My advice is to put him down, now" another man said, his voice resonating with authority, and a bevy of his brethren agreed. "Mark my words; this one is no weak-willed dog who'll roll over at your look of displeasure. This one is too stubborn to train."

I wrestled the beast raging within me as it tore at my soul, greedily feeding off my will. I raised my head, my eyes piercing into Juliana's. "Kill me now, for I will not submit."

A look of shock passed over her, and I dropped my head, concentrating on keeping the beast at bay.

The cool touch of Juliana's hand startled me as she placed her fingers on my spine. Her caress, from nape to waist, cooled my skin. Her words uncoiled in my ear, stirring up longings I fought to suppress. "Release the beast that is in you. Claim your new life and be by my side." She tilted my head until our eyes locked. Slowly, she placed a kiss on my burning lips; its sensation tender and sweet and not at all what I expected. She pulled away and whispered, "We will take all the pleasures we want and be satisfied forever. I give you my word, all the weaknesses of your former life will be gone. This is no curse, but a gift I give you."

The human within me hesitated. To be with Juliana forever, to take pleasure with her, to feel no more pain…I groaned. It sounded like heaven.

As my human side faltered, the beast within leapt at the chance to be free, and God help me, I submitted to its will. Pulling away from Juliana, a low, bestial howl rumbled out of my throat and, quicker than even Jakubek could change, my body altered from human to wolf.

Murmurs rose, some worried, some impressed and some, those like me, jealous at the speed of my turning.

Panting from the exertion, my mind sharpened. This transformation was meant to be. I could feel power undulate through me, feel every muscle and fiber of my new body. My other senses heightened even more. It was as if the last stitch of the tapestry had been sewn, creating a sensate image. One I always longed to feel.

Juliana held out her hand and I leaned into it, savoring her touch while I nuzzled her neck.

She stared at me, a smile of pure joy on her face. "My God, you're perfect."

A shadow stood over us. "Perfect until the dog doesn't appeal to you anymore," Jakubek sneered.

She unlocked the manacles and ruffled my fur; I luxuriated in her touch. "He will love me, always. As I will him."

"You're very sure of yourself," he pointed out.

"You just saw what happened. He is special, as I knew he would be." She lifted her face to Jakubek, pinning him with her gaze. "Maybe some pets think pissing all over themselves to do their master's bidding is attractive, but I like mine with a bit more bite in them."

"You always did like more earthy pleasures. He will suit you well."

My ears pricked to Jakubek's anger toward Juliana. The hair

on my back rose and I growled at him, warning him to back off.

Uncertainty flushed his face and he stepped back.

Juliana laughed. "Are your refined tastes offended, Jakubek?" She didn't sound at all upset, but I could hear her anger flowing through her veins.

He inclined his head in respect, though slightly mocking. "Never, my lady."

"You feel the constraints of your servitude, then? Four hundred years is a long time." She patted my head and stood. "I have a solution for you."

He bowed, his anticipation nearly palpable.

The air vibrated with her scent as she cupped Jakubek's cheek and then let her hand fall down his arm and away in a careless caress. My gaze followed her every move. Entranced, I could not look away.

"I think it's time to end your service…permanently."

A tray crashed to the floor and a woman leaned over the balustrade, her face pinched and pale.

"Permanently?" The man's usually placid face cracked. "But, you said—"

"I say a lot of things." She looked at me. "Kill Jakubek."

I swung my head toward the man. Juliana's command slithered through my body. Attack Jakubek. Kill Jakubek. His gaze fixed on Juliana, as if he couldn't believe what she had said. I leapt forward and attacked him before he could change. I knew exactly what to do, thanks to him. As he howled and dug his nails into my flesh, I ripped into his chest. My paws pounded and clawed at his ribs, and when I had broken through, I tore out his heart with one snap of my jaws. The carnage I wrought was over in mere seconds.

With the prize in my mouth, I trotted over to Juliana and lay down, letting the heart roll out of my mouth and into the dirt.

The woman from above had run from the chamber and appeared at the doorway. Without hesitating, she ran toward Jakubek, falling to her knees where she sobbed over his lifeless body.

"No, no, no," the woman moaned. "You said he could go free. We were to be together."

Juliana stared down her nose at the woman. "I kept my promise, Evangeline. He is as free as he shall ever be."

"Noooo."

I rose to sit on my haunches and cocked my head at the woman crying hysterically over Jakubek's body. In this form, I felt no sorrow for what I'd done. I had pleased my mistress and doing her bidding was all I wished to do. But looking at the woman, an unexpected wave of compassion curled through me. She would be beautiful if not for her tearstained face and ragged clothes.

Juliana pulled Evangeline to her feet and shook her until her eyes popped. "I told you not to get attached. But neither of you would listen. I didn't think I had to command you to stay away, but I guess I was wrong. So hear me now. From now on, you will only mate with whom I choose, and no one else. Do you hear me?"

The woman quivered in Juliana's hands. "Yes."

"You will obey me. Say it."

Her eyes slipped past Juliana's to mine. Her look of fear touched the human still lingering within me. But the beast ruled, and the flicker of humanity was quickly suppressed. I turned my back on her, snuffing at the blood drying on my whiskers as I rubbed my paw over them in an attempt to clean myself.

"Say it!"

The woman's gaze snapped back to Juliana. "I will obey you."

Juliana let her go and snapped her fingers. I instinctively knew she wanted me. Standing, I shook myself clean of dirt and trotted over to her side. She slid her fingers into my fur and I leaned against her leg. I couldn't get close enough.

"He wasn't good enough for you, Evangeline. Though his lineage was pure, he was a slave from the beginning and a slave to the very end. Your whelps shall have a nobler sire. Now run back to the castle and prepare my room."

The woman obeyed immediately.

With the excitement over, the tomb began to empty. Juliana bent down and examined the scratch Jakubek had imparted on my chest. She then lifted her glittering silver gaze to mine. "From now until forever, you are only mine." I licked her face and she laughed.

My heart soared. She loved me. She loved me. She loved—

I jerked awake, the image of Jakubek's ravaged body still fresh in my mind, but a more disturbing thought made itself very clear. Juliana knew about Maya. She had to. Even though I felt certain no one knew she'd been in my apartment last night, Evangeline would see to it that Juliana heard about the beautiful woman at the restaurant, and Stovall, ever sniffing at my heels, would get her the information on Maya.

I glanced at the clock. I'd slept through my alarm and night hovered at the edge of the city. In only a few moments darkness would descend to snuff out the light.

My heart thudded loudly in my ears. Maya was in danger. I'd been careless…no, I'd been a *fool* for letting her out of my sight.

I vaulted off of the couch and grabbed my keys. My staff, all unaware of my true nature and the danger they were now in, cast worried glances after me as I dashed through the rooms on my way to the elevator. "Take the rest of the week off," I called. "And I mean it. Go home."

As I waited for the elevator doors to open, my staff of eight gathered around me. "Is everything okay, Mr. Caldwell?" Mary clutched her hands in front of her. As my secretary, she knew something was wrong, considering I wasn't exactly my controlled self lately. Probably thought I'd finally cracked from the stress of running a billion dollar, international business.

"No. Yes." The doors opened, and I dove into the elevator. Turning, I looked at their startled faces. Mary had grown pale, making her look all of her sixty three years. "I've overworked you all. I've overworked me." My eyes pleaded with Mary to understand. She nodded. I could count on her to do what I asked.

I punched the button for ground level and willed the doors to close. "Go on a working vacation…all of you…to the Bahamas." We'd just bought a resort there, though I'd yet to visit it myself. "Use the company credit card, and put the new place through its paces. I don't care how long it takes. And take your families. Let's call this an early Christmas bonus," I said as the doors slowly closed.

Fool. Idiot. My brain had gone into overdrive. Adrenaline rich blood poured through my veins. Why hadn't I thought about this before? I knew why. I was well trained. Juliana would never allow me to walk away without punishing me.

How had I let myself forget? Her favorite mode of discipline involved attacking those closest to her pets.

Maya

CHAPTER TEN

My feet suddenly felt made of lead. Heavy and clumsy, they refused to move. I thought only the girl in a fifties B horror movie froze, a plot device to make it easier for the monster to kill his victim. Apparently not. I was the girl and my monster was a crazed psyche patient who'd killed my teammates in less than eight minutes.

"Don't go," he said, in a drug-laced voice, his pale hand almost touching my arm. "You want to hear the message, don't you?"

The ludicrous nature of the question snapped me out of my paralysis. Just like I'd been taught in self defense class, I lifted my leg and brought my heel down on his instep. His eyes glazed with pain, but I wasn't done yet. With the precision of a girl who took her marching band drills seriously, I slammed my knee high into his testicles. With a sharp intake of breath, he doubled over, clutching his crotch. Without mercy, I grabbed his ears to hold his head still, and rammed my knee into his face. I heard the satisfying sound of bone crunching. He cried out in pain and put a hand to his suddenly bloody face.

He wasn't the only one in pain. Sharp waves of heat ripped through my knee, and I hobbled back. Damn it! But better a broken knee than a broken neck. I ignored the pain, and with as much anger as I could muster, I planted a hard kick in the middle of his chest. He fell back, hit his head on the receptionist granite countertop, and tumbled to the floor with a heavy *thunk*.

He didn't move.

I stood gasping for breath, waiting for him to get up. He didn't.

"Oh, my God!" I blinked. "I did it. I beat the bad guy."

I was alive, but so was he. The thought of leaving my colleagues tore at my heart, but I had to get out of there. Favoring my good leg, I hobbled to the elevator.

My nerves were raw as I stood waiting, imagining the guy would get up at any moment and rush me. From where I stood, I couldn't see him, and I preferred it that way. I punched the elevator button a second and a third time when at the end of the hall, the emergency stairwell door smashed in. I screamed, and then nearly fainted with relief when Alden appeared.

His face had morphed into a mask of pure determination and deadly force. Seeing me, he rushed over, barely giving my attacker a glance. "Are you okay?"

My kick-butt persona broke, and I sagged to the floor. I didn't know why he'd come, but knowing I wasn't alone, that he wouldn't leave me to die, caused my emotions to pour out of me in loud, erratic waves. Alden pulled me into his arms and cradled me, actually lifted me off the floor and held me against his chest. Sobbing, I told him about Sean, about Mike and Eduardo and finally about Cal. "I don't know what happened. I don't understand any of this."

His lips brushed my temple, my forehead, my cheek, and he held me tighter. "I'm sorry. I'm so sorry," was all he said.

The doors to the elevator opened and the police rushed in, guns drawn. Alden held me close, protectively, and after several tense moments in which they made sure neither of us were responsible for the carnage, the police guided us to the waiting area. The calming décor did nothing to ease my mind. Alden placed me in a chair where the cold air of reality hit me. I stared out the windows and into the dark night trying not to think. I longed to be in Alden's arms, and as if he could read my thoughts, he took hold of my hand, anchoring me safely in the storm that whirled around me.

After a half an hour, a man dressed in a suit and a somber attitude approached. Why did detectives wear such dark suits? They reminded me of funeral directors. Right now I wanted someone who looked like my mother, dressed in an apron, leaning her hip against the counter and holding out a plate of homemade cookies and wearing a face of complete understanding.

This guy didn't smile, didn't even looked at me as I readjusted the icepack that Alden had made for my sore knee. He came right to the point. "I'm detective Carson with homicide. Tell me what happened."

No words of comfort or mention of my loss. I was a witness and he wanted information. I tried the best I could. My effort proved a terrible jumble of sensations wrapped in fear. The pictures etched in my head made me ill, they spilled out of my mind and infected my very being. As I came to the end of my story, another officer approached and the two whispered together before the officer receded back into the haze of dark blue uniforms roaming the office.

The detective's gaze sharpened on mine. "Let me see if I have this right. You said there are three bodies off the far hall and one in the main hall, just over there," he said pointing to where I'd kicked my attacker to the ground.

"Yes. Sean is in his office. Mike and Eduardo are in the hall and Cal…he was thrown out my office window."

"We accounted for him when we arrived."

Something wasn't right. Even Alden grew stiff.

The detective hesitated. "We've got a problem. There isn't a body in the main hall."

"What?" Panic locked the air in my lungs. I gasped and then choked out, "There has to be."

Alden's face grew fierce. "What are you saying?"

"I'm not saying there wasn't, Mr. Caldwell. We have blood evidence that substantiates Dr. Kelbeck's account. What I'm saying is there isn't one now." He licked his finger and pulled a page back, then looked at Alden. "When you entered this office through the stairway, did you see the attacker?"

"I saw someone lying there. I didn't go check on him. My concern was for Maya."

"Of course it was. So, neither of you noticed him leaving?"

Alden didn't sound amused by the question. "I think we would have noticed if he crawled by us, detective, if that's what you're getting at."

"I'm sorry, but I have to ask. Is there another way out of here besides the elevators and the emergency stairwell?"

I couldn't think. I couldn't breathe. He was gone. The man who had killed…no, who had ripped apart my friends was alive and wandering the streets of Boston.

Alden rubbed my back and air rushed in. He looked at the detective. "No. But have you checked the windows?"

"You think he left via the windows?" He chuckled. "That's a pretty good trick if he did. We're more than thirty floors up."

The detective's sarcasm didn't amuse Alden. He was a man used to getting respect from people, and it clearly didn't sit well with him to have this detective acting superior. His arms began to cord and his hands had gone from tender to tense.

"Have you ever seen a man in a full-on adrenaline rush?" Alden asked.

The detective gave him a condescending smile. "I've seen one or two."

"Now add the powers of the completely insane to it. It's amazing what man can do when he thinks he's invincible."

I glanced at Alden, surprised by his insight. The detective turned his eyes on me, and I confirmed the theory. "It's well documented that a disturbed mind can create illusions of invincibility, and along with adrenaline, it can make him unnaturally stronger than he would be in normal circumstances, although it rarely has a sustained affect."

With a quick twist of his wrist, he flipped through his notes. "This guy was drugged."

"Apparently not enough," Alden snapped.

A pair of officers ran for the stairs and another man, dressed similar to the detective questioning us, approached the lobby, excitement flushing his face. "Carson. We found his escape route. You won't believe it."

"Let me guess." The detective glanced at us and then back at his colleague. "A window?"

Surprise registered on the junior detective's face. "How'd you know?"

He snapped his notebook closed and stood. "Do you know where he is now?"

"I sent Ashworth and his partner down to see if we can pick up a trail. I don't know how the guy did it. If I didn't know better I'd think we have a real Spiderman on our hands. What kind of guy decides going out a window thirty floors up is a good idea…and then is actually able to climb down?"

I looked at Alden and he pulled me close.

I didn't know, and I didn't want to find out.

I swear I'm not lying, but my innocent bed shivered with ecstasy when it saw Alden enter my bedroom. It quivered with excitement when he placed me under the covers. It groaned with longing as he sat on its downy covers. It was more than ready for some action.

Sadly, I was in no mood to tear up the sheets. I was shell-shocked and Alden recognized the symptoms and reacted accordingly. Soothing voice, warm touch, no sudden moves. He babied me through a traumatic night. He hovered over my bed, held me when I cried out, and let me lie alone when I needed space to breathe. I'd never been treated so preciously. Not even by my mother.

In the morning, he entered my room with a cup of cocoa

and a hot buttered croissant. "Good morning."

I slowly sat up. "Is it?" I put my hand to my head. I had a terrible headache.

"It will be."

Confidence radiated from his voice. I wished I could believe him. How exactly did one bounce back from the nightmare of seeing your friends killed one after the other? Not just killed, but slaughtered like animals.

He slid the plate onto my lap and handed me the cup, its ear toward me. I gripped the warmed ceramic and a morose thought spiked my brain. "I have to call their families. God, Cindy will be devastated. She and Cal have been married for forty-eight years. And Lily and the kids," tears gathered in my eyes, "How can I tell them their daddy will never come home?" I couldn't do it. Not yet.

Alden sat on the bed and placed his hand on my calf. The heat of his fingers sifted through the silk to warm my muscle. "It's already done. The police took care of it."

The police. The blood. The terror. It all washed over me in a gigantic wave. The mug clattered on the plate, and I covered my face with my free hand. "I can't believe what happened."

"It wasn't your fault." I felt the bed tilt as he leaned forward. He peeled my fingers away from my face, and I looked into his soft brown, earnest eyes. "It wasn't your fault," he repeated.

I wanted to believe him. "Did I tell you, he came for me? I don't know why."

Alden didn't look at me. "Sometimes there isn't a clear reason. It's like you said. He was disturbed in the worst kind of way. How can anyone make sense of that?"

Disturbed. Delusional. Those words described my patients. They described Alden.

I looked at him with clear eyes. "Technically, you're disturbed." A man who claimed to be a werewolf couldn't be too far off from a guy who went on a killing rampage.

He snorted at the label. "I have an unusual problem. I'm not a mental breakdown waiting to explode."

Deep down, I knew that. I felt safe with him, safer than I had with anyone. I sighed. "What am I going to do?"

"You're going to take it one day at a time." He placed his hand under the cup and helped me lift it to my lips. "Take a sip. It's good."

I didn't want to, but I did, and it was. I lowered the cup. "You sound so sure of everything. I wish I could be."

"I'm sure because part of my job is to forecast trends and apply them to the masses for the best monetary gain." He lifted the croissant to my lips. "Bite."

Again, I did as he asked. It, too, tasted really good.

He lowered the pastry. "You are what people like me call a sure thing. You are what the masses need. Well, at least this mass needs you." He lifted my hand to his lips, and he gazed into my eyes. "Don't pull away," he whispered.

I should have, but I didn't. My fingers tingled as he gently kissed my knuckles and then the inside of my wrist.

He lowered my hand, but didn't let go. "You *will* get over this."

I would get over this. I don't know how I knew it, but I knew it was true. I had a purpose in life and that purpose revolved around helping others. I would go back to work. I wouldn't slide into the abyss of depression that so often followed such traumatic events.

But…

My sudden, newfound confidence began to crumble. "I can't go back there." The thought of walking those halls, seeing the empty rooms, hearing their last cries of life before they died made me sick.

He regarded me thoughtfully as if he knew exactly how I felt. "Then don't. When you're ready, why not see your patients here?"

"In my home?" I didn't like the idea of people traipsing around and through my stuff. "I don't think it's zoned for business." And I was thankful for it.

"I'll get you a special permit by tomorrow. We'll get the apartment next door…knock out a few walls, set up an office;

it'll be fine."

He couldn't be serious. "Mr. Garcia lives next door. He might take issue with your idea."

"I'll talk to him. You'd be amazed what a little money can accomplish."

He was moving too fast. I didn't want to think about tomorrow yet.

He looked deeply into my eyes. "Stop worrying."

All of the sudden, I did just that. I sat shaking my head, trying to remember what I was worried about. It only took a quick blink to bring it back, the office, the blood.

He had almost reached the door when I stopped him. "Alden. What if another patient—" I couldn't finish my thought.

"You're going to be fine," he said more forcefully as his warm gaze held mine. "You may not be able to forget, but you *will* trust me. You are going to be fine."

I put my hand to my head and laughed. "You're right. I'm going to be fine."

He smiled. "See? Trust me." He turned and left.

I did trust him. Something inside told me to, so I did. He was right. This had been an unspeakable, freakish event—tragic in the most horrific way, but still uncommon. I had to find a way to deal with it.

I rolled out of bed, and after smoothing the sheets and fluffing the pillows, I headed to the bathroom, a strange sense of well being cushioned my world. Though my bathroom lacked marble or a fancy tub, it held a hint of comfort with an array of candles, scented soaps and salt rubs. It was my version of a spa, small as it was.

Stepping into the shower, I turned it to hot until clouds of steam billowed all around me. I stayed there until my muscles relaxed and my mind cleared. After drying off, I sat to examine what I'd noticed in the shower. My knee had grown swollen, purple and green. It was unattractive. Odd how tragedy causes you to focus on the mundane. I found myself lamenting the fact that I wouldn't be wearing any skirts or even my lowest heels for a few weeks until the thing healed. Like I really cared.

I changed into a form fitting brown tee-shirt and an old pair of jeans, the kind your mama doesn't like because they ride too low, are slightly ripped and made your butt look good. Plus they were comfortable.

When I opened the door, Alden was there, stretched out on my bed with his eyes closed.

"Hey," I said. "What are you doing?"

"Looking at you."

Yeah, right. "Your eyes are closed."

"I know." A smile I could only call wicked spread across his face. "I can see what I wish I could see with my eyes closed."

I gasped and hit him with a pillow for that remark. He took it good-naturedly. Sitting up, his face grew serious. "I have something I have to ask you."

I didn't like his tone, but I nodded. "Go ahead."

"I have to leave, and while I'm gone, I want you to keep the door closed. Don't invite anyone inside. Okay?"

He acted so adamant, as if he expected the attacker to come find me. I shivered. "Trust me. I have no desire to see anyone."

His eyes softened and he brushed his fingers down the side of my face, just a whisper of a touch, but it meant a lot to me. He pulled his hand away. "I don't feel right leaving you just yet, but I have to go...sign papers, make some calls…business stuff. I don't know when I'll be back."

He had a business to run. I couldn't expect him to coddle me all day, even if that was what I desperately wanted. "Don't worry. I'll be fine."

He stared at me a long time.

"Really," I said, fluffing my wet hair as it slowly air dried, and trying not to panic. "I'll be fine."

He nodded, actually believing me. "I'll call you later."

And then he left. My hero, my savior, my anchor in the storm just…left.

Men. Why couldn't they catch on to subtle hints? My hands were shaking. My jaw had grown tight, and I bet if I looked into the mirror, my pupils were dilated with fear. No way would I be fine. My happy euphoric state had begun to fade the minute he said he was leaving.

I quickly locked the front door and ran back to my room. Though morning pushed through the curtains in slivers of brightness, I didn't feel its promise of warmth. A deep, cold dread had entered my body. I dove under the covers and pulled them over my head.

"Please, don't let him find me," I chanted over and over and over again.

If Alden didn't come back soon, I might very well die from fright.

Maya

CHAPTER ELEVEN

Hiding under the covers like a five-year-old wasn't very dignified. It isn't easy being your own therapist. I just realized I'm totally messed up. Granted, I had suspected a few bumps in my behavior before, but I never let them worry me too much. Who doesn't work crazy long hours these days? And who doesn't want the job done right? Exactly, precisely right the first time. In college I had the neatest notes. They actually inspired awe in my peers. Little did they know I went home and rewrote any and every page that had the tiniest flaw.

If I didn't get a grip on my emotional insecurities, and place what happened to me in wider perspective, I'd turn into an agoraphobic in no time. Victims of violence often retreated from society. I couldn't allow that to happen. Cal wouldn't have wanted me to crumble. Neither would Sean or even Eduardo. Mike? He would expect me to sink into a blubbering mass. I choked back a sob. What a hateful thing to think of the dead. Even if it were true.

I could go down to the newsstand and buy today's paper. I'd buy the *Boston Globe*, the *New York Daily News* and *USA Today*. Maybe even a magazine. A girly one. All about fashion and people-spotting and gossip that had nothing to do with anything.

In no time, I had my keys in my hand and a jacket slung over my arm and a tiny wad of money in my pocket. I curled my hand around the doorknob.

Keep the door closed.

My hand shook. Alden's command sounded startlingly clear, as if he stood right beside me and shouted it in my ear.

It was just down the street. That wasn't so far.

Don't.

A thin spiral of fear slithered through my body. It wasn't even noon. What was my rush? I had all day.

My fingers slid from the cold metal, and I took a step back. I felt better. A comforting warmth erased the dread. I needed a cup of hot cocoa. After that, then I'd go. I threw my keys into the bowl that sat on the table near the front door and folded my lightweight jacket into a neat square beside it.

And promptly forgot about going out for the rest of the day.

About one o'clock, a knock sounded at the door. My pulse jumped. I crept to the door and peered through the spy hole.

My visitor dressed just like the detectives I'd seen at the office. He flashed a badge. It looked real.

He knocked again. "Dr. Kelbeck? I'm Detective Sundquist. I'm investigating the crime at your office."

I took a deep breath, forcibly ignoring my instinct to obey Alden, and opened the door to peek out. "Yes?"

"May I come in?"

Don't invite anyone in.

My throat grew tight. Asthmatic tight. I didn't even recognize my own voice when I spoke. "I'm not exactly up for company, Detective."

"I understand."

He flipped through a notepad similar to the lead detective's.

"I have just a few quick questions. You told Detective Carson that Mr. Caldwell came into the office via the stairwell?"

"Yes. He kicked in the door. He said it was locked, but it's always open. I don't know why it wasn't last night."

"I see. Why do you think he used the stairs and not the elevator?"

"I don't know." I frowned, that wasn't exactly true. "Is it really that important?"

He pursed his lips and said, "Probably not. It just stood out to me, that's all. Now, about the bodies ..." He slanted an oddly focused and intense glance at me from under his eyebrows. "Two of them, Dr. Eden and Dr. Gregory, were drained of blood."

"What?" My body shook against the door. Mike and Sean had been drained of blood? A flash of lightheadedness overcame me for a moment as images I'd spent all morning trying to forget crowded in on me. "That's not normal, is it?"

He studied me for a moment. "Nothing about murder is normal. I need to reaffirm your timeline. You said all four were killed in eight minutes."

"That's right." Four dead in eight minutes. My mind shied away from the images. "That doesn't sound like a lot of time."

"It's not." With a heavy sigh, he flipped the notebook closed and pulled out a card, slipping it between the gap I gazed through. "Here's my card. If you remember anything else, please give me a call. Thank you for your time. I'm sorry to have had to bother you."

I took the card, puzzled by all of this. "Wait. That's it?"

"Just needed to clear up a few details."

Couldn't he have called? He took a step away and I stopped him. "Detective Sundquist?" He paused, and I took a deep breath, unsure whether or not I honestly wanted to know the answer to my question. "Did you find...the man who killed my friends?"

A glint of sadness shone from his eyes. "I'm sorry. All we have is the name he signed in with. John Smithson. It hasn't been helpful."

John Smithson? I'd never heard the name before. "Do you think it's an alias?"

"Probably. We haven't been able to locate anyone by that name with the description you gave us. If we do, I'll bring you a picture line-up. No need to come in unless we get a positive hit."

I nodded, not looking forward to seeing the murderer. And then I remembered something. "His eyes. They were blue. Sapphire blue. And they … it sounds stupid, but they sort of glowed."

He threw me an odd expression. Did he think I was crazy? I sagged against the door, all my energy drained. I just wanted to go to sleep now. "It's the stress. They couldn't have glowed."

He took a step closer to me, his face concerned. "Why don't you go lie down? You look exhausted. Do you need anything? Can I call someone for you?"

"No. Someone is coming over soon."

"Okay. Until then, don't answer the door."

It was odd how his advice echoed Alden's. With a smart nod, he turned and left.

I gladly closed the door and twisted the lock. A deep lethargy had entered my limbs. I went to the couch, picked up the remote and channel surfed. Nothing held my attention. I turned the TV off and picked up the book I'd been reading—a nice little autobiography about a doddering old woman who never felt threatened, and lived by herself in the middle of nowhere with only her cows and chickens and goats to keep her company. I fell asleep soon after.

The phone rang around four, jolting me out of my dreamless state. I shuffled to the kitchen where I'd last seen it, my mind soupy with an empty ache. "Hello?"

Alden's voice rumbled soothingly over the line. "How are you doing?"

I rubbed my forehead, trying to clear the fog. "Good." I wasn't about to tell him about my near escape into the outside world.

"Good." He sounded tense. "I'm sorry, but I've got a few

more things I need to check off my list before I can leave. I should be back before dark. In fact, I'm making it a point to be back before then."

"That's fine. A few more hours alone shouldn't push me over the edge."

"Do you want me to pick up something to eat? Do you like pizza?"

My stomach growled at his words. Did I even eat lunch? "Pizza with pine nuts, goat cheese and sun-dried tomatoes?"

I think he actually gagged. "I was thinking more like the meat lover's version, but we can have them split it."

"That's fine."

"Are you sure you're okay? Anything happen today?"

I didn't have to tell him, but it felt like lying if I didn't. "The police came by."

"You opened the door?" He didn't sound happy that I had gone against his advice.

"It was the police. You can't ignore the police."

"Yes, you can." I could almost see his look of irritation. "What did they want?"

"Sean and Mike didn't have any blood left in them. That can't be normal. The police don't comment on things that are normal."

"Their wounds were pretty bad." At my silence he added, "Listen, nothing about what happened last night was typical. Try not to think about it."

Not thinking helped for now, but soon I'd have to face what happened. My stomach did a little gurgling dance, and I rubbed it in an effort to calm it down. "Pizza would help."

"Then pizza we'll have. See you in a few."

I found a bottle of wine behind some beer Alden must have brought over. I uncorked it and set the table. I had time to kill and attacked the few dirty dishes I had, dried them and put them away. I mopped the floor, then washed down my growing thirst with a beer.

Soon it was past eight and the sun had begun to set. I didn't know what to think. I poured myself a glass of wine and stared out the window at the city lights.

By ten I'd consumed almost the whole bottle of wine and I was feeling woozy. I flopped lengthwise onto the couch and covered my eyes with my arm to block out the sight of the swirling ceiling. I didn't feel so good, and soon I drifted off into a dreary little miasma.

Sometime later, someone banged on the front door. I threw myself off the couch, and paid for the gesture with a massive head rush. What had I been thinking drinking like that? I shuffled to the door, and without warning, belched. The alcoholic aftertaste made me cringe.

Reaching the door, I peered through the spy hole. Alden. At least I thought it was him. He stood hunched, as if he'd just run the Boston marathon.

I unlocked the door and threw it open, ready to lay into him about not calling and worrying me half to death. "Do you know what time it is?"

Alden's right hand gripped the doorjamb to steady himself while his left hand pressed just under his heart. He looked up at me, one eye red and puffy, the other sported a deep cut to his eyebrow.

My anger evaporated. I took hold of his arm and helped him inside. "What happened?"

"I got jumped."

I kicked the door closed. "By who?"

"Someone who didn't like me walking in the dark."

"Are you okay? Do you want to go to the emergency room?"

"I'm fine. It looks worse than it is."

What more could happen? My gaze swept his face. Someone had given him a good beating. "It looks pretty bad."

"It's just a few cuts and scrapes. I'll be close to new by morning, but right now I need to lie down."

We slowly made our way to my bedroom. When we got close to the bed, he stopped short. I glanced up at him concerned. "What's wrong?"

He looked from the bed to himself. "I can't sit on your bed.

I'm all bloody."

He quickly switched directions, and we headed to the connecting bathroom. The small space felt cramped with Alden sitting on the toilet. I pulled out my first aid kit and rummaged around for an antiseptic wipe.

"I need a long, hot bath."

"I'll draw you one." I found a small packet and ripped into it. "Just let me take care of that cut above your eye."

He stopped my hand an inch from his face. "I'll do that."

"There's so much blood…"

"I'm okay. Juliana wanted me hurt not seriously harmed."

I lowered my hand. Juliana had ordered this done to him? "You know who did this?"

He nodded, then glanced up at me, his look pleading. "Do you think you could make me something to eat?"

Alden was a master at redirection. I could have insisted on knowing more, but I could wait. "All I have are pickles and some peanut butter."

"Toasted peanut butter on bread sounds good."

"Are you sure you're okay?" I tried not to sound too disappointed he didn't want my help.

"Trust me. Come morning, I'll look good as new."

I had my doubts about that. I turned on the tub before he nudged me out the door.

Putting together a sandwich was at the peak of my culinary skills, and it was ready in no time. With sandwich in hand, I went to the closed bathroom and knocked. "Alden? I have your sandwich."

I heard him grunt, like he was having a hard time moving. Why wouldn't he let me help? Helping people was what I did. He was just being stubborn.

"Put it on the dresser, will you? I'll get it in a second."

"Do you want anything else?"

A hopeful sigh sounded. "A good night's sleep?"

"I'll pull down the covers on the bed." My bed.

"Thanks. You're sweet."

I put the plate on the dresser, and hesitated. "If you need

me, just yell." He didn't reply, and I stifled the urge to knock on the door and ask him if he were okay. Somehow, I didn't think he'd be too pleased by my interference. Instead, I readied the bed and slowly walked out.

As I closed the bedroom door, I cast a jealous look at my bed. "Lucky you."

Alden

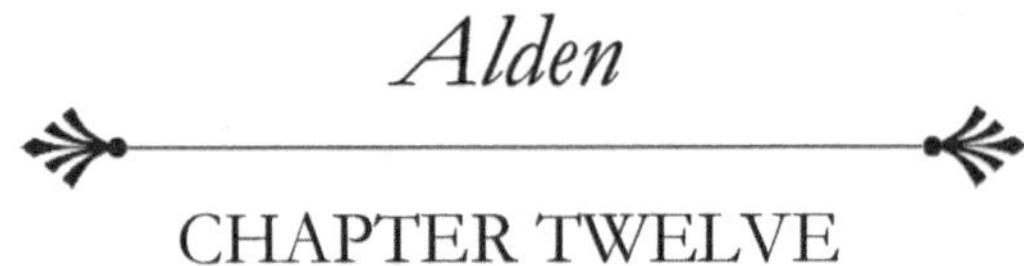

CHAPTER TWELVE

How many times must I suffer in this life before God granted me peace? My sins were many and loathsome to mankind, but I wanted to make amends. I longed to live my life free of evil.

Once I directed Maya into doing something constructive other than tending to me, I locked the door and proceeded to strip. The stab wound was deep. I poked it and blood seeped from it at an alarming rate. I had to concentrate. I needed to stay calm. With eyes closed, I visualized my wound. The injury was substantial. The worst was a tear to my liver. My curse had few perks, but being able to self heal at a rapid pace was one I'd had to use all too often over the years. I quickly fixed a few severed veins and moved onto the liver.

I couldn't help the groan. Healing myself took a great deal of effort. Minutes ticked by. The liver finally healed. Muscles repaired, the thin layer of fat smoothed and my skin knitted neatly where the wound had been. I moved on to the jagged slash to my arm. Thank God she hadn't seen it. I'd barely been able to staunch the blood flow before I reached her apartment.

It took me fifteen minutes to heal the worst of the damage Juliana's thugs had dealt me. Luckily, most of her men were too scared of me to really put in their best efforts. I studied my reflection and decided to leave the cut above one eye alone, but poor vision persuaded me to heal the other of its swelling.

I washed my clothes in the sink and laid them out over the toilet to dry. Only then did I sink into the tub filled with hot water and scrub every inch of my skin. When I finally emerged from the bathroom, a towel wrapped about my hips, an hour and twenty minutes had passed. I opened the bedroom door and saw Maya sprawled on the couch, her right arm flung over her eyes and her left arm dangling off the side, her breathing heavy as she slept. I eased the hair off her face. If she ever found out what I had done, what needed to be done, she would probably never forgive me. The papers would be filled with the story. Doctor's bodies disappeared from city morgue. Ashes to ashes, dust to dust. They wouldn't return to this world as demons. What had to be done was done.

Exhaustion from the encounter and from healing my wounds slid through me as I turned back to the bed. Settling in, I was asleep before I took my second breath, and fell into a waiting memory which rushed in to fill the void exhaustion had caused.

I trotted along at Juliana's heel, my face raised to see every lift of her brow and twist of her lips. I tried to anticipate what she wanted, how she felt and who I should keep away from her. The last wasn't too difficult. She was not a woman most men would willingly approach. Though her looks caused lust to flare in every man, her temperament cooled those fires on closer inspection. That was fine with me.

We came to a large door, and with a slight touch of her hand, it swung wide. The room was large, with high ceilings and no windows. Evangeline had lit candles and set a crackling fire in the hearth. I loped in after Juliana and she closed the door. My nose twitched at the barrage of scents, and I sniffed around the room, finding familiar scents here and exotic scents there.

Juliana laughed. "You are curious. That is good. I like an adventurous spirit."

After I satisfied my nose, I turned to her. She pushed away from the door and approached me. "I am pleased with the look of you. One never knows what one will get when a pet transforms. You look as powerful now as you did before. I should have you stay in this state for the rest of the night, but, my need outweighs caution." She knelt before me, placed both hands on each side of my head and said, "I need the man, not the beast."

I wanted only to please her. I had to please her. Blood pummeled my heart. Oxygen soaked my lungs as I breathed faster and harder. The change happened much more slowly, the process more agonizing, but within a few moments, I was a man. My head hurt and my body shook from the exertion of the change. My skin felt on fire as if it had been scrubbed raw. I blinked rapidly, finding it difficult to focus.

"Much better," she purred, sliding her hands up my sensitive arms and down my back. She cupped my buttocks and rubbed herself against me like a cat in heat. She traced each old war scar and licked my fresh wounds, sucking the blood from them and mewling with pleasure. I grew weak at her touch and then stronger as her desire fueled mine.

She stepped away, her enigmatic gaze calling to me. With slow deliberation, she disrobed until her pale body glowed against the touch of the candles flames. She was perfect, her body created to pleasure a man, and she knew it.

"Touch me," she commanded.

I needn't be told twice. I was a man used to his earthly pleasures and confident in the role she bid me play. Soon I stroked a fire in her as heated as the one raging within me.

"Kiss me," she demanded.

Her lips were like a drug. I couldn't stop. I couldn't breathe. I needed to possess her and have her scent fill me. As I lowered her to the bed she sighed. "Yes. This is what I long for. Tonight and every night. You will be mine."

As I tasted her skin and stroked her need, I echoed her thoughts. "I am yours. Forever."

My mind laid aside my will and I accepted hers. I no longer wanted what my old life had been. All I desired was to fulfill my mistress's needs, her fantasies, her desires.

Much later, spent and exhausted, I lay beside her, stroking her hair and gazing at her perfection.

She suddenly frowned and slapped my hand away. "Don't touch me."

Uncertainty replaced the beauty of our lovemaking.

A knock sounded at the door. Only then did I realize she had been lying there expectantly. Juliana languidly rolled out of bed and slipped her arms through a creamy silk robe lying nearby. I rose onto my elbows as she opened the door. A man stood in the hall holding a comely young maid by the arm.

Juliana smiled at the frightened girl and stroked her face. With soft, soothing coos, she pulled the maiden inside and closed the door. The girl, clearly a peasant, glanced at me. Her eyes were large and teary. She didn't want to be here, and her fearful gaze begged for help. I stole a quick glance at Juliana, unsure what to do.

Juliana cupped the maiden's chin and softly commanded, "Look into my eyes. Yes," she sighed as the girl obeyed. "That's right. Look at me. Am I not beautiful?"

The girl nodded.

"And so are you." She tilted the girl's head and ran a finger down her unblemished throat as if following a course on a map. The pale finger paused. "There it is. The sweetest spot just waiting for a kiss." Juliana closed her eyes, her body shivering in anticipation, but for what I didn't know. I was mesmerized by her actions, as was the girl.

She drew the maiden's trembling body close; I stiffened, a disturbing image of her sucking my blood flashed in my brain. Juliana licked the spot and then a flash of fangs showed before she sank her teeth into the girl's neck.

My body recoiled at the unholy sight. I expected the girl to cry out, to struggle, but she only sighed and allowed the invasion. As the seconds passed into a minute, she grew pale and finally sagged in Juliana's arms.

Disengaging, Juliana licked her blood tinged lips and let the girl fall to the floor, dead.

She turned to me. "Get off my bed."

Confusion stifled the horror at what I had just witnessed, but I obeyed. As Juliana threw off her robe and climbed back into bed, my gaze lingered on her nude body.

She pulled the sheet up and turned on her side, her back to me. "Put on your clothes and leave…and take her with you."

My clothes had been placed in the room, neatly stacked on a chair beside the fireplace. I skirted the bloodless body and dressed, trying to understand what I had done wrong to incur my mistress's wrath. When I slipped on my shoes, I hesitated.

Juliana twisted her body around and her passionless gaze landed on me. "Did you not hear me? Leave. Tomorrow night, you will come to me again."

I nodded, lifted the maiden in my arms and slowly left the chamber.

When the solid wood door closed behind me, I looked down into the ghostly-white face of the peasant girl. She couldn't be dead. I shook her. "Wake up. Please, wake up."

She lay limp, her chest still. The man who'd brought her stepped forward and took her from me. As he carried her away, I stared into the waning shadows of the morning.

Understanding hit me full in the chest.I had let Juliana kill an innocent. My honor cringed at my weakness that had allowed the maiden, more child than woman, to die. Humiliation and disgust roiled in my gut. I rushed to the window, ripped open the shutters and dry heaved until my throat grew raw and my eyes burned.

Even as my heart trembled at the evil I had witnessed, I knew as soon as the sun set I would see Juliana, and I would again take pleasure in her body as she did in mine. With my head in my hands, I slid down the cold, stone wall until I slumped onto the equally frigid floor.

There between dark and light, I wept for my soul.

Maya

CHAPTER THIRTEEN

A rogue ray of light squeezed through the drapes and slapped me square in the face. I groaned as pain lanced my eye sockets and shoved my hand over my face. The movement to save my sight hurt just as bad as the pain behind my eyes. I needed a lethal dose of pain killer...quick.

What was I doing on the couch? Last night was a blessed blank, and the empty bottle of wine on the coffee table made it clear what I had done. I hadn't had a hangover in years for one good reason—I hadn't had much to party about. In fact, my life as I knew it had become painfully static.

Never the most graceful in the morning, I stumbled to my room and into the bathroom. There, hanging on my toilet were a man's pants and shirt. I staggered out and glanced toward my bed to see Alden sitting up, his torso bare and the sheets puddled low against his lap. I blinked. The man was naked in my bed.

On seeing me, he swept a lean hand through his rumpled

hair and gave me a sheepish grin. "Good morning."

I couldn't stop staring at that sheet—at what it barely covered. I frowned, drawing a complete blank on the events of last night. "You're in my bed?"

"I was mugged last night, and you offered your bed."

"I offered my bed." I was still clothed so I was certain I hadn't offered anything else in my inebriated state. I put my hand to my aching head, remembering something about him being beaten up by Juliana's men and me trying to help him. "What's going on? Everyone I know is either dead or getting hurt."

He sighed. "It's all because of me. Because of what I am."

His delirium about being the pet of the living dead society was rearing its ugly head. "You didn't kill anyone. Some crazed man did. Unexpected, even tragic death is part of life. It's not fair, but life usually isn't."

"I'll make it up to you, Maya."

"Unless you can raise the dead, I don't see how. Some things can't be undone."

I went to the kitchen and stepped behind the small island that separated the cooking area from the living room and pulled out the bread and toaster. When Alden came out of my room—fully clothed—I looked up. His clothes were rumpled, ripped and blood stained. Though he'd tried to get the worst of the stains out, he'd only managed to smear them.

He flashed his dimple, and I wanted to sigh. How could a man in his condition still look as good as he looked? He took my hand and kissed my knuckles, staring into my eyes as he did so. "*Je mourrais pour un baiser.*"

The toast popped.

"You speak French?" I murmured. That explained the slight accent I heard from time to time.

"I'm originally from France."

"Your English is very good."

"I speak several languages. Fluently."

I slid my hand from his and turned away. Of all the languages he could speak, why'd it have to be bone-melting

French? Curiosity got to me. "What did you say just now?"

His laugh had a mischievous tint to it. "It's too early for French lessons. I'm interested in how you feel today."

I paused, holding a jar of jelly to my chest like a protective shield. He seriously wasn't going to tell me? I had no problem sharing exactly what I wanted to say in clear, plain English. "You want to know how I feel? I think it's safe to say my life is a wreck. Just the other day, I woke up to a promising new morning and today, I find myself cowering in my apartment." I faced him, my voice tightening on each word. His innocent question wound through me, causing the stress of the last few days to snap. "For a woman who's been dodging death, I can honestly say, I don't feel so hot."

He threw me a tentative smile. "You look gorgeous."

My hair fell around my shoulders in riotous disarray and my jeans and t-shirt were hopelessly wrinkled. Apparently he'd been blinded last night and didn't know it yet. There could be worse things wrong with a man.

Like thinking he was a werewolf.

I placed the jelly on the counter and wrangled my emotions under control. I sagged against the counter. "I'm…a mess. Can we *not* talk about me?"

He pushed a wild strand of hair away from my eyes and offered me something I didn't deserve. Compassion. I had to redirect my thoughts or I'd crumble.

Taking his hand in mine I asked, "How about you? How do you feel?"

"Much better than last night."

I took a moment to really look at him. The cut over his eye had scabbed and the puffy eye hadn't turned black as I thought it would and the swelling was gone. His knuckles still bore a few scrapes from the fight, but other than that, he looked right as rain.

"Great," I said, though without any true happiness to the word. Okay, I had wanted to know only if he felt as horrible as I did. I pulled my hands away from his, disgusted with myself, and confused. "Not only am I a victim, but I'm one of those pathetic weak ones."

He'd been attacked, just as I'd been, yet he seemed to have come out of it unscathed, while I felt my self-control unraveling at an astonishing rate.

Alden held out a jellied piece of toast. "This is but a moment in a lifetime."

But it was a huge moment. A defining moment. One I was failing to handle. I took his offering. "I don't know what's wrong with me."

Time would either see me better or push me completely over the edge. While I contemplated the two outcomes, I took a small bite of toast.

"So …" he hesitated, carefully scraping grape jelly over his toast. "I suppose I shouldn't ask about our next step in ridding me of Juliana."

Thankfully, I'd managed to swallow the bite before he'd said that or I would've choked. I didn't know what to think. Was I ready to help him? I barely felt capable of taking care of my own emotions let alone anyone else's.

Yet, Alden's wounds went far deeper than mine. He'd become an expert at hiding his true feelings beneath the suave, unruffable exterior he presented to the world. I couldn't blame him for wanting to break free.

Maybe focusing on his problems would alleviate my pain. It was worth a try.

I sank my teeth into the sweet toast and chewed, thinking his problem over. "Those men who jumped you, you said Juliana sent them?"

"She doesn't like it that I'm not available."

So this Juliana woman was getting testy and had decided a little push would get his attention. It certainly got mine. If Alden didn't pay more attention to his surroundings, the next time Juliana pushed, he just might break.

"Actually, I'm a little surprised she hasn't called here," he admitted and took a huge bite of his toast.

I snorted. "I'm not. My number is unlisted, for obvious reasons." I gave him a meaningful glare. "My patients aren't supposed to call my home."

That dimple reappeared. "I'm special."

I couldn't deny that.

His eyes mesmerized me. Flecks of gold richly colored the dark umber giving off a warm vibe. I took another bite of toast. "Does she know who I am?"

"Yes."

"Does she know what you're trying to do?"

"That I'm not sure. She may just think we met and that I've formed an attachment." His gaze warmed even more. "Which I have."

I looked away. "Alden…" I gently warned and started to step back.

He stopped me by putting his hand on mine. "You're my therapist. Of course I'm attached. I will adore you forever if you can help me."

I felt the coolness of the granite under my palm and the heat of his skin on the back of my hand. Slowly the granite beneath warmed. He was so obviously desperate. Little wonder why. Juliana had proven herself to be an unpredictable person, volatile enough to try and hurt Alden. I couldn't just pamper my own feelings and ignore his. I recalled what Cal told me the other night, and said, "I have a plan."

"I knew you would. You're very clever."

I fought the blush that threatened to rise. I knew only one way to tell him what needed to be done. Let it all out as quickly as possible. That way I couldn't change my mind, because frankly, Juliana terrified me.

I locked eyes with Alden. "I think we should visit Juliana tonight." There. It was out.

His hand tensed on top of mine. "No."

I wouldn't be dissuaded. "It's for the best."

"How so?" Of course he wasn't buying it.

"While you're here, you're separated from the cause of your problem—Juliana. There, we can face her together and break your," and here is where it would get painful, "your delusion."

He blinked.

Silence stretched out between us. Slowly, he stood. "You still don't believe me."

I took his hand in both of mine, willing him to stay with me, to hear what I had to say. "I want to, but how can I? Until you come to grips that your condition is a fantasy built on a network of complex lies, or I'm shown the truth of your claims, you will never be free of Juliana. I can't help you if I don't believe you, and you can't help yourself if you don't see the truth."

He yanked his hand out of mine and pushed away from the counter, his muscles straining as he breathed deep to control his emotions. His eyes snapped toward mine. "I know the truth, and it's far more evil than you can imagine."

"I can imagine some pretty horrific stuff. Most of my clients have been through hell. That's why they come to me. To find peace. To find the truth behind their fears."

He turned away and paced the confines of my living room. In that moment, I could well imagine the wolf that lived within him. He shook his head. "You don't know what you're asking me to do."

"Do you know what you're asking me to believe? It's outrageous. It's…insane."

He charged the counter and slapped his hands flat on its surface. "I can show you."

I stood my ground. Letting him see my sudden fear might escalate his anger. I had to keep control of this situation. "Then show me," I challenged.

He closed his eyes and after a moment, the scab above his eye fell off, and perfect skin, without any trace of a scar, showed beneath it. His eyelids flew open and he stared at me. "See? I can heal myself."

Disgusted, I picked up the scab. "Good trick. Frown, and a fake scab comes off." I threw the thing in the trash and rounded on Alden. "Don't you see how wrong this is?"

He stared at the trashcan, his face clearly portraying his shock. To see his delusion falter must throw a huge wrench in his fantasy. "I healed myself," he insisted. "I did!"

"You only think you did. Last night was all an act, wasn't it? While in your deluded state you feigned an attack. Then in the bathroom, you put the fake scab on." I was on a roll, letting the pieces of his bizarre puzzle fall into place. "Did you plant the alcohol too? You knew I would drink. Who wouldn't in like circumstances? I was so gone, I would've believed anything. A miraculous healing my ass. My God, Alden. Don't you see what you're doing?"

He rounded the counter. "I'm not insane."

Before I could stop him, he grabbed one of the gourmet cutlery knives I had hanging on a magnetic board beside my stove and placed the blade against his wrist.

Time warped in my mind. The kitchen blurred and morphed into a view of my office. I called out Alden's name and reached for him. I didn't know I was crying. I didn't know I was falling. My coworkers were dead. I saw blood, everywhere. The man was coming at me. He was covered in blood. Covered in so much blood.

I screamed. The sound ripped from deep within me. It tore through my throat. Rattled my teeth. It hurt my ears. No. This couldn't be real. This couldn't be real.

I dove for Alden, lashing out in desperation to save him. My hand slapped against cold steel, nicking me as I knocked it out of his hand. As the knife hit the floor, I looked down at my bleeding hand. A clean slice had ripped into my palm, though not large, it bled profusely. Numb shock gave way to tingling flesh and then to outright pain. I clasped my wrist, palm up, staring at what I'd done.

Before my eyes, stars flashed against a black void, yet the red slash of blood was all too clear. "I'm cut," I said stupidly.

My knees suddenly buckled. Alden sprang forward and caught me before I hit the ground. Pulling me firmly against his chest, he gently eased us to the floor. He pressed his lips to my temple, rocking me back and forth, shushing me as he wrapped my hand in a clean kitchen towel. "You fool. Why did you do it?"

Though the words were harsh, the sound of his voice

covered me like a soft blanket, comforting me. I became aware of tears rolling down my face. Confusion fluttered through me like a bird trapped in a cage, desperate to break free. I turned into his solid warmth that held me to this moment, and looked up at him. "I couldn't let you hurt yourself."

Sadness troubled his face. "God, I'm sorry. I shouldn't have scared you like that."

The glimmer of blood tingeing the knife caught my eye. I remembered the look in his eyes. "What were you trying to do?" I glanced back up at him. "Alden, I can't deal with that. I just—"

"I won't. I swear I'll never do anything like that again." He hugged me closer. "I'm frightened, Maya. You're asking me to risk too much."

He didn't say that lightly. This man wasn't used to being afraid. "If I take you there, you'll be in danger. I don't know if I can protect you. If Juliana should tell me to change, I may not be able to resist her commands."

I hugged his arm, his very human, masculine arm wrapped around my chest. He wouldn't change. Werewolves stood firmly in the mythical creature category. I gazed confidently up at him through the burn of my cut palm. "I'm willing to risk that."

Maya

CHAPTER FOURTEEN

The clutter of fabric strewn over my usually immaculate bed made me nervous. "Is this really necessary, Alden?"

"Light pink." Tossed on the pile.

"Baby blue." Joined the pink.

"Pale yellow. What are you, a Monet painting? No one wears this much pastel. You should be in warmer colors. Passionate colors. Not these insipid shades, and formless shells." He rummaged through my wardrobe, freely tossing out one outfit after another onto the bed in disgust. "To get in, you have to wear black. Don't you own anything black?"

My back stiffened at his censure. "Black is a depressing color and my patients don't need the visual cue to embrace their negative energies."

He turned to me, a look of disbelief on his face. "It's black. It's a non color. It's high fashion. Everyone wears black."

"I don't." No one would take me seriously if I walked into my office dressed like a Parisian runway addict.

He reached into the very depths of my closet, and after a long moment, pulled out an unadorned little black dress. His eyes sparkled when he held it out at arms' length. "Finally. It's black, chic and sexy." He held it up to me, and his grin turned greedy. "Oh, yeah. This is nice."

I'd forgotten I even had that. It had been an impulse buy, one my sister had encouraged me to get for my date with that gigolo she set me up with. It did not hold good memories. The cut of the fabric mimicked the curves of a woman and the neckline didn't leave much to the imagination. It was a dangerous dress, one to draw a man's attention, or so I'd thought. "I can't wear that."

"Why not?"

"I bought it years ago. It probably doesn't even fit."

He eyed me and then the dress. "It'll fit."

The man was irritatingly persistent. I plucked at the neckline and frowned. "It's too revealing."

"That would be the point. Where I'm taking you, women look like women, men are reckless…and everyone is wild."

My ears heated at the images of the decadent behavior I might encounter tonight. "What is this place called again?"

"The Black Dahlia."

I shivered. "That name is disturbing."

It conjured up the 1940 era unsolved murder of a young Hollywood starlet. The story never failed to give me shivers.

"It's meant to be. This isn't a cute little club where you'll meet the fun-loving people of Boston. These people are…dark and the Black Dahlia is their secret."

"Let me guess, black clothes, dark hair, dramatic make-up and depressing outlooks on life. They're moody and aren't shy about letting everyone know about it."

He stepped forward. The sheer bulk of him threw me into instant shadow. I had to tilt my head up to meet his gaze, and when I did, I was met by a grim expression that froze my heart. "I mean they're dark. There isn't a speck of light to their souls."

The hairs on my arms spiked. "You're trying to scare me

out of going."

"Is it working?" he asked in a rough voice.

"No." But I surreptitiously rubbed my arms.

He pulled back and held out the dress. "Then you'll be wearing this."

I grabbed it and snapped, "If that's what it's going to take, then fine. I'll wear it."

Cal had warned me that Alden would do anything, say anything, to protect his delusion, but honestly, this whole "we're about to walk into the gateway to hell" routine was starting to irritate me. I threw the dress on my pillows and began to re-hang all the clothes he'd pulled out of the closet.

Alden watched me, shaking his head. "This isn't going to work."

I turned on him, fed up with his negative attitude. "Fine, then stay Juliana's slave for the rest of your life."

I winced at the shocked expression on his face.

"You know that's not what I want," he said on a choked whisper.

I couldn't weaken now. "Good. We're going, because if we don't, our relationship stops here. Right now. I can't help you if you don't want to help yourself."

His eyes widened. "You would leave me?"

"You're not giving me a choice." I hated giving ultimatums, they rarely led to optimal outcomes, but he wouldn't stop trying to manipulate the situation, and I hated being manipulated.

His gaze turned from hurt into stony acceptance. "This is a mistake."

I groaned and pulled my hands through my hair. "Stop it already. Your worries are groundless."

He grunted. "I hope to God you're right." He suddenly pointed a tanned finger at me, his demeanor still holding onto a hint of aggression. "*Try* to blend in. And when I say we're leaving, you don't ask, you follow. Got that?"

So much for submissive tendencies. He sounded natural giving orders. Well, so did I. "Fine. You say leave, we go. But the command works both ways. If I say let's leave, then *you* follow."

A mocking smile tipped the edges of his lips. "You of all people should know men don't like being bossed around, especially me. I'm going to great lengths to stop a woman from doing just that, so it doesn't bode well for our date tonight." He turned to leave and said over his shoulder, "I'll be back around eight."

"This isn't a date."

He kept walking toward the door, ignoring my denouncement. The man was aggravating. I stood in front of my wardrobe and placed my hands firmly on my hips. "I mean it. This is a professional outing."

A hard laugh burst from his throat. "Nothing about what we're about to do will be professional, *Maya*."

I gritted my teeth at his emphasis on the familiarity of our relationship.

Stopping at the door to my room, he looked back. Only then did I glimpse through his anger to the shadow of concern. "You can't say I didn't try to warn you. I hope you're ready for this, because after tonight, we're both going to be in a hell of a lot of trouble."

I kept Alden waiting forty-five minutes. I didn't care. It'd been a struggle just to put on the dress. Not that it didn't fit. Oh, it fit all right. Too well. It was a struggle not to tear it off and scrounge for something a little less daring. Encased in this dress, there would be no doubt that I was a woman. It highlighted every curve and dip of my figure. I was actually shocked to see so many curves. Imprisoned in corporate suits for so long, I'd forgotten I had a female form. For all its body hugging ability, the dress was comfortable. I twisted my leg, looking for the hideous bruise decorating my knee. The hem hid it perfectly, and my strappy shoes made my legs look ridiculously long.

My real concern was the neckline. I must've been insane to buy this dress. A quick tug did nothing to cover the exposed cleavage, and when I took a deep breath to steady my doubts, the neckline dipped back to a dangerous level. A terse scan of my dresser showed I had nothing to camouflage what was on display. Heaving bosoms was not professional. I couldn't wear this. My hands went for the zipper when an insistent knock jolted my bedroom door.

"If we don't go now, we can just forget it. I'm all for that."

Great. By the sound of him, if I gave Alden a chance, he'd bolt. I snatched up my purse. "I'm ready."

God, I hoped I was. After giving the neckline another useless tug, I opened my bedroom door, finding Alden leaning against the door jam with his hand raised for another assault on my door.

One look at me and he pulled back. "Oh, hell no. We can't go."

A moment of uncertainty washed over me. My mirror had lied. I must look like a stuffed sausage instead of a sexy siren. I glanced away, trying not to show my distress.

"You look…"

His shaky voice brought my gaze back to him. He swallowed as his eyes drank in every inch of me.

"You look…" He swallowed again and finally his looked into my eyes. "Wow. You look amazing."

Relief unclenched my stomach. Until that moment, I hadn't realized how much his opinion meant to me. I smiled shyly up at him. "You do too."

Dressed in monochromatic black, he looked handsome. Dangerously so.

A delicate chain held a single large pearl that rested against the juncture of my breasts. I touched it, thinking it wasn't enough, but it was all I had. "This is the best I can do at blending in."

Alden didn't say anything. He didn't need to. His overly warm gaze said it all. I picked up my coat and stood by the door. Alden still hadn't moved; only his gaze followed me.

It had been far too long since anyone had stared at me like I was a desirable woman. “Come on. It’s nearly nine.”

It didn’t take him long to join me. When he drew near, he dipped his head toward my neck and breathed deep. Sighing, he muttered close to my ear, making my skin tingle, “You’re wearing perfume.”

It was my turn to swallow hard. “I am. I-it’s called Breathless.”

“Mmmm.” Pulling away, he opened the front door and took my hand. “How appropriate. I’ve no doubt someone will be left gasping tonight.”

I blushed as the memory of his kiss swept through me. There was no denying I found him attractive. Wildly attractive. I wanted…no, I *needed* to be near him. I was afraid of that need and of my insatiable longing. Every time we touched, the feeling grew stronger. If I weren’t careful, we’d end up in the back seat of his car before we left the parking garage.

I had to redirect my focus.

Disengaging my hand from his, I stepped into the hall. As I locked the door, I thought about tonight. Our venture was all about freeing Alden, about laying aside the fantasy world and showing him the real world could be just as exciting. This was going to be a big night for the both of us.

Expectations are so easily crushed.

It sounds crazy, but in the back of my mind, I looked forward to seeing a radical sub-culture. I felt completely safe with Alden. But once we were in his Mercedes with sumptuous red leather seats, a change came over him. He didn’t speak and his muscles grew increasingly tense the closer we got to the Black Dahlia. After parking the car in an alley behind the club—it looked more like an abandoned warehouse than a party palace—and opening my door, I noticed how his expression had gone numb. He was preparing himself for something unpleasant. He handed me the keys to his car. I looked at him questioningly.

“In case you need to leave without me.”

I wouldn’t abandon him. We were in this together. Still, I

put them in my purse to make him happy.

My heart rate rose when a man guarding the entrance to the club nodded to Alden and stared after me when we entered. Alden wasn't pleased. As he led me inside, his hand rode possessively on the small of my back while his dispassionate gaze swept the crowd. I tried not to let his dour mood taint my first impression. We paused on the uppermost landing. The club loomed massive before us, with multi-levels for dancing, drinking and lounging. I stepped close to the railing and peered down, letting my clinical eye study our surroundings.

What a disappointment.

Whoever had created this place had converted the inside of an old warehouse— in a less than favorable part of town—into a sleek, ultra-modern club. Handset stonework met cold metal and old-world carved woodwork in a modern twist on traditional. A massive sheet waterfall greeted us as we entered, and huge oil paintings, some post modern, some realistic, lined the walls at precisely six foot intervals. In between the paintings, sconces were illuminated by flickering gas lights, their sputtering glow warming the hard edges of the decor.

I had expected a gloomy atmosphere. The Black Dahlia was far from that. It radiated life. And the patrons were hardly the dregs of society. I expected the disappointed and rebellious faces of the young, but what I saw was a diverse mix of sexes, cultures and ages. A sea of black merged on the dance floor, which was located toward the back where a live band played loud techno music. To our left lay a long bar where people intermingled and looked to be having fun, and up above, a glass enclosure overlooked the crowd. Probably the VIP section.

I smiled, glancing up at Alden. "This doesn't look so bad."

His face took on a hard cast as he started us down the stairs. "We're not there yet. All this is the front to the real Black Dahlia."

A front? My steps faltered on the steps. My smile faded. If a club needed a front, didn't that mean the real thing had to be illegal? I, Maya Kelbeck, was about to enter an illegal establishment? I'd never done anything illegal in my life. I didn't litter. I didn't drink and drive, not even after one glass of wine. And I always obeyed the speed limits. My mother drove faster than I did. I was, without a doubt, the most law-abiding citizen in Boston.

Until tonight.

We pushed our way further into the club. Though crowded, everyone showed a polite veneer and made room for us to slip by. The loud atmosphere swelled with excitement. Laughter. Smiles. Bodies pressed together. A kiss here. A caress there. Everyone looked so happy. As we passed a girl not more than sixteen, I saw her accept a tiny pill from a woman and pop it into her mouth, her eyes already glazed with euphoria. The little pill promised love and acceptance, but it would end up delivering a broken heart. As we slowly made our way across the room, I asked, "Do these people know about the real Black Dahlia?"

"If they did, they'd run." Alden pulled me toward a break in the crowd. We found an empty space near the wall, and he nodded toward the masses. "Most everyone you see here are prospects we call postulants. Others are pretenders. They're here because of men and women like me. They're drawn to our power, or if you like, our charisma. This is a very exclusive club, and most of these poor souls can't believe they're lucky enough to have been invited."

"Who are they?" I asked spying a nearby glass table with rows of finely crushed powder. Illicit drugs were everywhere.

"Just regular people with no family, no close network of friends."

Then it clicked. These people were the disillusioned, the unloved and the lonely in our society, people who were searching to connect with others, to find a reason to wake up one more day. "Without family or friends, that makes them susceptible to social predators."

He looked at me, his eyes devoid of emotion. "Thank you Dr. Kelbeck. That's the whole point. Nobody misses them when they're gone."

I am an animal. A predator.

He had warned me what he was. What was I doing here getting ready to enter an illegal backroom? Reality made a small crack in my infatuation. I'd just met Alden Caldwell. I didn't know him. Not really. A niggling of fear clawed at my throat. I turned to him. "I have a family."

He glanced down at me. "What?"

I spoke up louder. "I have parents and a sister and a brother. If I disappeared, they'd move heaven and earth to find me."

He looked me up and down, and then understanding dawned. "You're not going to disappear. I won't let you."

Belief swept through me. Unreasonable calm took hold. I put my hand to his cheek. "We're in this together."

He closed his eyes, and when he opened them again, they were no longer empty. The man I had come to know and trust looked down at me. He turned me around and pointed toward the bar area. "Do you see that door? If there's trouble, use that one. It'll take you to the alley where we parked the car."

He pulled my attention back to him. "When we go below, I don't want you to trust anyone. If I tell you to leave, then do it. Don't go through any door but the one which we're about to use. You won't like what you see if you do. Don't wait for me. I can take care of myself. Just get out."

I wouldn't leave him. "I'll be fine."

"Maya …"

"I'll be fine," I reassured him.

My job would be easy. Show him there were no such things as werewolves, that this secret society was based on lies, and that Juliana had no real power over him. "Let's get this show on the road."

A flash of worry crossed his face, and his hand shook as he pulled me behind a screen and opened a concealed door. I followed him in, and when he closed the door behind us, darkness descended, thick and heavy. If not for my hand in his, I would have felt completely alone. The air had a tangy scent to it that tickled my nose and made me want to sneeze. After a moment, I noticed tiny specks of blue light a few feet ahead of us. They illuminated a flight of stairs that led down a curved stairwell. Listening, I could hear the music from the main club echo somewhere below us.

Alden pulled me close, and I let him. We stood there, his body pressed against mine, his lips against my ear, his breathing ragged. When he found his voice, it had become whisper soft and rough, like he fought just to talk. "Whatever you see, it is real. This isn't a joke, Maya, or a trick. These people are the ancient ones. Demons. God has forsaken them because they forsook him. They live to terrorize humans and fulfill their own needs. Don't say anything. And for the love of God, don't stare. Act like you've seen it all before."

My knees began to shake. Demons? What kind of secret society did he belong to? My mind skittered across a host of disturbing evil images. I needed to narrow the field. "What am I going to see?"

"A taste of hell."

I instinctively stiffened. "Okay, you're scaring me now."

"Do you want to leave?"

I heard the hope in his voice. Was this his way of protecting his delusion? It had to be. Whatever was down there, I could handle it. I'd seen and heard too many real-life horror stories to allow Alden's fantasy to shake me now. "No."

The door behind us suddenly opened and Alden yanked me to him, hooked one hand beneath my right knee and hiked it up toward his waist while his other slid over my hip. His lips burned against my skin as he bent me back. I gasped, but I didn't push him away.

Two men entered and started down the stairs. The younger one stared at us with eager eyes. "Oh, man, this is going to be awesome. I didn't know there was another part to this place."

"It's the best part," his companion said. "By morning, you won't want to leave."

"That's fine with me. I don't have any place to go."

Alden's lips finally found my mouth and nothing mattered after that. Nothing but him. My arms wrapped around him. I could hear my blood rush through my veins, feel every minute muscle within me shift in a harmonious dance of seduction. I could smell every nuance of his spicy cologne, and the underlying scent of his bare skin. I could hear the blood rush in his veins. In mine. His hands moved along my body, pressing me closer…and then he pushed me away, his breathing loud and labored.

I blinked, fighting my way back to sanity. What kind of crazy hold did this guy have on me? I completely forgot everything and everyone with just a touch. I stumbled back. "Does this happen with every woman you kiss?"

"No. You're the only one."

How could that be? I put my hand to my fevered skin and focused my attention on why I was here. If all went well, Alden would be free. My heartbeat slowed. My mind cleared.

"Damn it," he growled, pushing a hand threw his hair. "This is wrong. We –"

I dared to step closer to him. "It's going to be all right." I couldn't allow him to talk me out of this. "Let's just get this over with and go home."

He nodded. "Keep your eyes on me. Act as if I'm the only one who exists for you."

That wouldn't be a problem.

"And don't look directly into anyone's eyes but mine. If you find you have to look at someone, stare at the tip of their nose or their eyebrows."

An amused smile hovered at the corners of my mouth. "Are you trying to tell me they'll hypnotize me?"

"Something like that."

"Oh." It sounded like those magicians in Vegas who called on audience members and had them crowing like roosters every time they flicked on a flashlight. Maybe something like that had caused Alden to believe he was a werewolf? If that were true, it was a mean trick to pull.

He slipped my hand within his arm, gave me one last look and all his doubt evaporated. I could feel the power of authority pulsing off of him. The unexpected transformation caused me to arch and eyebrow at him. He flashed a deeply dimpled, wicked smile. I didn't have time to wonder at the sudden change before we started our descent. Strange noises rushed up to meet us. A flash of panic seized me just before we entered the room…and then it was too late to turn back.

The girl looked dead. She hung in a cage in a room decorated like a medieval dungeon. Her pale body had been stripped. Her skin was dotted with dozens of bite marks. A shiver bolted down my spine, followed by a deep chill of foreboding.

We passed by a group of men and women. They nodded at us. No one approached, but everyone watched. I hadn't expected such an extensive social network. There were at least fifty people. Their voices grew quieter, like a buzz of insects instead of the loud roars of the wild beast they wanted to emulate. Everywhere I looked, I saw men and women engaged in one form of seduction. Some nibbled at the necks of their partners, others caressed their skin as if fascinated by it.

I leaned closer to Alden. "Why is everyone staring at us?"

He shrugged as if the stares didn't affect him. "It's been a while since I've obeyed Juliana's summons. I've become a curiosity."

So this was where he went when Juliana called. As I scanned the crowd, I couldn't say I liked her choice of company. They were all beautiful, yet most of them carried a brittle quality that reminded me of porcelain dolls–white skin and dead eyes.

My gaze faltered on the young man we'd seen coming down the stairs. He looked dazed. Two scantily clad women sat on either side of him literally undressing him, their eyes glittering as his skin came into view. The woman on his right kissed his chest. He flinched, and when she moved on, she left behind two small, weeping wounds. She'd actually bitten him and he'd let her.

The man who had brought him below hovered close by, as if on guard.

I faced Alden and whispered, "All these people think

they're werewolves?"

"No." He nodded to a table where a man held a girl straddled on his lap. He pushed her hair off her neck, lazily, almost reverently. I then saw what I hadn't noticed before. Fangs. The man slowly sank his pointed teeth into the girl's neck. She shuddered and moaned as if she enjoyed the invasion.

I reared back, unable to conceal my shock. "These people think they're vampires?"

"They are vampires."

The man continued to drink from her vein. Repulsed, yet fascinated by the behavior, I asked, "Why doesn't she run?"

"Can't you guess? She's entranced. Needy. She wants to belong. Some of these are postulants, hoping to be turned into immortals, so they let them feed. Others are a food source, brought here for the purpose of feeding until they end up like the girl in the cage.

"This is what I've been afraid to tell you. Juliana is a vampire. She's my master. I do exactly what that guy did tonight," he said, nodding toward the guard hovering by the young man and the two women feeding off him. "It's disgusting and perverted and I want out. But I can't. Not on my own."

Disturbed by what he was telling me, my gaze slipped back to the girl in the hanging cage. She was dead. Really and truly dead. My stomach lurched with disgust. This couldn't be real. It was a sick joke. I looked around, desperate to find the smoke and mirrors that made this all seem real. It was then I noticed the glasses filled with blood. At one table, a woman's wrist had been sliced and her blood was being collected in a cup. In a last tremble of life, she fell over and those at the table cheered, passing the cup between them as a man who'd been watching collected the body and carried it toward a back door.

I didn't just see what I thought I'd seen. I couldn't have. Yet the girl hung limply in the man's arms as he pushed through the door. My chest grew tight. It was suddenly hard to breathe. Even as the door began to close, I couldn't look away.

"What's back there?" I whispered as the door finally closed with a soft thunk.

"The slaughter house."

Nausea rippled through my stomach.

"Oh. My. God." I clutched Alden's arm as a wave of lightheadedness rolled over me. "This can't be happening."

A man entered through one of the doors near the back of the room and Alden cursed. "He's not supposed to be here." Turning me around, he pushed me back the way we'd come with a harshly whispered, "Go!"

I stumbled forward, obeying him without question, feeling his distress. With my head down, I methodically made my way toward the stairs.

"Caldwell!"

My ears perked at the man's voice. He sounded familiar. How could that be? I didn't know anyone who would visit a place like this.

"So, you finally decided to show yourself. We have some prime flesh tonight."

I dared a quick glance back and saw Alden staring after me. He shook his head before granting the man his full attention. "I'll pass."

The man looked my way. Stovall! I hurriedly darted out of his line of vision, praying he didn't get a good look at me.

"Pick out someone from above?"

"No. They're all trash. Juliana wouldn't be pleased."

"I don't blame you. You've displeased her too much already. Vilmos was happy with the girl I brought. He's giving the body to me. You're welcome to join me. Don't say no. I'll give you first bite. So young, she's bound to melt in your mouth."

My ears burned with outrage at the nonchalant way Stovall offered to share a dead girl with Alden. An image of the two of them tearing the flesh from the girl's bones made the bile rise in my throat, and I tripped on the bottom step. I was going to be sick. Lightheaded, I clung to the wall and turned back to see Alden take a step forward, his eyes now solely on me.

"Later," Alden said. But before he could take another step, a group of men converged on him so abruptly, I barely saw them move, and they were vicious in their attack.

When Alden was beaten to the floor, Stovall bent over him and grinned nastily. "It looks a lot like you want to leave."

Alden fought to free himself, but there were too many. I clung to the wall, wanting to leave, sickened by all I'd seen. Alden raised his head and our eyes met. Horror etched into his face at seeing me.

Stovall's gaze followed Alden's and he smiled, bringing everyone's attention to me. "Well, now. Won't Juliana be surprised? I think she'd enjoy a little snack before she rips into you. Don't you think so, Caldwell?"

Terror clawed its way through me when a pair of men lounging in a booth suddenly vaulted to their feet and started toward me.

Don't look into their eyes.

But I wanted to. Something inside me demanded I look at them. I gritted my teeth. No! I wouldn't look. I wanted out of here.

I didn't wait to see what would happen next. Alden had been right. We should *never* have come here. I bolted up the stairs toward the door, the steep ascent a challenge in my heels, but one I was determined to achieve. A deep bestial roar rumbled from below and I heard the clash of furniture being thrown.

"Oh, God. Oh, God. Oh, God," came my prayer. I concentrated on the sound of my heels puncturing the stairs in a hard metallic pop as I frantically climbed to the top.

Alden

CHAPTER FIFTEEN

They knew better than to touch me. Last night they had irritated me; I could handle a few thugs in my human skin. The beast inside me had raged to be freed, yet only Juliana could release it.

But tonight they'd threatened Maya.

I changed. Without thought, without command, I changed. Clothes ripped and the men leapt back, their lips pulled back in growls and hisses and yelps of surprise. Not even the vampires dared approach me now. I was too strong, with a reputation that sent their cold, evil hearts into a deep freeze.

Tables flew across the room and the men staggered away. Screams from the women and yells from the men threw the room into chaos. Stovall put his hands up, his weasel eyes growing larger than I'd ever seen them, and backed away. "Now, Caldwell…this isn't the way to handle the situation."

I cared as much for him as I did a pile of excrement. My senses honed in on the men charging up the stairs after Maya–Vilmos and one of his ilk. I bounded through the crowd and up after them. At the top, the door flew open and Maya dashed through it. I concentrated on the man in front of me. He was a lesser vampire, a new one, and he didn't know the danger he had just put himself in. I pounced on his back and tore into his throat. For the instant of awareness remaining, he knew he'd made a mistake. I snapped into his neck bones and ripped his head from his body.

I scrambled over the quickly deteriorating corpse. At the door, Vilmos turned. He was one of Juliana's favorites, and Stovall's master.

"Down, boy," he sneered and kicked me in the chest. I stumbled backwards, lost my balance and tumbled down the stairs. Lying in a heap at the bottom, I blinked back my surprise. When I gained my focus, the stairwell was empty. I started to rise, when a pain lanced through my head, turning everything black.

I drifted on a river of violent dreams. If I dipped my head under the current, I observed one human death after another. I had killed them as surely as if I, and not Juliana, had drained them of their blood. Whole villages were laid to waste, blamed on the Black Death, and quickly set to flame.

It was too easy. We moved from country to country, ravaging its populace like a tide of doom. Some areas were rich in humans, others sparse. It didn't matter to Juliana. If the nearby human populace grew low, I sought out slave markets. I bought human cargo from as far away as Persia and even on occasion along the rim of Africa. Some, the violent and hateful, I took as a service to the community. Other times I was approached by parents. A child's life was only worth as much money as a father could get for it. We treated them like cattle. Fed them, used them and then disposed of them. Oh, yes, it was so very easy to feed Juliana's appetite.

And for my obedience, I was rewarded. Juliana's love was the one thing I lived for; to be in her presence, to bathe in her attention. But as the years turned into decades and decades slipped into centuries, the pleasure I received from Juliana's body couldn't heal the misery, the loneliness, the sharp bite of humiliation or the sting of shame I felt after being with her. That was when I knew.

Juliana was incapable of love.

She and all of her kind were demon possessed, and the demon which had possessed her on the day she'd given away her soul fed not only on human blood, but on human pain and suffering. Pleasure was given as a last resort and taken without regard to anyone else.

Though werewolves still retained their souls, we were tainted, poisoned by the demon that owned us, and though I lived with an immortal curse, my humanity clung fiercely to a tiny edge of my blackened soul. I could remember love. I could remember goodness. But they were so far out of my reach, I dared not believe they were possible. So I devoted myself to Juliana's empty love. I told myself, her corrupt love was better than none at all. And as the love-starved beast I had become, she could kick me and I'd return to her side, spit in my face and I would whisper sweet words in her ear. She could whip me and I would forgive her. But worst of all, she could torture a human and I would look away just so long as she would favor me with a soft caress and the feel of her body pressed to mine.

The goodness that had once been in me was on the verge of being snuffed out. Until the day Evangeline came to me.

The year was 1657. We were ensconced in a pretty little French castle outside of Rouen which had been abandoned when a lord and lady never returned from their trip to Italy. Juliana had met them in Venice. Their end tragic. Two bodies found bloodless and bloated, floating in the brackish water of an obscure canal. I watched as they were fished out, laid side-by-side in a barge on that crisp spring morning, their hands touching in death as they had in life. They had been a loving couple, enchanted by the sight and feel of each other. Juliana hated such blatant shows of affection.

The castle they had left behind had all the accoutrements of a privileged life, from barns and outbuildings to a training yard where I drilled Juliana's men in all manner of weaponry. Years earlier, after a falling out with Juliana's father over her self-indulgent ways, we had set out on our own, and Juliana lost little time building her own "court" of admirers and slaves.

That day, the sun spilled its warmth over the land, heating my skin until it grew slick and salty. Our training session had gone well. The combination of my former life as a soldier and the alpha male I had become mixed to create a fierce opponent.

Most of the men I trained, I had turned. They were young and eager and easily controlled. Only a few had come with their masters when Juliana had left her father. Men like Stovall, who were soft and felt more at home under the table at their master's feet than in defending the group. I had left Stovall on the field, panting and groaning as if he would die.

The heat of the day wrapped itself around my body as I left the field. My men scattered in the opposite direction where a stream lay a few miles away. I preferred to let them go and cool off where they could curse my name for the sore muscles and outright pain they were likely feeling without thought of retribution. I headed toward the largest outbuilding, a barn. The sun slipped through the cracks in the walls and dissected the stalls with yellow strips of light, yet the shadows provided a respite from the heat. I quickly threw down my dueling sword and parrying knife, stripped and doused my heated skin with cool water from the bathing trough. A massive puddle developed on the cobbled floor at my feet. I didn't care. My mind was focused, alive with pure energy. Only after a rigorous workout or heated battle were my body and mind at peace. I almost felt human again. Almost.

I smelled her before I saw her. Her essence was that of lemon oil and cinnamon. It brought to mind candied apples. She wasn't supposed to be here. Saturated with young virile males, this part of the castle grounds was off limits to the females for their own safety.

I didn't turn around, but continued to bathe away the sweat. "What do you want, Evangeline?"

To her credit, she didn't shy away. She boldly stepped out from her hiding place. Too boldly. "I was just out for a walk."

"Then I suggest you walk out of here."

She didn't obey me. That was Evangeline's problem. She didn't have a head for common sense. Life, to her, was a never-ending game. Irrepressibly playful, she pushed until she got a reaction; whether for good or bad, it didn't matter. She craved attention, and Juliana gave it to her–outrageously spoiling her or severely punishing her. Evangeline didn't seem pleased until all eyes were on her.

So why had her eyes suddenly fallen on me? I had always believed she hated me for killing Jakubek. I rarely gave the woman–any woman–a second look. Juliana was more than a handful for me.

I could feel Evangeline inch closer, and I became wary when her voice slid into a husky whisper, sexy yet tinged with sadness. "Don't you ever get lonely?"

As casually as I could, I slipped my hoses back on. With a sharp tug to the tie, I turned around. My gaze honed in on Evangeline, barefoot, dressed in a thin, yet chastely white chemise cinched tightly at the waist by a corset. Juliana would not be pleased to see her pet romping around in her underthings even if it were broiling hot outside.

Willowy to the point of looking fragile, Evangeline bore herself with an air of serenity, an aloof carriage that only came from being born into nobility. Slight chin, high cheekbones and big brown eyes surrounded by a riot of honey blonde hair, she looked innocent and untamed all at the same time. It was a heady mixture for any man to ignore.

She drew closer, her gaze skimming over my chest, across my shoulders and then finally to my face. What was she up to? Never had she dared to engage me in conversation let alone done so in private. I would ferret out her intent. I crossed my arms over my chest and threw her a careless grin. "Loneliness would be a blessing. This place is filled with people. I can't even bathe without an audience."

"I've been watching you." She stepped closer. I let her, curious as to what she thought she could get for her boldness. Since I didn't tell her to leave, a flash of confidence flared in her eyes, and she circled me, probing with her eyes and her senses.

I fastened my gaze on her as I immersed myself in her essence. Searching. I found fear, hesitance, and excitement lying beneath her brave front. She had entered a dangerous dance, but I wondered if she knew exactly how dangerous it had become?

I attacked, grabbing her arm and yanking her in front of me. Her eyes grew even wider as I growled into her face, "If you have been watching me, then you will know what pleases me and what does not. I do not need the headache of my men panting after you." I was leader of this pack and to get on my bad side would be a deadly mistake.

Both our bodies stood quivering in the variegated light. Hers with fear, mine with tightly held anger. She raised her arm hesitantly. Her fingers fluttered near my temple, the promise of a touch so near. I was stunned by her persistence. "I could please you, if you'd let me."

And then her fingertips grazed my cheek. Startled, I jerked back, though I didn't let go of her. I plundered her eyes, desperate to know her game. Only innocent curiosity stared back. Though my grip must surely be painful, she didn't pull away. Instead, she laid her warm hand against my cheek. It had been so long since I had felt a woman's warmth, it surprised me. A stab of desire for what I had once been sliced through me.

Seeing my distress, her eyes softened. She stepped closer, a gentle whisper on her lips. "I can feel your pain."

I would never admit to a weakness. "I don't know what you're talking about."

Was that my voice? It sounded broken, uncertain. My heart pounded against my ribs as the humanity that was left within me began to push the beast aside.

Her fingers traced over my lips as she brought her body in contact with mine. A sweet, long-forgotten ache arched through me. "Let me heal your wound," she rasped just before her lips touched mine.

That was all it took. My battered and bruised humanity desperately reached out for something warm, not cold. I could barely contain my feverish desire as I crushed her to me. I was enamored with her skin. It was so warm. Silky. It beaded with sweat and trembled with desire. We tumbled onto a pile of hay, our clothes gone and our bodies wrapped around each other. No thought to the punishment I would receive entered my mind. I only thought of Evangeline–of finding pleasure that touched my soul instead of draining me of life. I nearly cried as I experienced what it was like to be human again.

"Evangeline," I whispered against her earlobe, tasting the salt of our lovemaking, and the pulse of her sated desire. "Why? What made you come to me?"

She placed my hand against her left breast and the rhythm of her heartbeat pulsed against my palm. "I needed you. I didn't want to, but I knew. Only you could fill the void."

I shuddered at what she was saying. "We can never do this again. If Juliana were to find out…"

Jakubek's fate flashed in my mind.

"She won't. And we *will* do this again."

As soon as she spoke the words, I knew she was right. And I knew now why Jakubek had tempted death. Like him, I had been given a taste of heaven while living in hell. I would risk anything to taste it again.

Somebody had hit me with a sledgehammer. That had to be it. My head throbbed and there wasn't a part of my body that didn't ache. I cracked open my eyes against a light that felt like it could burn holes in my retinas. Blinking, I forced them wider.

Golden satin sheets crumpled around my hips as I lay naked

on a bed. Juliana's bed. I groaned, and put my hand to my forehead. How did I get here? The bed dipped, and cool fingers slid against my tender skin.

"Finally, my beauty awakes." An exquisite face, surrounded by perfectly coiled, mahogany curls, hovered over mine. She wore a daring, icy-blue, silk gown that hugged her lush curves. Tiny buttons ran up one side and across her chest. Leave it to Juliana to neglect so many of the lower buttons that the gown split wide to show more hip and thigh than a high-priced call girl. My heart constricted, and a pulse of longing quivered through me. The blatant sexual hunger rolling off her fueled my own.

A flawlessly executed frown appeared, enhancing her delicate features as she grazed her fingers up my ribs. "I am disappointed."

What had I done? I held my breath, wary of her mood.

She bent close to my ear as her hand slid over my collarbone. "You're a very naughty boy."

Icy dread filled my heart and gooseflesh rose along my skin.

She nuzzled my neck, her hand stopping at the juncture between muscle and bone. "What have you to say for yourself?"

My mind searched for a reason for being here. "I, um…I don't know…"

"Why didn't you come when I called?" Her grip suddenly tightened, lighting my nerve in a painful spasm. "And who was that woman with you?"

My memory slammed into me, speeding through the events that found me here. The last thing I remember was Maya flying up the stairs and then Stovall standing over me with a massive piece of wood raised over his head and a look of hate in his eyes.

I'd killed one, but the other one, Vilmos, was still after Maya. I had to find her.

Juliana eased her grip and her hand began a sensual descent. "But how can I stay mad at you?" she purred just before her cool lips took mine.

I closed my eyes, and slipped beneath the flood of her onslaught. I clutched her to me, kneading her curves. She could be more intoxicating than the finest wine. More exciting than any woman alive. I found myself succumbing to her will. Disgusted by the ease with which I fell, I fought against her lust, chased it down and tore into it, decimating the feelings she ignited in me.

Feeling my desire wane, she pulled away, cold anger flashed in her steely silver eyes. "What are you up to, my naughty little pet?"

Too late, I realized my mistake. I needed to play her game, outsmart her. Maya's life depended on it. Juliana was no ordinary woman to trifle with. She had powers beyond the norm and her anger usually culminated in someone's death.

I grabbed Juliana's arms and flipped her onto her back, pinning her against the mattress. I nipped and kissed and caressed her to new heights of passion. After I had her purring with need, I slanted a hot gaze at her. Calmly, as if I had nothing to hide, I said on a deep growl, "I am ever your faithful servant."

She arched her hips into mine, her eagerness to play hovering just below the surface. I continued to torture her with nips and caresses until I was sure I had distracted her anger. "Have I not always given you exactly what you asked for?"

A throaty laugh erupted from her. "Lately, your service lacks attention to certain details."

I froze, as if insulted. She wiggled her body enticingly, "You are doing much better now."

I pushed off her and rose, heading for the armoire where I kept a change of clothes.

"Do not pout," she called from the bed.

"Nothing I do pleases you." I slipped on a pair of pants. "I brought you a present, but the boys were a bit too eager to carry out your orders, and she ran away."

Juliana huffed, and pushed up on her elbows, one shoulder strap of her silk gown fell, baring enough of her luminescent flesh to draw my eye. "So that's your excuse?"

I rested my hands on my hips. "Last time we spoke you said you were bored with the usual. You asked for something different. Unique."

"And what is so unique about her?"

"She's smart."

Pulling the strap up, she threw her legs over the bed and stood. "My body yearns for a challenge and you would bring me a pale intellectual?"

I bowed. "I'm only following orders."

"Was it my order to take her to lunch?"

"You don't get different by snatching someone randomly off the street. I had to woo this one, but now…" I turned and grabbed a shirt, "…I must start again."

She took the shirt from me and threw it to the floor. "Do you think I'm an idiot? You haven't been home for days."

I allowed my anger to finally show. "So you send Vilmos to fetch her, but instead, he kills her co-workers and brings the police on our scent. Do you know what you've done? Your kind has no self-control…especially Vilmos." My gaze bore into hers. "Have no doubt, your jealousy will get us all killed if it persists."

She knew I spoke the truth, but I would get no apology from her. Instead, she asked, "How did you know it was Vilmos?"

"I saw him lying on the floor imitating a bloody mess. One of your best men botched a job I could have done with one hand tied behind my back."

"Fine. Bring her back."

I must be calm. She mustn't guess my intent. "Why should I bother? Vilmos is still after her. He probably has her as we speak." The thought of Vilmos's hands on Maya, his mouth raping her neck, made my bile rise. I swallowed hard. "He'll rip into her before you even get a taste. You know he will. He is ever pushing the limits of your orders."

Her jaw tightened, but she went to the phone and called Vilmos off. I tried, but I couldn't withhold the ragged sigh of relief. I could only hope he hadn't done his worst.

She returned to me, her face a frigid mask of anger. She didn't like to be proved wrong, and I would suffer for stinging her pride. "Remember, no one makes me wait. And that includes you."

The cool silver of her eyes flared with an eerie evil light, but it didn't faze me. I had perfected the technique of defusing her anger. Slowly, I trailed my fingers down her cheek until I cupped her chin. I held back for just a moment, extending her anticipation, and then pressed my lips to hers. The kiss grew in intensity. Her hands slid up my nape, digging into my skin as she pressed herself to me as if she would enter my very body. She pulled at my heat intent on warming the ever-present cold that pierced her heart, fascinated by my pulsing body, and craving the warmth above all else. I was nothing more than a prolonged shock of energy, stimulating ghost feelings of a life she couldn't find on her own.

I broke away, fighting against the pull of her need. Was it only yesterday that I couldn't live without her? Yet today, I could actually feel the beast within me sneering, pulling me toward Maya.

Maya. Only Maya filled me with the deep, soul-stirring longing. I pushed my fingers through Juliana's hair and lied, "There's no need for jealousy. I only did what you asked."

She wrapped her leg around my hip and slipped her hands along my body, finally compliant to my ways. "I wanted you, and you were gone."

"Wanting only heightens desire," I reminded her.

Her hand slipped to my pants and she tugged down the zipper. "I am done waiting."

Maya

CHAPTER SIXTEEN

"Oh, crap. Oh, crap. Oh, crap." My breathing turned ragged as I pushed through the tightly packed dance floor. The music jumped through my veins, urging me toward freedom. I needed to get to the bar. Freedom lay at the end of that bar.

I glanced behind me like a "B" movie actress, gauging the distance between freedom and death. "Just run!" I always yell at them. But now, I knew why they looked back. Sheer terror made them do it.

I tripped and fell against a tall man. He had a pale, almost ethereal, look to him. I knew that look now. He was one of them.

"Sorry," I said. "New shoes."

I pushed out of his hands. The shoes had to go. Feigning a drunken dance just for him, I ripped the shoes off. Hooking my fingers within the straps, I twirled off, and the crowd swallowed me from his hungry gaze.

Toward the edge of the dance floor, another guy wrapped

his arms around my waist, causing me to yelp as he pulled me close. I glanced into his flushed face. A human. Dazed with drugs and sweating from the heat of the dance, he had attached himself to the nearest form. Me. As I peeled away his grip, I saw the man who had been chasing me.

An unexpected vision of a body covered in blood flashed in my mind. It was him! The man who'd killed my friends. I nearly fainted as his gaze raked the crowd, searching for me. I instantly sagged against my new best friend. Shaking, I somehow managed to move to the beat he carried without collapsing into a blubbering ball of fright.

My dance partner's rank breath and slick skin made me want to vomit, but I held on. My pursuer turned his back to me and headed for the stairs. He needed a better vantage point. Once he reached those stairs, I had no doubt he'd find me.

I slipped out of my buddy's arms and pushed him toward a new partner. He accepted the change without a backward glance. I quickly headed to the raised tables and chairs situated near the bar and mingle-walked toward the door at the end of the room. Just a few more steps and I'd be out of here. The coolness of the knob slid within my hand.

"Let it be open. Please, let it be open."

A quick twist and push and the door opened. The light above it began to flash and I glanced back, over the crowded expanse, and right into the eyes of the killer who'd been chasing me. He vaulted over the stair railing, his eyes pinning me to the spot.

"Look away, Maya. Look away." With effort, I pulled my gaze away and slipped within the dark hallway, slamming the door closed.

Blind, I ran. I ran until I saw another lit placard signaling the exit. I refused to look back. I yanked that door open and tumbled into the empty alley at the back of the warehouse. Alden's car sat innocently at the end, illuminated by a sole streetlight. Nothing ever looked as wonderful as that car.

I hitched my dress further up my thighs and ran. My purse thumped at my side, my shoes slapped against my wrist. I felt every lump in the uneven pavement, every rock that met my feet. I didn't care. I couldn't stop. I had to reach the car.

My body slammed into it, forcing the air from my lungs in a violent *whoosh*. With horror, I watched my purse skitter across the hood and to the street on the other side. I scampered over the hood and dropped to the ground just as the man appeared at the far corner of the warehouse. I huddled against the car as I searched for my purse. Finding it, I snapped it open and dug out the keys, chanting, "Oh, please, oh, God. Oh, please, oh, please."

The keys jingled in my hands as I fumbled with the automatic car lock. I pressed the button and heard the lock pop. It sounded like a gunshot in the quiet night air. I yanked the car door open and slid in, locking myself inside. The bite of cool air caused my breath to come in quick painful puffs as I pushed the key into the ignition and gave it a hard twist. The car rumbled to life. Yes!

The car suddenly rocked and I looked up. The man had landed on the hood of the car and squatted right in front of me. His eyes were burning orbs of blue. Iridescent and compelling.

"Hello, Maya," I saw him mouth.

I screamed and threw the car into reverse.

Don't look into his eyes. Don't look. Don't look. Don't. Don't. Don't.

I closed my eyes and punched down on the gas. Tires squealed as the car shot back, tumbling him from the hood. I slammed on the breaks, threw the car into gear, and raced forward. The man stood, blocking the narrow alleyway. I would hit him. I was going to hit him!

I screamed as the car made contact. He rolled over the hood, slammed into the windshield–cracking it–and then over the roof. I didn't stop to check on him. My foot had seared itself to the gas pedal. Nothing would get me to slow down.

As the end of the alley approached, I heard a terrifying sound. The rivets holding the seams of the roof to the main body of the car began to pop. It sounded like a giant can opener slowly ripping the top off.

I came to the end of the alley and spun the steering wheel, sliding the car out of the alley and onto the street. The man tumbled back and managed to hang onto the car by digging his fingers into the metal surrounding the trunk.

My rearview mirror had to be lying to me. No way could he still be attached. The tires spun, and I skidded down one street and up another, tossing the guy this way and that. Tears burned against my eyes, making it even harder to see out of the cracked windshield. It was eerie seeing a huge city like Boston so lifeless. Where the hell were all the people?

I had no idea where I was. I just drove, hard and fast, in a full-blown panic to offload my unwanted passenger.

I yanked on the wheel and the car spun in a tight circle. A loud thud shook the side of the car, and I pulled the wheel straight and punched the gas pedal. The car sprang forward in a cloud of burning rubber. I glanced behind me and saw nothing but the dark gray, rank cloud hovering over the pavement.

Somewhere I had made a wrong turn and ended up along the docks in South Boston. The grounds were rife with machinery that loaded and unloaded cargo from the ships. I drove without a plan, until I found my car racing along in a darkened dockyard, its deserted state the result of a week-old labor dispute.

Metal groaned against the rev of the car's engine.

My heart was pounding so loud, it took me a moment to realize the sound was coming from the roof. I looked up just as a pale hand grabbed hold of the interior of the roof.

"Are you kidding me?" I yelled. I couldn't believe he was still attached. What would it take to get this guy off the car? The metal groaned and cracked. I quickly glanced up and saw the contorted face of the man. He stood and pulled the top back as easily as a page in a book.

I screamed, the only thing I felt capable of doing with any amount of success. A warning stripe of yellow slashed across the road. I didn't slow down. The tires hit the speed bump and the man went airborne. My gaze slanted toward the rearview mirror, and I saw him execute a perfect flip from the car and land on his feet in the road behind me.

My foot shook, feeling the roar of the engine through the gas pedal. I zipped around a corner and raced out of the quay. The car roared up one street and down another, making my pattern of escape as illogical as possible. To my utter relief, I spotted a police station. Without a second thought, I skidded to a bone-jarring stop and threw the car into park.

My hands shook as I pawed at the door handle. Finally, the door sprang open and I tumbled out. Without a backward glance at Alden's destroyed car, I ran toward the station. I must have been a sight with my hair windblown, my eyes wide, my breasts heaving over the low cut of my daring black dress and my bare feet slapping against the cold linoleum of the police station floor as I dashed inside. At least I'd had a recent pedicure to suggest that if I was a prostitute, I was a highly paid one.

The officer at the front desk, Officer Lebinski his badge read, took one look at me and stood. "Whoa there. Slow down. Are you okay?"

I pointed behind me and stuttered, "I-I-I..."

Officer Lebinski's gaze focused behind me, and I whirled about expecting to see the man who'd destroyed Alden's car standing at the door.

"Is that your car? Have you been in an accident?"

"Yes. No. I mean yes." I turned back to Officer Lebinski. "Do you know Detective Carson from homicide? I need to see him. I've been accosted, nearly killed!" My hands shook so badly I would have dropped my purse, if I hadn't left it in the car. I didn't care. I wasn't going back out there for a tube of lipstick and a few credit cards."

Officer Lebinski eyed me suspiciously and sat. "This isn't Carson's district. He's uptown, but I'm sure–"

"He's working on the psychiatrist murders." That's what the papers were calling it.

His eyes sharpened on me. "How did you know?"

"That's my case. I'm Maya Kelbeck. Dr. Kelbeck," I added.

He no longer looked at me as if I was a possible problem child. Over the walkie-talkie attached to his collar, he said, "Peterson, take a look around outside." An affirmative answer sounded and he motioned toward the door to my left. "Come on back," he said, pushing a button which buzzed the side door open.

I lunged for the door, breathing a sigh of relief once I was safely behind it. Officer Lebinski looked me up and down. "Looks like you've been through a lot lately. Are you sure you don't need a doctor to check you out?"

My teeth had begun to chatter. "I-I need Detective C-Carson."

Officer Lebinski led me back to a wide room stuffed with desks and littered with piles of paper. He ducked into one of the few cubicles along the wall and pulled out a chair. "Sit." He left and returned with an ugly green blanket. More gently than I expected, he tucked the wool around me. "Better?"

I nodded…but I wasn't better. I felt sick and disoriented and confused by all that had happened tonight. My eyes must have related my emotions, because the officer gave my shoulder a gentle pat. "I told my superior about you, your car, and I've put a call in to one of the detectives familiar with your case. I'm not promising Carson will swing by, but someone from that case will be here shortly."

I nodded. My voice had deserted me. I couldn't think clear. I still felt vulnerable, like the undead would spring up from the carpet, or seep through the cracks in the walls. I was in a full-blown crisis, unable to reason myself through it.

A short, skinny guy came to the door and Lebinski stood. "Mac, this is Dr. Maya Kelbeck. Dr. Kelbeck, this is Officer McBride."

The officer nodded, his hands gripping two Styrofoam cups of steaming coffee, and smiled, causing the skin at the corners of his eyes to crinkle merrily. "Hello, Dr. Kelbeck."

Lebinski left, probably went back to the front desk, as Mac entered the cubbie. He sat behind the desk and put one cup in front of me and the other near him. "I guessed, but you look like a coffee drinker. One who could really use a good jolt about now."

I wrapped my hands around the cup but didn't dare pick it up. I was still shaking too much. Instead I sipped at it, barely tilting it to reach the hot liquid.

Mac pulled out a notebook and pen. His gaze never left me, and I could feel his inspection, probably wondering what kind of trauma I had sustained to bring me here. "I'm only slightly familiar with your case. We all are. It was terrible. I'm sorry for your loss."

"Thank you," I said, finally finding my voice.

"Does your being here relate to the murders?"

"Yes, and no." I shivered. "I saw the man who killed my coworkers."

"Where?"

"At a club…The Black Dahlia."

"I'm not familiar…" He swiveled his chair to his computer and punched in the name. "Nothing's coming up."

"I think it's an illegal establishment."

His eyebrows rose. "You went to an illegal night club? Why?"

"I can't tell you. It has to do with a patient of mine, but I didn't know it was illegal, not until I was there. People were doing all sorts of things."

"Like?"

"Drugs, and…"

I couldn't finish the thought. It seems so unreal to me.

"And…"

"Murder. They killed someone. Right in front of me. She was beautiful. So stupidly beautiful and they just killed her." I could feel the hot sting of tears enter my eyes.

"You witnessed another murder?" At my nod, he stood and with a snap of his fingers a group of officers quickly crowded around us. "A murder at this club?"

"The Black Dahlia. It's an underground club in a converted warehouse. There's no sign outside. I'm sorry. I got lost. I'm not sure where it is. I'm not even sure where here is."

He looked at his fellow officers. "Anybody heard of this place?"

A chorus of "no's" sounded.

"Okay, people. Let's see if we can find it." He turned back to me. "Do you remember street names? Anything you give us will help."

I tried to remember, but all I saw were blurs of buildings and that man, that inhuman thing peeling back the roof of the car. "I'm sorry. All I remember is ending up at the docks nearby.

"Taylor! Check the Harbor area. Creegy! Go south from the channel. Eunice, get a sheet going on all abandoned warehouses in the area. Let's see what we're dealing with."

Eunice, a big-boned black woman in her forties, shook her head, her big hooped earrings slapping against her neck. "We're in a recession. Do you know how many abandoned warehouses there are in this city?"

Mac sloughed off her irritation. "Keep your search close to the water. That should help."

She snorted, insurrection coloring her voice. "Not much, but you're the boss."

His gaze swung back to me. "Did you know the victim?"

"No."

He regained his seat and leaned forward. "How do you know she's dead?"

"I know a dead person when I see one."

"Did he shoot her?"

"No."

"Strangle her?"

"No."

"Bludgeon her?"

"No." How could I tell him? When I looked back, it didn't feel real. Nothing about that place felt solid. Nothing but Alden.

"Okay, you tell me. How?"

"You won't believe me. I don't believe it myself."

"Try me." He gazed earnestly into my eyes. His whole being, the little boy face, the sweet smile, the gentle voice, all conspired to drag the impossible from me.

"They drained her body of blood." There. I'd said it! Relief shook my shoulders. I'd said the unthinkable.

His pen hovered over the paper. "What?"

"They took her blood. All of it."

He didn't move. His eyes had grown dark, as if he couldn't believe he'd heard me correctly. "How do you know that's what they did?"

"I saw it. They slit her wrists and collected her blood in glasses."

"Why would they…do that?"

He looked as stunned as I had been. "To drink it. I told you, it's an underground club."

"Underground." He rocked back from his desk, his hands toying with the pen as he studied me. "Goth movement? Wiccan? Satanic crap? That kind of underground?"

"It's worse than that." So much worse. He wouldn't believe me. I started to shake again. My stomach roiled with nervousness.

Mac leaned forward. "You're safe. Nothing is going to happen to you here. Trust me. I want to help you."

He did. I could see it in his eyes. The rough wool of the blanket scratched my skin as I pulled it closer, needing its security. I felt breakable, as if any moment I'd fall to the floor and shatter into a million pieces. Had Alden felt like this before he'd told me? Had desperation driven him to the same point I now faced? I had to confess what I saw. I had to purge my mind of the nightmare or I would go insane. I drew in a deep breath. "It's…it's filled with vampires."

His hands stilled and his mouth grew tight. Silence rang in my ears. Slowly, Mac's trusting face turned into a sardonic mask of a hardened cop. "When was the last time you snorted?"

"Excuse me?" His question caught me off guard.

"Got a fix." At my continued shock, he sneered. "Come on,

doctor. You know, sniffed a line? Smoked some crack? Wrote yourself a prescription to la-la land? Is that how your car got totaled? There are a million ways to get a buzz these days. What are you on?"

Oh, my God. He didn't believe me. How could he? What I'd voiced was inconceivable. I didn't believe me either. I put my hand to my head, confused by the images swirling within my brain. "I don't do drugs. I barely even drink."

His hand shot out and gripped my wrist. He turned my arm up and ran his thumb down toward my wrist. I yanked my arm free. "What are you doing? I told you, I don't do drugs."

"Your eyes are dilated and your story is getting a little freaky. Listen, I get all sorts of whacked out crazies coming through here thinking it's fun to play hide and seek with the cops. I don't need another boogieman story."

My heart thudded in my chest. I thought I'd found a person who would help me, instead, I'd made myself out to be a joke. One thing I knew, I had seen a girl murdered. Whether by mortal or monster, that was hardly the point. "I'm not telling a story. I'm telling the truth."

Officer Mac stood, threw the pen on his desk and snapped, "I get the stress you're under. Seeing your colleagues murdered. Seeing them dead. But taking drugs and inventing a crazy story isn't the path you want to go down. I could arrest you for giving a false statement."

"I'm not." I sat frozen to my seat, heartbroken and disillusioned. He wouldn't help me. I'd messed this up by delving into Alden's fantasy world and believing it to be true. Logic fought with what I saw in that underground club. Logic told me they were human, just like me. Evil humans bent on evil sport.

But what of the man? I knew that face. For eight minutes I'd lived in absolute terror because of him. And he knew me. He'd chased me down and ruined Alden's car. Logic couldn't explain that away.

Could monsters exist? Could Alden be right?

A shadow fell across Officer McBride's desk and I looked

up. It was the detective who came to my door the other day, Detective Sundquist. He nodded at the red-faced officer. "Hey, Mac."

"Finally!" Mac slouched back into his chair. "Take her. Get her out of here."

Maya

CHAPTER SEVENTEEN

Sundquist turned to me. His eyes held a shadow of sadness bordering on pity. Had I sunk so low, into the throes of delusion that everyone around me thought I'd gone crazy? He didn't move to shake my hand, only nodded at me and said in a quiet voice reserved for the unstable, "Hello, Dr. Kelbeck. Why don't you come with me?"

It wasn't an offered choice, but a nudge that said my time here was done. I stood, my legs still shaky, but now more from anger than fear. I had *never* been summarily dismissed. *Ever.* Alden had been right. Going to the police had been a bad idea.

Eunice approached with a pile of paper. "Here's the list of warehouses you wanted, though—"

"Give it to Sundquist," Mac said without looking up. "We're off the case. Call everyone back."

Eunice lifted an arched brow and slanted a curious gaze at me. I shrugged off the blanket and handed it to her with a soft thank you. I felt like one exiled, infected with a terrible disease, never to be included again. Sundquist, with papers in hand, motioned for me to precede him.

Outside, the night air slapped at my face, it's cold anger at my stupidity seeped through my tiny dress. I shivered, though not from the chill. My paranoia still clung to me. What if *he* were here, watching me? Waiting? Surely he wouldn't attack me in front of an officer right outside a police station. I needed help. Not just for me, but for Alden. I hadn't forgotten him. Though he said he could handle himself, how could he possibly do so against those monsters?

"That your car?" Sundquist asked casually.

I glanced at the bizarre shape, its metal roof half peeled back and the hood indented in front of a cracked windshield. Alden would be horrified to see what had happened to his car. "I borrowed it from a friend."

I opened the door and began searching for my purse. It had to be in here. I wanted to go home, to see Alden and make sure he was all right. I found my cell phone on the passenger side floor. I dialed home. The phone rang and then my answering service beeped. "It's me, Alden. Are you there? Call me so I know you're okay." I ended the call and continued the search for my purse.

Sundquist hovered just outside the car door. "That's quite a sunroof it's sporting. Recent addition?"

At my glare he shrugged. "Well, I hope that friend is real understanding. By the way, you left these in the ignition." He held out his hand.

I looked over my shoulder at him. Alden's keys.

"I turned the car off when I got here. Most people aren't in that much of a hurry to see a cop."

I'd left the engine running? Not only was I seeing monsters, but I'd become completely irresponsible. Embarrassed, I took the keys from him. "Thank you. I wasn't myself earlier." What was I saying? I still wasn't.

He shoved a pack of cigarettes in front of my nose as an offering. I looked at him and declined. He pulled one out for himself and lit it with a flick of his lighter. Breathing in deep, he blew the smoke out. "Do you mind telling me what happened to you tonight?"

I snorted and resumed my search. Finding the little black purse with a skimpy shoulder strap, I eased out of the car and turned to him. "Apparently, I'm on drugs. At least that's what they think." I nodded toward the police station.

He held out his cigarette and smiled bitterly at its burning tip. "Most people are. I am." He smiled and sucked on his cigarette and blasted out a stream of smoke. Then his eyes grew more serious. "Are *you*?"

"I don't even take aspirin if I think I can grit my way through a headache."

He nodded. "Okay. Then tell me what happened."

I sat on the edge of the driver's seat and rummaged behind me for my shoes. Finding them, I strapped them on my tender feet. They'd begun to throb from my dash to the car. "You won't believe me."

"That's a risk, but I'll let you in on a secret."

A secret? Didn't he know? I was a pro at hearing secrets. With my shoes in place, I stood. "Oh yeah? What's that?"

He drew in another long breath of toxic smoke and let it out slower this time, gauging his words. "I have a better imagination than most. What seems impossible to most cops is perfectly plausible to me."

I laughed at that. He was in for a shock, then, because my story came straight out of peoples' nightmares. I cocked my head. "Really? How about vampires and werewolves and the boogieman?"

He threw his spent butt on the pavement and ground it out with the toe of his shoe. "Bloodsuckers, shape shifters and pure evil? What's not to believe there?"

I was about ready to accuse him of littering when my gaze snapped to his. "Don't tease me. It hasn't been a good night."

"I wouldn't do that to you. Why don't we go get some coffee at an all-nighter just down the street? If we do, I'll let you in on another secret." He opened the passenger door to his car and waited for me to get in.

I stalled. He'd shocked me with his admission, and now he

promised me another secret–the one sure thing to draw me into a trap. My hand clutched the warped roof of Alden's car while the other slipped to the door. Good ol' Detective Sundquist looked normal, but…

"Are you a walking nightmare?" I had to ask.

He laughed. "Hell no. I'm as normal as a guy can get."

Normal was subjective, but for some reason I believed him. He, unlike Mac, wasn't put off by the bizarre. I sighed, stepped away from Alden's car and slammed the door closed. I didn't bother to lock it. What would be the point?

"I could use a dose of normal about now." I slipped into Sundquist's front seat and buckled up as he closeted me in the stale air of his car. It took him less than five minutes to drive to a 24-hour diner. They were the longest five minutes I'd ever had. My brain, still flipping out over what I'd seen, spotted potential evil everywhere I looked.

He parked in front of a collection of flashing neon signs advertising all sorts of delicacies. Chicken fried steak. Deep fried Twinkies. Various types of sodas. Dirt seemed to cling to every surface of the exterior–at least the parts that weren't chipped, split or peeling. It was a bona fide, straight-from-the-movies, den of grease. How very cliché for a cop. I bet they had doughnuts.

The waitress, with her buttons declaring "smile" and "Have you called your mom today?" on her apron, showed us to a two-seater booth. The vinyl, riddled with cracks, shone fire engine red while the linoleum underfoot blazed a bright yellow–whether from age or 1950's aesthetics, I couldn't tell. I suspected cockroaches congregated beneath my seat, but I refused to tip myself upside-down to see if it were fact. Instead of ordering a late night snack like Sundquist, I opted for a clean cup, mine had remnants of an earlier patron's bright pink lipstick along the rim, and a half cup of coffee.

When the bagel and cream cheese arrived along with my coffee, Sundquist looked over at me. "So, what's your story?"

I stared at his shaggy hair thinning along the top, the oval face, the big hands and the suit that didn't fit. Either he had recently gained weight or he had gone to Goodwill and picked out the closest thing to a good suit he could find. He reminded me of a scruffier, heavier-set version of my brother. God knew, I missed my brother. He'd always been my great protector.

The tension I'd been carrying all night eased a bit. "What's your secret?"

He waggled a finger at me like I was a naughty child. "After your story."

I shrugged. "Fine." The memories were so jumbled, I had a hard time pinning them down. "A friend and I walked into this club. Wait, it was a warehouse that had been converted into a club. But this club was only a front for another one, an illegal one though I find it hard to believe the other one was above board. It was piled with drugs, like that candy store you see in the mall with bins stuffed with sweets. Well, not that bad, but you know what I mean." I stopped. He was lazily chewing his bagel, looking slightly bored. "Aren't you going to write any of this down?"

"That depends on what you tell me. So far, it's not been noteworthy."

Fair enough. I cradled the warm cup in my hands and blurted out, "I saw a girl murdered tonight."

"Where?"

His response to my announcement wasn't nearly as dramatic as Officer McBride's, in fact, it was taken in with a sleepy eyed look of acceptance.

Danged if that didn't piss me off just a bit. "At The Black Dahlia."

He nearly choked on his cream cheese laden bagel. That was more like it. He wiped at his mouth, his eyes glued to mine. "You were at The Black Dahlia?"

"You've heard of it?"

"It's got a reputation for devouring people. People go in and never come out." He pulled out his notebook. "What did you see?"

"That's the problem. It was all so surreal, like a nightmare."

The more I thought on it, the more bizarre it appeared to me, as if I had made it up. And now, in the bright florescent lights of the diner, I was afraid I had.

I shook my head, puzzled. "I don't know if everything I saw I actually believe, but I do know, without a doubt, they killed her…slit her wrists and bled her dry."

He put his notebook down. "I know how you feel. Sometimes, I think this whole world has gone crazy and I'm the only sane person left. I see things that don't make sense. Things that shouldn't exist.

"So here's my secret. Reality isn't as predictable as people think. We've been told the creatures roaming the dark are all in our heads. But they're not. They're real."

An image of fangs sinking into flesh flashed in my mind. A shiver passed over my skin. "Monsters?"

"Pure evil. Society has been deceived into believing none of that scary stuff really exists. But I know people who know the truth. They fight evil everyday and win."

A champion. That's what I needed. I needed someone to believe in me. Someone who could make sense out of what I had seen. I glanced at my phone. It had been more than a few hours since I'd run from The Black Dahlia. Alden hadn't called. Something had gone wrong.

I couldn't mess this up. "I think my friend is still at The Black Dahlia. Actually, I know he is. He would've called by now to check up on me. He's very protective. I need help in getting him out. Can your friends help me?"

"If he's still there, then he's as good as dead. I'm sorry."

Alden dead? It was unthinkable. He radiated life.

I shook my head. "I don't think so. He's special."

"Why do you say that?"

I threw him a sly smile. I wasn't the only one who couldn't resist a lure. "That's my secret. But I'll tell you if you take me to your friends."

He flipped his notebook closed and slipped it into his breast pocket, a grudging look of respect on his face. "You learn pretty quick."

"I try."

He motioned me forward as he slid closer, his upper body engulfing the width of the table. I put my coffee down and did as he asked. Our faces were an inch apart. Creases in his skin marked his years, along with the slight graying of his stubble, and the pull of weariness on his face. He had a nice face. A bit too world worn, but trustworthy.

His voice reached my ears on a puff of air tense with warning. "You sure you want to go through the looking glass, little girl? The other side of the mirror isn't pretty. Once you go though you can never go back."

Little girl? He had to be kidding. He had no idea who he was dealing with here. The horrors I had heard, the things people told me. I was never a little girl.

"You don't understand," I whispered back. "I'm already on the other side."

Alden

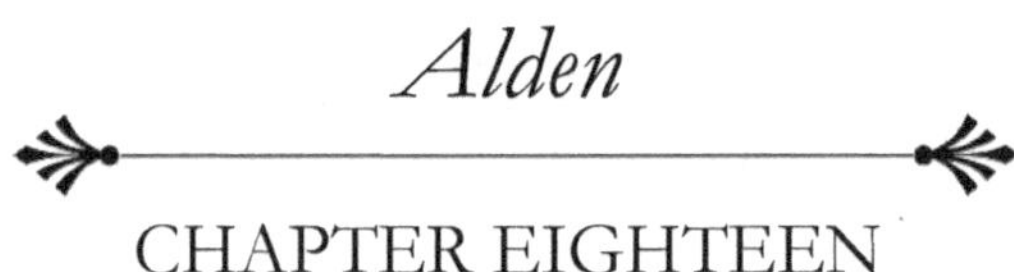

CHAPTER EIGHTEEN

Juliana fell back against the pillows; her pale skin radiant against the golden sheets, her breath slowing, her hardened eyes calculating. She was still angry. Angry at me.

I raked my hair back from my eyes and stared at the coffered ceiling. God, had I not suffered enough? Endured countless humiliations for my folly? When would this nightmare end?

Instead of choosing a noble path on that fateful night so long ago, I had passively accepted my fate–to change into the beast. Regret at allowing the transformation pinched at my soul. I should have refused to follow Jakubek. I should have waited for the promised execution. Death was preferable to this endless existence. I had surrendered to my weakness, to my lust for Juliana. I had gained a prolonged life, but what good is life without love? Instead of being cradled in the loving arms of God, I now made my bed with the devil.

I closed my eyes and pictured Maya. Warm and pure and

without an endless list of selfish demands I must perform. How cruel to present her to me now when I was so far beyond redemption. I would surely go to hell for all that I had done.

So why present me with hope? Why chance her ruin? I shied away from the strange bond we shared. I had purposely left it unexplored for fear of disillusionment.

Still…I grew stronger in her presence–renewed by life. With Maya near, this sucking void that threatened to suffocate me vanished. I could breathe. Naturally. Freely.

A cool hand slid down my jaw. "Who do you think of when you close your eyes?"

I could hear the jealousy, the childish insistence she had been unable to control in all these centuries. How could one live so long and remain so selfish?

"No one." My heart had long ago been shattered by her probing mind and vicious tongue. I now guarded the pieces that were left by encasing them in stone.

"Do you know that when you lie, your eye twitches?"

My lids flew open; my gaze collided with the liquid silver of her eyes. "What?"

"Just barely," she whispered as if giving me the most delicate of secrets. Her fingers glided down my neck and to my shoulder. "In fact, if I was not looking for it, I would not see it. But I did."

I grabbed her hand, stilling it. Ever since those first years living in a sensual haze, I had developed an aversion to her touch along my old scars. She played with them, sometimes opening them to watch them bleed anew.

At my interruption, her gaze flared, causing the silver to deepen, a visual warning of the flood of emotions lying just beneath her control. She was toying with me. She always did. "No it doesn't."

"And there it is again."

I let my eyes close against her milky visage hovering so close to mine. "You're mistaken."

I felt the sting of sharp nails puncture my skin and draw blood. On a voice laced with derision, she snapped, "I did not give you leave to speak your mind. It is a habit you have developed over the years that chafes. Get up."

Gladly. I pushed off the bed and stood looking down at her superficial perfection. My eyes only saw an ugly creature bent on evil. With a struggle, I said, "What would you have of me? I am always your obedient servant."

She stood, wrapping the sheet from the bed around her body, the fine satin trailing behind her as she headed to the phone. "Obedient? Hardly. You have a mind of your own–one that needs purifying."

A cold sense of dread rushed through me. Purifying? I had never heard her use that term before.

She lifted the receiver. Though the words were mouthed quietly, I heard her. "Come get him."

"Who comes for me? What have I done to displease you?"

She stood before me in a blink of an eye and slapped me full across the face, sending me flying into the wall. "Be silent."

I crumbled to my knees, clutching my head and tasting blood in my mouth. She had crushed my cheekbone. Pain lanced through my face, but I refused to cry out. I forced myself to stand, though my legs shook beneath me. Her strength was awe inspiring and terrifying to witness. I glanced over at her beneath lowered lids.

"We have shared together more than others thought prudent. I laughed them off. You were my pet. My special one. Your loyalty would be forever. How do you think it makes me look to hear of your behavior?"

She paced, driving her heart rate up, sending a wave of anger to shake the walls. Her powers had grown since the first years I had known her. She had always delved into magic. At first I had thought it amusing, her tricks and potions. I should have paid more attention. Now even I did not know how far her powers extended.

"What have I done?" I managed to cautiously mutter past the pain.

"You changed. Without my consent, you changed and attacked Vilmos's apprentice, killing him."

I had changed? Why didn't I remember that? My heart pounded in my chest at the news. "I-I don't remember. Are you sure they do not lie?"

"Very sure."

A knock sounded and she called admittance. Men I had hand-picked and personally turned for her army, men who had sworn faithfulness to me, entered.

"Take him. I'll be there shortly."

I did not fight them; I hadn't the fervor to get away. My head ached, not only with pain, but with the realization that I had somehow changed from man to beast and back again without Juliana's consent. No wonder anger poured from her.

Concentrating on healing my facial bones, I detached myself from the humiliation of being dragged half naked through the club and down the stairs. They pulled me through a back door and into a room. Juliana's chamber of shame. It was the largest room beneath the club. It had to be to accommodate all of Juliana's "toys", for this was the room where she played with her special victims, torturing them until she became bored and killed them.

The air in the room smelled of fear and death. Flashes of unpleasant memories bombarded me as the chains encased my wrist much like the first time I had been captured by Jakubek. I fought off the feeling of helplessness and continued repairing the damage to my cheek.

When they were done chaining me, the man to my right squeezed my shoulder. "I'm sorry," he whispered and backed away.

Vilmos entered. His superior swagger hard to watch. "Well, now. Finally. I've waited far too long to see this."

The healing complete, I smiled, denying him a show of fear. "I'm so pleased you could make it. I worried you might not."

"Do you refer to your little friend? True, she gave me a good chase."

I longed to know if she were still alive. "How did she escape?"

"What makes you think she did?"

"You're as pale as chalk."

He nodded, accepting I obviously knew the look of a vampire who had just fed, no matter how small a bite. "I could have delivered her to Juliana."

"We all know you can't hunt without tasting."

He laughed. "True, true. She is quite clever, really. And brave for a human. I don't think there is a weak bone in her body. Her blood will be a pleasure to savor."

"I doubt you'll get any."

He grunted his agreement. "So do I."

We both knew Juliana never shared her victims. They were almost a sacred thing, to be drained and burned, only the most special were turned.

The room began to fill, werewolves and their masters, until the scene reminded me of a seventeenth century beheading I had attended once. The whispers rose. Why was the master's favored pet chained? Why had they been summoned?

All speculation ended when Juliana appeared. She entered like royalty, her stride commanding, her face unreadable and her body dressed all in white, from the pants and thin white shirt to the jacket lined in artic fox fur that ended in a collar that brushed against her pale jaw line. She looked gorgeous, and those who rarely saw her gaped at her beauty. Even I found it hard to look away. She stopped before me, her eyes chips of ice, sharp and biting, and came directly to the point. "For your disobedience, I will administer two hundred lashes." A gasp rose from the crowd, which she ignored. She motioned two men forward. "Hang him from the beam."

My men hesitated for only a second before stepping forward. The chains I bore were attached to a beam from which a hook dangled, waiting to accept its prisoner. My toes brushed the floor, teasing me with the thought of safety. I stood taller than most, yet I was far more muscular. The stress on my position would add to my torture. Juliana held out her hand for a whip.

Grasping it in her slim, white fingers, she turned to those gathered behind her, her voice resonating total authority.

"Hear me, all of you. When I speak, you listen. When I give a command, you obey." Her gaze slanted toward Vilmos and his once relaxed position stiffened. "These are my rules, and to challenge them will bring my wrath upon you, and very possibly your death. Do not think you can leave and survive on your own. You need me. You need what I give you. Anonymity to feed. To gorge yourselves without fear. Without me, you would be dead within a week, for there are those who hunt us–our own kind as well as those of the human realm. I give you the luxury of life without consequences. Think on that the next time you play with the idea of disobedience."

Turning her back on her devotees, she approached me, her hips swaying seductively. Hanging there, I had begun to sweat with the effort to keep the bulk of my weight off my shoulder joints. Her eyes followed a trickle as it wandered down the side of my face and down my neck.

"Has it been so terrible?" she murmured, whisking the droplet away. "Did I not give you whatever you desired?" She stepped closer, sliding her hand into my hair as she brought her lips to mine. I jerked, feeling her leach my body of its will. I strained forward, my mind suddenly my enemy. *Obey. Submit. Yield to her desire. She is what you really want.*

Her lips broke away, yet I strained forward, my eyes glazed with need, with the obedient hunger she expected. She leaned forward, and sighed. I buried my face in her hair, breathing deeply of her cool scent. The old obedience stirred, coming to life in the stale, fear-soaked air of the chamber. The old words of obedience poured forth. "Whatever you desire, I desire."

"I gave you the world," she whispered in my ear. "It's time you understood that gift comes with a price."

She stepped back unfurling the black coil and said, "This pains me as much as it will you, my sweet." She shook out the whip in front of her like a snake charmer controls a cobra, delighting in its beauty, its sleek design. With a flick of her arm, the leather whistled through the air and slapped the skin on my chest a bright pink. Again and again the whip flew, ending its swift journey on my flesh. Welts rose and then turned into cuts. Some shallow, most deep. Blood began to flow, dripping down my body to pool on the floor. I bit my lip, refusing to cry out. I moaned and my body jerked involuntarily. Again and again my limbs shook against the strikes, my mind shrinking from the agony being inflicted on me. I tried to heal each cut as it appeared, but they were too many. My body burned from throat to toe as the lashes melded into one another. A stroke. Another one. Another and still more. And then…nothing. I moaned with relief. She was through.

But she wasn't. I had one hundred more to endure. She stepped to the back of me, her once pristine white clothing spotted with blood. Without a word, she began the torture again. The first lashes felt almost pleasant compared to the ones that followed. I gritted my teeth, the beast howled at the pain.

Give in. Obey without question.

I would rather die. I could make that choice. My bond with Juliana had somehow been broken. I could do as I pleased now. I could stop this madness, refuse to heal my body and let nature turn me into ashes. No longer submitting to Juliana was a tempting prospect. Yet, an image of Maya floated through my mind. I couldn't give in. I couldn't die. Maya's life was now at stake. If I died, that wouldn't change. They would hunt her and kill her for sport…and it was all my fault. I had brought her into their sights and now that they knew of her, they wouldn't rest until she was theirs.

The lash bit into my spine, and I let out a short ragged yelp. God have mercy on me. My mind began to fade. Have mercy, I implored. Keep me alive long enough to see Maya safe.

The slash of the whip carved my back, forcing pain to rip through my body. I began to think the lashes would go on forever. Indeed, they did. Again and again the leather tore into my flesh until a moment of intense clarity dawned.

I would die.

Under another vicious lash, the wretched shell that was my body spasmed. I gasped, flooding my lungs with air. The cords in my neck strained against the agony I wished to hold in, but at long last, it wouldn't be denied. On a pain-roughened voice I cried out. "Mercy!"

Whether the plea was to God or to Juliana…I could not say.

Maya

CHAPTER NINETEEN

My doubtful gaze encompassed the ground floor of the derelict building Sundquist had brought me to. "Are you *sure* this guy can help rescue my friend?"

"I'm more than sure," he said, leading me onto an old freight elevator. He pulled the decorative, wrought-iron gate closed and pressed number three.

The old freight elevator shimmied like a rattlesnake's tail as it began its ascent. I could see a century of dust in the air; its unique smell telling me the history of this place—old tobacco and…was that garlic?

Sundquist leaned into a corner, his hands gripping the side of the cage as if he were the only thing holding this rat trap together. His stance didn't inspire confidence. We slipped into the darkness of the elevator shaft and the sound of grunts and yells drifted down from higher up. That couldn't be good. "Seriously. Are you sure?"

"Just wait. I've known him a long time. He's a character. So is his brother. Both tough as nails kind of guys."

The elevator shook even more violently if possible, slowing

to a crawl as it came to the second floor. Sundquist kicked at a piece of metal that snagged the rim of the elevator platform and the cage rattled past the second floor. I grabbed hold of the grate door as the elevator suddenly picked up speed. I slanted a worried glance at him.

He smiled. "It's fine. She just needs a little tap now and again. Can you believe there's a guy who wants to convert this place into a bunch of high-priced lofts? Who'd want to live in this dump?"

Obviously, appreciating the finer points of old architecture escaped the detective.

The grunts and yells grew louder as we neared the third floor. The elevator slowed, and gradually, the wooden floor came into view. The old, wide planks groaned with the stomp and slam of a fight.

I had no doubt my eyes showed my alarm. Sundquist stepped forward and pushed the gate open even before the cage came to a full stop. "Welcome to the slayer's nest. It's not very homey, but it gets the job done."

I peeked out from the elevator and saw a group of people, six at the most, gathered at the far end of the cavernous room. Sure enough, a fight was in progress. A man flipped past a boy who tried to fly kick him in the chest, only to have the man deliver several punches to the boy's torso. Not to be denied, the kid went into action, spinning and jumping and kicking like a kung-fu movie on steroids. The man encouraged and deflected the hits, and every-so-often, he landed a brutal hit of his own, landing the boy on the mat.

The four people gather around them hooted encouragement at the pair. The boisterous uproar didn't seem to bother Sundquist.

"What's going on?" I asked as I stepped into the room. Everything looked old Army surplus—dingy, greenish-gray and dented.

"Looks like di Taro is testing Wiggy."

"Wiggy?"

"Just a little snack he pulled off the streets a few years ago."

"Snack?"

"A group of vampires got hungry and Wiggy got caught. If not for di Taro, he'd be drained cold and six feet under. He's a wiry little kid, black as midnight with the biggest afro under that rag I've ever seen this side of the seventies."

I looked more closely at the group. di Taro was the only adult. "Where's the rest of his group?"

"Around here and there."

"Are they all kids?"

"Not all. There's di Taro. His brother Ryan. Then there's Anara. And…I'm pretty sure Cade and Snap are over twenty," he said as if three more adults would alleviate my worries. It didn't.

A slim, young girl, no more than twelve, broke off and strode toward us. Her jeans were too big, ripped, but clean, as well as her racer-back, baby-blue shirt with a hem that scrunched low on her hips. She took one look at me and shook her head, sending her blond choppy layers swinging, which emphasized her pixie looks. She raked her intense blue gaze along my wrinkled black dress.

Planting her feet wide, she placed her fists on her slim hips and pursed her cupid's bow mouth as if she were preparing to spit on me. "Drag in a pretender?"

Her innocent looks clashed with the smoky, adult voice. She sounded as if she'd already hit the hooka one time too many tonight.

Sundquist smiled. "Be nice, Baby. This is Maya, a friend of mine."

"You don't have friends, Chubby."

He put his hand to his heart as if wounded by her words. "Aren't you my friend?"

"No." She stared at me, her eyes hard, her beautiful, baby face unyielding. "Beau won't like her."

My analytical brain went into therapy mode. A street kid. Protective and belligerent. Typical posturing, like a cobra expanding its hood to make itself appear more threatening.

My gaze went from her to the group, and I took a step

back. "No. This isn't going to work. They're just kids. I need…well…big people. *Really* big people." I shook my head. "No. Let's go."

Sundquist must have suddenly seen what I was seeing. "Yeah, they're kids, but they aren't your homegrown, normal kind of jots and tittles. Just give them a chance."

"I don't care if they're the offspring of Chuck Norris and Lucy Liu. There's *no way* they can help me."

The girl dropped her threatening posture, but her dislike of me still lingered in her tone. "Come on, Chubby. You know what we can do. We're the right choice…" she slanted a glance at me, "…if she's for real."

He fluffed the girls cropped hair as he passed by, expecting me to follow. "She's for real."

Baby took another long look and snorted. "Okay, then. Come on."

She waved me forward. I hesitated. What could a bad-tempered brat and the lollypop gang really do?

Stopping at a chair, she twirled the seat about and looked back at me. "You coming or leaving, lady?"

Good question. Sundquist seemed to believe we were in the right place, and frankly, I'd run out of options. I nodded, though my steps weren't exactly enthusiastic.

"Sit." She shoved a squeaky wheeled chair toward me. "They'll be done in a bit. I suppose you want coffee?"

Not the most pleasant hostess, but considering the cheerless atmosphere she hung out in, I couldn't expect more. "Thank you."

I sank into the chair, grateful for its utilitarian support. All my adrenaline from the night vanished. It was getting harder to stimulate a response from my brain to my limbs. I forced myself to call my apartment again. No answer.

The yells and grunts continued on the other side of the room. What I could see of di Taro was impressive. About six feet tall, head shaved clean, with the look of an athlete. Not bulky like he lifted weights, but lean and strong. The constant motion, the continuous flexing and contracting of his muscles, had sculpted a lean, hard-planed shape. The more I looked at him, the more I saw a weapon instead of a body.

A man carrying a duffle bag, appeared and said something about leaving. A beautiful woman with white blond hair adorned with tiny braids and silver beads joined him, slipping her arm around his waist and hiking her own bag higher onto her shoulder. Beau barely acknowledged them. As they left, the man glanced my way, his eyebrow rising in question. It didn't matter. He didn't stay.

"Who were they?" I asked Sundquist.

"Beau's brother and sister-in-law. Ryan and Anara come and go." He shot a quick glance around and said quickly, "They've been looking for Baby's older sister. She up and left a couple of weeks ago. No word and no reason for the Irish goodbye. They heard about a witch, and Anara needs to speak to her."

There were dozens of reasons why a child would run away. Witch or no witch, by the looks of this place, the first reason that came to my mind was a desire for a normal childhood.

A cracked cup suddenly appeared in front of my face. No use breaking out the good china for a temporary guest. I glanced up. Baby's eyes were glued to di Taro. "He's totally bad ass. I've never seen a body move like his."

I took a sip and nearly gagged. She'd given me the bitter dregs. It tasted more like lukewarm bile than coffee, the little imp. I thanked her and set it on the nearby desk. My gaze returned to the fight. She was right. The guy had moves Jet Li didn't know existed. "He's fast."

Baby gasped. "Hell no, you didn't just say that. He's not just fast, he's like lightning."

"Sorry." Far be it from me to get in the way of a girl and her hero. "You're right. He's amazingly fast."

"That's why he's the best at killing them. They don't think he's real."

I narrowed my gaze on the unfolding fight. "I don't understand."

Sundquist cleared his throat, bringing my attention his way.

"Let's put it this way. Vamps may scare us, but the di Taro brothers scare them. In less than six years, they've become a legend, sort of a myth within their world. The vamps don't know who the brothers are, what they are, or how to catch them. They just know the Brother's Grimm are out there, waiting for them."

A look of hate flared across Baby's angelic face. "I love to see vamps piss blood."

"Excuse me?" I didn't even want to think what trauma caused such a sweet looking child to have such violent thoughts.

She twirled my chair around. Her strangely flushed and animated face hovered close enough to mine that her hair brushed my cheek. She smelled of lavender and sugar. Such a little girl scent for such adult eyes.

"Look." She pointed to a wall just behind us. The unfinished plasterboard was covered with unusual items—not otherworldly, but unusual in their commonness—in a haphazard design. Pieces of clothes, odd looking jewelry, knives, pieces of spiked metal, fur pelts and…

I leaned forward. "Oh, my God, is that a finger?"

I jerked back certain it was, but I just had to hear it. "Is that someone's finger?" I demanded to know.

Baby walked to the wall, and flicked the yellow and curled finger hanging morbidly by an old tack. "Vamps usually pop to dust after they die, but di Taro got a piece of this one before the big event. He's the only one who's ever done that."

I turned to Sundquist who'd propped his hip on the edge of the desk, and whispered, "Serial killers keep victim trophies. This child needs help. It's not a healthy atmosphere for her here."

"I agree," came a deep voice I didn't recognize.

I turned around. None of us had noticed the fight had ended. Two of the kids had left, and the other two, along with di Taro, joined us. Wiggy guzzled water from a bottle, while di Taro went to an old sink and splashed himself clean before wiping his arms and torso down with a gray towel. A big guy of obvious Samoan descent sporting long dreadlocks pulled into a ponytail, slipped past me to sit at a nearby computer. He was at that awkward stage…two steps past a teenager, but two steps away from an adult. Still, from what I could see, the group was a ragged lot, mismatched and tinged with an intensity most normal people would never experience.

di Taro straightened, the waistband of his loose pants sported water marks while his torso gleamed golden in the dim overhead light. He slung the towel around his neck and carefully wiped the expanse of his shaved head dry with the edges, all the while staring at me. "Get off my desk, Sundquist."

His dark, brooding gaze quickly uncovered every dip and curve outlined by my tiny dress. "*Who* are *you*?"

Sundquist stood. "Nice to see you too, Beau. This is Maya Kelbeck. *Doctor* Maya Kelbeck," he emphasized.

Interest showed on di Taro's rugged face, a face that seemed to flirt with handsomeness, but couldn't quite relax long enough to enjoy the effect. His was a manly face. Tough, though a bit too cruel for my tastes. He quickly expelled a lungful of air, his stomach muscles flexing, displaying his washboard abs. "The lone survivor of the psychiatrist murders?"

"Yep. She's in need of your services."

"How so?" he said, walking behind my chair, though I felt his eyes on me as he did. "I thought the local cops were on this one?"

"You know nothing is going to show up," Sundquist said.

"Most likely not…but what I really want to know is how she fits in."

Sundquist was about to enlighten him when I put my hand on his sleeve and stood, facing my inquisitor. "I'm the one who drop-kicked the man who killed my friends."

His gaze lazily swept me from top to toe and then back again. A wicked smile broke free. "Not in that you didn't."

My eyes narrowed, unimpressed by his attempt at wit.

His smile widened, though I got the impression he didn't

use it often. "Ease up, sweetheart. You're damn lucky he was drugged."

"They're…" I suddenly stopped.

They who? Vampires? My mind still couldn't wrap itself around that. Something strange—very strange—was happening and all I wanted to do was close my eyes and wake up. But I couldn't. I had abandoned Alden. I had promised him I wouldn't and I did. I couldn't live with that. I took a deep breath. "They're holding my friend against his will at the Black Dahlia."

"Well shit!" Wiggy blurted out, lowering the water bottle he held.

His outburst conveyed the group's feelings. Even the linebacker turned around to gape before giving me a you-dumb-outsider head shake and turning back to the monitor. The hopelessness of my situation threatened to overwhelm me. I couldn't let that happen. "It's not impossible. I got away."

"You were there? In the Black Dahlia?" Baby didn't look or sound convinced. None of them did.

Whether they believed me or not didn't matter. It was the truth, and I knew I had precious little time to argue the point. "I don't want to go back there, but I have to go back for my friend." I stared directly at di Taro. "I'll do it with or without your help."

"Who's this friend?" he asked, pointing to a shirt hanging from the back of a chair near Baby.

He just *had* to ask that. "I'd rather not say."

He took the clean shirt Baby handed him, and shook it right-side out before putting it on. "Listen, if I'm gonna give of my resources, you can at least give me a clue as to who's being held at the Black Dahlia."

He had a point. Sundquist was suddenly all ears. This was the tease that had gotten me this far. I swallowed and let the name fly. "Alden Caldwell."

"Alden Caldwell." Sundquist scratched his thumb along his lower lip. "Why does that name sound familiar?"

It wouldn't take him long to connect the dots.

"Caldwell? Alden Caldwell? Hold on. You mean that guy who topped the chart as the richest Bostonian this year? He's worth something like 21.3 billion. That Alden Caldwell?"

I nodded. If I failed to help Alden after all I'd put him through, I couldn't live with myself. He wouldn't be in trouble if not for me. I'd made him go there. Me. He'd warned me it was dangerous, but I didn't listen.

My stomach grew tight and my eyes started to sting with tears. I had to control myself. If I broke down now, I'd be no use to Alden.

Sundquist whistled. "Do they know who they've got, because this could spin into a huge ransom opportunity?"

"They know," I said, "but they won't ransom him for money."

di Taro crossed his arms over his chest, but it was Sundquist who asked the question. "You sure about that?"

"He's never come out and said it, but I think he might be the one investing for them."

"They're actually biting the hand that feeds them? I can't see it." Sundquist eyed me. "So that's why you don't think he's dead? He's their moneymaker?"

That was my guess, one that made the most sense to me. I cast him a quick glance. "He's important to them."

di Taro, not having said a word, just stared at me long and hard. Finally, he asked, "Are you in love with him?"

I blinked back my surprise and stared back at him. "He's my friend."

His lips tipped in a knowing smile. "That's not what I asked."

Everyone's eyes were fixed on me. I couldn't reveal that Alden was my patient, nor was this the time for me to delve into whether or not I had compromised my conduct. I took a very firm, but vague road. "Him being there is directly my fault. I pressured him into going."

"You wanted to see the freaks?" Baby accused. "Are you really that dumb?"

di Taro slanted a look of disapproval at his little charge. She cursed under her breath, but she backed off.

She was right, though. I'd been an idiot. My defense was weak at best. "I didn't know they were for real. I went because I needed to see for myself that vampires actually exist. I still can't believe it."

"Believe it," Wiggy said. "The vamps mess with your head. Convince you they aren't real even while they're sinking their teeth into you." He rubbed at a spot on his neck. "Once you accept the reality, they have a harder time convincing you they're human, but that doesn't mean you're safe."

Wiggy had been bitten. The tiny, even pricks on his neck stood out when he lowered his hand. I couldn't suppress a sudden shudder.

di Taro whipped off the dingy towel from around his neck and tossed it into the nearest corner. "Do you know if your guy went there often?"

"Pretty often." I hesitated as I got to the heart of my dilemma. "There's a small problem. I'm not exactly sure where the Black Dahlia is located."

With a snort of disgust, Wiggy kicked the trashcan and di Taro frowned. "Yeah, that would be a problem."

"I noticed his car has a GPS system," Sundquist offered.

As fast as the frown appeared, it was gone. "Perfect. Snap," di Taro nudged the big guy at the computer, "go with Sundquist and divest the car of its travel history."

After the initial shock of my dumb luck in escaping The Black Dalia, Snap had been completely uninterested in our conversation, apparently more enamored with his computer game than a sob story of some rich guy gone missing.

At the order, he swung away from the monitor, leaned back in his chair, and met di Taro with an indifferent gaze. "Are you asking me to hack into it and pull up the coordinates for the club? I'm just clarifying your orders, because if I remember correctly, you just got onto me yesterday about hacking into the city's electricity, water and waste management site and erasing our bill."

"What I'm asking you to do id nothing like that, and you

know it. Now get going."

He smiled and heaved himself out of the chair. "It's always the gray area with you." He passed the detective. "I need to get my kit. Be back in a second."

Sundquist clapped his hands together. "So this means you're going to help?"

Baby gave Sundquist a sarcastic glance. "Duh. We've been looking for The Black Dahlia longer than you, Chubby."

An authoritarian look entered the older man's eyes. "Detective Sundquist to you, Infant."

"It's *Baby.*"

A slow smile crossed his face. "I rest my case."

Anger flushed her cheeks and she hauled back her arm as if to strike, but di Taro caught her wrist. A quick whisper in her ear and a smack on her butt sent her off in the opposite direction. He cast a censorious glance at Sundquist. "You shouldn't tease her. She's still hurting over Sage's disappearance."

My ears perked at that. di Taro didn't appear to be the mother hen type.

"She's pissed at her and is taking it out on everyone," Sundquist accused as Snap rejoined the group. "She needs to be in foster care, not hanging around here with you degenerates."

"She won't go," Snap said. "She's threatened to run away if she even smells Child Services."

Wiggy nodded. "It's what I'd do."

di Taro fixed Sundquist with a serious eye. His words weren't threatening, but his stance said it all. Baby was his business. "She'll run and end up exactly where we rescued her, only next time, we won't find her alive...exactly."

I shivered, disturbed by the thought.

"Yeah," Wiggy said in a barely audible whisper, drawing all our eyes to him. He twisted the cap on and off the bottle, his nerves stretched thin as his eyes followed Baby around the room. "Except they won't kill her right away. They'll keep her until she's all grown up…and then they'll turn her. She's too pretty to just kill."

We all stared after Baby. She would be a beautiful woman one day. Startlingly beautiful. I remembered the faces I'd seen in the underground room at The Black Dahlia—all shades of human perfection, all almost too beautiful to believe. I looked away, unwilling to think about it and noticed di Taro's face. His jaw had grown hard and the muscles spasmed as he watched Baby.

He suddenly turned away. "We're in all the way, Sundquist." He nodded toward me. "While you're out, why don't you drop Dr. Kelbeck off at a friend's house?"

My lips grew tight. The child could stay, but I had to go? That was ridiculous. I evaded Sundquist's hand and planted my feet firmly to the spot. "I'm not going anywhere."

My challenge brought di Taro up short. His countenance darkened; his steps were precise as he closed the distance between us and placed his face right into mine. His eyes glittered with tightly held power. "Do you think this is a game? These guys are real. They kill for fun."

I glanced at the wall of trophies, then back at him. "It looks like you do too."

He shoved his face close to mine and snarled, "Hell, I don't care what you think about me."

Intimidation didn't work on me. I got even closer, my voice dead serious, aggressive even. "I'm the only one who knows how to get around in there. You need me."

Silence, heavy and thick, gripped the room. None of his little band of outcasts dared to breathe as they waited for what di Taro would do next. But I knew. His hands were tied.

"Damn!" Sundquist said, the word as loud as a shout in the still air, drawing our eyes to him. Admiration shown on his face. "You learn *real* quick." He motioned Snap to him. "Come on, mop head. We've got a car to strip."

Snap tucked his kit into his back pocket. "Where's it at?"

"If we're lucky, right in front of a police station. If not, how do you feel about hopping the fence at the impound yard?"

His lips split to reveal a beautiful, bright smile. "Awesome!"

Maya

CHAPTER TWENTY

When Sundquist left, I found myself in a world I didn't know and with people who didn't exactly like me. It's an odd feeling, knowing you are being held at arms' length, judged by some measure you don't understand. I needed their trust, but I didn't have a clue how to gain it.

I didn't have to guess how to gain it for long. di Taro showed me to the middle of the room where a long table sat crowded by a handful of chairs. He pulled out a seat.

Obviously I was supposed to sit. Fine.

Throwing my purse onto the table, I sat, in perfect viewing of the workout mat. The whole right side of the room was dedicated to fitness. Punching bags, weights, inclines, and a climbing wall lined the space. On the far side of the room hung an odd assortment of weapons— knives, swords, exotic blades of odd shapes. And guns. More guns than I'd seen in one place, and what looked like an area where they made their own bullets. I nervously shifted in my seat as he left. Exactly what was I supposed to do? Just sit here quietly with my hands in my lap and wait for him to return?

I felt di Taro behind me before he came into view. With an unwarranted amount of dramatic flare, he slapped a few pieces of blank computer paper in front of me and held out a pencil, his face a mask of indifference. "A layout of the club. Please."

I hesitated and stared into his eyes. They were the color of melted chocolate. I imagined they could be warm, but unfortunately for me, they weren't. "If I do, will you still take me?"

His eyes hardened into opaque chips. "If you don't, I certainly won't risk going into a place blind. You'll be on your own."

He didn't like to be challenged. Point taken.

Sadly, our association was bound to be an unpleasant one.

I grabbed the pencil. "I'm going with you."

"It's your decision," he said dispassionately and straightened. "Baby, take the mat."

Somewhere behind me, I heard her squeal with delight. Her fragile, little body streaked into view. She ran onto the mat and executed a perfect cartwheel, which morphed into a round-off backhand spring with a twist, the tumbling run ending at the wall of weaponry.

I turned to di Taro, my instinct to protect the girl even though she'd been nothing but hateful towards me sprang to life. "Don't you think she's a little young to get slapped around by you?"

He let loose a big laugh. "Nobody slaps Baby unless they want to get slapped back. All I'm doing is teaching her to defend herself." He glanced back at his pupil and shook his head. "Too big. Take the one next to it."

I peered around him and saw her pull a knife from the wall, one with a long glittering blade. She began a series of controlled moves, brandishing the knife in sweeping arcs and precise lunges.

I shook my head at the sight. She was so young. So tiny. Seeing the deadly weapon in her hand looked macabre—indecent. I refused to watch.

Turning my attention away, I slipped my aching feet from

my shoes, pulled the paper close and began to draw, guessing at the dimensions of the warehouse. Layer-by-layer, I delved back into The Black Dahlia. The room around me ceased to exist as I concentrated on reproducing the layout of the club. I shivered a few times, my heart pounding at unexpected memories that sprang to mind as I retraced my steps.

Warm fingers gripped my shoulder, snapping me out of my self-induced trance. di Taro hovered over me, studying the map of the first floor. I had drawn a basic blueprint, yet in the margins I'd sketched out certain key positions I'd noticed. The door. The bar. The stage. The huge window that overlooked the club and the hidden door to the underground rooms.

"You have artistic talent."

I frowned. "Enough to get by." I pointed to the hidden door, showing him on the map where it was located. "This is where we go down into the real Black Dahlia. It's not pleasant."

"I bet not." His gaze rose from the paper and stared at me. His fingers tightened against my shoulder as his eyes probed uncomfortably into mine. I felt vulnerable. Trapped. The paper crumpled in his fingers, suggesting at the war of emotions within him. "I have to ask myself, what's a big-time guy like Caldwell doing associating with the undead? Not exactly a match made in heaven—or one normally found on earth."

I didn't blame his suspicious nature, but I couldn't let him link Caldwell to Juliana. He didn't strike me as the type to rescue the enemy. I swallowed, my tongue darting out to quickly moisten my suddenly dry lips. "I don't know much. What I do know is that the things he's discovered about them have disturbed him to his core. He wants out."

Baby, now slightly breathless after an hour of prancing around the mat, pursed her lips thoughtfully, then jabbed her knife repeatedly at an invisible opponent. "He's got to be dead. You don't piss them off and live."

The paper and my shoulder were suddenly free from di Taro's hands as he went to Baby. "Hold up, Baby." He repositioned her stance, saying, "Don't act like you're going to shank him like some stupid prison hoodlum. Use your brain. Train your muscles to obey without question." He stepped back. "Again."

She repeated the move, this time smoother, more controlled. "Good," he praised. He held out his hand and she placed the knife against his palm. If she were angry, all she'd have to do was jerk it back and his fingers would be sliced off. The blade was that sharp. He didn't seem to notice. "Do some tumbling runs and then hit the shower. It's almost time for bed."

It was then I noticed at some point, while I'd been drawing, di Taro had slipped away and taken a shower and it was now almost four in the morning. Bedtime obviously was a subjective time of day for this group.

I waited for him to return the knife before I asked, "What are the odds of her getting attacked again?"

"High. She's exactly what they look for." His gaze inspected me again. "In fact, so are you."

"Excuse me?" I hardly met the criteria for the exceptional beauty I had witnessed. "I don't think so."

"You said yourself they let you go."

"Not on purpose. You should see the car. The guy chasing me pried the top open with his bare hands."

"If he wanted you dead, he would have punched through the metal and ripped your head off."

A vivid mental picture accompanied his words. One moment my head was attached to my body, the next it was gone. I couldn't stop the frightening footage from repeating, over and over and over…

My mouth gaped in an attempt to breathe, but I couldn't seem to get my lungs to work. di Taro gave my shoulder a quick shake, and I sucked in a big breath. He put his face in front of mine and sneered, "Panic at the Black Dahlia, and you die. I guarantee it."

He was trying to scare me, just like Alden had, trying to keep me from going back to the club. This time it would be different. I knew what I was getting into. I had to see Alden safe. I'd promised myself I would.

I lifted my chin in the air. "Thank you for instilling confidence in me." Even he couldn't mistake my sarcastic tone.

"You want confidence? Get up." He motioned me to my feet.

"What?"

He plucked the pencil from my hand and pulled me out of the chair and to the mat. "Let's see what you've got."

The man had lost his mind. I was a thinker, not a fighter. I pointed out the obvious. "I'm in a dress."

A very revealing dress one should avoid stretching to its limits at all costs.

He didn't seem to care. "Do you think they're going to wait until you've changed into sweats and a t-shirt before they attack you? Come on. Let's see what you've got."

He was serious. I looked around, but Wiggy had disappeared, along with Baby. We were alone.

Well, if I embarrassed myself, at least I would do so without witnesses. I pushed my hair out of my face. "I don't street fight."

"Really? I would've never guessed that."

There was no need to be so snarky.

"So how did you disarm your man the other night?" he asked.

Now he was just ticking me off. "Self defense classes with a smattering of kickboxing I learned off a video."

"That's very DIY of you. So let's see your moves."

I shoved my hands on my hips. "I don't have any moves. I just—"

He suddenly rushed me, and I jumped out of his way, planting my foot against his side as he sped by. He quickly pivoted and swept his foot out, catching my lone leg and jerking it from underneath me. I went down, hard, but I rolled away before he could dive on top of me.

Springing to my feet, I pushed my hair out of my eyes. He was nearly on me again. As he spread his arms out, I ducked and he vaulted over me, rolling out flat on the mat, face up. He had a perfect view up my skirt. Grinning, he grabbed my ankles, flipped to his stomach and pulled. I fell, forcefully twisted sunny-side up in mid air before I hit the ground.

Slammed against the mat, I kicked out in an attempt to get free. His hands grabbed my waist and slid me against the mat at an amazing speed until I was pinned beneath him. I pushed against his chest, trying to dislodge him, but he quickly trapped my hands in one of his and pressed them above my head.

Breathing heavily, he glared at me. "We're not playing around. You fail, you die."

As I struggled to get free, he slowly forced my head to the side. The nip of his teeth made me gasp. "You're a liability, plain and simple," his harsh whisper entered in my ear.

Clapping erupted.

"Nice!" a very male voice called out, joined by a whistle from someone else.

I tilted my head to see two guys standing at the edge of the mat. di Taro stood and helped me up. I could feel a blush heat my face. I tugged my skirt to a more modest level and adjusted the neckline. What an exhibition. My mother would be mortified.

With a wave from di Taro, the two approached. "This is Cade, my chemical expert," he said pointing to a good-looking and grinning twenty-something year-old dressed in fatigue pants and a black t-shirt before pointing to a boy in his late teens. "And this is Poison. He likes to dip his knives in some pretty nasty stuff before he goes on the hunt."

They'd been hunting vampires with poison dipped knives? I turned a suspicious eye on him. "I thought vampires were immortal."

He stared back unaffected. "Almost."

Now that I thought on it, all I knew about vampires I had learned from horror movies. Probably not the most dependable of sources.

Poison thrust his hands in his pocket and pulled out a cross, tossing it to di Taro. "They're immune to disease, famine and most natural disasters."

Well, that was consistent with what I knew. "I don't get it, then. You can't kill them with poison, can you?"

"Naw," the boy said, unbuckling his belt that had a wicked looking blade handle sticking out on one side. "But it'll cause them enough pain to disable them for a while."

Cade sidled close, his eyes definitely focused lower than my face, his grin growing even wider. "He's not the most popular person in their circle of acquaintances. Actually, none of us are."

di Taro smacked Cade on the back of the head and shoved him away. "Mind yourself. You can go blind looking there."

He threw an embarrassed glance at di Taro just before his mentor grabbed him in a headlock and raked his knuckles across his crown. I turned to Poison. He handled himself well for someone so young. "Doesn't causing them pain irritate them more?"

"It's one of the reasons they started the club."

"We scare them," Cade managed to say before he and di Taro began to wrestle in earnest. Baby appeared from out of nowhere. With wet hair and wearing pajamas, she clapped her hands, urging Cade on. No wonder di Taro was built like he was. It took a lot of energy to subdue such a rowdy bunch. In no time Cade was pinned to the mat and di Taro stood, offering his hand to help him up.

Poison placed his gear on a shelf. "Now they mostly send their pets to do the dirty work."

Pets. Like Alden. "What do you know about their pets?"

"They have several kinds. Most are werewolves. Some are postulants, readying themselves to become vampires. Others are demons."

This was no ordinary kid. He was a walking encyclopedia of the vampire sub-culture. I was still having a hard time believing this was all real. I knew what I saw, but my mind just didn't want to accept the impossible, and now he was talking about creatures who I'd only heard about in horror movies. "Demons? What kind?"

"Does it matter?" di Taro said as he drew near.

My gaze swept him as he stepped past Poison to check his gear. Confident with a dangerous edge, di Taro's arrogance set my temper toward a fast burn. I crossed my arms over my chest. "Humor me."

He sighed as if I were one more annoying child he must deal with. "The Fallen Ones come in all shapes and sizes. Dead and alive. Zombies and ghosts and creatures so bad and ugly, I don't even know what to call them."

I wanted to laugh. "You're kidding." He had to be. I'd only just started to believe werewolves and vampires were real, but now zombies and ghosts? They only existed to scare people around a crackling bonfire in the middle of the woods.

He threw me a warning glance. "I never kid about this. Evil uses whatever is at hand to gain a foothold in your head."

I stared at him, my mind blank. I didn't want to think. I missed my innocent, deluded life. I liked thinking vampires, werewolves and the evil uglies were elaborate Halloween costumes instead of scary beasts that lived to kill, maim and destroy our lives.

Cade drew closer. "Dude, I think you just blew her mind."

"Good," di Taro said as he finished examining Poison's gear. "Maybe she understands now why she needs to go home."

Go? After all I had been through I was just supposed to go and forget? Forget about Alden? Forget about the girl and The Black Dahlia? Forget about the man who ripped apart Alden's car with his bare hands? My whole being screamed for me to do exactly that, but I couldn't. I knew too much. Seen too much.

I wrapped my arms tighter around my torso, fighting the panic that told me I was in over my head. "I understand more than you know. It's just hearing it said out loud...that you believe what you're saying…that *I* believe what you're saying…it's surreal."

"Welcome to the world of weird. Most of us pass demons on the streets and don't even know it. They're good at camouflage."

Baby came up close, her eyes glittering with delight. "They'll promise you anything," she whispered.

Cade moved to the other side of me. "Your heart's desire," he breathed close to my ear.

"Then…" Poison suddenly leaned toward me and shouted, "Bam!"

I jumped.

"They've got you," he said, pulling away. "All you can do is surrender and die."

Why did I feel like I'd been dropped into an urban telling of the *Children of the Corn*? I wouldn't be scared off. "*You* all fought."

"We were saved by the Brothers Grimm," Poison said, and they all turned to look at di Taro who had wandered off to wipe down the mats and do other general maintenance work. "Now, we're a team."

They idolized him. Why not? He may not be their father, but he was their provider, their mentor, the reason they were alive. He and his brother may have rescued them from imminent death, but neither of them couldn't save these kids from the nightmare they now knew existed. "He can't save everyone all the time."

Cade's eyes grew serious, his face guarded. Within this rag-tag bunch, he was old enough to know di Taro wasn't invincible, that he was only human. Yet his confidence in the man was unshakable. "Maybe not, but he'll die trying."

Alden

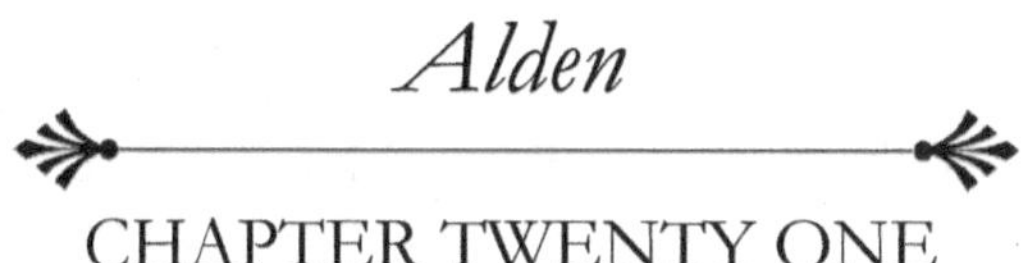

CHAPTER TWENTY ONE

Thankfully, I didn't remember the last dozen flails of the whip. No skin had been left on my torso. Juliana had gleefully stripped it from my body with each precise stroke. Neither did I remember the room quietly emptying after the last slash fell, nor the sound of the chains as I was lowered to the blood-washed floor. I had become a shadow of myself. A mere wisp of flesh and blood. My body so damaged that I couldn't think where to begin the repair. My mind had gone numb, retreating into the bowels of my subconscious.

Physical pain often brings nightmares. I tried to not think, but my mind, too focused on avoiding physical pain, let in a moment of mental anguish I had sworn to keep buried forever.

It was the summer of 1858. Our band of predators found itself along the balmy shores of England's lake country. The light that filtered through the clouds in that portion of England was truly spectacular. It glimmered with a life of its own. Evangeline and I lay on the mossy banks of Lake Windermere under the spreading arms of an old elm, her head on my stomach as I stared at the clouds rolling by. The voluminous fabric of her dress engulfed our tiny patch of earth, yet seeing her in her fine silk, demurely covered like a lady of means should be, made me proud. I could stay there forever.

Evangeline and I had been lovers since the moment she stepped into the converted stable area during the spring of 1657. Our moments were few but treasured. Not only must we hide our relationship from Juliana, but from those who would gladly carry news of our affair to her. Which was almost everyone. There is nothing sweeter to a man's eye than to see one who has been placed in charge fall from grace. I had to be especially careful of Stovall. His gaze was ever present, and his heart ever lustful for power and prestige.

Our horses grazed nearby, and the waters of the lake shone bright, calm and reflective, mirroring the sky above. The book in Evangeline's hands shifted as she turned the page. Her voice rose and fell on the lilt of the love poem as a tinge of sadness pervaded every syllable.

"*… Which, when it has been seen, is such that it*
Alone and always lights the fire of love."

The silence that followed her words gave weight to the air and seeped into my bones. She sighed and let the book fall against her stomach. Tilting her head so as not to muss her carefully coiffed hair, she gazed up at me, her face flushed with delicate color.

"Did you have family…before?" I asked. I don't know why I asked. In all these years we never spoke of our past.

"I had a twin sister. We were opposites in every way. She right-handed. I left-handed. We were like mirror images of each other." Her eyes grew distant, melancholy. "She was the best part of me."

"What became of her?"

"She died soon after I was turned," she whispered.

The brittleness of her features caused my heart to sink. "You didn't…"

I couldn't finish the thought. I had heard how some of our kind had turned on their families, but I had always put that down as myth.

"No," she assured me, blinking the memories away. "I loved her dearly. I would have never hurt her."

I nodded and faced the lake, suddenly regretting my invasion into her past. What if she asked about mine? It wasn't a memory I wished to explore.

Her knuckles slid against my ribs, and I returned my gaze to hers.

"Do you love me?" she suddenly asked.

I was taken aback. This had become a day of firsts. In all these years, she had never once asked me such a thing. I gave no thought to love. I had grave doubts I would ever feel that gentle passion again. Evangeline's eager face made my heart constrict with regret. I chose my words carefully. "I see beauty when I am with you, Evangeline. Beauty I had forgotten ever existed."

A sweet frown puckered her brow. "But do you love me?"

I could not lie to her. "No. I do not."

Surprise and hurt warred for dominance on her face. Yet mixed within the fray shone a dose of disbelief.

I hurried to allay her fears. "Do not think me cruel. I fear I cannot love anyone. My heart is too damaged for the emotion."

"I love y –"

I placed my finger against her soft lips. "Don't. It is folly to waste something so pure on someone as filthy as I."

We lay there, each within our own thoughts. After a moment, she asked with a hesitant tone, "Is that how you view me, Alden? Am I filthy because of what we are?"

"Of course not." I was truly shocked by her question. I looked skyward, peering past the clouds and into the highest reaches of the crisp blue sky. How could I explain to such a simple heart? "You are nothing like me. I have done things no good man would ever think to do or ever admit to doing."

"I care nothing of that. I know you must obey, just as I must." Her voice turned frail, as if it would break if she pushed it one notch higher. "What of me? Do you feel nothing for me? Have I been only a diversion?"

My tongue froze. The day had lost its appeal. The lake no longer looked gentle, but eerily quiet as if it only waited for me to wade in and accept its depths as my tomb.

A diversion. That is exactly what she had been. A retreat from what my life had become; a desperate search for what my life had been. I had used her; shame sealed my lips.

The book fell to the ground as she rolled away. "I am a fool."

I sat up and grabbed her hand, stopping her. "Never say that. You gave me something beautiful, something I will always cherish."

She wrenched her hand free. "I cannot believe you duped me," she said, her chin quivering with suppressed emotion as she collected her shoes.

"I never promised you love. I never sought it from you. There is no promise broken that you can claim foul."

Her fingers stilled on the hooks of her shoes. "You are right." Her shoulders rounded in defeat as her arms wrapped about her body. "You never promised me love. But I sought it. I willed you to give it. You knew what I expected. I need it. Now more than ever." She turned her golden face to me, her eyes pleading. "Why can't you love me?"

I didn't know. I longed for love. I had thought all those years ago that I loved Juliana, but that was a lie. I lusted after her…I still did. I floundered in the trap of her making, forever longing for the warmth of her love, yet receiving only cold desire.

"How can I explain to you why when my own understanding escapes me?"

Her large, doleful eyes grew moist with unshed tears. "I thought you above all would know that to find love is a noble quest."

How easily she sat there spouting ideals of love and happiness, of a knight's pursuit for honor, chivalry and power. She had been born in a time when the world was dark, entombed in the tragedies of warring kings. When noble ladies were bartered like sugar to entice an alliance from an enemy lord. After all these years, she still waited to be rescued. I would have laughed if it weren't so tragic, for how could I rescue her when I couldn't rescue myself?

Bitterness at my own limitations infused my soul. "My nobility was taken from me long ago. I am damaged, Evangeline. Damaged beyond repair."

Hearing my words, she hunched her body forward as her shoulders shook with tears. I placed my hand on her back, wanting to hold her, to tell her it would be all right, but it would be a lie. From today on, nothing would be the same. "I am sorry. Hurting you was never my goal."

"You are willing to let me go?"

I scooted close to her, tucked a stray tress behind her ear, and said gently, "Never would I force you to do what you do not want to do. We have few choices in our lives. I give you this one. Do with it as you will."

Sadness shadowed her eyes. The riot of perfectly twisted curls called to my hand, yet I resisted and let my hand fall away. My gaze drank of her beauty, mayhap for the last time.

She gathered the many layers of skirts in her arms and stood, letting the rich fabric cascade to the ground. Turning, she gazed at me for a moment. "You are wrong."

"About what?" Was that my voice? It sounded wounded, like a lamb before the slaughter, bleating for its life.

"You are nobler than any man I have ever met. It is you who have chosen not to love."

As I watched her go, I wished with all my heart she were right. But I knew differently. The small scrap of humanity clinging desperately to my heart had shriveled to an unseeable size.

I stood and my foot nudged Evangeline's book of love sonnets laying where it had fallen. I picked it up. "False promises of love forevermore." I drew my arm back and threw the book as far out into the lake as I could. It landed with a loud slap, rupturing the glassy water and causing ripples to mar its surface.

There would be no love forevermore for me. Juliana had seen to that.

I woke to a burning hell. The skin that remained skipped with pain. My bare muscles cried out for moisture. I could feel each ribbon crackle as it dried out in the stale air of Juliana's torture chamber. I would soon fall into a deep sleep; the coma of the wicked. Whether I would ever awaken would depend on Juliana. When I was at my weakest, she would either kill me or wait for the healing process to complete itself and call me forth from the abyss.

I took note of my injuries. From head to foot, I was astounded by the severity of the whipping. Deep sleep was inevitable. I could not heal so much damage in one night. I prepared myself to journey to the center of my being when a soft hand pushed the hair from my eyes.

Evangeline had come—sweet and soft as the morning dew, as I had once known her to be. Gone were the hard edges the modern world had imprinted on her. Pink lips instead of cherry red. Soft unbound curls instead of the sleek twist. Flowing pale clothes instead of the gaudy flash of fashion she had adopted over the centuries.

She bent her head to examine my wounds, and I dared to touch what I thought was a dream, yet my fingers found the silken tresses were real. She turned her head and stared at me, her eyes full of unshed tears.

"Evangeline," came my hoarse rasp. "Beautiful Evangeline."

Tears rolled from their prison, streaking her pink cheeks with pale stripes of sadness. "How could she do this to you?"

"Far too easily." I moved my leg, and white heat lanced

through me, causing my sight to dim and a deep moan to claw from my gut.

"Don't move. You're so weak." She said this as if it were a shock. "What have you done?"

I knew what she meant. What had I begun to heal? I could barely say the word past the pain. "Nothing."

"Why? If you do not leave this place by morning, she will only torture you more—in every way possible."

"I cannot—"

I couldn't voice what I needed to say. The pure torture wracking my body sapped all the strength from me. I closed my eyes and concentrated on breathing. Though I longed for the bliss of unconsciousness, my mind would not comply. The only comfort I received came from the silken tresses wrapped around my fingers. I don't know when I realized it, but I knew she had changed. Her hair had taken on a wiry texture against the back of my hand as my fingers slipped against a downy soft undercoat.

"How?" I rasped, cracking my eyes open to see her soulful eyes staring down at me. How had she changed without being commanded? I still didn't understand how *I* had done it. Evangeline and I were the oldest of Juliana's lycans—Evangeline captured and turned a mere ten years before me. There was so much we didn't know about our species. We knew we grew in strength, but could it be we grew in power?

I closed my eyes, longing for the black shadows to close in on me. Juliana would be displeased to know two of her favorite pets no longer needed her to instigate a change. We were doomed. It was best I die now than to prolong my pain.

Evangeline's nose dipped, and then I felt the cool touch of her tongue as she lapped at my broken and bleeding skin. I winced. I would push her away if I had the strength. I couldn't survive. I wasn't meant to live. Surely she knew, of all people, the suffering I endured.

Yet, my moans of agony did not deter her. On through the night she licked my wounds. Slowly, they began to close, to heal. My thoughts became more concentrated. Maya. I must live to save Maya. Only then, when she was safe, did I dare allow this cursed life I was forced to lead end.

My pain grew less unbearable, yet I was as still as a babe. Weak from loss of blood.

Near dawn, the last of my open wounds closed and Evangeline pulled away. My skin glowed pink and new and throbbed with life. When she returned, she had regained her human form and was carrying a bundle of clothes for me. She helped me dress, pulled me to my feet and led me out of the room. I followed because I hadn't the strength to refuse. We exited the terror of the back rooms and entered the common area. To my surprise, it was far from deserted. Those who had witnessed my punishment had gorged themselves on their human sacrifices until they had passed out along the tables.

She pulled me toward the stairs. I resisted, stopping her. "Where is Juliana?"

"In her room."

"Then I go this way," I said, nodding toward a far door that would take us through the labyrinth of the underground passageways and finally to the surface a few blocks away.

Her brow prickled with worry, yet thankfully, she didn't hesitate to do as I asked. Though my strength was returning, it was happening far too slowly for me to get around by myself. I needed her strength a bit longer to achieve my freedom. I understood her dilemma and strove to ease her mind. "Don't worry, Evie. I only seek to delay the encounter. I will see Juliana soon enough."

We lumbered through the door and down the halls, traveling along a hidden passageway deep beneath the buildings above us. Finally, we entered a room at the back of an industrial machinist shop. We fell against the wall, both breathing heavily, exhausted from the process of healing. The door that led to my freedom stood only a step away.

I looked at her, unable to understand why she risked her life for me. "Thank you."

Her lashes fluttered down, hiding the smoky gray of her eyes. "You promise to come back?"

Still looking for someone to care for her. Still the lost and lonely child at heart. The goodness that had governed her human existence warred with the selfish needs of her immortality. I tipped her chin up until she looked at me. "Did you care for me on her orders?"

Evangeline quickly looked away. "She commanded me to stay by you until you either healed or slipped into a coma."

"So, you disobeyed her. You helped me." It was hard to believe. Evangeline had always given the impression of being a true lap dog of our mistress, eager to please, eager to obey without question.

She smiled—a sad, hopeless tip to her full lips. "I did not. I translated her imprecise orders to suit the situation presented to me."

Her admission shouldn't have surprised me. Since the day she had come to me, I had believed she did so against our mistress's wishes. As a favored pet, Evangeline had never been as well trained as the rest of us—typically doing what she wanted—while Juliana, more times than not, humored Evangeline's little fits of fancy with a tolerant hand.

"How long have you known you could change without her knowledge?"

"A few years ago. It happened purely by accident. I hadn't attempted it again until last night. What of you?"

"I didn't even realize I'd changed until Juliana told me."

Her large doleful eyes peered up at me. "What does it mean?"

I could smell the fear on her. We had been through the same hell, her and me. We had been used, disrespected and violently abused. We'd had a child all because of Juliana's warped sense of destiny. I had blamed Evangeline for the disaster of that union, for betraying me, for the birth of our son and his ultimate death. But how could I? She'd obeyed because Juliana had not given her a choice. Now the power of obedience had become subjective. That freedom would be our downfall.

"It means we have very little time to live."

Fear spiked through her gaze and caused her to shiver against me. "You won't tell her about me, will you?"

I slipped my hand through her hair and pressed her head to my chest, inhaling the clean scent of her. Memories of happier times rushed in on me. She tipped her head to look at me, and I kissed her forehead, pressing my lips firmly to her skin and muttered, "I would never hurt you. Never doubt that."

She continued to cling to me, fighting the need to see me safe and the desire to keep me near. Finally, she let go. The door squeaked on rusty hinges as I opened it and fell into the wet, dark morning. I left her there, staring after me as I stumbled and fell and picked myself back up again, determined to get to Maya. Protect Maya. I could not bear to see another innocent life, one I had come to care for so deeply, be crushed by the indiscriminate hand of Juliana.

It was time I ended this nightmare once and forevermore.

Maya

CHAPTER TWENTY TWO

I could hear the elevator before I saw it. It rattled to a stop, and Sundquist and Snap emerged no worse for wear. di Taro looked up from studying the map I'd drawn and glanced over at them. "Did you get it?"

Snap's thickly tangled hair fell over his shoulder as he bent and dug a small box from a side pocket on his cargo pants. "This model not only records where you've been, but the times and dates for up to three months. It's more of a spy tool than a GPS system. Only an idiot would put this in his car."

"Or someone who wanted to know where someone else was every minute of the day," I muttered, thinking of Juliana. She would want to know where her pets had gone while she slept. Modern technology made that invasion of privacy all too easy to accomplish.

di Taro straightened and put both hands on his hips. "Can you break into it?"

The big guy snorted. "Please. They can't make anything I can't hack into."

"That's my boy," di Taro announced like a proud parent.

Everyone converged on the computer station except di Taro, Poison and me. I can't lie. My curiosity over these kids was getting the better of me. I leaned against the shelves stacked neatly with countless containers full of God knew what inside of them and spotted a few clear bottles filled with shimmering yellow liquid stamped with the word "flammable" beside a couple dozen tin cans labeled "danger". It smelled bad in this area, like rotten eggs and chocolate covered pretzels.

Poison squatted and pried open a can. With slow purpose, he counted out twelve red balls—like stink bombs—which he tucked into his belt. I cleared my throat to get his attention. "What is all this stuff?"

"A little bit of this and that. Cade calls them evil deterrents. He likes to mess around with chemicals and make up nasty surprises for the bad guys. Keeps 'em guessing. These," he said, holding up one of the tiny red balls, "explode and spread red dye everywhere."

"What's the point of that?"

"It's awesome!" he said, his face lighting up with excitement, causing his freckles to turn darker. "It also colors any non-visibles hanging around."

"Non-visibles?"

"You know. Ghosts. Demons."

"Oh." I was sorry I asked. I turned my attention to the canisters lining the shelves. Guns, swords, knives and now explosives. What was there for a teenage boy not to love? "Then you're *happy* here?"

He stood and looked at me as if I were crazy. "Well, yeah. Why wouldn't I be?"

"Right." I nodded. "This is a pretty cool thing you've all got going here, huh?"

He dipped his curly blond head and stared at his hands. He was actually blushing. "We're like superheroes. Fighting evil. Protecting the innocent and all that crap."

"I get it. Poison is your superhero name." Clever. Give the kids an altruistic reason to stay, which makes them more pliable. Not a comforting picture of di Taro. In fact, it was disturbingly manipulative. "So, what's your real name?"

He looked away, his jaw tense, his arms suddenly interlocked across his chest in a defensive posture. "It doesn't matter. The last time I heard it was when my dad tossed me out of the truck along I-75 and told me to go to hell. Two weeks later, a vamp pegged me for his next snack and Ryan saved me." His gaze snapped back to mine as if he'd told me something he hadn't intended.

I touched his arm, empathy softening my stance.

The clear blue of his eyes grew muddier. The veins within the whites began to brighten. He was on the verge of crying. He nodded and muttered, "I gotta go clean up."

"Okay," I said to his rapidly retreating form.

I'd seen too many kids like Poison. Abandoned like an unwanted puppy. He'd become disposable. His normal demand for attention had probably irritated an already unstable situation and…BOOM! Out he went. With no thought of how he would survive lingering in his father's mind. *That* was true evil.

Out of the corner of my eye I saw di Taro coming straight for me, his face tight, his body tense. He stopped only a step away, crowding me in a place that had nothing but space. I thought he'd been engrossed studying the layout of the club. My mistake. He obviously had both eyes on the map and one ear tuned to me. I guess I should've felt special. I didn't. I refused to let him intimidate me. I held my ground and stared steadily back at him.

"I'm only going to say this once, *doctor*. Don't go searching for root causes to their problems. You'll be leaving when this is all over and whatever you unearth I'm gonna have to deal with."

"Playing on their need to feel needed?" I narrowed my eyes. "That's very slick of you."

"How so? Even you do what you do because you want to help people. Why can't he feel the same? Because he's a kid? He needs an outlet for all that anger he's got. Going toe-to-toe with monsters that prey on kids gives him a reason to live. Gives him a sense of honor. I'm not going to take that from him."

His reasoning was horribly flawed. "What I do doesn't get people killed, and if I'm to believe all the scary, crazy stuff you've all been saying, which I do, then what you do places children directly in harm's way. How exactly is that honorable?"

"They're safer here, doing what I've taught them to do, than where they came from."

He was right. I knew he was right, but his methods were frightening. I shook my head a sudden headache rearing toward the base of my skull. "Sorry. It's none of my business, right? It's just…" How could I explain what I felt? "Children need to feel safe all the time. Loved, not used."

He stepped closer. "You're prying where you have no business. Before we found them, they weren't given a chance to feel anything but cold. It's because of me and my brother they have a semblance of a home life. Because of us, they have three meals a day, clean clothes—can sleep without crying."

Enough indignant heat radiated off of him to boil water. It was time to back off. I threw up my hands and offered a truce. "Okay. I won't dig."

di Taro stepped back, but the kids weren't the only distrustful souls crashing this paramilitary party, and I found my mouth opening and words spilling out before I could stop them. "Except, I'm more than a little confused. Exactly how are these kids going to help me? Because, I don't know if you noticed, but they're *kids*...you know...not adults."

"Look beyond the age," he advised. "These guys have lived hard and know how to take care of themselves. I made sure they'll never be the victim again. I trust them with my life."

Snap stood and pumped the air with his fist in victory. "Got it."

di Taro's attention honed in on the computer whiz. "What'd you find?"

"An address in South Boston. The rich guy has been there

nearly every night for the past three months except recently—and then, of course, he was there last night."

"That's got to be it," Sundquist said. "It's the address right before she arrived at the police station."

Cade slapped his hands together and grinned. "Looks like we've got ourselves a nest to clean out."

It was strange to see them all excited over finding The Black Dahlia's location, like they'd just been given a free movie pass that included a bucket of popcorn, candy and a soda.

"Settle down. From the doctor's drawings, this place is big. It's going to take a little time to figure out the best way to clear it."

I hated to dampen their mood, but my agenda had priority. "Getting Alden comes first."

di Taro slanted a surprised look at me, irritated I had voiced yet another opinion. "Maybe for you, but that's not our mission. Killing the bad guys is what we do."

"Not this time. Our focus has to be on getting him out."

"Look." A pacifying dash slanted his lips and a touch of condescension wrinkled his forehead. "I know you're worried, but—"

"I'm not waiting, and I'm not compromising. A man's life is at stake. You've got all these kids convinced saving lives is your purpose." I got right into his face. "Well, now it's time to prove it."

di Taro looked at Sundquist, obviously searching for backup. The detective shrugged. "I wouldn't push it, Beau. She's been through a lot lately."

di Taro looked like he longed to strangle Sundquist. Instead, a long, drawn out groan emerged from his chest. "Fine. We'll get your boy and pull him out. But so help me if this whole thing backfires, if they pull up stakes before we can finish them off, I'll have your head."

Rain. It hit the road in heavy droplets, springing up against the side of the van parked near the entrance to the alley. I leaned my head against the headrest, regretting the unavailability of a change of clothes. I still wore my ridiculously high heels and tight black dress. Black may be the universal color for swat teams, but I doubt any professional siege organization would be calling me for referrals to my stylist.

I shivered, pushed my heavy mass of curls out of my eyes and turned to di Taro. He held a pair of night-vision goggles to his eyes as he slowly searched the area. We'd been there for a good twenty minutes, and my patience abruptly came to an end. I turned to him and snapped, "What are we waiting for?"

He placed the goggles on the dashboard and pulled out a gun. "The sun. Unless you'd rather we go in there with all of them awake. It'll be bad enough when we meet up with their pets. I'm not fond of fighting them *and* the vampires."

"Oh." I suddenly felt stupid for asking. The click and snap of metal against metal caught my attention. I glanced behind me to the interior of the van where Sundquist, Snap, and Wiggy lounged, though to be fair, Snap was actually staring intently at a computer screen and not tossing marshmallows into the air and catching them in his mouth like the other two were doing. Sundquist was such a twelve-year-old. Not exactly the army of rescuers I'd envisioned, but at least they each had a gun.

I glanced at my hands. My empty hands. Then it hit me. I didn't have a gun. Worry escalated my nerves. I held out a shaking hand toward di Taro. "I need a gun."

He arched his brows in a you've-got-to-be-kidding-me look. "No gun for you."

"You have plenty," I said as he holstered the first one and pulled out another. I spied one more riding along the middle of his back. Three for him—zero for me. How was that fair? I leaned toward him and wiggled my fingers like a child greedy for candy. "Seriously, I need one."

"You shouldn't even be here." He shoved another magazine into the second gun and slanting a jaundiced eye at me. "You're not trained *plus* you're still wearing a dress and high heels. That equals liability which says no gun."

He couldn't be serious. "You don't expect me to go in there without a weapon, do you?"

"I don't expect you to go in there at all."

"But—"

"You," he interrupted my whine, "are going to watch the van, and when we bring out your friend, slide open the side door. That's your job."

"But…" That was not what I'd planned.

"It's either that, or we leave. I won't risk my boys' lives because you have some misplaced sense of duty to this guy, got that?"

The finality in his voice came across loud and clear. I nodded.

Snap swore and looked up from the laptop he'd been typing on. "Not good. Sun's up."

I stared out the front window, but all I saw was gray and wet. "Looks like this storm is getting worse."

A marshmallow disappeared into Sundquist's mouth. "Vamps get extra playtime. Lucky us."

"Maybe we'll get lucky and the clouds will break." Wiggy's optimism sounded forced.

A harsh snort from Snap followed. "Yeah, like we've ever been that lucky."

"We don't need luck. Ashes to ashes," di Taro said and held out his hand. They each placed theirs on his and said, "Dust to dust."

"God be with you." His gaze looked at each of them. They broke apart and di Taro opened the door and stepped out, sliding a knife in a scabbard he had strapped to his leg before he disappeared down the dark alley. Sundquist cast me a meaningful look and quickly headed into the alley behind di Taro.

"Here," Wiggy pulled off a bag he had slung over his shoulder and thrust it in my hands. I peeked inside to the small cache of tiny plastic bottles. I looked up confused.

"It's water."

They expect me to be their water boy during the big game's timeout calls? This was humiliating.

He must have seen my irritation because he quickly explained, "Holy water. The bottles are easily crushed so be careful. If you see anyone with fangs, throw one at 'em, and don't miss. There's nothing worse than a vamp with a splatter burn."

He hopped out and followed di Taro and Sundquist around the corner. I looked over at Snap. "Really. I'd rather have the gun."

Snap, stoic and unimpressed, shook his head. "We'll be their targets, not you. Beau's right, you know. He's always right." With that, he left.

I stumbled out of the van and came up short as a burst of cold rain bit into my exposed skin. I clutched the bag to my chest as I stood with rounded eyes, feeling like the next victim in a horror movie. "Isn't there some code of conduct that stipulates the group should never, ever split up?" I whispered loudly into the gloom of the early morning.

No one answered.

If popular culture dictated life's outcome, then the one left behind always got killed first. Me left holding the proverbial bag couldn't be a good sign.

di Taro had parked at the far end of the alley, nearly two blocks away from the club's back door. The sun had yet to make an appearance, and as I looked up into the rain-laden sky, I realized it wouldn't. Dark clouds, heavy rain, deserted streets. My life had gone from comfortable PG-13, parental guidance suggested to R-rated, heavy violence and possibly disturbing images with a smattering of Maya-is-in-trouble sprinkled within.

Gloom penetrated the area; penetrated me. I grabbed a dark gray hoodie lying on the back seat and shrugged into it. I shivered as the cold rain grew harder, and I gave up trying to zip the hoodie closed. I hugged the bag to my chest and peered through the rain.

I couldn't see the guys anymore. They had slipped into the

dark alley like four disreputable thieves. My distress rose, causing my heart rate to speed up. I could feel the blood rush through my neck, flooding my brain with adrenaline...my blood pressure rising toward a full blown panic. I couldn't stay here. Not alone.

"Please find, Alden," I whispered like a prayer.

I took a step toward the alley. Did I dare follow? I glanced back at the van. It presented itself as a safe haven, but I had seen firsthand what vampires could do. I was no safer in there than standing in middle of The Black Dahlia's dance floor. I took another step forward, peering into the darkness. With shaking hands, I slipped the bag's strap over my shoulder and pulled out a vial. My fingers wrapped tightly around it. "Snap?" I called out in a scared whisper.

"Crackle. Pop."

I yelped and whirled around. Standing behind me was a man with pale skin and strangely glowing eyes. The air around him fairly vibrated with evil intent. I staggered away.

He caught my arm and pulled me toward him. "Don't I know you?"

Our eyes locked. Images of me falling into his arms flashed in my head. Feelings of past contentment, of unfolding lust exploded within me. I wavered toward him.

"Yes," I said, convinced I had searched for him my whole life. "I love you."

"And I you. Rest your head here," he said, pulling me even closer and easing my head onto the black leather jacket he wore. "You are so weary."

My legs were suddenly wobbly as if I couldn't hold my own weight. He held me tight, and I did as he asked. Like mine, his jacket lay open making it easier for me to cuddle into him as I slipped one hand around his waist, and the other one up his chest.

"What do you hold?"

"You," I said with all sincerity.

His chuckle reminded me of the sound of icy rain hitting glass. He ran his hand up my arm and to my fingers. "I meant here."

I opened my fingers, revealing the small plastic vial. "Water."

I stared at the vial. Holy water.

Reality crashed in on me. I was being held by a vampire. I stiffened.

"Water?" he dumbly repeated before he, too, stiffened.

We pulled away from each other. His gaze lowered to my hand. Before I lost my nerve or he snapped out of his shock, I slammed the bottle onto his chest. The thin, waxy plastic crackled apart, soaking his shirt with holy water.

A gasp of surprise sprang from him. I stumbled back, digging in the pouch for another bottle.

His eyes widened, and he started to scream, raking his hands at his clothing. He fell to his knees and ripped off his expensive leather jacket, tossed it to the ground before tearing his shirt from his body. I stared horrified at his chest. It was disintegrating before my eyes, the holy water eating the flesh over his heart and burning the skin everywhere the water touched.

The rancid smell of burning flesh drove me back. His screams brought another man to the edge of a far building. He sprinted straight at me. I screamed again and pitched two bottles at him. They hit dead center. He didn't stop coming. I was truly trapped between two evils.

And then I saw di Taro and the others appear from the same alley, guns blazing at something behind them. I called out and he turned, leveled his gun at the man running toward me and shot him, propelling him forward, right into my arms.

We toppled to the ground, yet I ended up on top of him, my stash of holy water bursting between us. There was no stench of burning flesh wafting up, no scream of pain, only a slight moan. I pushed away and looked down into a pair of familiar pain-racked eyes.

"Alden." I glanced back at di Taro and his small band as they rushed forward. "You shot Alden!"

"Kill him," Alden said through tight lips.

I frowned. "I can't. He didn't know it was you."

"Not him. *Him*." He nodded to where my attacker still lay.

My gaze snapped to the vampire. His skin had already begun to mend. I sat up, sputtering inanely as I pointed to the vampire.

di Taro was already one step ahead of me. While the others continued to fire rounds down the alley, he pulled out his blade and with a single swipe, the vampire's head flew off his body, and both pieces exploded in a cloud of ash.

Sundquist rushed up. "Time to go."

With Wiggy's help, I stood. Sundquist and Snap scooped Alden up and tossed him in the van as di Taro reloaded both guns and poured a round of bullets into the shadows. I wanted to be in the back with Alden, but di Taro shoved the door closed and motioned me up front. "Very convenient of your guy to come out just as we got here."

Exactly what was that supposed to mean? I watched as he grabbed the leather jacket on the ground in one quick motion. He slid behind the wheel and threw the jacket on the floor between us.

As we sped away, I couldn't help the sneer that entered my voice. "Another souvenir?"

"I can get two hundred for it. Baby needs to go to the dentist."

"Oh."

I turned just as Sundquist ended his examination of Alden's wound. "You're a lucky man," he said. "The bullet hit your shoulder and it went clean through."

"I hope he won't be insulted if I don't thank him," Alden said, nodding toward di Taro.

The man in question looked back through his rearview mirror. "Sorry. I tend to act first, and ask questions later."

Alden grunted, closed his eyes and sagged against Sundquist. The detective looked up at me. "That's weird. He's fainted."

And then I knew. di Taro used silver bullets.

Maya

CHAPTER TWENTY THREE

"Are you sure you don't want to take him to the hospital?" Sundquist asked as he finished dressing Alden's bullet wound. Poison had scrounged up a first aid kit when we arrived back at the loft, and Sundquist had used nearly everything in it to make Alden more comfortable.

Sitting in a chair by the bed, I bit my lip and stared down at Alden. I squeezed our interlaced fingers. He still hadn't woken. Or moved.

Stripped of most of his clothes, he looked like a marble sculpture, pale and perfectly chiseled, yet carrying the artist's rendition of a man who'd lead a hard life. I was familiar with those scars…and knew the curiosity they caused.

Next to me, di Taro shrugged as he, too, stared down at Alden. "You said it was a clean shot in a benign area."

"Yeah, but I think he's been tortured. Look at all these bruises. What's weird is some of them look old. And will you get a look at this scar on his chest? I don't know what chewed him up in the past, but it wasn't pretty."

Alden's chest rose and fell in deep rhythm as our eyes followed the white puckered scar that slashed across his torso. Slowly, I pulled the sheet up to his shoulders, shielding him from their curiosity. It proved a pointless gesture.

"You know what I think is weird?" di Taro whispered heavily.

Sundquist cocked a curious eye, and I forced myself to casually look di Taro's way. His face had a placid, almost unemotional quality to it, but his body, as always, tensed for immediate motion. He hadn't taken his eyes off Alden. He was studying him. Watching him. Judging him. "He's been in that house-of-hell all night and there isn't a bite mark on him."

Sundquist quickly glanced back at Alden and shrugged. "It looks to me as if they weren't all that hungry, just really pissed."

"The question is; did he learn his lesson?"

I suddenly stood and turned on him. "Your skepticism doesn't speak well of your upbringing."

His mouth twisted into a dark smirk. "My skepticism has kept me alive."

I had no doubts that if he knew exactly what Alden was, he would kill him…without remorse. I'd seen the hate that pierced his eyes when he'd killed the vampire. I'd seen the unrelenting determination to stop whatever was in the alley chasing after them. di Taro would be a ruthless enemy.

He nodded toward Alden. "We did what you wanted. Now it's our turn to do what we need to do. It'd be nice if your guy could give us a picture of what to expect in there. Show his gratitude..."

For what? Alden had gotten himself out of there and di Taro had promptly shot him. I gritted my teeth and swallowed back a nasty remark, and said instead, "I'm sure once he wakes up, he'll do whatever he can to help."

"Peachy. By the look of him, I shouldn't expect much." He headed to the door. "I could use you, Sundquist."

After di Taro left, my gaze locked with Sundquist's. He

knew I barely held myself together. He watched me as his hands continued their work. "I know what you're thinking, Maya, but don't be so hard on Beau. Him and his brother are the only ones keeping evil at bay these days. No one knows what they know. No one would believe them if they tried to get help."

I didn't want to feel sympathy for di Taro. I didn't want to think about him at all.

"I know." It nearly killed me to say it. There was so much about him I didn't like, but I knew he operated under the best intensions. "It's just…he's a little too rough around the edges."

"With what he deals with on a daily basis? I'd be irritable too. If his brother and Anara were here, it would be better, but they won't be back for a while." Sundquist stood, letting out a heavy sigh. "Well, that's all I can do."

Putting the first aid kit back together, he gave me one last look. "This isn't over. The vamps are pissed off now." With that, he left.

It was over for me. When Alden woke up, we'd leave. That had been my original plan, and that's what I intended to do.

I tucked the sheet firmly around Alden. Seeing him in such a state of vulnerability worried me. I didn't know what to do. I was confident no doctor had ever had a werewolf as a patient, and I wasn't keen on being the first person to bring the species to light. Alden certainly wouldn't thank me. I knew if he began to heal himself as he claimed he could do, which I now believed he could do, di Taro would know he wasn't mortal. Just as she said, he'd act first and question later.

My hands were tied. I could only wait and make him comfortable. To that end, I needed to go to Alden's apartment and get a few things. Maybe if I were lucky, he'd have a few books or notes on "what werewolves should do if shot" lying around.

I left the little room. All the kids except Cade and Snap were asleep. Neither were really boys anymore. In their early twenties, they were on the path to become mini di Taro's. I had no problem eavesdropping on their conversation.

"So you did the rounds and Sage was a no show? What makes you think she would?" Snap asked.

"We had a deal. She wouldn't do anything stupid. Not without me. Not after what happened last time."

Snap clapped Cade on the back. "Remember what Beau says. Never trust a pretty female."

"He didn't mean her," Cade said and pushed off Snap's hand.

"Let it go. She'll come back. She always does."

The look Cade gave Snap told me he didn't think so.

Snap returned to making new bullets, and di Taro motioned Cade to him, giving him instructions to keep an eye on their new guest. I went to Sundquist. His big hands patted his pockets in a search for his pack of cigarettes.

I put on my most charming smile. "Could you drop me off at Alden's apartment?"

"Why?"

"I was thinking about getting him a change of clothes."

He found the pack and tapped it against his hand until one stabbed out. "Okay."

Before he could light it, di Taro appeared, yanked the cigarette out of his hand and snapped it in two. "I'll take her. I think I want to see where this guy lives."

Heat infused my cheeks. I hadn't expected he'd want to go along. Suddenly my brilliant idea had become a serious liability for Alden. I didn't have a clue what I'd find in the apartment, and I didn't want di Taro along to find what needed to stay buried. "That's disgusting, poking though his life while he lies here defenseless."

di Taro only smiled. "That's the best time to go poking around, sweetheart."

Ruthless. Didn't play by the rules. I had no doubt he'd steal, lie and do just about anything to get what he wanted.

Sundquist jabbed his pack back into his pocket, took the destroyed cigarette from di Taro and pitched it in the trash. "I've got to check in." He put his hand to his head. "Man. What am I going to tell Carson about what I've been doing all night? I can fill him in on the whole car wreck and weird story, though by now I probably won't be telling him anything new."

di Taro readily jumped in with a solution. "Tell him the truth. You've been searching for The Black Dahlia."

He scratched his head and heaved a heavy sigh. "That I took her story seriously will tick him off."

"He'll get over it. Eventually."

The big man laughed as he headed to the elevator. "That's reassuring."

My eyes blurred as I slipped the key into the lock. The drive over to Alden's apartment had been tense, neither of us talking and me holding on for dear life as he sped along the back streets in his ugly little car. I hesitated. This was a mistake. I shouldn't have asked to come here, but I couldn't invent a reason to take it back.

"Is it stuck?"

I whipped my head toward di Taro and saw his right eyebrow rise with suspicion. I quickly looked away. "No." I jiggled the handle and pushed the door open. Morning light poured through the windows that housed an unobstructed view of Boston and the harbor.

di Taro whistled. "Nice. Your boyfriend has no problem showing his wealth."

"He's not my boyfriend," I said wearily as I closed the door behind us.

"Right. And I don't believe in things that go bump in the night." He picked up a stack of unopened mail next to a vase of long stemmed red roses and began to rifle through it. "I'm sure Alden Caldwell is an innocent bystander caught in the crossfire of our supernatural war."

"He *is* innocent." My gaze swept the apartment. It looked exactly as I remembered it. Sleek, sophisticated and clean.

He looked up from the mail. "If it walks like a duck and talks like a duck, it's a duck with an agenda."

I shoved my hands on my hips and faced him, tired of

hearing his suspicious mind grind like a rusty wheel. I needed to know exactly what he was thinking. "And what do you mean by that?"

"He's in too deep to be innocent."

I let loose a huff of contempt. "Look around you. He's a rich, brilliant man. He got caught up with people who are beyond evil and he wants to leave. But that's not so easy. Even you know that. They can control people." I remembered how the vampire had so easily placed thoughts into my head. It scared me. How much worse would it be for Alden, being bound to Juliana by some strange power. "They can make people say anything. Do anything."

"Not if you're on to their game."

"Not everyone can claim that privilege. You have to believe in the impossible before you can control it."

His mouth gave a sharp twist. "Shouldn't you be getting him clothes?"

Sore loser.

I made my way through the apartment, past an office and to a door slightly ajar. With a push of my hand, it easily swung open revealing Alden's bedroom. It was nothing like I expected. It looked like a page taken from a medieval manuscript. Ancient tapestries lined the walls. A tall canopied bed, its steepled peek rising majestically to the high ceiling, sat in the middle of the large room. Luxurious fabric hung from the frame to sweep the floor. A few pieces of armor stood behind large glass encasements one would find in a museum, while a collection of old swords, crossbows and knives hung over a large fireplace, its ornate mantle depicting a wolf hunting a man. Or maybe it was the other way around. But I doubted it.

It was the year 1150. I was a soldier. One of the best.

These weapons weren't hard won prizes of an avid collector. These ancient bits of armor and weaponry were Alden's. He had worn them. Fought battles with them.

"What the hell?"

I spun around, my heart racing. "What?" I cried, my hand

going to my chest.

He entered, fingering a vase atop a tall pedestal as his gaze swept the room. "What is all this?"

"He's a collector, obviously." I returned my gaze to the weapons. "Actually, it looks a lot like your place."

He pulled down a blade hanging from the wall. "Except my stuff is new and his is old. These look really good, though. Like they've been cared for."

"Put that back." I glared until he re-hung the sword. "And isn't condition the point. A collector wants his antiquities authentic, yet functional."

A lopsided smile tipped his lips. "Aren't we the expert? I wonder if he knows how to use any of it?"

I had no doubt he did.

A row of worn-down horseshoes ran along the top of a pair of doors, which I opened to reveal a huge walk-in closet. The built-ins were made of rich cherry wood accented with ebony. The epitome of a man's closet, and one who knew who he was and what he expected. Painfully neat and orderly. His suits lined one section, his casual clothes another. A large armchair sat in the middle with a table beside it. A floor to ceiling mirror covered a section of the back wall.

I let out my breath. "Wow. *This* is a closet." It put mine to shame. I pulled my finger along the clothes like a harpist does the taut strings until I came to a pair of jeans. I pulled them out, followed by a button-down green shirt and a brown leather jacket that matched a pair of laced leather shoes I'd spotted earlier.

di Taro entered. "You'd think he'd have a butler."

"Why?"

He shrugged. "Just seems the type. Obviously he can't take care of himself."

"That doesn't describe Alden at all."

"Come on. He needed a woman to rescue him, didn't he?"

I rolled my eyes. "Alden got out of the club all on his own, remember?"

di Taro shrugged, determined to find fault. He opened one

drawer after another. "What the hell is this guy's issue? No respectable dude has this much underwear." He pulled out a silky pair of black boxers with bright red lips all over them. "What does this tell you about the guy, doctor?"

I snatched them from him and shoved them back into the drawer, glaring. "That he has a sense of humor, unlike you."

"Believe me, I'm laughing on the inside."

As I finished gathering Alden's clothes, di Taro left. That worried me. He wouldn't be content until he unearthed something suspicious about Alden. I quickly opened every cabinet and door, searched every drawer and shelf for anything that would help me understand Alden better. I found nothing. To all appearances, he was a rich man who liked to collect ancient war memorabilia.

I gathered everything in my arms and left the bedroom. As I passed the office, I saw di Taro sitting in front of Alden's computer, pecking at the keys. "Hey," I said, hovering at the door. "What are you doing?"

He nodded to the flash drive. "One of Snap's hacks." He jabbed at one last key, and sat back, his eyes boring into mine, challenging me to stop him. "You may be content to believe everything he says, but I've learned a different tactic. To get at the truth, you have to sneak in the back door."

He returned his attention to the computer, and I stepped closer. He stuck another flash drive into the computer's USB port and with a few more taps, the screen zipped along, revealing file after file being downloaded onto the hardware. The second stick suddenly stopped glowing.

di Taro pulled both free, and looking up at me, he stuffed them in his pocket. "Trust me. People don't reveal their true selves very often."

His blatant theft of Alden's private information irritated me. "So what does that say about you?"

He stood, and as he passed, he said in his gravelly voice, "That you don't really know me. And you probably never will."

Personally, I liked it that way. Our relationship couldn't end quickly enough for me. I followed him out of the apartment and to his car. His ugly little car.

He popped the hatchback and I placed Alden's things in the back. I had to admit, he kept the car squeaky clean. "What kind of car is this?" It looked more like a squat refrigerator box with headlights than a car.

"A Mini Cooper." He closed the back.

"But Mini's are cute. What happened to yours?"

He unlocked my door and held it open for me. "It's an old model. It'll be a classic so don't gouge the vinyl."

"Well, darn," I said, slipping into the seat. "I don't' know how I'll control myself. Vinyl gouging is my favorite pastime."

"Funny," he said and closed the door.

He was a horrible driver, darting in and out of traffic more like a motorcyclist than a motorist. I threw an annoyed glance at him. He didn't seem to notice my irritation. When we hit Congress Street, he let loose a heated curse. I cast a frown at him. "What?"

He made a quick, jarring right down a small alley, his eyes glued to the rearview mirror. I glanced back. Suddenly, another car slipped in after us.

"Shit!" di Taro ground the gears, and our Mini shot forward.

"Who's that?"

"I don't know, and I don't want to find out."

A series of loud pops sounded and the side mirror on di Taro's right flew off. I screamed and ducked. di Taro cursed and stomped his foot on the accelerator. When we hit the next street, he spun the wheel, and we skidded to the side and squealed forward.

Anger flared within his eyes. "They shot my car. They freakin' shot my car."

He leaned toward me, popped open the glove compartment and pulled out a gun and a fully loaded magazine. Steering with one knee, he slammed the magazine in the handle.

"What are you doing?"

"Just hold on." He punched the clutch, shifted gears and made another sharp turn down an alleyway. I looked back just as the other car spun into the alley.

"Grab the wheel!" he ordered.

I took it, my heart slamming hard enough to crack a rib. He turned, aimed out the back window and pulled the trigger. The glass shattered into the alley. He let fly five more shots, hitting the other car's windshield.

"Street," I cried.

di Taro spun around and grabbed the wheel just as we hit a bump and vaulted into the street. How we didn't get hit by oncoming traffic was a miracle. We swerved and raced away. I stared at the alley entrance, but the other car didn't emerge.

"Did you hit the driver?" My own breathless fear greeted my ears.

"I was aiming for him."

I sunk low in my seat and put my hands to my head. "What is going *on*?"

di Taro cast an angry look at me. "That's what I'd like to know."

Alden

CHAPTER TWENTY FOUR

Lying there with the trace of silver poisoning my body, and my wounds from Juliana's scourge still raw, I had no more power to heal myself. Too weak. Too broken. I needed sustenance. I needed fresh, bloody meat. Without it, I would lay here for weeks, exposed and vulnerable to anyone. All I could do was collect what energy I could in case I needed to defend myself. My wounds would have to wait. Numbing sleep swept over me, covering me in memories best left buried.

Evangeline faded from view for nearly two years. Not that she had left. Her enticing scent lingered wherever I went, mingling with the new and the old and the unlucky. Nay, Evangeline purposely made herself invisible, keeping to herself, avoiding contact with anyone other than Juliana. Our mistress abetted her in this bizarre game of hide and seek, for I did try and find her. To talk. Only talk. Our last time together had been marred by my inability to give her what she so desperately wanted, and I felt badly.

Then, after years apart, she came to me. The shock of seeing her froze me to the spot. Without a word, she led me to a shadowed alcove. Our coupling was heated and quick, yet it satisfied the need I had buried since she left. I had forgotten the redemption I found in the softness of her skin.

Seeing her, being with her, gave me pleasure. Yet…she had given me the distinct impression that I had disappointed her beyond measure. I hadn't expected her to forgive me. Worse, I hadn't expected to want to be forgiven.

Then something happened. Our trysts suddenly became more frequent, more daring. I tried to talk sense into her, but I feared she steered a course with the intention to either make me fall madly in love with her or see me destroyed.

The industrial age had grown deep roots by 1860. England had entered its golden age. I had dipped my hand in whatever pursuits interested me; from Ireland to India, I sought out challenges, set standards for the era and pushed man forward. I had a legion of workers within my company, had accrued respect and honor throughout the Empire, and even the queen's favor. And in the underbelly of London, the riches of my labors caused a satisfied smile to soften Juliana's cold lips.

How wrong I was. Her smile had nothing to do with my success. It was her own ambitions that made her smug. I had played a central role, although I had no idea. I still believed my resurrected affair with Evangeline was a well-guarded secret.

After one of our encounters, when my lust was well sated, and I had given Evangeline pleasure, I donned my pants, thinking of her return to me after her strange absence and not understanding the why of it. I could no longer tolerate the hole in the canvas. I needed to fill in the picture. I sat to the side of her, slid my hand over one plump breast and to her chin. I kissed her, until her breathing turned rough and her eyes grew dark. I pulled away. "Why?"

She frowned. "Why what?"

"Why this desperation? Why are you never satisfied? We cannot keep this going. We risk too much."

Panic infused her eyes. "No. We must do this."

I pulled away. "Must?" That was an odd word choice.

"I need you," she said simply. She rolled from the bed and began to dress, not an easy chore in this day and age. Women were more tightly bound than at any other time. She expertly donned her delicate lace embellished undergarments, slipping a glance toward me every-so-often.

It was an enjoyable pastime watching her cover her luscious curves, but today I was more interested in the why of the matter. A tight smile slid across my face. "You need no one, Evangeline."

"I do. I need you. What you can give me."

I studied her movements as she gathered the whalebone corset about her and started the arduous task of connecting the hooks running down the front from breast to hipbone like tiny tin soldiers ready for duty. Her actions were sharp and clumsy, not the elegant motions of the petted woman she was.

I feared she once again wanted my love. And once again I would disappoint her.

Hesitantly, I asked, "And what is it that I can give you?"

Her fingers stumbled over the intricate hooks of her corset, which pressed her breasts into high fullness. She turned away, shaking her head.

She had a terrible secret. I could smell her misery, her overwhelming anxiety. Evangeline was not a woman who naturally kept her thoughts to herself. That she refused to tell me spoke of some evilness afoot. I slid off the bed and rounded its rumpled end, coming to a stop before her. With the last hook finally fastened, I grabbed her shoulders and forced her to look up at me. "Tell me. Why have you come to me? What do you want from me?"

She visibly paled. "I dare not say."

Fear sprang from her very pores. I'd never seen her so scared, or so miserable. I instantly wished to ease her mind. "Have I not kept every promise I ever gave you? Have I not told you I would protect you so long as I had breath in me?"

She nodded.

"Then speak."

She opened her mouth, but her voice would not obey. Moments past until she stuttered over the breathy words that finally tumbled out. "I-I want another child."

"Another child? What…?"

When had she ever had a child? I didn't even know it was possible. Who? Why? The thoughts racing through my head would not coalesce into a rational explanation.

She began to quiver. Her eyes welled with tears and her lips trembled with suppressed emotion until the dam burst and the tears flowed. Falling against me, she clung to my shoulders. Her forehead touched the base of my throat as she sobbed into my shirt. "I couldn't say no. She made me. I swear, if I could have stopped her, I would have. I tried for so long, and then it happened. When I had thought I was safe, it happened, and then she took him. I'm sorry. I am so very sorry," she cried.

I peeled her hands from my shoulders and held her back. Staring into her face, I tried to understand what she had said, and when the pieces fell together, my gut tightened. "Are you telling me we have a child? A son? I have a son?"

She nodded and a fresh wave of tears cascaded down her cheeks.

"When?" I yelled, my fingers digging into her arms.

"I tried to tell you. I asked you to love me."

By the lake. She had known of her pregnancy then. I had noticed how soft she looked. How gentle her behavior, and how sad she had sounded. She had begged for my love, and I had denied her request.

As if she could read my mind, Evangeline moaned and sagged within my hands like a rag doll bereft of cotton. "I would have done whatever you said, but you didn't want me and now it is too late. She has taken him and I know not where."

A son. I had a son. Incomprehension swirled through me, raking my gut and squeezing my heart. A child. A family. It was the one thing I had never allowed myself to hope for. I didn't even know it was possible. I had been denied my future. A legacy.

Sudden roiling hate boiled to the surface. My hands shook as I shoved her from me, disgusted by what she'd done—what she'd allowed Juliana to turn us into. As she fell to the bed, I snarled, "I am not a dog to breed with any willing female."

She looked at me, her eyes filled with sorrow. "To her that is exactly what you are. Just as I am."

I flung open the door and turned to the beautiful woman who had betrayed my trust in the deepest way. I pointed an accusing finger at her. "Never talk to me again. Ever."

I stormed from the room as she sobbed my name, her cries following me like a malevolent specter. I pushed them from my head. My target was the woman who'd planned this evil.

When I reached Juliana's door, the men guarding it saw the murderous look on my face and stepped aside. I barged into the dark interior and shouted, "What have you done with him!"

Midday found her asleep. At my yell, she rolled to face me, her face cool and serene. My disheveled appearance didn't seem to surprise her. She sat up, letting the sheet fall from her body to reveal a scrumptious confection of lace and silk that hugged her body. If she thought to entice me to lust, she thought wrongly. Visions of her imminent death floated through my head.

I strode to her bed and yanked the covers from her. With a rough hand, I pulled her to her feet. "Tell me."

Though my fingers dug into her arm, she easily pulled away. Her face clouded with annoyance. "How dare you barge into my chambers."

"Where is he?" I demanded.

"Who?"

"My son."

At that, she smiled. Her wicked core flared to life at the pain she had caused in me. "So she told you. I feared she never would."

She glared past me to the open door and the guards standing at odds as to what to do. "You must truly inspire fear in your pack. They seem to forget who they call master."

I didn't allow her to change the subject. Though the doors closed, I kept my eyes glued to hers, and repeated, "Where is he?"

She rounded on me, her eyes sparkling with silver hate. "You are lucky I do not have you killed for your actions. Do you think me blind? I know what you do. Always. I have known since the first. But I tolerated the act. You kept her pliable. Content. Something Jakubek could never do."

This was not about Evangeline. "I don't care about her."

She flicked her hand at me and slouched into the cushioned chair by her bed. "I know that. It is why I allowed your pleasures. Only after I saw the potential of such a union did I openly encourage her to continue the affair." She sat forward. "Was it not exciting thinking you were disobeying my orders, though?"

The truth of that statement speared through me, yet I stood stoic in the face of her cruel teasing.

"No? Leave it to you to feel guilt while taking pleasure. You hid the affair well. Not one of the others reported you. That should brighten your countenance."

"Tell me."

She sat back, staring at me with the look of a well fed cat. "Or what?"

I stood silently before her, my heart hammering in my chest, sweat pouring down my temples. I had no threat to offer. We both knew it.

She sighed and leaned back, savoring my defeat. "I wanted a child and you provided me with one. He will be a new breed of servant. One who will not agonize over whether or not to obey because he will have been born into service. He is the perfect combination of beauty and obedience."

I winced, the pain of loss acute within me. I was not above begging. "Can I at least see him?"

"You long to see what you've created, is that it?" She

twirled a lock of hair and stared at me. After a moment, she tucked her feet beneath her, the movement graceful in its precise positioning. "I can understand such a longing. I have children of my own. Not the babe of your creation, but the blood ties of my kind. Your instincts tell you to protect the seed of your loins, but he is in no danger. I would as much hurt him as I would myself."

My chest ached, as if my heart would burst forth. I could not bear to have my son perverted by Juliana's evil. He was an innocent. One of a kind.

Grief blinded me. I hung my head and shook it back and forth. "Why us? Why now?"

"You are not the first to breed. Others have gone before you…but their progeny were not strong. The females were usually killed—being the weaker sex. And when the time of change came over the young men, they went mad and died."

Horror filled my body. I lifted my head; my lips had gone tight with fear. "None survived?"

"None. But I have high hopes for this child. He is strong and handsome like his father and perfectly malleable like his mother. Be cheered. I see a bright future for him."

I fell at her feet, head bowed. "I beg of you. Please allow me to see him."

She stretched out her leg, touched her big toe to my shoulder and tapped along with each word. "Should I or shouldn't I?"

I kept my head bowed, my eyes on the floor, yet I willed her to say yes. She suddenly stood. "Your attachment to this babe is already strong even though you have yet to see him. How much stronger will it be if you do?"

I knew what she was after. She weighed the advantages of my pain. Would it be worse to let me live without seeing the child or let me see him and then forevermore deny me the sight of him.

I dared to lift my head and look into her cold silver eyes. "Much stronger, but I care not. I must see him."

She sat forward, dragged her cool fingers down the side of

my cheek and cupped my chin in her hand. Bending she kissed me, full and insistent. After a moment, she said against my lips, "Your request is…denied."

I awoke to a strange room, utilitarian in design and execution. In a word, ugly. The burning near my heart matched the ache I felt for my lost son. How I had lived through that time I would never know. I looked down at my body and felt the familiar pain of silver in my veins. I remembered being shot, using the last of my strength to force the poisonous bullet from my body, being hauled into a van, and then nothing. A hiss of pain leached through my lips as I peeled away the bandages, destined to suffer this pain until I regained my strength.

The door opened and a kid entered—a young, blond and beautiful girl. I knew exactly who she was. I'd helped save her years ago. She hesitated. "Does this mean you're going to live?"

"I guess so."

She looked down her petite nose at me. "Doesn't matter. di Taro will most likely kill you anyway. He hates anyone who hangs with the vamps."

Her forthright announcement caused a small laugh to bubble up within me, though I paid for it in the end with a burning ache in my chest. I closed my eyes and asked, "What do you know about vampires?"

"I know you hang with them. I can smell them all over you. It's disgusting."

I forced my eyes open. "You can smell them?"

She leaned forward, her small face puckered with disgust, and said fiercely, "All over you."

"Do you know what I smell?"

She frowned, her bravado cracking just a bit. "What?"

"Maple syrup." I smiled. "There's some on your lip still."

Her tongue dashed out and dabbed at the offending spot.

She leaned back. "Why does she like you so much?"

"Who?"

"Maya."

"Because. I'm likable."

"Cade says she pretty, but I'm prettier."

"I heard my name." A good-looking kid poked his head in and pointed at the girl. "You're not supposed to be in here. Out."

"He's going to live," Baby said as she passed him on her way out. "Be nice to him, Cade. He's not so bad."

The guy glanced at me. "Sorry. She thinks she's special."

"I am," came her strident voice from the other room.

I struggled to sit up when a commotion sounded from the other room. Cade glanced behind him and immediately stepped out of the way as a man came striding in, his face wreathed in anger. Within a second he loomed at the side of the bed and nestled his gun muzzle directly between my eyes. It was a Beretta semi-automatic pistol. A bit of an over-kill for the job of blowing my head off.

"Why do they want you?"

"Stop it!" Maya cried from the doorway.

Cade held her back, along with the little girl.

di Taro flipped the safety off. "Talk."

Maya

CHAPTER TWENTY FIVE

Alden's facial expression didn't change. Only his eyes darkened to an eerie black. Though he lay in a vulnerable position, he didn't look at all defenseless. An unseen veil of power radiated from him. "I don't typically respond to threats."

"Lucky you," di Taro growled. "This isn't a threat."

They were at a standstill, two powerful men taking measure of each other. One with a definite advantage, the other facing him unafraid. Alden didn't know di Taro. He didn't know how fiercely he hated his kind. di Taro didn't know Alden; didn't know he was different and just as lethal if pushed hard enough. I struggled against Cade's restraining hand, my heart in my throat, my body breaking into a cold sweat.

Alden shot a quick glance at me. "It's okay, Maya." He then sighed, accepting the responsibility of the moment. "You want to know why they want me? They don't. Not anymore. Apparently, my uncooperative attitude of late negates my worth."

"Then why aren't you dead?" di Taro growled.

That was a good question, and one I wanted to know just as badly as di Taro.

Alden's gaze returned to mine and it visibly softened. "I have a guardian angel."

Baby glanced at me, then snorted and walked away, muttering, "Gross."

Somehow, that little word coming from Baby neutralized the tension in the air.

Alden's gaze returned to di Taro. "Honestly? I'm as surprised as you I'm still alive."

di Taro reluctantly pulled the muzzle off Alden. "You expect me to believe that, don't you?" The frustration in his voice sliced through the air.

"Believe what you want. That's all I know."

I pushed against Cade's arm, and he let me pass. Shouldering by di Taro, I stepped in front of Alden. "That's enough. He's not the enemy. He's lucky to be alive."

"We'll see." di Taro turned toward the door and then stopped. "You owe my car some body work and a new paint job, Caldwell. As I see it, that's the least you can do to thank me for rescuing your ass." He stormed out, nudging past Wiggy who stood rubbing sleep from his eyes.

"What's going on?" the boy asked.

"Everybody, take the mat," di Taro yelled from the main room.

"But I just woke up," Wiggy whined.

"Now."

He groaned and followed Cade out.

Alden sagged against the pillows. "Nice friends, Maya."

I placed the clothes I'd brought from his house at the foot of the bed and sat beside him, my fingers itching to touch him, to see if he were truly okay. "He's not so bad, really."

At least I hoped not. In all honesty, I hadn't seen him in any other mode except that of supremely ticked off to actually know that for certain. Surely the guy knew how to relax.

I gave in to my desire and brushed back the dark hair from

his face. Sweat trickled down his jaw, a testament to how difficult it had been to act unaffected. I peeked under the bandage and saw that his wound was still bright red and sore.

I got up and closed the door. Returning to him, I asked in hushed tones, "Why haven't you started to heal yourself?"

"So you believe me now?"

I rolled my eyes. "Please. I may have been a bit skeptical at first, but I'm a true believer now. That happens when a couple of vampires try to kill you."

He looked away, self-disgust coloring his cheeks. "I never should've taken you there."

I put my hand to his chest feeling the warm, lush beat of his heart. I took comfort in the steady rhythm, and my own heartbeat slowly synched with his. "I made you do it. Not one of my finer moments." I thought of all that had happened in the past twelve hours, and added, "It was a really *stupid* idea."

"Seeing is believing."

His sarcasm wasn't lost on me. I quickly changed the subject to the one I worried about most. "So, why can't you fix this?"

He took my hand that lay on his chest and interlaced our fingers. "There are a few problems. First, if I suddenly walk out of here with nice pink skin over a new bullet wound, I'm sure *Baldy* will have my head. Second, he shot me with a silver bullet. One won't kill me, but you start loading me up with those things, I'm down for good. Third, I..." he broke eye contact, and his voice grew quiet. "Well, Juliana wasn't exactly happy to see me last night. The superficial damage is healed, but the deeper wounds are still there. That, along with the injection of silver, I'm about as weak as one of my kind can be."

So Sundquist was right. Alden had been tortured. I slid the sheet down his chest, bringing to view the bruises and barely healed scars. My gaze returned to his eyes. Something within him called to me. I could feel the power in him seep beneath my skin and pull me closer.

I placed a kiss on his cheek. The warm flush of his skin

tingled my lips. I moved to his other cheek. Pulling away, I stared into his eyes. I didn't want to hurt him. I only knew a deep desire to be closer to him. I hesitated. His hands pulled me closer. I closed my eyes. When our lips touched, my senses sharpened. I was aware of myself in a way I'd experienced only with him. The power was seductive in itself. I heard snippets of conversation in the other room, knew the combined smell of those in the building, yet all that fell away when the kiss deepened.

Alden's pain, his doubts, his deep feelings of failure and ultimately his search for redemption flavored the kiss.

I wanted to ease his emotional suffering, show him I cared, but this was not the time or the place.

"You're not crazy," I whispered against his lips before pulling away.

He combed his fingers through my hair, and I could sense the fight within him to cover his vulnerability. He laughed bitterly. "Are you sure?"

"Don't," I urged, taking his hand and pressing it between my palms. "You are one of the strongest, bravest men I've ever met."

A look of self-loathing flushed his face. "You have no idea how often I pray this isn't happening, that it's all some hellish nightmare I can't seem to wake from." He stared straight into my eyes, fighting the grief threatening to overcome him. "But it *is* happening, and I can't stop it."

"We'll stop it. Somehow. Before we can, you've got to get better. What can I do to help?"

He didn't answer. He turned my hand up and kissed my palm, hopelessness clouding his eyes. He'd stopped believing in miracles. From his perspective, the problem appeared too big. How did one climb out of a hole one had been digging for hundreds of years? I had to show him every solution started with the first step. A simple step.

To heal the mind, face fears. To heal the body…

"How about some chicken soup?" I offered. "Every mother swears by chicken soup."

He grimaced. "So did mine, but what I *need* is a big bloody slab of meat."

I chewed on my bottom lip. From what I'd seen, di Taro and the kids were just getting by. I could almost guarantee ground beef was the red meat of choice for this crew.

Alden's hand tightened against mine. "Take my car and go to Savenor's on Charles Street. Tell one of the guys at the meat counter that Alden Caldwell wants the usual. It'll take them a while to get it together, so you'll have to wait a bit. They'll put it all on my tab."

His car?

"Ummm," I disengaged our fingers and stood, "about your car…it got towed to the police impound lot."

His gaze sharpened on me. "Why?"

Breaking the news to a guy about the misshapen appearance of his once flawless car was like telling a woman her precious newborn baby looked like the spitting image of Quasimodo. My brother had freaked when I'd gotten a teeny tiny dent on the side door of his stupid $1200 second-hand Jeep. I couldn't even guess how Alden would take the total destruction of his McLaren. I'd rather walk a mile on glass shards than tell him, but there was no way around it.

I winced. "Let's just say di Taro's car isn't the only car that's going to need body work and a new paint job, but let's not dwell on that. You rest." I backed toward the door. "Don't worry. I'll get the meat."

Like a coward, I left, ignoring his calls to come back.

Everyone stopped their workout and stared at me as I darted out of the room. I gave them a weak smile. "How about some lunch? I noticed you've got an indoor grill on your stove. How does steak sound?"

"Maya," Alden called from the room. "Why did my car have to be towed?"

My smile waned. "Okay. Steaks it is. And Alden's paying, so you can't say no," I said, cutting off di Taro's objections before he got started.

I went for my purse where I'd stashed Sundquist's business

card and my cell phone. Leaning my hip against the table, I punched in his number.

I told him what I needed and he agreed to get the meat. He was coming over in a little while anyway. He had to talk to di Taro about the raid.

I'd almost forgotten. I took a good look around. The kids were practicing, some with swords, others with daggers, and still others with throwing stars, all within a very tight space. A fight simulation of sorts. Controlled chaos is what it looked like, and their accuracy was frightening.

After I hung up with Sundquist, a rush of weariness invaded my body. I'd been up for over twenty-four hours now. I could barely think straight. I caught my reflection in the mirror di Taro had affixed near the workout mat and cringed. I hated my dress, despised my not-so-clean hair, and I'd abandoned my shoes somewhere and I wasn't even worried if I ever saw them again. I glanced at the table. Without thinking, I pushed everything off and stretched out on its surface. I fell asleep before the last pencil fell to the floor.

Someone shook me. "Wake up, Sleeping Beauty."

My neck ached and my head swirled in a thick fog as the hateful person kept insisting I get up. I shrugged off the offending hand and pushed myself up on my elbows, feeling every bump and bruise I'd received over the past few days. "What?"

Sundquist pushed his face close to mine. "I've brought you a carriage filled with magical things."

I peered grumpily up at him. "Are you drunk?"

"Follow me," he said, crooking a thick finger close to my face.

Reluctantly, I left my bed of torture and followed him, braving the rattling deathtrap down to street level. Dodging puddles and tire sprays, we approached his car amid clouds of exhaust from the constant flow of semi's and delivery trucks purging and filling the surrounding warehouses. Sundquist pointed to the back seat.

I cupped my hands around my eyes and leaned close to the window. "Okay. What am I looking at?"

"Mostly meat, a bit of wine and a few choice vegetables, and a change of clothes for you."

I opened the door and leaned in for one of the bags. Sure enough, one of them held women's clothing. I pulled it out. "Where'd you get this?"

"I made a few calls…pulled a few strings…" He sounded pleased with himself.

I rifled through the bag—jeans, a cami, a dark shirt, an olive green jacket and a pair of black biker boots. "You're the sweetest man ever. I mean it, but I doubt any of it will fit."

"It'll fit. I'm a cop. Observing is my job." He nudged me out of the way and pulled out the other bags.

I stood in shock. I couldn't believe he'd thought to get me clothes. "Where'd you get all this?"

He shoved a bag in my hands and frowned. "Does it matter?"

"I guess not." They still bore the price tags.

He kicked the door closed, and while he juggled the bags, I snuck a kiss to his cheek, startling him. "Thank you. Really."

He ducked away and turned a brilliant shade of red. "I have sisters, okay? One of them owns a clothing store. I know how you women get when you don't have a change of clothes."

Not just sweet, but smart. "Why aren't you married?"

"I am," he said, and then added softly, "we're separated. She says I don't love her enough. Says I enjoy being a cop more than being her husband, but that's ridiculous…she's having an affair."

"I'm sorry." There wasn't much else I could say.

He swept his hand through his hair. "I don't know why I said that. I haven't told anyone, and I mean no one. How would it look if I admitted I love a woman who's sleeping with another man?"

"Like you love her," I said gently.

A soft snort greeted my words. "Yeah. And that's pathetic." He abruptly turned away, and I followed him inside.

The atmosphere in the warehouse had changed while I'd been asleep. Wiggy and Poison had gathered containers from the shelves and were "reloading" everyone's belts. Snap was at the computer, Baby was packing cartridges with silver bullets and Cade and di Taro were pouring over my drawings of the club.

Sundquist went to see what plan di Taro had come up with, leaving me to cook. I'd rather see what di Taro had planned. As I threw the steaks on the grill and microwaved the garden veggie mix, I tried to listen to their conversation. Only bits and pieces reached my ears. "Objective" and "explosion" and some mention of "not much time" floated my way before my task of feeding the group took over. I shouldn't care. Taking a bunch of kids into that hell hole was crazy. It made me sick thinking of them welding swords and dodging fangs.

I slopped the veggies in a bowl and threw the steaks on a plate. Then I quickly seared each side of a particularly large steak, slapped it on a plate and started toward the bedroom door. "Food's ready. Help yourselves," I yelled and ducked into Alden's room.

"He's really going to do it," I ranted as I kicked the door closed. "That maniac is taking those kids into The Black Dahlia. I'd call the police, but Sundquist is already here and he's all for the idea. I don't know what to do. They're both so stubborn, and…" I looked up and fell quiet.

At the sight of the still bleeding steak, Alden's eyes had grown intense. Suddenly, the thought of those kids safety was supplanted by my own. I felt like a lion tamer caught in the cage at feeding time. I eased the plate onto his lap and backed away, moving to the farthest part of the room. Picking up the knife and fork, he cut the meat in civilized portions and chewed before he swallowed, yet the plate was empty in under a minute. He glanced sheepishly over at me. "Sorry. I was hungry."

I'd actually never witnessed a raging appetite before. "That's okay. Do you want more?"

"Can you get me another one…or two? The rarer the better."

My eyebrows rose at that. "Okay"

Since everyone else was happily eating, I placed two more steaks on his plate—I didn't bother searing them this time—and sneaked them back to his room along with a bottle of wine and two glasses.

He thanked me, and dove in. All I could do was sit back and watch, sipping my wine and thinking he would surely explode from so much food. When he finished, he settled back and sighed.

Picking up his plate I looked from it to him. "Have you ever considered a life on the county fair circuit? You could make a living entering hotdog eating contests."

He grinned. "I feel much better."

"So I see."

Suddenly an excited cry filled the air. I exchanged a surprised glance with Alden and left. Baby was clearing the table of empty plates, and Snap rolled his chair away from the desk, a huge grin on his face. "Look what I found."

"What?" di Taro asked from the kitchen where he was rinsing off the plates.

Snap jabbed a finger at the screen. "A bank account."

I put Alden's bloody plate on the table and went to Snap. I peered over his shoulder at a screen filled with bank account numbers. "So?"

"Here," he said, pointing at one in particular. "This one isn't linked to any business. It's a personal account for someone else. Pretty odd to have that just sitting there."

He didn't need to act as if I were a total idiot. I looked closer at what he'd done and came up short. "Wait a second. You hacked into Alden's personal files?"

"I wouldn't call it hacking, not using my awesome, grinding-on-the-rim decrypting program. It's more like, welcome to the company. Come on in and take a look around. Hardly challenging."

Okay. They'd hacked into Alden's financial statements. "So? It could be an account his employees use for business expenses."

He clicked on the document and it sprang open. "A thirty eight million dollar employee account?"

"Thirty eight million…" My eyes nearly bugged from my head. "Okay, I can see your point, but it's not like we already don't know he's rich."

Stepping back, I slanted a quick glance at di Taro who came up behind me, wiping his hands on a dish towel. His gaze flicked from the screen to me. With stunning accuracy he assessed my sudden discomfort. "You know whose money this is."

I had my suspicions.

di Taro clamped his hand on Snap's shoulder. "Drain it."

"Wait!" I shot him a horrified look. "How's draining it going to help us?"

"Money talks, even in the realm of the living dead."

I'd seen the lavish lifestyle in which Juliana and her crew lived. They would definitely miss the money. They would also know exactly who had taken it. "Let's say this is the coven's account. Won't draining it put Alden at risk?"

"It's their account and it won't matter." All eyes turned to where Alden stood with his arm draped over Baby's shoulders for support. They slowly walked toward us.

I rushed over and helped him to a chair. "What are you doing? You shouldn't be up."

"That's what I told him," Baby announced, concern shadowing her pixie face.

Sweat dampened Alden's hair, but his attention stayed firmly on di Taro. "I'm not the only one funneling funds their way."

di Taro flung the dishtowel over one shoulder and crossed his arms over his chest. "Who else?"

"I'd be easier telling you who isn't. The coven has been around for centuries. They consume money like we drink water. The network they've established is more complex than one person. It's more complex than one country. They're global. You can bring one vampire down, maybe even a coven, but it won't affect the others."

"I don't care about the others. I care about the one running The Black Dahlia. Who's in charge?"

Alden hesitated. His job had always been to protect Juliana. Now he was being asked to betray her. I didn't know if he could do that.

I opened my mouth to answer the question, but to my surprise, he answered before me. "Her name is Juliana Taman."

"A woman?"

Alden shook his head, obviously irritated with di Taro's cavalier attitude. "She's more than that. She's a powerful demon. A witch. She's nearly indestructible. About five hundred years ago, she was banished from her father's presence and expected to die. But she didn't. She prospered. If her own father can't control her, how do you expect to do it?"

"I don't want to control her. I want to destroy her." di Taro turned to Snap who looked at him expectantly. "Let's cut off this she-demon's tail. Send an anonymous donation to that children's home in Wyoming."

Snap's fingers blazed across the keyboard.

Alden paled. "I don't think that's wis—"

He swallowed the rest of the word when Snap punched the enter key and looked up. "Done."

Alden shook his head, the horror of what just happened etched onto his face. "God help us."

Maya

CHAPTER TWENTY SIX

Baby helped me get Alden back to bed and safely tucked in, swaddled like Moses in his reed basket. I stood over him frowning, hands on my hips. "What's wrong with you?"

"Yeah, what's wrong with you?" Baby repeated.

I glanced over at her, at her exact mimic of me, frown and all, and sighed. Apparently I had competition for Alden's attention. I scooped up the bag of clothes Sundquist had given me and glared at Alden. "You need to do what you need to do."

Alden gave me a confused look.

I slanted my eyes over at Baby, then back at him. "You know what I mean. Just do it. And stay put. For some reason, you annoy di Taro and that's not good. We might need him. I don't care if you agree with me. Just stay put and…take care of yourself."

"Yeah, stay put." Baby pushed me toward the door and whispered, "Don't worry. You kinda smell. You should do something about that. I'll keep an eye on him."

One moment I was staring at Alden's defeated face and the next I stood staring at the closed door. She'd kicked me out. She had her eyes on Alden and she'd eliminated her competition for the time being. That little girl would be all trouble when she grew up.

She wasn't wrong about one thing. I needed a shower. I looked around for someone to help me. Where was everyone? Poison, happily chatting with Wiggy about some comic book hero who could dematerialize into shadows, came into the room. "Wouldn't that be awesome?" he said enthusiastically.

"Until someone invents perpetual daylight. Then he'd be trapped." Wiggy threw a fake karate chop to Poison's throat for emphasis.

Poison knocked the hand away and huffed, "What do you know?"

The boy's fascination with superheroes verged on the obsessive. "No one's invincible," I said. "People have limitations."

The pair glanced at me as if I'd lost my mind. Wiggy smiled. "We're not talking people. We're talking superheroes."

"Everyone, even superheroes, have weaknesses that can bring them down. Take away their onesies and girlie capes and they're like anyone else. Alone and scared and acting out."

That came out a little harsh, but I wasn't in a happy place at the moment and these kids seriously needed a dose of reality.

"Oh, that is so wrong." Poison's horrified expression turned to Wiggy. "She has no clue."

Wiggy just stared at me and nodded like a little Zen master would, giving my idea room to breathe. It was more than what Poison did. His freckles brightened against his pale skin as he realized Wiggy wouldn't defend his position. Turning to me, he immediately went on the offensive. "If everyone has a weakness, then what's yours?"

Feeling out-of-control.

Whoa. Talk about a message stabbing me in the chest to get my attention.

I was a fixer. If I saw a person holding an emotional time bomb, I had to defuse it; rewire it for safe handling. I felt so compelled to reconnect people I believed were broken that I worked long hours. Ridiculous hours.

Controlling every aspect of my life had become paramount to easy living. When I was younger, I would get overwhelmed with people and their problems. I felt their pain as if it were my own. It was the reason I became a psychotherapist. I couldn't *not* help. Over the years, I learned a few tricks, found ways to survive the emotional upheaval. If I lived my life without developing any emotional attachments, then I didn't have to worry about getting emotionally bruised. Safety meant being uninvolved. I lived within a strict code of ground rules, and until now, that fierce control had been an exercise in perfection.

My clients suffered because they engaged in relationships. I rarely suffered because I never truly let myself live.

Oh my God. My breath caught in my throat. I looked away. Panic clawed along the ripples in my brain. My hands shook as I peered at the boys staring at me. They were waiting for an answer.

"Dirt," I blurted out and looked away. "I need a shower."

"Huh," Wiggy grunted. "Baby says a lot of girls have that weakness. That's why she doesn't like them." He pushed Poison in the arm. "You show her. I gotta finish this."

Still grumbling under his breath at my derision of his superhero, Poison led me to a large bath area. There was an old claw-foot tub, a large glass enclosed shower and a line of lockers. Poison pulled out a towel and handed it to me. We stood staring at each other, me waiting for him to leave and him gnawing on his lip. Finally, he said, "That guy we rescued. You think he's pretty smart, huh?"

"He's made a lot of money, if that's what you mean."

"Yeah, but he got used by the enemy. That makes him part of the enemy, right? I mean, super villains always start out with good intensions, but end up turning bad."

What was with this kid and comic books? They were like his

Bible. "Alden is nothing like them. He recognizes where he's failed, and he's doing something about it."

"He thinks we're stupid going after the bad guys tonight," he accused. "But we have too. They know we're onto them. We can't wait."

How could I explain this to him? "Juliana isn't a run-of-the-mill bad guy. She's very powerful. It's a mistake not to take her seriously."

Poison's mouth tightened. "You're new to this. You don't know. di Taro doesn't make mistakes."

With that, he turned and left.

di Taro and his little sidekicks all had the same weakness. They were human. Superheroes and arch enemies. That's what this boiled down to in Poison's head. He wouldn't lose because he was a hero. In his mind, the good guys always won.

I wished that were true. Especially tonight. "God, let it be true."

With robotic measures, I stripped and entered the shower. I attacked my hair, soaped my body, and let the hot water pound my skin clear of lather, wishing my worries about tonight could be so easily washed away. I'd done what I needed to do. I'd rescued Alden. He was safe…sort of. I could walk away knowing I had every right to do so.

Who was I kidding? It was my nature to help others. I placed my hands against the wall and hung my head while the water beat down on me. Poison's earnest face kept intruding on my thoughts. What if something went wrong? What if one of them died?

I had to disconnect. I shook my head, willing myself to not think. "I'm not di Taro. Or Alden. I didn't choose this."

I punched the water off and pushed myself straight. Stepping onto the mat, I dried off and dumped my new clothes onto the short, wooden bench that ran in front of the lockers. Bundled within the black shirt was a cream colored cami and…yes, underwear. Bright red underwear edged in black lace. Astonished, I held them up. "What kind of clothing store does his sister own?" I glanced at the bag. *Blue Ocean Boutique:*

where fashion meets fabulous.

Obviously one trendier than I'd ever visited. I shouldn't complain. Clothes were clothes. I slipped on the panties and bra, hurriedly covering my underwear with the frayed jeans, and a soft, deep scoop-necked cami. No matter how much I tried to cover the bra's black lace edging, the cami wouldn't stay put. I chewed on my lip and threw on the transparent black shirt. The body hugging cami and lace were still visible, but the whole affect wasn't so in-your-face.

I stepped in front of the wall mirror and swiped my hand against its sweating surface. Stepping back, I stared at my reflection. I definitely projected a rocker chic look. Thankfully, all the vital parts were covered and everything fit.

"Huh." Sundquist had obviously been staring where he shouldn't.

I cocked my head, not recognizing myself in the mirror. With my hair down and no makeup on, I looked younger and far too unworldly to be trapped in an otherworldly nightmare filled with vampires and demons. "I shouldn't be here," I told the woman in the mirror. "This isn't me. None of it is."

She only stared back, challenging me. Condemning me. *You can't run now. They need you.*

I shook my head. "This isn't my fight."

My world consisted of reason and logic, not the love of weapons and hero worshipping.

I quickly turned away and pulled on the socks and boots. I stuffed my dirty clothes in the bag, grabbed the jacket and headed out.

Cade saw me first and let out a long, high whistle, as he snapped on a belt with a double holster over his lean hips. "Damn. Don't you look nice? Not at all like a suit with a brain."

"Thanks, I guess." I studied the group who'd changed into dark clothes. All except Baby. She pouted in a chair, her legs slung over one of the arms, her fingers drumming against the table as she glared at everyone. di Taro strutted among them, checking this bag and that belt, ordering changes and repeating each member's duty, basically being a commander. I cocked my head at them, seeing the fresh clean faces of the boys.

And they were boys.

A beep sounded and everyone turned to Sundquist who let the drawings I'd made slide on the table in front of Baby before snatching his cellphone from his belt. "It's Carson." As he separated himself to answer the call, di Taro gathered his boys around him.

"Keep a clear head. We go in. Mingle. Cade, you keep our exit clear. Snap and I will find the security system, shut it down and mess with their communications. That's when the fun begins for you two," he said nodding to Wiggy and Poison. "You know what to do. After you set the timers, get out fast and be slick. I don't want any surprises except the ones we're springing on them."

I sidled close to Baby. As di Taro continued to check the boys gear, I whispered, "So, what's the plan?"

She gave me a disinterested look before turning her petulant gaze back to the group. "They're gonna kill the vamps…without me. Again."

Sundquist ended his call and slid a worried glance toward di Taro. "Damn it. I have to go."

"You're coming back, right?"

He chucked the van keys at di Taro and shook his head. "Not tonight. There's been a homicide and kidnapping. I've been called on it."

di Taro caught the keys. His gaze turned dark and unsettling. "Tell them you've got a new lead on the psychiatrists' murders."

"Sorry, Beau. Priority is on the living." Picking up his jacket he nodded my way. "Why don't you take Maya? She handled herself pretty well last night."

"What?" I could feel my eyes grow big with alarm as I watched Sundquist enter the elevator.

di Taro took a step toward the detective. "Sundquist…" The name faded as the elevator took his friend away.

He tossed a horror filled glance at me and cussed. Pulling

his hand down his face, he groaned. "I'm gonna regret this, but how about it, Maya?"

Baby leapt up, her blonde hair bouncing wildly against her animated features. "You're picking her over me? You all suck." She stormed off, her face clouded with disgust.

"Baby." My call was met with a string of foul words no child should know punctuated by a series of crashes.

"That better not be my CD collection," di Taro yelled.

I faced the group. "She sounds really upset."

"Baby's a bit of a hot head," di Taro said. "She'll get over it." He held up the keys, and then looked at me. "Well?"

My brain spun with excuses. "I can't go. You said yourself, I-I-I'm not trained."

He narrowed his dark gaze on me. "This morning you were all up in my face about taking on the vamps and now, suddenly, you're not trained?"

He was right. I'd expected him to risk his life for me, and I wasn't prepared to do the same for him. It wasn't like me, but The Black Dahlia wasn't just a scary place. It was pure evil. "Only an idiot would want to go back there."

"Somebody's got to get their hands dirty saving this city."

Wiggy hefted his rucksack higher onto his shoulder. "It's the right thing to do."

Ouch. That hit home.

"Fine," I agreed, but without any real conviction. "What do you want me to do?"

"Can you drive?" he asked.

"Yeah," I said warily.

The keys came flying at me. I caught them, the cold metal unnaturally heavy in my hand, warning me to run. I still remembered the stench of holy water burning flesh. My stomach did a tight, earth-spinning flip before I glanced at di Taro and shook my head. "Not the van."

Seeing my hesitation, Wiggy bounded forward, flinging an arm around my shoulders. "You're not bailing on us, are you? I mean, you can't. Not after we risked our lives for you."

My gaze landed on each of their expectant faces. He was

right. How could I say no? But that didn't mean I had to be happy about it. "Fine. I'll drive the van."

Poison came to stand on my other side and grinned. "Great. We can use her as bait. While she distracts the vamps, we can do our thing."

My mouth hung open at his idea. "Bait?"

"Scared?" he taunted.

"Yes. I am."

My admission took all the nastiness out of him. "Oh."

"She's staying with the van," di Taro announced. "Give her a dagger and a bag of holy water."

Snap got the bag, and as he slung it over my shoulder, he said, "Don't worry. The bad guys will be inside with us."

"Aren't we risking a lot doing this at night?"

"We don't have a choice. They know we know where they are."

Right. I stared at the blade. "What am I supposed to do with this?"

"Shove it where it hurts." Cade handed me a belt for my new, never-before-been-used-by-me dagger.

Poison showed me how it fit in the belt. "Don't worry so much. There'll only be five maybe six outside looking for unmarked vans with defenseless women in them."

Cade smacked him aside the head, and Wiggy pushed him away from me.

"What?" Poison held his hands out innocently. "What'd I do?"

"You'll be fine," Snap said. "Remember to stay low. Stay quiet, and don't panic. We'll be their targets, not you."

I was pretty sure that's what he said last time.

I hadn't said goodbye to Alden. It seemed wise not to worry him. He would've only tried to talk me out of going to The Black Dahlia, and I just might've listened.

Our small group huddled in the van, darkness covering our

position along a side street not far from the club.

"I'm still not sure about this." I felt it my duty to be the Debbie Downer of the group seeing as I dealt in realistic outcomes on a daily basis.

di Taro glared at me, then looked at the boys. "We sneak in the back way, blend in and do this as quick as possible."

I had to admit, they looked the part, all dressed in black. They had on heavy coats that hid their weapons.

di Taro slanted a serious look at me. "We'll be gone anywhere from thirty to forty-five minutes."

My pulse skipped into high gear. "Forty-five minutes?" That sounded like forever.

"At the most. If we're not back by then, call Sundquist." I'd forgotten my cell, so he handed his me his, and pointed to Sundquist's speed dial number. "Press three and yell for help."

I could do that. "Forty-five minutes, then call Sundquist."

He held out his hand and said, "Ashes to ashes." Everyone put theirs on his and he stared at me until I put mine on top. "Dust to dust," everyone else said. They'd purposefully included me. I wasn't sure how I felt about that.

"God be with you," di Taro said, looking at me last. Could he see the fear I tried to hide?

As they all got out, each squeezed my shoulder. I didn't feel comforted, especially when, with the whisper of feet on pavement, they disappeared down the alley, leaving me alone.

Just me, a knife and a bag of holy water.

I moved to the middle of the van, into the shadows it provided, and sat on the floor. I promptly began to chew my bottom lip. My nerves stretched taut. I slanted the flashlight down and clicked it on, just to give me a moment of light. A second to feel safe. I clicked it off and a shiver slithered down my back.

After a while, I glanced at di Taro's cell phone. Ten minutes had passed since they'd been gone. I peeked out the window and squinted toward the alley. Nothing but shadows.

A door slammed somewhere. I jumped and swallowed around my heart now lodged in my throat. Someone else wandered the night. Sweat popped out along my hairline. Although my eyes had long ago adjusted to the dark, there wasn't much to see. Just a deserted street, the collective bulk of ugly warehouses and the interrupting slash of inky darkness at odd intervals indicating alleyways.

A series of pops sounded, startling me. I sat frozen in place. Gunshots? My senses went into hyper-drive. It could have been gunshots. I sank deeper into the interior of the van. A few more minutes brought footsteps my way. Voices. Visions of vampires danced in my head. I pulled out the dagger...and promptly dropped it.

I gasped and quickly slapped my hand over my mouth.

The voices stilled. Surely they could hear my heart beat. I stretched out low, scooting halfway beneath the back seat in my search for the dagger. The floor was anything but clean. My hand encountered a bag of chips, a bottle of water, and a sports bag. As I patted along the surface for my dagger, I felt the outline of a gun. Screw the knife. I needed that gun.

A beam of light slanted through the drivers' side window. I eased back, hiding behind the bag as I slipped my hand into it.

The light went away and scratching sounded. Closing my fingers over the gun, I pulled it free. The butt was empty of a clip. The voices started up again. They were arguing. I couldn't tell about what, but it couldn't be good. In a full blown panic, I dumped the bag's contents and out poured a loaded magazine.

Suddenly, the drivers' side window crashed in, showering splintered glass all over the driver's seat. A hand snaked in and popped the lock. Shaking, I slammed the magazine in the gun and pointed it at the hand. I closed my eyes and pulled the trigger.

A high-pitched scream rent the air. I opened my eyes to see my aim had gone astray. The front window had been shattered by the bullet and two guys were high tailing it down the street.

I let my breath out, not realizing I'd been holding it. My heart pounded in my ears. They ran. I'd scared them off.

I slowly lowered the gun, one thought uppermost in my mind. They weren't vampires. Just regular delinquent humans.

I could still hear the echo of the gunshot ringing in my ears, like a clanging alarm saying, "Over here, vampires. Look. The slayers are back."

"Oh crap." They'd know in mere seconds we were here. I had to warn the others.

I frantically slung the bag of holy water over my shoulder, and searched the floor for the clips I had dumped out. I found my knife and slid it into the sheath. Next to it was a gun holster. I buckled it over my hips, securing it against my thigh and thrust the gun in the holster. I lobbed whatever I could find that even remotely looked like a weapon into the gun bag—guns, ammo, wooden stakes, even a can of pepper spray.

I moved toward the door. Sweat dotted my skin and my heart rocked against my ribs in a punishing rhythm. My gaze widened when a shadow, cold and malevolent descended on the street, cloaking the area with non-visible evil. Poison's excitable voice boomed in my head.

Ghosts. Demons.

My head suddenly grew light, as if all the oxygen were being pulled out of me. My stomach roiled, causing my throat to burn. I grabbed the door handle for support as I doubled over, gasping for breath. I couldn't be sick. I couldn't pass out. Not now.

I glanced behind me and saw the shadows converge into that of a man. His face, carved into a mask of death, boney and grim, thrust through the broken window; his eyes glowed red. His hands outstretched in grasping claws as he drew closer. The stench of rotting, diseased flesh filled the air.

Fighting against the terror spiraling through me, I yanked the door open and stumbled out of the van and ran. I blindly sped down the alley, tripping over nothing. The darkness enveloped me in cold fear. Shadows gathered in a tight, tumbling knot ahead. That *thing* jumped from the van to the alley in less than a second.

My head grew light again. My lungs heavy. My feet slowed. The door to the club seemed too far away to reach, yet I knew it was only a few steps away. As the shadows merged and burst toward me, I ripped open the door and fell through the threshold and onto the cement floor. I pushed myself to my knees and brought out a vial of holy water. Looking up, I came face to face with the shadowy figure. It opened its mouth and drew in a breath, emptying the area of oxygen. My strength to live began to slip away. As I fell to the floor, I slammed the vial against the base of the door jam, swiping the holy water from one side to the next. An ear-splitting screech pierced the night, shaking the ground as a violent rush of air burst through the doorway and slammed the door closed.

A brutal shiver swept my body from head to toe. I knelt there on hands and knees, panting as if I'd just sprinted a marathon, and stared at the glistening streak of water.

What just happened?

Holy water had saved my life.

I was in *waaay* over my head.

Shaking, I stood, supporting myself against the wall. Something evil knew I was here. I'd made myself into a walking target. Not just me, but all of us. I had to find the others and warn them. With gooseflesh crawling over my skin, I hurried down the dark corridor.

By the time I got to the club's emergency exit, I could feel the bass line through the walls. The beat thumped and boomed like a living thing. I squared my shoulders. di Taro had said I could control the vampires' influence over me by remembering who and what they were. They weren't people. They were demons.

"Demons," I said as I cracked open the door and peered into the club.

Lights flooded the stage in red, gold and blue. The band jumped and howled out lyrics that the crowd screamed to hear. The rest of the club lay in dim shadows as if all the energy was being used to highlight the performance. I slipped through the crack and stood still, watching and listening to the music. The words filled my head with visions of love. Sweet, sexy, desperate love. It was happening again. That feeling of being controlled. I recognized it and pushed it away, scanning the area for Cade. If I remembered correctly, he should be guarding this door, securing their exit.

A dark hulking shape loitered within the shadows to my right causing a sliver of fear to wedge itself in my mind. I snatched a bottle of holy water and faced the figure. But it was no ghost, only Cade, his arms wrapped around a girl and his lips happily attached to hers. "Cade?"

It took him a few seconds to react. "Maya? What are you—"

The girl tried to latch back onto his lips, and he guiltily disengaged her limbs and pushed her toward a nearby group. As if in a trance, she walked up to the nearest male and planted her lips on his.

Cade pulled me into the darkness, and I slapped his hands off me, afraid the music had infected him. He sighed and grabbed my hands. "Relax. *She* kissed *me*."

"Uh-huh. I know a tongue dance when I see one."

"Fine, don't believe me." He suddenly grew tense. "Why aren't you in the van? What are you doing here?"

"I was attacked by something I've never seen before. It came into the van and then chased me in here."

He stepped deeper into the shadows and pulled out a gun.

I pulled out mine. "We have to warn the others."

"Is that a gun?" he asked. "Don't point that at me." His grip slipped over mine and pointed the gun down. "Do you even know how to use one?"

How hard can it be? "Point and pull the trigger." As I said the word, my finger jerked against the trigger and the gun fired. I jumped and stared down at the floor. A splintered depression marred the polished wood between Cade's and my feet.

I snapped my head up, eyes wide and wary. The music came to a string-twanging halt. The dancers and gropers grew still. Everyone blinked. The pale hosts disengaged from their empty-headed victims and focused on the darkened corner where Cade and I stood.

Cade let out a nervous chuckle. "My bad."

In one single bound, the bartender leapt over the counter.

Cade pushed me behind him and leveled his gun on the crowd, sweeping it back and forth. Others moved so fast, they seemed to appear out of thin air. We were outnumbered in no time flat.

Cade threw me an angry look. "Get out of here." He swung his gaze back to the gathering crowd of immortals and started firing as he charged into them.

Screams ripped through the club. People began to dash for the exits. Some turned to fight, defending their would-be killers. I couldn't move as I watched Cade enter the crowd. One guy against all of them. The odds of his survival were hopeless.

The back door was only a few steps away, but I couldn't abandon him. Not like I had Alden.

I made to follow, but the bartender blocked my way. A triumphant smile tipped his pale lips. His eyes burned unnaturally bright, drawing my gaze to his. A flurry of soft French spilled from his lips, and I could feel myself soften. "Bon, mon cheré. Let it go. Come to me."

I glanced at the innocent people trapped by monsters. Adrenaline flooded my veins. There was only one outcome that would free them. I raised my gun and shot him. The force of the bullet only twitched his stance.

He glanced from the blossoming bullet wound to me, surprise coloring his face. His jaw flexed, and his eyes burned even brighter. "It'll take more than that to stop us."

"Fine by me." I pulled the trigger, again and again unloading the weapon into his chest.

He fell to the ground, blood soaking his shirt and pooling on the floor. My gaze searched for Cade. I had to help him. Thrusting my hand into the duffel, I pulled out a loaded clip. Stepping past the bleeding vamp, I reloaded the weapon the way I saw di Taro and his gang of kiddie heroes do more than a dozen times.

I didn't get far. The downed vamp tripped me to the floor. My gun went skidding toward the bar. Rolling onto my back, I kicked him in the face, my sturdy boot heel imprinting his cheek and cracking the bone. But he wouldn't let go.

I reached into my bag and pulled out a vial of holy water and smashed it into his face. He immediately let go, screaming as the skin and muscle bubbled and burned, but even that pain didn't keep him off me for long. His long white fingers grabbed my jacket and pulled me to him.

The smell of scorched flesh made me sick. I gagged, pushing against his hold. His hands wrapped around my throat. I stopped pushing and raked my fingers against his.

I couldn't breathe. My cheeks felt fat, my head heavy. My eyes bulged and my ears rang. His head dipped toward my neck. I couldn't stop him. Spots appeared before my eyes.

I would die. Here. Now. In the lap of evil. As I struggled for breath, my life didn't flash in front of my eyes. I had one thought. Alden.

Alden

CHAPTER TWENTY SEVEN

Though deep in a healing state, I knew something was wrong. It was quiet. Too quiet.

Maya's scent had slowly grown weaker. So had those of the men. The only active smell I could detect was that of Baby…and coffee. Rich, sweet, creamy coffee. She was close. Very close.

The sound of a cup clattering to the floor, jerked me fully awake, and I opened my eyes. Baby's horrified face registered in my brain. Her wide, terror-filled eyes were locked onto my chest, my bare chest. I must have torn the bandage off while asleep. New pink skin glistened where the ragged bullet hole had been only hours before. My gaze popped back to hers.

She pointed at the spot. "You can't do that. You can't." Her eyes rose to meet mine. "You can't be one of them. You can't."

I eased myself up on my elbows, keeping my expression gentle, my voice quiet. "Hush, Baby. It's all right. I'm—"

Her face paled and her hands shook as she staggered back.

"It's not all right. You're one of them."

She turned and ran from the room.

I bolted to my feet, sliding against the now wet floor as I made my way to the door. She was in a panic, and I didn't know what she'd do. As I entered the main area, a cold piece of metal whipped past my head. I heard the thunk and hum as it embedded itself into the wall behind me. The hairs on the back of my neck rose, feeling her anger, her resentment like a tangible entity stalking me. Another *whiz*, and I dodged another steel star.

"Stop it, Baby." I dove behind some shelves, my mind racing. I had to calm her down, but hormonal tween girls weren't my specialty. "I'm not what you think I am."

"I'm not an idiot," the high-pitched voice cried out from her hiding place. "You're an immortal."

"I am. But I'm not like them." I poked my head out, scanning the area for her. I saw nothing. "I won't hurt you."

"They all say that."

She'd changed positions. Smart girl. She knew not to stay put, to skitter around, keep me off balance.

I had to make her see I wasn't like the rest of them. But how? It had taken me days to gain Maya's trust, and she didn't have any prejudice I had to fight against.

"I'm a werewolf," I admitted.

A high-pitched, out-of-control laugh ricocheted through the room. "You're a pet? A damn dog? That's pathetic."

That she understood the trap I had lived within, that I was nothing more than a slave, even had her—a child—feeling superior to me. "Tell me something I don't know."

"Easy," she said, her voice nearer than I expected. I whipped my body around and there she was, a gun pointed straight at my head. "You won't get out of here alive."

I had to give it to her. She was a pro at stalking her prey. I straightened to my full height, though I kept my body language non-threatening. We stared at each other for a long time. Her breathing heavily, me praying she would collect all that she had learned about me over the past few days and listen to her heart.

"Don't do it."

"It's loaded with silver bullets."

I smiled gently. "It'll take more than what you've got to kill me." Unless she hit my heart, I could survive a handful of silver bullets.

Her face had taken on a deep, silent, secret pain. Her eyes welled with tears. "I bet it'll slow you down enough for me to reload."

Maybe it would at that. I couldn't believe I was being brought down by a child. My heart sank. I could take her out with one swipe of my arm, but she wouldn't survive. I couldn't, *wouldn't* hurt her. I slowly sank to my knees before her, my head bowed in surrender and put all my feelings into the next few words. "Don't do it. Please. I have so much to make up for. I can't die before I see Juliana dead."

Her lips tightened. I could feel her surprise, her struggle to remain aloof. "You're a little late, then."

My gaze zeroed in on Baby. "What do you mean?" She didn't answer, and I leaned forward, my voice hard with suspicion. "What do you mean?"

She took a step back, her hands tightening on the gun. "They left hours ago. By now, Juliana is dead. And without your help."

"Where's Maya?" I had a sinking feeling she hadn't gone home to bake cookies.

Baby's mouth turned down in disgust. "They took her with them. Her," she bit out. "Not me. Her. What does she know? I'm the one who's been training forever, and what do they do? They take her."

A wave of nausea swept me. "They couldn't have been so stupid."

"They're boys. You'd be surprised how stupid they can be."

"But she has no idea what to do." Real panic took hold of me. "What kind of idiot would take her? She'll die."

"I know that. But they wouldn't listen. They really do think I'm a baby."

One thought crashed through my brain. "I've got to go. I-

I've got to go." I jumped to my feet and headed for the bedroom. I needed to scrounge up some better clothes than what Maya had brought.

"Hey! Stop! I'm the one with the gun. I'm the one in control here. You do what I say."

"I'm done being someone's pet," I shot over my shoulder. "You can come along, but if you do, you do as I say. Got that?"

She lowered the gun. "I can come along?"

"I could use someone with your skills."

"You're not playing with me, are you? You mean it?"

She wanted to have fun with the big boys? Fine by me. I'd give her exactly what she wanted to hear. "You're the one with the gun. Now get ready. We leave in ten."

I pressed my back against the side of the building a few feet from the alley. I could sense the evil roaming the dark. It had made its presence known as soon as we got out of di Taro's little car, and the closer we got to the alley, the stronger its force became. It shouldn't bother us, I was one of them, but with ghosts one always risked it finding a way to expand its mission. It was the reason I didn't encourage Juliana to use them, yet after what happened the other night, she had obviously panicked and forgotten my advice to steer clear of them.

I turned toward Baby. "Are you afraid of ghosts?" I whispered.

Her face puckered with distaste. "Ghost don't scare me. What can they do but scream at you anyway?"

Poor baby. If this thing had found a way to expand, she was about to get a lesson in exactly what an evil spirit could do.

"Listen, it feeds off fear. Just try not to…"

"Be afraid?" she offered. A soft snort followed and she actually rolled her eyes at me. "I won't."

She had no idea. "Good. We'll make for the door about

halfway down this alley. Whatever happens, keep moving. Get inside as quick as you can."

"You got it."

She looked so cute with her blonde hair framing her face as it poked out from beneath a black beanie. She wore a long coat that covered the dark sweater, skintight pants and the weapons she'd strapped to her body. She was a walking arsenal. Her bravado scared me to death. I suddenly had doubts about bringing her along.

"This is going to get rough."

"No shit."

The fierceness of her reply took me aback. So much for a sweet, innocent little girl. I nodded. "Okay. Let's go."

We entered the alley at a run, Baby in the lead, me following close behind her. My eyes and ears were attuned to every sound within a block of the club as we followed Maya's scent trail. She'd come this way. I could smell her fear. Damn. That would have triggered the ghost, and once triggered it would linger.

It didn't take long to come out and play. I could feel its presence to my left. A dark shadow moved along the opposite wall. Suddenly, a large dumpster flew across the alley, straight for Baby. I raced forward. Baby's eyes widened. She put her hands up as if to ward off the ton of metal bearing down on her. Before it hit, I slipped between it and Baby, took the heavy container in my hands and shoved it away with a force so hard, the dumpster slammed into the opposite building and smashed through the wall. Bricks and mortar rained down into the gaping mouth.

I didn't stop. I turned to see Baby approaching the door. She gasped and tripped, falling to the ground, her hands skittering against the pavement. She quickly rolled against the building, plastering her back against its solid surface and whipped out a gun.

Bad idea. I shouted her name just as the ghost materialized through the wall and wrapped its arms around her from behind. Surprise registered on her face as the ghost squeezed, pulling her against the rough bricks. It would crush her in no time.

I rushed forward, but before I could reach her, the smoky hands covered hers and the gun went off twice. The silver bullets struck me— once in my arm and once in my stomach. The force of such a close range impact knocked me off my feet. As I went down, I kicked out and the gun she held arced away from her. I hit the ground and rolled. In one lithe motion, I grabbed her and yanked her from the ghost's arms. Bounding to my feet, I ripped the door off its hinges and we fell inside.

I lay there, hurt.

Baby pushed away from me and rolled me to my back. "I shot you. I didn't mean to. Really. I didn't."

"I'll be okay. Just give me a second."

As I lay there, I went deep into myself. One bullet had gone clean through; the other lodged against bone. Her eyes widened as the bullet in my arm suddenly reappeared and fell out, silver pinging against the concrete floor. Within a moment my wounds were healed.

She blinked. "That is so cool."

I rolled to my feet and helped her up. "Getting shot is never cool. Are you ready?"

She pulled out a wooden stake and flipped it into the air before catching it in her small palm. "I'm ready."

This little bit of fluff was turning into quite a warrior. I grabbed her free hand and we ran down the corridor. I could hear the clash of metal and the pop of gunfire. I prayed we weren't too late.

Yanking the door to the club open, we were met by total chaos. As Baby rushed forward, I saw my worst fear coming to life. Maya lay sprawled on the floor with a vamp choking the life from her.

She managed to hit him with a bottle of holy water, but that did nothing but anger him more. He only squeezed harder. As Baby passed, she rammed the stake into his heart from behind and the vamp burst into ashes.

Maya climbed to her knees coughing amid the swirling vamp ash. Baby thrust the wooden stake into Maya's hand. "Ditch the holy water. Wood to the heart." She shook her head, muttering, "What an amateur," before she dove into the crowd nearest her.

I helped her to her feet. Her throat was already beginning to bruise and a look of disbelief shadowed her eyes. I touched her cheek, concern for her pulsing against the adrenaline of the moment. "Are you all right?"

"I thought I was dead," she managed to croak out.

"I need to get you out of here."

She resisted. "I can't go. They need help."

I was about to dissuade her of that warped sense of logic when a huge blast rocked the club. As one, the people ducked. A new concerted effort to reach the doors began. Yet before anyone could take two steps, another blast ripped through the place. Smoke and fire engulfed the deserted stage area.

From out of the crowd ran Poison, Baby and Cade, dragging a kicking and screaming Wiggy.

"Time to go!" Cade shouted at us.

"You've got to listen to me," Wiggy pleaded.

Poison shot him a confused look. "What's wrong with you? You know we've got to get out before the last bomb goes off. This whole place'll go up in smoke. Hell, Wiggy. Even the vamps are smarter than you."

"We can't go yet."

Something in the kid's manner didn't set well with me. "What's wrong?"

His desperate gaze slammed into mine. "It's di Taro and Snap. They have them. Upstairs."

I closed my eyes. This wasn't good.

Maya touched my arm. I opened my eyes to her questioning look. I needed to say only one word. "Juliana."

"Oh, no."

Maya knew what damage the vampires could do. I turned my gaze to Wiggy. "How long ago?"

"I don't know."

"Think."

Wiggy looked about ready to cry. "Five minutes, maybe a little more. It was right before the first blast."

Five minutes. A lot could happen in five minutes. I didn't tell them that. But I think they knew from looking at me. How could I tell them their hero was as good as dead? Juliana rarely wasted time. She was gluttonous. She could drain a body in less than two minutes if she wanted. Rarely did she prolong the feed for more than an hour. If she did, it was usually to torture the victim in between sips.

I pushed past them. There was no time to waste. My preternaturally enhanced speed had me at the top of the far stairs. I looked back and saw the group fighting their way across the club. It was slow going. I couldn't wait.

I burst into the room that overlooked the club and found Juliana, two of her guards, and Evangeline waiting. di Taro sat slumped in a chair, his eyes staring blankly before him, his hands bound behind him. Snap lay at Juliana's feet, pale and lifeless.

The woman who had held me captive for so long looked up and wiped the a line of red from her lips with a finger before sucking it clean. "There you are. Evangeline said you would be back. I threw this little party just for you, but I was beginning to think you'd miss all the fun."

I was too late. One more person I couldn't save. I went to Snap and touched his warm skin rapidly cooling beneath my fingers. My jaw tightened. There was no helping him now. He would turn. She'd created another monster. My gaze flittered toward di Taro. He'd hunched forward in the chair, his eyes wide with horror, his muscles corded with tension, as if he couldn't believe he'd lost.

Of course. Juliana had done the one thing that would hurt her enemy the most. She had turned one of his kids into one of hers.

I stood, my vision honed on Juliana, and growled, "I'm no longer your slave."

Juliana only smiled. "Really? I think differently." She waved her hand at the two men as she stepped out of harm's way.

I wasn't surprised. She'd never willingly let me go. I took hold of Snap's arm and pulled him toward the door. Then, in one long fluid motion, I shrugged off my long coat and drew my sword. I stared at the men, both whom I'd handpicked for my army. "Step aside. This isn't your fight."

They tensed. I thought for a moment they might agree. How could I forget the pull of Juliana's will? As a unit, they stepped around di Taro and drew their swords.

Though unfamiliar with the sword I'd borrowed from di Taro's wall, it proved sound. Its balance rang sure as I brought it down on one man, twirled it around my body and brought it up against the other. Sparks flew as the blades clashed.

I tested their worth and found they had grown lazy in this modern age—their reactions slow. I kicked one away and as he fell back, I drove my blade through the other's neck, severing his head from his body. As he fell, I swung about and plunged my weapon into the other's heart and twisted. As he gasped for breath, I pulled the blade free and ended his life in the same manner as his friend.

I turned toward Juliana. She clapped, slow and mocking. "Well done. I see you haven't lost your touch for killing."

Dark anger swirled within my chest. "I'll never kill for you again."

"I would not be so sure of that." She snapped her fingers and Evangeline drew close to her. Juliana cupped her chin and cooed brightly, "Bring me the stone, my sweet."

Something was wrong. Evangeline did as Juliana bid. Where was the strong woman of yesterday? I watched as she pulled out what looked to be a chunk of polished amber and brought it to Juliana. The cold silver eyes never left mine as she accepted it from her pet. "You've been a naughty, naughty boy. But we can fix that now."

Disgust coated my tongue and I snapped, "I'm done with you."

She clutched the stone tighter. "*I* say when you are done."

"Not anymore." I slashed di Taro's bonds, freeing him and

gave him my sword. "Take the boy and go."

He took it, his eyes wide with disbelief. "Who are you, really?"

"A friend. Now go."

He did as I said, throwing Snap over his shoulder and disappearing through the door, while Juliana watched with interest. "How very sweet. Let him go now so we can hunt him tomorrow. I like that."

A series of loud blasts rocked the floor beneath us. I smiled mercilessly. "There'll be no tomorrow. Look out there. This place is burning down around us. Everyone's gone. They ran. Abandoned you like rats on a sinking ship."

"Oh, but there *will* be a tomorrow. This is just a building. They were just play things. I can make new ones. We can create anything we want. *Do* anything we want."

A layer of brittle cold encompassed my heart. I didn't like the way she said that. With such conviction, as if I were still a part of her plan. I shook my head. "Not with me."

I would have to change. Only in my wolf form would I be able to strike her down.

Just as I prepared myself to change, Juliana's emotionless voice turned hard, "I find humor in that. Evangeline said much the same this morning when I found her. But I fixed that little flaw. She's better now. Aren't you, my precious?"

Evangeline nodded, her eyes glassy pools of obedience.

I couldn't fathom her sudden change. We were finally independent of Juliana. Evangeline believed as I did. We would rather die than be Juliana's puppets again. My gaze narrowed; my voice snapped with accusation. "What did you do to her?"

"Nothing really. Just a little trick I unearthed." She held out the stone, and with a strange word, tossed it into the air. It hovered there, spinning, and began to hum. The sound brought a pain to my chest. As the spinning grew faster, the amber began to glow.

I tried to change, but I couldn't. My body wouldn't obey my command.

"Don't try to fight it. If you do, the pain will only get worse.

Trust me."

I sank to one knee, fighting the spasms of pain rippling through my limbs. I glanced at Evangeline for help. Begged her to come to my aide.

A sad smile tipped her rosy lips. "Trust her."

I dropped my head to my chest. Not again. I would rather die than lose my soul a second time. "Never."

Maya

CHAPTER TWENTY EIGHT

Ours, unlike Alden's, was a slower journey across the club hampered by one immortal bent on killing us after another. Wiggy and Poison buzzed around like killer bees, obliterating anyone that came in contact with them. Cade's attention centered on fighting anyone stupid enough to get between us and our goal and Baby protected the rear of the group, her knives flying in the air, creating a wall of steel. By the time we made it halfway across the floor, a line of dead bodies and vampire ash littered the area. I had a newfound respect for these kids. They were lethal.

As I looked around, there was no one left to fight. We stood in the middle of a burning building. Not the smartest place to be. As the smoke thickened, my thoughts clouded with doubt. "There's not much time left. Come on."

Just as we reached the bottom of the stairs, di Taro appeared with Snap draped over his shoulder. A huge blast rocked the bar area and slammed us together as a wave of heat rolled toward us. We all crouched and turned our backs to it.

My lungs burned against the sudden sweep of searing air. Wiggy quickly gained his feet and cried out, "There's one more set to go off. It'll be the one to bring it all down."

We all stood just as di Taro's rapid descent met up with us. "Let's go!"

I stared passed him. "Where's Alden?"

He turned to me, his dark eyes filled with pain and accusation. "You didn't tell me. He's one of them."

I planted myself in front of him as he turned to leave, not averse to begging. "Please. You don't know what he's been through."

"I bet you're pretty pleased with yourself getting me to save him. Bet you had a great laugh, you two. That's not a joke I like."

How could I make him understand? "All he wants is to be free. He's come so far. I can't leave him now."

"I can," he said darkly.

Baby pushed forward. "You have to go back. He's not like the other ones. I swear it. He's not bad."

"The hell with him. I'm not going back." He shoved past us. "We're gone. Come on. Baby, that means you, too."

She lingered for just a moment, indecision showing on her face.

I nodded toward the rapidly retreating group. Her place was with di Taro. "Go."

Tears welled in her eyes, but she turned and followed the boys.

I didn't lose any time climbing the stairs. When I reached the door, I saw a beautiful woman, pale skin and dark umber hair luminescent in the strangely lit room, her lips moving in a slow cadence. Juliana. It had to be, though I couldn't believe it. She was a vision of ethereal beauty. Perfection come to life. How could someone so innocent looking be so evil?

Beside her, the woman from the restaurant, Evangeline, the golden goddess, stood with eyes only for Alden. She professed to love him so much, yet she just watched as Alden slipped to his knees, paralyzed. A look of absolute pain unfurled across his face. Above him, a swirling glow began to stretch out from a yellow stone that spun in the air. If I listened hard enough, I could hear a low, warbly hum coming from it. Juliana was not the cause of Alden's pain. It was the stone.

I didn't believe in magic, but it was hard to deny a spell was being cast, and one I sensed would change Alden for the worse. Without thinking, I sprinted forward, leapt into the air, and with a single bat of my hand, knocked the stone to the floor where it skidded lifeless toward the far wall.

The room fell into darkness, and a sharp scream rent the air. Juliana stood instantly before me, her face a mixture of rage and pure disbelief. She grabbed me by the arm and tossed me across the room like a paper airplane.

I flew until I hit the wall. My head slammed against the thin drywall, crushing the underlying brick while bright light burst in front of my eyes. Stunned, I slid to the floor, my legs buckling easily beneath me. My hand landed on the stone and I grabbed it, a reflexive move. My whole body felt broken, snapped in two. I knew I wasn't dead, but the pain ravaging just beneath the surface told me I would be soon.

I watched Juliana turn and face me. Time slowed as if to prolong the agony of my impending death. I could only blink and pray for a miracle.

My miracle came—in all its frightening, amazing glory.

Alden changed. One moment he was man and the next, his clothes were flung from his body and a wolf, massive and beautiful, emerged. I'd never seen anything so incredible. It defied logic. It went against everything I'd ever read. *Lycanthropy is a mental state, not a physical one.* My God, how stupid those of us in my profession could be. Blind and arrogant. I'd had to see to truly believe.

He lunged at Juliana. Surprise registered on her face. Until that moment, I don't think she believed he'd ever turn on her. She had bullied him, demeaned him and rendered him a mere object—a possession—instead of a man. She had sealed her fate long before this day.

As they fought, I could feel my soul wrestling to be free, to fly to the heavens and be at peace. I smelled the tang of blood, heard the rent of flesh, saw the violence of their hate played out in front of me, but my body couldn't respond. It fought its own war. My heart pounded against my cracked ribs, sending wave after wave of pain through me. The scent of smoke, of burning rubber, the sound of scorched metal as it groaned against the heat of the fire slowly but surely consuming the club, entered my subconscious.

The immortal battle continued to rage. Neither could gain the upper hand, and for the second time this night I felt the haze of death draw close. As their fight grew bolder, all hope faded.

The wall I leaned against began to sag. I could feel flashes of heat ripple behind the drywall. It would be only moments before the floor gave way and we would all fall into the fire. I tried to yell out a warning, but there was too little breath in me to create sound.

The floor suddenly tilted. The beams had become dangerously weak. Juliana managed to wrestle free of Alden and in one bounding leap, she crashed through the wall and out into the night.

Alden ran toward the gaping hole.

I willed him forward. *Go. There's no more time. Save yourself.* Blood, hot against my cooling skin, dripped down my neck from the crack in my skull and onto my clothes. I was no longer worth saving.

He turned back to me and changed. In the blink of an eye, he was in front of me, scooping me up to cradle me against his bare chest. He ran for the stairs and grabbed his coat on the way out. He threw it over me, shielding most of my body from the flames. Still, the heat of the club attacked my lungs, burned my eyes and prickled against my skin. Yet the torture he carried me through only lasted for a second as he sped through the inferno, our passing barely noticed by the hungry flames. He took me to di Taro's ugly little import and gently tucked me in the back, his fingers tenderly sweeping against my broken body. I could smell burnt hair and charred skin, feel the lassitude of my limbs. I wanted to retch, but I couldn't move. I wanted to see him, but my vision had blurred. My thoughts grew sluggish and disjointed. A massive blast rocked the street. Lights flickered, and then complete and utter darkness descended. As the car rumbled to life, I took one last breath. Between the roar of the engine and the rush of my breath, my heart stopped.

Dead.

My spirit hovered over my body, connected only by a wisp of thought. The lights of di Taro's warehouse had become bright, the colors unusually intense. Even the sounds of life had grown richer in a way that mocked my passing. Alden's footsteps, as he rushed into the room with me in his arms, carried a note of despair. His cries for help were sonorous, scarring his path like a shooting star. A moment witnessed, a lifetime remembered. He dropped to his knees and laid me gently on the floor as di Taro watched from the bedroom door.

I could feel everyone's emotions in every inhale and exhale. Their hearts were like those of myth. They truly were heroes. Their combined sorrow rippled against the air, muting the colors around them when they realized I was gone.

It was Baby who refused to believe the obvious. She placed her arm around Alden's shoulders. "She isn't dead," I heard her whisper. "She's just asleep."

Alden put his hand to Baby's bright blonde curls, his eyes shimmering with unshed tears. "She'll awake soon. To a better place."

"No. I can still feel her. She's here."

"Baby." di Taro's deep voice called. "Don't start that again."

"I'm not starting anything. Snap isn't dead, not really and truly, and neither is Maya."

di Taro took a threatening step toward her, his face writhed in agony. "I said stop it."

"You never listen to me." Her eyes relayed her upset.

Baby could feel me. She knew I existed in a strange state of suspension. I didn't know how long I would stay, but I wanted desperately to comfort her…tell her not to be sad, to stay strong. I reached out a wispy hand to Baby, and then stopped. A tingle filled my spirit. I looked back at my body. Something wasn't right.

Suddenly, a burst of light swept my body, and it twitched. Everyone gasped. One moment I was omnipotently aware of everything and everyone, and the next my spirit returned, encased in warm skin. Golden heat pulsed through me on quick bolts of energy. A lovely humming entered my veins. Suddenly, my heart jumped to life. It quickened and embraced its mission of renewal. Energized blood flooded every organ, every capillary. I grew warm, my skin flushed.

"See?" Baby cried. "It's that thing in her hand. It's glowing. It's bringing her back."

"Don't touch it," Alden warned.

I could feel everyone back away. I felt gloriously free. My body thrummed with energy; my mind quickened. The damage done to my body repaired itself. Hot impulses swept through my limbs, bringing what had been damaged to life again.

The heat slowly ebbed and I opened my eyes. I felt stronger than I had ever felt in my life, yet confusion blurred my thoughts.

"Maya?"

Alden sat stupefied on the floor a few feet away from me. I eased myself to a sitting position, still clutching the rock in my hand. Slowly, I unfurled my fingers and let it slip to the floor.

I glanced up. The kids just stood there staring wide-eyed and open mouthed.

"It could be some kind of space rock," Poison quietly mouthed to his cohorts.

"So…" di Taro dragged out as he drew nearer. "How do you feel?"

Did I look different? Was that why everyone stared at me? My heart rate rose a bit. "Is there something wrong with me?"

Poison took a step forward. "Maybe you should tell us?" He held out his arms and turned around slowly, saying, "Can you see through my clothes?"

He was such an odd boy. I frowned, and leaned away from him. "Why would I be able to—"

He dropped his arms. His face wreathed in disappointment. "That means it's probably not from space, like kryptonite."

Cade rolled his eyes. "How many times do I have to tell you, kryptonite isn't real?"

Poison gave Cade a nasty look. "That's what the government wants you to believe."

Cade shook his head. "Crazy doesn't even begin to explain you."

"She was dead. Not just sort of dead, but really dead. Now she's not. That's out-of-this-world kind of stuff going on."

Baby approached and picked the rock off the floor. Both Alden and di Taro yelled at her to drop it, but she didn't. She looked from the rock, to me and then the bedroom door. That split-second warning was all she gave before she sprinted across the room. Everyone shouted for her to stop. di Taro chased after her, but she was too quick. Darting into the bedroom, she slammed the door closed and locked it before he got there.

He brought his fist down on the heavy wooden panel. "Open the door, Baby. You don't know what you're doing."

I tried to make sense of the chaos that filled my head. I remembered being in The Black Dahlia. I remembered seeing Alden in pain. The stone. Juliana. That's when things got a little fuzzy. And now di Taro was chasing Baby. I looked to Alden to fill in the blanks. "What's going on?"

"It's Snap." Alden stood and held out his hand to me. "Juliana turned him into a vampire. He hasn't awakened yet. He won't for five more days."

A loud bang drew my attention toward di Taro. He kicked the door near the knob, trying to break into the bedroom. The wall shook, but the thick, locked door stayed firmly closed. He reared back and kicked it again with the same results.

I went to di Taro and touched his shoulder, bringing his desperate gaze onto me. "Let me try talking to her."

He struggled to do as I asked, priding himself on always maintaining control, but this situation was beyond his experience. He nodded and stepped away.

I faced the door. "Baby? You're scaring us. We love Snap just as much as you do. Please let us in. Together we can find a way to help him."

There was no reply. Silence was the universal girl language for go away. I gently rapped on the door. "Baby?"

No reply.

I could feel di Taro's impatience rising. Alden came up behind me, put his hand on the knob and twisted. The metal bent and snapped. The door opened. He looked at me as di Taro pushed past us. "I'm good at more than just making money."

Baby rushed at di Taro, the stone in her hand. "It's not working. It's not working!"

She suddenly chucked the stone our way and I shot my hand out and caught it before it hit Alden in the head. I blinked my surprise and slid my widened gaze toward Alden. I was the least athletic girl I knew. I couldn't catch a ball to save my life.

di Taro stood calmly amid Baby's emotional cyclone. "He's been turned, Baby."

"No. It has to work." She took the stone from me and placed it in Snap's hand, but it just lay there, silent and dull, causing Baby's tears to flow faster.

di Taro gently guided her out the door. "Don't cry. We'll find a way to fix this. I promise."

He left the room, burdened not only with Baby's feelings of failure, but with his own. His mental anguish at not being able to save Snap settled on the room like an emotional parasite. It jumped from one person to the next until we were all infected with despair. I pushed away from Alden. *Why me? Why had the stone healed me, but not Snap?* I wanted to ask, but was afraid to know.

Wiggy felt no restraint. His questioning gaze fell on Alden. "Why didn't it work?"

"I don't know."

Cade's gaze followed di Taro and Baby, and when they were far enough away he whispered, "We're gonna have to bury him. Either that or burn him."

"Don't say that," Poison snapped. His face turned an angry scarlet. He showed his back to us and stood in the doorway, staring at Snap.

"Do you think I want that? For any of us? It's a risk we all take," Cade shouted. "God, Poison. Grow up!" He knew he shouldn't have said that. We all knew it, but it was too late to take the words back. Instead, he clenched his jaw, snatched up his coat and headed for the elevator.

"Cade," Wiggy called out. But the older boy didn't stop. Wiggy sighed. "He shouldn't go out alone. It's not even light yet, and the city's crawling with homeless vamps." With his head down and his hands shoved deep into his pockets, Wiggy slowly wandered off.

Baby crying. Poison fuming. Cade gone off alone. Wiggy shuffling about in a lost fog. God knew this kind of trauma could tear them apart easier than it could bring them together.

Alden leaned close and whispered against my ear, "I know what you're thinking, it's not your fault."

I nodded. I knew it, but knowledge didn't always make everything better.

Poison unexpectedly hit the door, causing me to jerk away from Alden. I watched the door bounce off the wall. Poison clenched his fists to his sides and spat, "This sucks."

He cast me a quick, accusing glance and stormed away, his face pinched with unshed tears.

Maya

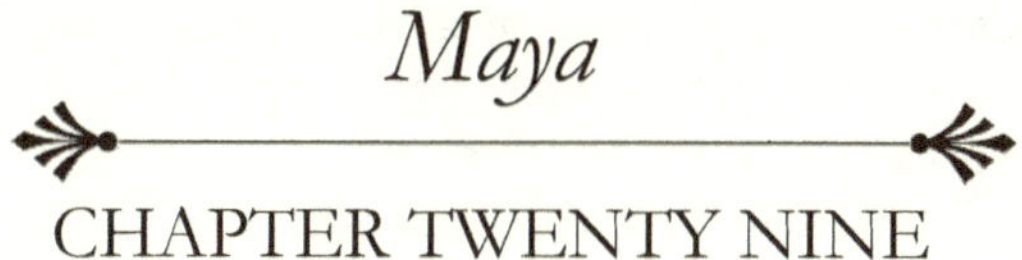

CHAPTER TWENTY NINE

As dawn colored the sky orange, Sundquist arrived. His face held the ashen color of self disgust mixed with deep bereavement. "God," he whispered to me hoarsely. "What a mess. I shouldn't have left."

"You couldn't have stopped Juliana. None of us could. If not for Alden, none of us would be here." I made to show him the room where Snap lay, but Sundquist stopped me.

"Don't get me wrong," he said, "I want to see him, but...is he...has he started to turn? I've never seen that happen, and I don't think I want to."

I looked away, aware of the life I held, and wondered if Sundquist resented me being alive too. "No. It should happen in a couple of days." Against my better judgment, I peeked up at him. His lips were thinner than usual and his eyes were suspiciously red. "I should warn you. He's unnaturally pale."

"I've seen plenty of dead people in my line of work. Just not ones I care about."

I knew what he meant. I pushed open the door and walked

in. The room was dark—mausoleum dark—with the only light coming in from the open door. I could have flicked the lights on, but for some reason that seemed inappropriate; as if light, even artificial light, would be an insult to Snap's death. A slap to his face. A taunt to what he'd never feel again.

My gaze settled on the body stretched out on the bed as if he were only asleep. I didn't understand. Why was I alive? It should be me lying there. Not him. He didn't deserve the fate of never seeing the sun again, to always lurk in shadows.

I hung back as Sundquist stood over the body for a long time. He looked tired. Dark circles ringed his eyes. "I'm sorry, buddy. I should've been there." After a moment he swept his hand over his face, pushing away the misery, the regret and gathered the detachment his profession used to make it through another bloody, senseless day.

"Right," he finally sighed. Leaning over the body, he peered at Snap's neck where the bite had been. He touched the wound and quickly drew his hand away. "God. He's ice cold. And look at this. Rigor has set in." He glanced at me. "You're sure he's not dead in the mortal sense of the word?"

I nodded.

He scratched at the stubble on his chin. "He sure seems dead to me. If he is, I need to take him to an abandoned building and call his body in for pick-up."

"He's not that dead. Baby can feel his spirit."

"Since when is she clairvoyant?"

"I don't know that she is, or if it's just wishful thinking, but she said she knew I wasn't dead when Alden brought me here. And I wasn't."

"What's this?" he asked, pointing to the stone in Snap's hand.

"That's the stone I told you about."

Sundquist held it up toward the window, and it immediately became a prism, scattering yellow stabs of light within the room. He frowned. "Did you see this? It's got what looks like three dots of red ink embedded in it." He squinted harder, and then snorted. "Unbelievable. I've read about resurrection stones, but I've never seen one."

His easy observation caught me off guard. "A resurrection stone?"

Sundquist grunted. "Since you were dead and now you aren't, that's my guess."

My heart sank. "You don't know for sure, though."

"I'd say it's a pretty good guess, but yeah, I've no concrete evidence to the theory..." he shot a measured look at me, "...except you."

What was Juliana doing with it then? Alden wasn't dead...but his desire to serve her was. She'd figured out how to use magic on it to create what she wanted.

He placed the stone back within Snap's stiffened fingers and tucked a wayward clump of hair over the boy's shoulder. "Poor kid. What's Beau got planned for him?"

I glanced past the open doorway at di Taro ensconced on the couch, furiously typing on his laptop, and then back to Sundquist. "He won't say."

"I'm not an expert, but I'd say there isn't much we can do."

"I'm afraid he's going to do something stupid."

"Like?" he prodded.

"Let him turn."

He shook his head. "I can't see that happening. He wouldn't jeopardize the others like that."

"He's been on his laptop all morning. When I ask him about Snap, he just mumbled that he's got a plan. It's starting to worry me."

"I'll talk to him."

That's another reason I'd called Sundquist. He was stable. It was in his nature to ask questions and not stop until he got answers, plus as far as I knew, he was the only friend di Taro had. Before he started toward di Taro, I asked, "Did you find Cade?"

"Not yet. I've checked all the normal teenage haunts, but then I remembered, Cade ain't so normal. I came by for Poison or Wiggy. Hopefully one of them can point me where the guy's been hanging out lately."

"Take them both. A change of scenery will do them good."

"Sure thing." He cocked his head at me. "What about you? You've got your man now. What's keeping you here?"

I glanced around the room. Everyone had retreated into their own misery. "I want to help. They seem so lost. I just want to be here for them."

"When Sage left, that hurt, but she's technically an adult and can do what she wants. Snap's death…well, I'm not so sure there's much either one of us can do. Why don't you go home and get some rest?"

"I don't know…" I looked at the kids. It felt like I would be abandoning them.

"What are you gonna do? Hang out here forever?" With that, he lumbered off to find the boys.

Alden appeared from the back rooms just as Sundquist approached. They stopped, shook hands and a moment later Sundquist went about his business. Alden came to me, his eyes warm and caring. "He said you want to go."

I knew just by the look on his face that he was ready to leave. I had my doubts. "Is it safe? Juliana's still out there."

"She's weak and alone, and bound by the restrictions of her kind. She can't enter any private residence unless she's invited. If you want, you can stay with me for a while until we know exactly where she is and what she's doing. But I understand if you want to stay. You feel safe here."

Safe? Yes. I felt safe here, but not relaxed. Slowly I intertwined my fingers with Alden's, feeling the calluses, the warmth of his skin, and the strength of his fingers. The scars were pale against the tan of his hands, as pale as my skin, and when our palms were pressed tightly together, I looked up. His gaze had grown cautious. Was he really that clueless? "If you leave, then I leave."

He gathered me close. I could feel his body warming. His voice broke as he whispered near my ear. "Are you sure?"

I didn't know anything anymore. I didn't know what exactly the stone had done to me or if I could even be classified as human. Yet, when I looked into Alden's eyes, I wasn't afraid.

I pulled away and cupped his face with my hands. "Very sure."

His gaze shone with a warm intensity that had my stomach doing little flips. "Then I'll call a cab while you say goodbye. When you're done, I'll be over by the swords. He's got some pretty nice ones. Not like mine, but I will say his are very shiny." He suddenly grinned. "And you know how dogs love shiny objects."

That brought out the first smile I'd had all morning. "By all means, go and drool."

As Alden left, I looked over at di Taro. Baby had cried herself to sleep on the couch and di Taro sat close by, typing away on his laptop. I hesitantly approached. "We're going, now."

He looked up. His eyes were red rimmed with weariness. "Where?"

"Home. I think it's time."

His gaze shot past me to Alden. True to his word, he'd found a cell phone and had a local cab company on the line. di Taro looked back at me. "Don't go with him. It's not safe. I'll take you home, or Sundquist."

I sighed. "You can't be serious."

He closed the laptop and stood, his face carved with worry. "He's a werewolf. Baby told me. He'll kill you. That's what his kind does."

Was he listening to himself? "His kind? From what I hear, you're not so innocent yourself."

"I protect the innocent. I don't gather them up and present them as dinner. His kind can't help but be evil. They aren't sweet cuddly pets. They're monsters primed to kill."

I suppressed a bone shuddering shiver and forced myself to stare into di Taro's eyes. "I know what he is. I've seen it. I know what he's done. He's told me. But he's different."

I truly believed that. I knew Alden. I knew him deep down to his core. He was good.

"Different?" A coarse laugh rippled hatefully from his throat. "That's what he wants you to think. They call it charisma, but that's a lie. They have the ability to persuade, to suggest you do something out of character, like go off with them to a dangerous night club or willingly let a vampire drain you dry. God, you're falling right into his trap."

I turned my head away and refused to look at him. I didn't want him to see my surprise at learning Alden had the same kind of power as vampires. The ability to place suggestions in people's minds was a far cry from being charismatic.

di Taro sat back down and returned his attention to his laptop. "Whatever. Don't say I didn't warn you."

I wanted to scream, he was so irritating. I didn't want to leave on a sour note. I cared and believed in what they were doing. They needed someone to look out for them, to balance the craziness their lifestyle created.

I crouched and put my hand on di Taro's knee. Our eyes met over the screen; mine pleading, his hard and unyielding. "He saved your life," I reminded him. "He saved mine. He saved Baby's life. What more proof do you need?"

He leaned over the monitor, a snarl twisted his lips. "He put Baby in danger. I should kill him just for that."

Curled on her side, Baby slept on the couch, her lips puckered sweetly in sleep. She exuded innocence, but I knew differently. "That little girl is a walking killing machine. You've seen to that. If not for her, I'd be dead. Several times over. These kids are amazing. I don't know if I should congratulate you or curse you for what you've created.

"But I'm thankful. They were there when I really needed them. The same goes for Alden. He isn't what you think he is. He's different. If you can't see that, well then, I don't have any more time to waste on you."

I didn't want to say it, but it needed to be said. I couldn't allow him to try and control me. I wasn't one of his kids, nor was I incompetent. I sought help when I needed it. In view of that, I was far stronger than di Taro would ever be.

"That's it? You came here and inserted yourself into our lives and now you're just going to leave? Fine, then. Walk away."

My hand stiffened on his leg. "What do you want from me?"

His stare grew intense. "You've just been given a gift. A new life. I saw you catch that rock. No one else could have done that. Who knows what else you can do." He turned the computer to face me and it showed an intense training regime specifically created for me. "I can train you to fight. You could help lead these kids. Save countless others."

He thought I had some kind of supernatural power now? It didn't matter. "I'm not a violent person. I can't do that."

He put the laptop aside and leaned forward. "Is that what you think of me? That I enjoy this? I do what I have to do. I'm proud of what I've been able to accomplish. I'm not gonna get a medal. Hell, no one knows I risk my life everyday to keep them safe, but it's something I have to do."

"That's your choice. I save lives in a different way."

The muscle in his jaw spasmed. "But if you could intercept the demon that's hunting them before it takes hold, isn't that a better calling?"

"No. It's a different calling. One I'm not keen on answering." I stood, gratefully breaking contact with him. "Any time any of the kids need anything, I'm here for them."

He sat back, his gaze suddenly dispassionate. "Fine. I'll tell them you just couldn't stomach the fight. They'll understand...eventually."

He could be such a jerk. "You know what? You do that."

I turned and headed toward the elevator. My steps echoed sharply against the polished concrete floor. I entered the elevator, and before I could slam the gate closed, Alden appeared. He stepped in beside me, took my hand and closed the gate. I stared at di Taro, saw his frown, his disappointment, but I couldn't help him. I clung to Alden's hand as the elevator began its descent, and my gaze finally broke from di Taro's darkly brooding one. When the cage moved halfway into the shaft, I let out a deep sigh. The ride down to street level couldn't come fast enough.

The elevator stopped and Alden pushed the gate open. I

was so tired, my mind so traumatized, I couldn't put two words together. I stood directionless, drained of all thought. I could hear the soft pitter-pat of rain outside and longed to lie down and sleep. Alden slipped his fingers between mine and led me to the cab, dirty yellow against an angry sky. The early morning orange horizon had been gobbled up by thick black clouds which had rolled in from the sea. The gentle rain of minutes past quickly turned violent. We got in the cab, and I laid my head back. I blinked once, twice, and by the third one, my eyes refused to open.

Confusion laced with weariness pulled me into a deep sleep where an image of Snap, alone in the bedroom, flashed in my head. Again and again, the image popped, like a strobe light bringing the curious to a carnival oddity. Darkness, and then Snap. Darkness, and then Snap. Darkness, and then Snap, but then I was there, standing beside him.

"Wake up, Snap," I said.

He lay utterly still. His soul leached from his body.

I trailed my hand down his arm. So cold. He felt so very cold. I picked up his hand, the one holding the stone, and I called out to him, again. Nothing.

I glanced at the stone, plucked it away and held it before me. Hot pressure gathered behind my eyes and I closed them tight. "If you have any power left in you, do this for me. Heal him."

I wished for a miracle, yet the stone lay just as lifeless in my hand. Defeated, I placed it within Snap's palm and wrapped his fingers around it.

"It's wrong. Unfair." Hot, unbearable emotion flooded my eyes, and I sank to my knees beside the bed. "You know it is. He's so young. If I'm worth saving, then so is he." A tear slid from beneath my lashes. I clasped Snap's hand in mine and laid my forehead against his cool fingers. "Save him. Please."

A moment past, and then…his hand shook. I drew away. The stone had begun to glow. I could feel the warmth of it, could see the energy ripple under his skin. I drew away as his body began to shake uncontrollably.

Within moments, the stone's light began to fade, and as I took a step toward Snap, he bolted upright, eyes glowing amber bright, his mouth opening in a frigid hiss as fangs sprang forth.

Alden

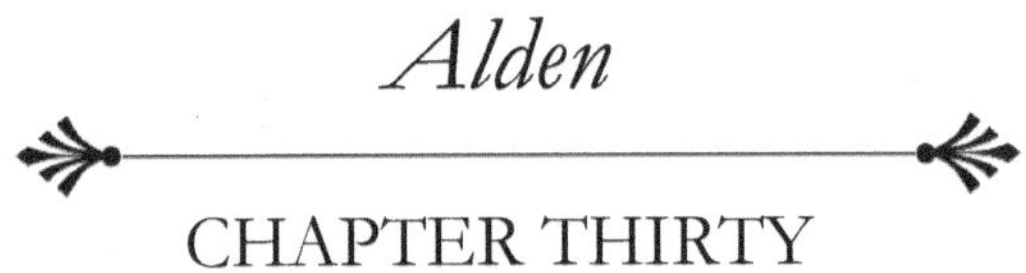

CHAPTER THIRTY

Since the cabbie insisted on swerving in and out of traffic, I slowly eased Maya's sleeping form against mine. She curled into me; her hand rested against my chest, twitching every so often as her warm breath slid against my neck in quick jabs. A sleeping beauty. Yet a beauty who fought against troubled dreams as Boston shuddered under a heavy thunderstorm. I gently pushed her hair away from her wrinkled brow. Its silken strands clung to my hand, and I brought them up to my face. Jasmine. She smelled of jasmine and honey.

I moved my hand to hers. Since she woke up, di Taro had honed in on her like a hound on the scent of new prey. I wouldn't allow her to agree to his ridiculous plan. God knew she had a big heart, but she shouldn't have to be a fighter. Not like him. Not like me.

But from what I'd seen so far, di Taro had a persistent streak. Like a gnat on a hot summer day, he'd buzz around her, wearing her down. He would appeal to her empathetic nature.

She would naturally give in to the temptation to cleanse the world of evil. And then her life would be ruined. Evil would be her constant companion. She would never know a moment's peace again.

I gazed down at her sleeping face, my heart breaking to see her struggle through an unpleasant dream. If di Taro succeeded, the ugly side of mankind would forevermore torment her sleep, delivering nightmares from which grown men shrank.

I ran my fingers along the smooth slope of her jaw. So beautiful. So courageous. But hunting evil was not her destiny. I wouldn't allow it. She'd had just a small taste of my world, and it had already killed her. She was too good, too pure of heart to survive what di Taro wanted to thrust upon her. Let the fallen angels such as di Taro and I deal with evil. Maya deserved a life devoid of such pain.

Thunder boomed, and Maya jerked awake amid a jagged rip of lightning. Her eyes were wide against the bright flash, and she gasped, turning her hazel eyes on me. I gathered her close, pressing my lips to her temple. I wanted nothing more than to erase the last few days from her mind.

Her body shook uncontrollably, and she drew in a deep, unsteady breath. "It was just a dream. Just a dream." Pulling away, her eyes flared with determination. "We have to find out where that stone came from."

"We will."

A weak answer for such a grave moment, and certainly not enough of an answer to ease her fears, but it was all I had to give her right now. I glanced out the window at the mix of old brick and modern sparkling glass buildings. Gray colored the horizon as rain speckled the morning. This would be a day of hunting. Juliana loved nothing better than to attack in the damp shadows of a stormy day. By pure habit, my heart accelerated at the thought of the hunt. She would need to feed. She was alone and hurt.

I nodded more assertively. The safety of my apartment lay just around the corner. "I know about some books. Maybe one of them can help us."

"Books?" I could hear the sneer in her voice. "Somehow I doubt the local library will have what I need."

I smiled. A little of her fire had returned. "They're mine, and they're more like ancient scrolls."

"Ancient is good," she said, looking out at the raging storm.

The cab barely rolled to a stop when Maya opened the door and jumped out. I paid the man, and in no time we were before my apartment door. I ushered her in. The rush of familiar scents eased my mind…except…

"di Taro's been here," I rumbled. His scent made my jaw clench.

Maya whirled about. "I needed a ride to get your clothes. We were here for just a couple of minutes."

The hair on the back of my neck rose. My eyes narrowed and my nostrils flared. I followed his scent to my office. I touched the soft leather of my chair. He'd sat in my chair. My fingers slid over the keyboard. His hands had been there as well. Lightning lit up the sky, illuminating the office with a slash of white heat. "God only knows what he's done to my files."

Maya worried her lip from the doorway. Her curls, damp from the dash into the building glistened in the muted light. "I couldn't stop him. I'm sorry."

I didn't say anything. I re-entered the hallway, following di Taro's testosterone-laden scent into my bedroom. Only a thin shield of gauzy fabric covered the windows, its weight unable to block out the brilliant rips of lightning marking the sky. The scent trail twisted about the place in a random pattern. di Taro had wandered the whole room, poking into my life. He'd even gone into my closet.

I stopped at my underwear drawer. I slid the third drawer open where a pair of silk boxers had been shoved inside. I pulled them out and tossed them into the hamper. I glanced back at her. "I see he made himself at home."

"He doesn't trust you."

Her defense of him suddenly irritated me. I shouldered past

her and snorted. "He wants me dead. I'd say I have even less reason to trust him."

Maya followed me back into my bedroom where metal and glass sparkled as the lightning flashed. "Can you blame him?" she asked.

I pulled down an old sword, and in a swift series of moves, whipped it about my body, ending the display with the blade pointing straight up in front of me. Thunder boomed in the distance, but its sound rattled the window panes. The storm was gaining strength. I slanted my gaze past the blade to Maya. "He had his eye on this."

Surprise registered on her face. "How do you know that?"

I had become a wizard in her eyes. I knew the impossible. But it was just the trail of his scent that had led me to the accusation. I pulled out a cloth and began rubbing the blade down to erase di Taro's touch.

"And now he wants to use you," I said as she cautiously watched me buff the blade and wipe down the handle. "Make you one of his minions."

The curtains were backlit with another flash of light. Its insistent pulse pulled at my baser side. I fought the beast that longed to come forth. It wanted to tear at di Taro and keep him far away from Maya. I couldn't control my anger, and I snapped. "I heard him talking to you before we left."

"How?"

Thunder sounded. I glared up at her. She'd pulled back until she drew even with the bedpost. Her fingers appeared to toy with the wood, but I could see the whiteness of her knuckles. I made her nervous. Did she think me angry with her? I wasn't. Yet I couldn't control the seething injustice that di Taro had roused. "Werewolves have good hearing. Exceptional hearing, actually."

"Then you know what he believes, what he wants from me." I could hear the hesitance in her voice, the fear of the future. Her own insecurities slithered on the air to wrap around me. di Taro had done this to her. His idea had set in motion a cruel war within her mind.

"He wants to make you a killer, just like him." I let my anger enter my eyes, and I couldn't control the bark of laughter that echoed within the room. "It's ridiculous. You're the last person I would recruit for such a job. We don't even know what the stone did. Quick reflexes don't make you superhuman. It could be a temporary side effect, gone tomorrow."

"I hope it is," she said quietly.

The room burst with light, revealing her doubt in the harsh flash. I re-hung the sword and looked at Maya, my eyes haunted by the past, by the path I had chosen. "I would give up what I've been given to be human again. di Taro shouldn't have asked you to join his dysfunctional little party. You have a life—a good life."

"He shouldn't have asked," she said, "but he did."

Thunder shook the windows, and she raised haunted eyes toward me. "I should be dead." She pushed her hands through her hair, her body shaking like an abandoned kitten. "I can't deal with this. Not on my own."

In an instant, I stood before her. "You don't have to."

I ran my hands up her arms until they rested on her shoulders. I gave her the chance to pull away, but she didn't. Instead, she stepped into my arms and clung to me, her body quivering. Tears wet my shirt as she burrowed closer. "What else has changed inside me?"

I gathered her face between my hands, willing her to step beyond the pain and listen to me. "You are who you've always been, do you hear me? No one can steal our essence from us, no matter what people do to us or how far we stray."

She closed her eyes tight, her mouth stiff against her inner anguish. "I'm different now. I feel it."

"Look at me," I commanded. When her eyes met mine, I allowed my form to shift, just slightly, and then return to full human form. I let what she saw sink in, and then asked, "Am I irredeemable? Have the sins of my past placed me beyond the reach of love?"

"No." Tears swam in her eyes. "No. You are the best man

I've ever met. Even with all you've been through, you still have a soul that longs for good."

"And so do you," I whispered fervently. "And di Taro is preying on your goodness."

Those tears hovering on the edge of her lashes sprang forth and rolled down her cheeks. Her gaze searched for any doubt that lingered in me. I gave her no escape. I held her captive, my fingers tangled in the thick coils of her hair. "You are the same woman who you've always been. That's what I can feel. That's what I *know*."

I gathered her slender form to me, feeling the rise and fall of her chest against mine. I wouldn't let her go. She was emotionally distraught. She walked the edge. One misstep on my part and she would crumble, but I had to take that chance.

The violence of the storm lashed at the windows, mirroring the storm raging inside her, matching the longing raging inside me. I had only one way to show her the truth. "Don't think, Maya, just feel."

I pressed my lips to hers, willing her to see what I saw, a woman, fully and completely loved.

I sought her soul and when I found it, I gave it no mercy. I demanded it prove itself, and just as I had hoped, it didn't disappoint me. It blossomed and filled her being, lighting her every corner until the darkness had nowhere to hide. And then it did the unimaginable. Her soul wrapped around my mine and repaired the damage I couldn't bear to touch. Maya chased away the last trace of the monster that hid in me.

How had this happened? My intent had been to comfort her, but instead, she had healed me. I felt renewed. Rebirthed. The beast no longer controlled me.

I jerked free and peered into her warm eyes. For the first time since the night that changed me forever, I felt completely human.

Maya entwined her arms around my neck, and urged me closer, her words soft, but firm, "Don't pull away. Never again."

"I would die first." She had become my greatest desire.

Our lips joined and I lifted her, molding her soft curves along my harder angles. I nibbled along her jaw and traced a path along her throat until I came to the curve of her neck. I buried my face there, my breath unsteady, my heart a thudding giant ready to burst free.

"Alden?"

I lifted my head and allowed the truth to show in all its raw power. "Love me, Maya. I can no longer live without you."

Our breathing melded together, quick and heavy as her lips captured mine. I pressed her back to the bedpost, slanting my mouth over hers, delving deeper, wanting more.

She gave of herself. A gift so pure it was nearly my undoing. My mind swirled with exploding sensations, yet I clung to the feel of her soft lips, and the taste of her warm mouth that was sweeter than any I had met. Her fingers eagerly slipped into my hair as mine found the hollow created by the small of her back. Slowly, I splayed my hands lower and fit her securely to my hips.

She pulled away, her eyes glazed, her face bathed in wonder. "How is it that I can feel my own blood rushing under my skin when I kiss you?"

"I don't know." I didn't. Everything about Maya was unique. Every touch a new experience. Even my empowered senses were heightened. "Does it frighten you?"

"It used to," she murmured, her gaze locking with mine, "but not anymore."

Her words sparked a rush of pleasure that flushed my skin. A growl of need tore from my throat, and she gasped as I jerked her from the bedpost. Holding her tightly, I spun us about and we fell to the mattress. Our mouths joined as we sank into the downy softness of the bed.

Without breaking contact, I trailed my hand down her leg and pulled off her boot. With a careless toss, I dropped it to the floor. She hooked that leg around my thigh and I quickly removed her other boot. I kicked off my shoes, and in one motion, rolled us to the center of the bed.

I hovered over her, my hands entwined in her hair as I

nibbled at her bottom lip, and then kissed her more deeply. Her hands were at my upper back, and then lower where she slipped her fingers beneath my shirt hem and began to slowly creep it up my torso. I wanted nothing more to be rid of my stifling clothes. My impatience showed as I ducked my head free and zealously shook the fabric off my arms.

She pitched the shirt and brought her hands to meet the bare flesh covering my ribs. There she found a scar that rippled across my torso, and her fingers gently explored its length, eradicating the memories of Juliana's abuse. I let her touch what she willed until I shuddered and groaned against her lips with desire.

I sought her skin, and when the satiny texture of her belly greeted my hand, I thought I'd gone to heaven. She inhaled, her ribs expanding under my touch as I exposed one glorious inch of skin after another. I nuzzled the silkiness of her nape, and I lifted my head to stare down at her face.

Lightning flashed, highlighting the rich color of her hair and the creaminess of her skin. I wanted her so badly, but…

"I don't want any regrets." I knew how hard it was to live with an unalterable choice.

Her heart beat faster against the palm of my hand. "Neither do I."

I could smell the pain I had unwittingly delivered, pain she so bravely fought to control, yet it revealed itself by the sadness darkening her eyes. She dropped her gaze to my mouth and said on a shaky voice, "I died for you. Doesn't that tell you anything?"

It was the one thing she had given me time and again. Without her, I would be physically alive, but dead—a mere puppet of a cruel demon whose one desire was to sate her insatiable need for power over everything and everyone she encountered. My feelings for Maya were strong, but I needed to know hers matched mine. "With this…I can't be wrong."

She pushed me away and rolled to her knees. I followed her lead. We faced each other in the center of the bed, kneeling only inches apart, yet not touching. I felt the heat of her skin, and the strength of her purpose. I probed deeper and sensed a profound vulnerability, as if no one had ever seen her this emotionally exposed. Her thick lashes brushed her cheeks, and when she finally looked up, the long fringe accentuated the slant of her eyes. The clearness of her honesty reflected there burned into me.

"I love you," she admitted in an emotionally thickened voice. "If you asked me to follow you into hell itself—"

She shook her head, unable to finish, yet begging me with her eyes to understand what she found herself unable to say.

My heart constricted. I leaned forward and I kissed her cheeks, her eyes, her mouth. I laid my forehead against hers and said, "You already did."

She cupped my cheek and blinked back a sudden wash of tears. "Then how can you not see? Nothing will separate me from you."

I had to be honest with her. She may now see me through rose-colored glasses, but when she realized how difficult our life together would be, she may well decide against it.

Her eyes softened. "Don't be afraid. Real love is rare, and I have no intention of letting you go." Her lips found mine and the kiss she delivered fogged my head, heated my skin and drove my hesitance away. Pulling back, she said in a confident voice, "From this moment on, I am yours. That's all that matters."

Maya

CHAPTER THIRTY ONE

How could I not love him? Noble and chivalrous, he would deny himself everything to give me respect. It was that, his inherent goodness, his lifelong battle to reclaim his humanity, which I loved.

"If you will have me, I will be yours forever," he whispered raggedly.

"Forever," I repeated, and as soon as I said it, he pulled me to him and sealed the promise with a heated kiss.

I finally felt the full power of desire flooding through him. It attacked, delving into every inch of me until I knew every emotion, every thought, he possessed.

There was so much I didn't know or understand, but when it came to Alden, I had no doubts. He was my love, my protector, my life. If he ever left me, I would die of a broken heart.

He broke free, hovering only a hairsbreadth away as he swept my shirt from me with one pull, exposing my lacey, very girlie bra. "I will never abandon you," he said huskily.

He had read my thoughts as I had his. I placed my hand on his chest, his muscles vibrating with expectation, the angular planes of his body a pleasure as I ran my hands down and around him.

He clasped me to him, kissed the top of my head and murmured, "I love you."

My embrace tightened. I had waited so long to hear those words. Never had anyone said them to me. I couldn't help the tears welling in my eyes, afraid this might all be a dream.

He eased me to the bed and began a gentle assault, kissing and nuzzling every inch of my skin until I couldn't think straight. The rest of my clothes were slowly stripped from me, one after the other until I lay completely exposed to his sight.

Neither of us were able to deny ourselves the feel of the other for long. The more we explored, the more I became aware of myself. A simple touch created a dozen sensations. I revealed in every kiss, every stroke. As our bodies merged, so did our thoughts.

This was what I had waited for so long for, this pure give and take. I felt cherished. Adored. And as our bodies found release, a deep contentment washed over us.

But it didn't last. On the crest of pure joy came a wave of terror.

My sight suddenly blurred and the next moment, a scene invaded my mind. It showed two lovers passionately embracing in an alleyway. Yet something was wrong. The man's arm, once tightly wrapped around the woman's waist, slowly fell to dangle limply at his side. The woman raised her head, and I stared straight into the silver bright eyes of Juliana. She stared back at me, a dark secretive look that chilled me to the bone. A ruby red smile slowly emerged, growing into an evil sneer.

"I never forgive. And I never forget."

The gruesome scene vanished as quickly as it had emerged. Alden froze. I could almost taste his panic. My heart, so recently pounding with passion, grew heavy with fear. "Alden?"

"Oh, God," he moaned into the pillows. "What have I done?"

My fingers clutched at his shoulders. My own sense of panic joined his. "Did you see her?"

He raised his head to reveal his face wreathed in alarm.

"You did see her." I forced myself to re-imagine the scene. "She killed a man, and then she said—"

"I never forgive. And I never forget."

My heart constricted, and I began to shake. "What just happened?"

"I don't know." He pushed away and sat at the edge of the bed, confusion wrinkling his forehead as his hands gripped the mattress like he would fall off the edge of the world if he let go. "Maybe it's the bond."

I sat up and put my hand on his shoulder, refusing to let her poison him. "It's broken," I insisted..

"A remnant, then, of what we once shared. She was feeding. Cresting on an emotional and physical high…" He slanted a cautious glance at me. "I don't know. It's never happened before."

He got up and went to his closet.

"What are you doing?"

He didn't answer, and that worried me. I sat in the middle of the bed and wrapped the sheet around me, feeling exposed and unsure. "Alden? What's going on? Talk to me."

When he reappeared, he wore dark jeans and a dark shirt. Apprehension caused the back of my neck to tingle. "Where are you going?"

He paused and looked over at me. "She'll never leave us alone. She proved her point by what she just did, and it's sealed her death. I have to find her. I have to end this."

He strode to his weapons and pulled down a mean-looking sword and a thin dagger.

I scooted off the bed as alarm bells went off in my head. "You can't. Not now. She wants you to find her. I know that for a fact. I felt it. Be smart about this. Call di Taro. Have a back-up plan."

"The longer I wait, the stronger she'll become." He slid the sword into a decorative scabbard and buckled it around his hips.

"Don't do it. She's trying to control you again." When he went for the door, I stood before him, blocking his way. "She's desperate. Unpredictable. Going after her is a mistake."

He ground his teeth and shook his head. "I know you're right, but she's weak. She's weaker than she's ever been. I felt her pain. Her loneliness."

"What of her bitterness," I quickly pointed out. "Her anger? Her lust for revenge? Take time to think this through. Please. She's not going anywhere. That's something we both know."

I waited, my breath shallow and uneasy. I couldn't lose him so soon.

His jaw flexed as he warred against his instincts. I willed him to follow his decision to its logical, disastrous conclusion. After a long moment, he looked at me and held out his hand.

I didn't hesitate. I place mine in his, peering up at him and wishing I could see into his mind like I had before.

"You're shaking."

I nodded. I wouldn't try to deny my fears.

He tugged on my hand and brought me closer. "Not so long ago, I would've done what I wanted. Now I find myself thinking about you. I want to end this for you. Keep you safe."

"I am safe. Here. With you."

"It won't always be so."

"We'll deal with that when the time comes."

He pulled me into his arms and kissed my temple. "Your confidence in my abilities is appreciated."

His hands casually kneaded the tense muscles in my shoulders, and he pulled away, frowning down at me. "You're tense. I've done that to you, haven't I? I didn't intend to upset you."

I sighed as his fingers pushed and pulled at the knots. "Just so long you're with me, I'm happy."

He lowered his head to my ear and whispered seductively, "You want me to draw you a bath. Sprinkle rose petals in the water. Light scented candles all around you while beautiful music fills the air."

I pulled away, a sudden urge overtaking me. "You know what I'd like?"

"What?"

"A bath. With rose petals in the water, scented candles and beautiful music."

He smiled, though it had an edge of weariness to it. "I think I can arrange that. Grab hold," he said as he swept me into his arms. He carried me into the master bathroom and set me on a padded bench near the tub. To me, it looked more like a small indoor pool. Along the back edge, beautifully carved candlesticks and a host of stands held all sizes of candles. He picked up a tapered lighter and touched it to each wick until a soft glow circled the tub. He then turned on the water and glanced over at me. Holding up his finger, he left, but returned a short time later with a handful of red roses. They were the ones I'd spied on the entry table the other day. I suspected he had fresh flowers delivered every week. With grand flourish, he plucked the petals off the stems and let them float down into the water where they swirled on warm eddies.

He stepped back and waved a hand toward his handiwork. "Will this do?"

"Not quite." I tipped my head and smiled. "I don't hear music."

He pointed to a panel with buttons on it. "The third button down controls the stereo. The first is for the TV and the second is for the DVD."

"How very…indulgent of you."

"A man likes his comfort."

"And what will you be doing while I'm in here?" I asked as I let the sheet slide down my body and stepped into the tub. The steam hugged my calves and then my hips as I lowered myself into the water, rose petals scurrying out of my way.

His eyes brightened as he watched me. "Thinking of you."

"That's very sweet." I picked up the sea sponge lying in a nearby basket and began squeezing water over my shoulders and down my back.

He sighed and dimmed the lights. As I closed my eyes and leaned back, he quietly left.

I soaked in the tub until the water cooled. After drying off, I found a shiny gift bag filled with women's clothes on the bed. Tags still attached. "Lucky me," I muttered, wondering where they'd miraculously come from.

I sifted through a dozen shirts in various styles, slacks, high quality jeans and a selection of very feminine underwear almost too pretty to wear. Almost. I quickly changed, put my hair up into a messy updo and sought out Alden's whereabouts.

I found Sundquist lounging on the couch, gnawing on a deli sandwich and watching *The Hallmark Channel.* His presence explained the sack of new clothes.

He threw me a quick glance. "Hey, beautiful," he said around a mouthful of steak and sautéed onions before returning his attention to the show.

I picked up the remote on the coffee table and clicked the TV off. "What are you doing here?"

"Your guy called me."

I hadn't seen Alden in his office or in any of the other rooms I had passed. Apprehension tingled just under my skin. "Where is he?"

"Out."

Out? My stomach tightened into a hard knot, and I grabbed the back of a nearby chair to steady myself. "He's gone?" I said past a tight throat. "Where?"

Sundquist sat a little straighter, his eyes on me. "You okay?"

"Where, Sundquist? Where'd he go?"

"Relax. He went to the office. Said he had things to take care of. He'll be back."

He went to the office? Today? I couldn't be more stunned…or more suspicious. "Are you sure he's at his office?"

Sundquist snorted against his full mouth. "Okay, you got me," he said between swallows. "I didn't follow him there, but I didn't think I needed to."

His sarcastic tone snapped me out of my panic. What was wrong with me? I had to calm down. I swept a trembling hand through my hair. "Sorry. I-I'm just surprised he left."

Why hadn't he told me he was leaving?

Sundquist popped the last bite of his sandwich into his mouth and wiped his hands clean against his dark slacks. "Found Cade if you're wondering."

I hadn't. I bit my lip as a blush heated my cheeks. "How is he?"

"A lot like everyone else. Talked to Beau, too." He slanted a curious eye at me. "He's always been a man with a plan."

How could I forget his plan? I slouched on the couch next to him. "He's crazy."

"Agreed. But his kind of crazy has kept Boston relatively safe from the devil's underlings."

I threw Sundquist a surprised look. I didn't expect him to agree with di Taro. "You're not suggesting I take his offer seriously? We don't even know what happened to me."

"I'm not suggesting. I'm just commenting. It's your life…and it's been one hell of a ride lately. I can see your point. Find out what's happened to you first. Then think about it."

I relaxed a little bit. At least Sundquist was being reasonable. di Taro reminded me of an action figure, posed for movement and bigger than life. His mind never stopped clicking, and he was raising a bunch of kids to be just like him.

Plucking at a crease along the arm of the couch, I asked, "What's he going to do with Snap?"

"Cage him."

I cocked my head, peering over at him dubiously. "What does that mean?"

He let out a heavy sigh. "It means he won't kill him, he can't bear to bury him, so he's going to cage him."

"Where?"

"In the warehouse. Better to keep an eye on him there."

"But what if he gets loose?"

He slapped his hands on his thighs and stood. "Listen, *I* know it's insane. *You* know it's insane, but Beau isn't thinking with his head. We can't stop him, so we might as well help him. I'm thinking, we find out how that rock fixed you and maybe we can figure out how it can fix Snap."

I'd never been able to turn down someone who needed help. "Alden said he had some books…"

He held out his hand to help me up. "Let's get to it, then."

The book slipped from my fingers and thudded to the floor, waking me. Startled, I sat up, my vision darting about the expensively decorated room before I found my bearings. I'd been searching ancient texts. Dull, dry, unreadable ancient texts. I mostly scanned the pictures while Sundquist searched the internet.

He thrust out his arm and snapped his fingers to get my attention. "Come see."

I went to stand beside his chair and gazed down at the screen. There, in an old pencil sketch, was a stone.

"Look familiar?"

Sort of. I bent closer. "What's it say?"

"Not much. Most of it is about this creepy little church in the Carpathian Mountains, but," he scrolled down the page and pointed, "then it talks about some weird guy who brought the stone there sometime in the middle ages. Then, during an eighteenth century rebellion, the stone wound up lost. Here's where it gets interesting. They claim the stone carries the blood of an angel."

I snapped my gaze to him and he nodded. "I know. It sounds crazy, but we've been dealing with demons, which are technically fallen angels, so it's not that farfetched."

"What else does it say?"

"Legend says a sorcerer summoned the angel and stole the blood. Somehow, he was able to place three drops in pine resin and…a little hocus-pocus later, our stone was created, capturing the blood and evidently a portion of God's power. He then died. Just fell down dead.

"Over the centuries people found the stone difficult to control. Apparently, it's been known to kill the one who tries to use it. Anyway, it landed in the hands of some knights, and those lovely gentlemen didn't want anyone else to mess with it, so it was taken on a long journey, far into the wilds of no man's land where they built a creepy little church."

As legends go, it was on par with the Holy Grail and just as farfetched. "I don't get it. If it kills those who try to use it, how was Juliana able to use it?"

He leaned back in the chair. "She's already dead?" he offered.

"Okay, I'll buy that, but then there's me. It didn't kill me."

"Technically, you were already dead."

"But why bring me back to life?"

"I don't know." Sundquist clicked on the print button and the printer hummed to life.

His "I don't knows" weren't what I wanted to hear. Frustrated, I began to pace, and rubbed my thumb within the hollow of my palm. A sorcerer had harnessed the power of God? It was too outrageous to be true.

The thunderstorm had abated into a dull gray shower, reflecting my morose mood. I didn't like unanswerable questions. Alden's library held a world of knowledge on its shelves. Surely something here held my answers. The pictures I had unearthed were intriguing, but I needed to know the text. I should have taken that Latin class in college. But *noooo.* Cal told me it would be a waste of time. I needed Alden. I glanced at the clock again. Three thirty-five. Where was he?

Collecting the papers, Sundquist stapled them together and handed the pile to me as I passed by. "It's a weird little stone," he said. "I've got to go with Poison on this one. It's like Kryptonite to us humans. Obviously God isn't too pleased people are trying to use it for their own purposes. I say we take it back to that creepy little church and be done with the whole weird thing."

"You believe the legend?" I said as I rolled the papers into a tight cylinder shape.

"It's fantastical, I'll give you that." He nodded to the rolled up papers in my hand. "You've got to admit, the legend has all the elements to explain what happened to you."

"If you're right, we can't take it back. I'll never get any answers, and I need answers."

"Look. You were dead," he said as his gaze followed me around the room. "Somehow, for some reason, you were brought back. Be thankful. And if that hunk of rock is what they say it is, then trust me, something that pure wouldn't pervert you."

I slanted a fearful gaze at him. "Juliana used the stone to control Evangeline. That's not good *or* pure."

He shook a thick finger at me and turned back to the computer. "Funny you should mention her. I kept coming across her name on a ton of websites. She's got some bizarre fan club going. So, I did a little research." He pecked at a few keys and another webpage popped up. "Juliana was an evil woman when she was alive. She delved into all sorts of magic and devil junk. That makes her not your ordinary vampire. She's had centuries to gather knowledge, practice, and play with her bat wing and lizard tongue collection."

I wasn't surprised by any of that.

"She used her bad juju on a holy relic, which takes some serious nerve."

"She didn't have anything to lose. Like you said, she's already dead."

"And loving it." He pushed away from the desk and stood, blocking my way. His big face grew heavy, and his eyes pleaded for me to stand still. "I know you want answers, so here's what I think. That rock chose to help you, and it gave you something really special in return."

I threw him an apprehensive glance and shouldered past him. "Rocks are inanimate objects. They can't choose. Geesh! You're starting to sound like di Taro."

Sundquist shrugged. "di Taro's not all crazy."

"Oh yes he is."

"We talked, and..."

I didn't like the way he hesitated. "And?"

"Maybe...you're supposed to be looking beyond yourself."

Oh, that was unfair. I twirled around and got right in his face. "I've *always* looked beyond myself. For as long as I can remember, I've dedicated myself to helping others."

"So what's your problem?"

"What's my problem? Are you serious?" He acted as if I should shrug my shoulders and carry on like nothing happened. How could he say that? He'd freak too if he had some unnatural, life-altering event redefine who he was.

The keys in his pocket jingled as his phone vibrated. He held up his finger for me to wait and fished out his phone. Peeking at the sender, he cussed and glanced back at me. "I guess that's all the time we have for today, doctor. We can take up this conversation tomorrow if you like."

Turning on his heel, he answered his phone. "Sundquist. What's the crisis?"

I stood gaping at him as he walked away without a backward glance.

Maya

CHAPTER THIRTY TWO

I squashed the rolled papers in my fist and threw them in the trashcan as I heard Sundquist leave the apartment. He didn't know my history, the pain that tore at my heart every time one of my patients told me another story of lost hope. Sometimes I wanted to give up, but I couldn't. Helping others came as naturally as breathing to me, and just as necessary. I had to help. But this? I slanted a hateful look at the papers in the trashcan. This was beyond my scope of understanding.

I turned toward the windows and saw my reflection in the glass. A feeble image, blurred and scarred by the slashes of rainwater, stared back. To me it was a true image. I wasn't the perfect hero. That destiny took more courage than I possessed.

Where was Alden? I needed him. His comfort. His strength. I found my purse on the credenza near the front door and pulled out my cell phone. The battery flashed low. Probably good for one more call. I went back into the office and found the number for Alden's main office. Two rings and a friendly voice answered.

"Caldwell Industries. How may I help you?"

"May I speak with Alden Caldwell?"

"I'm sorry, he isn't in at the moment."

I wasn't sure if that was code for he wasn't taking calls or if he really wasn't there. "Do you know when he'll be back?"

"I'm sorry. I don't. But I can connect you to his secretary's voice mail. I'm sure she'll be happy to call you back and make an appointment for you."

"I don't want an appointment. I just need to talk to him."

"I'm afraid he's not taking calls."

"My name is Dr. Maya Kelbeck. If you just tell him I'm on the line, he'll want to talk to me."

"This is his answering service. As far as I know, his office is closed. It has been for the past few days. If you'd like, I can connect you to his secretary's voice mail."

"Then he's not there?"

"I don't know. All calls have been diverted to our service. All emergencies are being handled through his secretary's line. Would you like me to connect you so you can leave a message?"

The woman was absolutely no help. Though human, she had all the resources of a prerecorded message. "No. Thank you."

"Have a nice day," she chirped cheerfully.

"You too," I muttered and hung up.

I should've called his cell phone. And then I remembered. I didn't have his cell number. I tossed my phone in my purse. I hated not knowing where he was. My gut told me something was off.

I picked up my phone again and punched in Sundquist's number.

The deep voice of the detective sounded in my ear. "Sundquist."

"What were Alden's exact words?"

"Maya? What are you talking about? When?"

"Did he say he was going to the office?"

"He said he had some business to take care. Where else would he go?"

"Oh, no."

"What?"

"Oh, no!" I hung up, my brain racing.

He couldn't have gone after Juliana. He promised me he wouldn't. I had to be jumping to conclusions.

My phone rang.

I pressed it to my ear. "Hello?"

"Okay," Sundquist's voice roared over the line. "Never do that again. You can't say 'Oh, no,' and then hang up. I'm a cop. Do you know what that does to my heart?"

"Sorry. It's just…" I didn't want to say it. I believed if I did, it would show my distrust of Alden. But if I kept quiet, I would burst with worry. Better to let it out and hear Sundquist tell me I was reading something into Alden's behavior that wasn't there. I took a deep breath and gave life to my worry. "I think Alden is in trouble. Big trouble."

Silence met my words. Long silence.

He thought I was an idiot. I'd felt silly saying it, but that didn't mean he had to act all dramatic. "Go ahead. Tell me I'm paranoid."

Nothing.

"Sundquist?"

Still nothing.

I pulled the phone from my ear and looked at the screen. Totally blank. The battery had died.

That was just dandy. I threw the phone into my purse, and when I did, the lights in the apartment flickered, yet they stayed on. The last thing I needed was for the electricity to go. Silvery rivulets raced down the window panes diluting the view of the city. The storm which had begun that morning hadn't dispersed. Wind still churned the clouds. Rain still slapped angrily at the tempered glass. The darkening harbor was just a blur in the distance. Because of the storm, the shadows of night spread quicker, grew deeper.

Visions of Alden lying dead in an alleyway seemed all too

real. I shuddered and clasped my arms around my torso. If I wasn't careful, my imagination would quickly get the best of me. I had to trust that he wouldn't do anything stupid.

The lights suddenly flickered off. The hum of the refrigerator sputtered silent. The heater's pings and soft moans grew quiet. The whole apartment building seemed to shudder as it fell into a dead zone. Only my annoyed breathing greeted my ears as darkness closed in on me.

I expected such temperamental outbursts from my part of town, but not in the heart of the city. I stood cut off from the world at the height of Boston. Alone. I shouldn't be alone. Alden should be here.

I looked out the window to the other buildings. Their lights gave off a soft glow against the stormy night sky. My gaze swept right then left, encompassing the immediate area. The outage didn't seem to affect any building but this one.

"For a high-priced place, you'd think they could afford regular maintenance," I muttered.

My eyes adjusted quickly to the lack of light. The apartment should have been pitch black, but somehow I could make out shapes. Distinguish one shadow from another. I made my way down the hall and into the bedroom. My quest for light brought me into the bathroom and to the stash of fragrant candles surrounding the tub. I picked up a sturdy candle stick, touched the lighter to the wick and was immediately greeted with a cheery little flame.

I carried the candle into the bedroom, and by chance, I glanced at the wall where Alden hung his swords. I stopped cold. Several were gone.

They'd all been there this morning. My breath stilled, halted by a deep fear. He'd done exactly what I'd asked him not to do. He'd gone to look for Juliana.

My lungs burned, and I released the trapped air in a violent burst. My heart throbbed, its beat painful in my neck. I had to find him and stop whatever he planned, but I didn't know where to start looking. I stood, a newborn lamb, in this preternatural world where the night held more than darkness, where nightmares, more real than the flame, burned a hole into the dark. I knew what I had to do. I had to go to di Taro. He knew Alden's world almost as well as Alden. He was my only hope in finding him. I had no doubt there would be a price to pay for the favor, and one I would willingly pay—whatever he asked.

I turned toward the bedroom door and came up short. Evangeline stood in the doorway. The single candle flame revealed a woman more beautiful than any Hollywood starlet. The overly made up woman I had seen in the restaurant had given way to a vision of purity, sweetly innocent with her long golden hair spilling down her back in lush waves.

A cold smile crept across her lips. "Hello, Maya."

I watched her warily. The candlestick in my hand shook, causing a few drops of wax to land on my skin. I barely noticed. My whole body shivered like a mouse caught by the tail. She did notice, and her smile grew Cheshire-cat wide.

She took a step forward. "We've met, but we've never been properly introduced, have we?"

I couldn't speak. I only watched her slow progress into the room, one carefully placed footstep at a time, a macabre dance that sent threatening tingles down my back.

"Let me rectify that oversight. I'm the woman Alden loves. Not you."

Her smile turned hard, chilling me to the bone. I was in deep trouble. Though she glowed like a blonde goddess of mythical legend, a stain had blackened her heart, pushing her over the edge of reason.

What Alden had told me about Evangeline wasn't much except that she was Juliana's pampered pet. Pampered or not, she wanted to kill me. Malice poured from her like a river fed by bitter disillusionment, and I had stepped into her path, disrupted her plans. As she saw it, I had stolen her man.

Why was this happening to me? Hadn't I been through enough? Something inside me snapped. Her confident stance suddenly irritated me. My hands ceased their trembling. My senses sharpened, and my gaze slammed into hers. "You know what? You had 800 years to make him fall in love with you." I stepped forward, no longer the victim. "I managed to do it in less than a week."

A growl of hate erupted from her chest. She lunged toward the wall and grabbed a sword. I blew out the candle, plunging the room into darkness. She lashed out with the sword, and I brought the candlestick down, blocking the thrust. I spun to the side and hit her over the head with the heavy base.

She fell and rolled, springing to her feet. Blood oozed from the back of her head, but in no time the wound healed. "Good try, but who do you really think is going to win here?"

My candlestick suddenly seemed more like a weapon fit for a Looney Tunes character. I searched the room as we circled each other. When I drew near the bed, I took hold of the sturdy post and swung myself onto the mattress and scrambled over to a glass encasement which held a small shield and an old sword. I broke the glass and grabbed them, twirling away as she brought down her weapon and shattering the rest of the enclosure.

The battle was on. I did the best I could, ducking behind the shield and chasing her thrusts with ones of my own. I saw surprise enter her eyes when I refused to yield, giving back as good as she delivered. Neither of us were adept sword fighters, and my confidence grew with every minute I played her game.

And then I made a fatal mistake. To avoid the tip of her sword sweeping near my legs, I jumped atop the bed. With amazing speed, she cut the canopy frame down on top of me. As the steepled structure tilted and clattered down the bed posts, I ducked and slid to the side, my body catching in the opulent hangings. As I fought blindly to free myself, her blade ripped through the fabric and stabbed into the mattress a mere inch from my head. My weapon and shield snagged on the fabric and I abandoned them.

Throwing off the heavy fabric, I quickly came under attack. Evangeline's sword flashed in every direction, stabbing, thrusting, blurring before my eyes as I dashed behind the bedposts and other furniture in an attempt to protect myself. A cut here, a wound there; my injuries were adding up. I was running out of time. In a last ditch effort, I jumped behind the pedestal holding a vase and pushed it on top of her. As it fell, I ran for the door.

Evangeline grabbed hold of my hair and pulled, wrapping the strands within her fist. I swung about and punched her in the face. Her head snapped back, and she let go. But not for long. With a growl, she brought the heavy hilt of her sword against the side of my head. Light exploded behind my eyes, and I staggered back. When I straightened, she was bringing the sword down toward my head in a sweeping arc. I grabbed her arm, slipped to the left and shoved my knee into her stomach as hard as I could.

Evangeline bent over gasping and dropped the sword.

I kicked the weapon aside and pushed her face first into the wall, holding her arm behind her back.

She glared over her shoulder at me. With a snarl, she reared back. Her shoulder snapped awkwardly and I let go, stumbling back to catch my balance.

Free, she pulled out a gun, pointed it at me and pulled the trigger. Again and again and again.

Alden

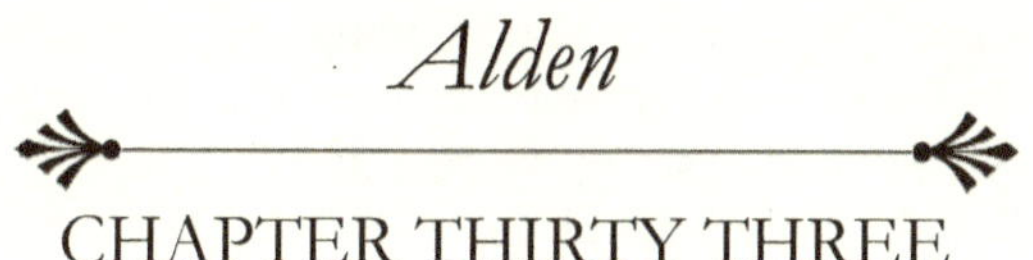

CHAPTER THIRTY THREE

The bathroom door closed, and I placed my hand on the slick wood, breathing in the scent of Maya just beyond the portal. "Forgive me."

I had redirected her thoughts, causing a need she couldn't deny to spring forth. I wasn't proud of what I'd done, but I didn't regret it. And knowing she would hate me for tricking her, I still walked away. It was the hardest thing I'd ever done. As I collected my favorite sword and a dagger, I thought of the promise she had wanted me to make. I could only hope she would understand. I didn't want to leave, but I had no choice. As long as Juliana was out there, Maya would never be safe.

Oddly, my soul swelled with peace at the thought of confronting Juliana. I would do anything, suffer anything, to see Maya safe.

Love can make a sensible man into a fool, but I was no fool. I knew love could also show a lost man the way to freedom. What I had to do would free not only Maya, but myself. No longer would I flail in doubt. After today, my decisions would be my own, with no visions of evil to taint them.

I rarely gave my trust, but I recognized a good soul when I'd met Detective Sundquist. I called in a favor. I needed him to stay with Maya until I returned. I had work to do. He didn't ask much and assumed everything. As we passed, he entering the apartment and me leaving, our gazes met. He nodded. "Good luck."

He knew.

"I'll be back as soon as I can."

"I'll give you as much time as I can."

He would stay with her, watch over her until he was called away. "It'll be enough. I'll make it enough."

With that, I left. The predator within me sprang forward. I ran, my strides strong, my mind determined and alert. I kept to the deepest shadows, passing as quickly as a ghost.

I smelled The Black Dahlia's smoldering ruins before I saw them. Firefighters had responded to the burning building, but too late. The place was unrecognizable. As I skirted the area, I heard the police talk about disturbing finds. Handcuffs. Chains. An underground labyrinth. Human remains.

"Something evil went down in this warehouse," one officer said.

The man he talked to only shrugged. "I've been down here plenty. This area is crawling with homeless."

"What about all that stuff they're digging out?"

"How green can you be? The homeless are scavengers. They'll pick your trash clean one day and outright steal from your house the next if you turn your back to them long enough."

"What about the skeletons?"

"Simple, if one of them dies, they just roll him into a corner and cover the body up. Ain't that right, Jones?" he said to a guy from the morgue who sauntered past. "You're always pulling dead bodies from buildings, huh?"

The guy paused by his friend, a number of empty body bags clutched in his hands. "Especially lately. Seems Boston has become the place where the homeless come to die."

"That'll bring the tourists in." The three continued talking, unaware I was near. I quickly moved on, shaking my head. Their callous attitude implied they'd seen it all. They had no idea the horror that threatened this city.

I picked up Juliana's scent on the far side of the building and followed it. The rain muted the odor, but hadn't washed it completely clean. I smelled her disbelief, her fear. And then her scent subtly changed, grew stronger, more confident. She'd picked a victim. She'd fed. I found him in an alleyway slumped beside a dumpster, his pale face shiny with rain, his sightless eyes lifted to the sky. In a few days, he'd turn. Hunger would nag him, evil would drive him. He would feed and the infection of evil which had been terrorizing Boston would escalate.

Without a second thought, I drew my sword and plunged it into his heart, interrupting the change. Now he would be just one more mysterious death found in the wrong part of town between two old brick buildings. I stared at the macabre sight I had created; disgust coated my tongue. I closed my eyes, blocking out the image.

I'd done him a favor.

A whistle of wind sounded behind me and I turned, my sword at the ready. Juliana landed graceful as a cat on the hard, slick pavement. Her hair settled about her shoulders, her eyes glittering with rage, her face glowing with pale innocence. I would never be swayed by such deceit again.

Her mouth tipped in a tender smile, and she cast an appreciative look at her victim. "I thought he might lure you here. At least I hoped. I'm glad to see I was right."

I didn't say a word, I waited. She thought to lure me here, but I no longer lived by her rules.

She cocked her head. "What? No comeback? No righteous indignation?" She posed elegantly in the gray shadows and gently pursed her lips, deciding how best to goad me. It wouldn't be difficult. She knew me well. "He had a family," she finally said. "A wife. Two small children."

I only blinked, never taking my eyes off her as she slowly

moved closer. Her gaze raked the man's body, and then slanted back to me. She let out a sad sigh. "And you killed him. Do you never think about that—that I don't actually kill them? *I* give them long life. It's always been *you* who've ended their time here on earth."

It was true, in a way. After she fed, I either disabled them, buried them, or burned them. Burying them might seem kinder, but I preferred to end their suffering before their living hell began. "I deliver mercy."

"That's right," she jumped on my explanation. "That's how you've always been able to justify your predilection for murdering the innocent."

"I'm not a murderer, and after you're through with them, they most certainly aren't innocent. If not for you, he would've lived happily."

"Why do you even care?" she asked. "I enlighten them. They see I can give them what God never would. Eternal life."

"By draining their souls and letting evil in."

"They hardly miss it. I certainly don't."

I could smell the lust on her skin, the indecent surge of want. Never satisfied. Her kind were *never* satisfied. "If you call being a parasite living."

"If it's been so bad, what has kept you here so long?"

I winced inwardly. She circled me, like a jackal looking for a weakness before launching her attack. And whether she knew it or not, she had found one. She pressed further. "No comment? How very typical of you, my stoic, proud pet."

I was *not* her pet. Not anymore. I shook my head. "I never wanted this life."

"But you chose the path. You were given an out. You could have chosen death."

My heart thudded in my chest. I could feel the blood rushing in my veins, adrenalin sweeping into my limbs. "I didn't understand." I'd been too young. Too naïve. Sweat tickled my nape as cold dread swept my body. "I didn't," I repeated, trying to convince myself.

"You did," she snapped. "You found what I offered more

to your liking."

A shiver spiraled down my spine. I couldn't deny it anymore. She was right. I saw what I would become and had walked into my bondage with open eyes. I'd been a coward, choosing a life of constant servitude over a death which offered freedom.

And I'd regretted that choice ever since. It nearly destroyed me. Stripped me of honor. I felt sick just thinking of it. But I was no longer under her thumb. I'd broken free, and I intended to stay that way. I cast a cold eye on her. "You're right. I was weak. But not anymore."

My muscles sprang to life. I swung my sword in her direction. She flipped back, head over heels, landing in a crouch a few feet away with a hiss on her lips. "You never were the perfect pet."

I smiled. "My thanks. That is the first true compliment you've ever given me."

Juliana pounced, and I jumped back, but not soon enough. Her foot landed on my chest like a wrecking ball, and I flew backward into the brick building, my sword flying out of my hand. It clanged to the ground near the entrance to the alleyway.

I leapt sideways, just missing Juliana's fist. Her knuckles smashed into the bricks causing a cascade of red dust. A snarl of hate pierced the air, her silver gaze whipped to mine. I ran full out toward my sword. As I splashed through murky puddles, the rippling cadence of her spell followed me. A grinding sound warned me of an even greater danger. Mortar against brick scratched the humid air just before the first brick loosened and flew from the building on my right. Another brick came loose on the left, and then another and another until the bricks launched from the buildings on either side of me in rapid succession, their aggressive intent clear. I heard the violence of their flight and smelled the chalkiness of their failure as they slammed into each other, disintegrating on contact. I was able to keep a step ahead of them, but not for long. The pavement suddenly shifted, then started to buckle and lift from the earth. Soon, I was running uphill. Behind me, the bricks flew closer, as Juliana stood with her hands outstretched, a spell on her lips.

Halfway up the hill, I spun about and slid back, my legs outstretched before me as I quickly slipped under the flying rubble. My feet skated over the powder that had mixed with the rain, coating the alley in a muddy film that turned my pants a thick reddish brown. She gasped just as I slammed into her, knocking her down. The pavement shuddered and fell into a buckled path as the bricks dropped in mid-flight.

I rolled on top of her, my grip bruising, but she broke free and pushed me back. I flew into the air, and in mid-flight, a steel fire escape uncurled from its staid shape, its iron biting into the flesh of my ankle to hold me aloft.

I'd thought her powers weak, but it was as Maya had said. Juliana had tricked me into believing what I wanted to believe. She had lured me too easily into her trap, had warped my sense of power, had played on my desire for freedom. I now dangled helplessly, the bite of iron an all too familiar punishment.

"You," she said on a heated note as she glared up at me, "are a disappointment."

She stretched out her hand and my sword skittered across the wet pavement and into her hand. She glared up at me. "Alas, you know I don't tolerate disappointment well."

The iron groaned as Juliana called it down. It was an unpleasant journey. The iron twisted harder against my ankle, and I clenched my teeth to interrupt the moan of pain that pushed against my lips. My descent stopped a foot or so above her.

She cocked her head and smiled, though it was far from pleasant. "It is clear to me now. You have lived past your prime. Simple as that. Though I had hoped to reclaim you, it's a useless quest. Replacing you shall be difficult. For the time being, I must rely solely on Evangeline. Yet, because of you, I find it hard to trust her. You've tainted my most beloved pet. And for that, you shall suffer.

"There is, however, one mission I trust her to perform

without complaint." She took a step forward. "Shall I tell you what that is?"

My heart skipped a beat. I already knew.

"Evangeline's penchant for irrational jealousy has always been a glaring fault in her otherwise docile nature, a fault I'm more than happy to see her exercise. Poor Maya. Do you think anyone will recognize her once Evangeline is done?" Again, she stepped closer, like a moth to a flame. In her desire to see my pain more closely, she was moving into a dangerous position. I held my breath, praying for just one chance.

When I didn't say anything, her face curled with anger. "Maybe it's not Maya you really care for. Maybe you care for someone else?"

I had no idea what she was talking about. Excruciating pain clawed up my leg from my ankle. Blood continued to rush to my head. Concentration became a chore I strove to hang onto.

Juliana noticed my struggle and her guard eased as she took another step closer. "Try to stay alert, for I believe you'll find this interesting. I have sent Vilmos to find a young woman. A very special young woman, one with golden hair, much like Evangeline's, and a sweet disposition. Unselfish. Caring even. Evangeline's opposite, in fact, which I find humorous, since she is Evangeline's daughter."

"You bred Evangeline to another?" I didn't believe it.

"You do not seem to understand what I'm saying. Let me help. When Evangeline gave birth to your son, she also gave birth to your daughter, a small, frail thing. I had no use for a female at the time, and one so obviously flawed, so I sent the little whelp away. Evangeline had no idea, and I didn't see the need to tell her the other child lived. After all, she's hardly the motherly type, more suited to getting affection than giving, do you not agree? I felt it best to save her the inconvenience of seeing the child die."

The pain in my leg was suddenly surpassed by the pain in my heart. I had a daughter? It couldn't be. Juliana was just being cruel. "You're lying," I spat in her face.

"Why would I? You'll not live past this hour. Why not

speak of what I've always viewed as a distasteful episode, especially since it has now transformed into such a pleasure. You see? You are not the only one who had a secret all those years ago."

I ground my teeth against the delight twinkling in her gaze. She could not be telling me the truth. I had proof. "You lie. You had no reason not to kill the child when she was born, if she ever was born."

"Is my nature so transparent? She lives due to an oversight, or perchance fate. I simply forgot about her." A throaty laugh escaped. "And who would've thought the weakling would be the stronger sibling? Not I."

Juliana moved closer, almost close enough for me to reach down and touch. I warred with the need to kill her, yet something held me back, forcing me to listen to this mad tale she wove. My body quivered as I fought to hang helplessly upside-down, the picture of a victim submissive to her will.

Juliana blinked up at me, and her voice lowered to soft, lush tones, those she used to seduce her victims. "She lives, confused and frightened, unwilling to admit the truth of what she is. That will soon end. Vilmos will find her. He will show her what she is, toy with her for a while, and then put her out of her misery. Her fate has become far more entertaining than the quick kill I had wanted after her birth, don't you agree?"

Oh God. The pleasure wreathing her face made it all to clear. I had a daughter, and she was alive. I fought to retain consciousness, afraid in that moment Juliana would succeed. "No!"

Juliana breathed in my pain as if it were a heady wine, and sighed.

I allowed all the pain and misery of a lifetime to fill the space between us. My eyes welled with hot tears while my mind shied away from the horror she planned. I couldn't allow it.

One step closer. Just let her take one step closer.

"You see, it has become my deepest desire to wipe out your existence on this earth. Everyone you have loved, cared for or thought about will die. Your print on this world will be erased. There will be no successful business left behind, no grateful employees, no family heritage to be lauded. I have made sure that Vilmos will interrupt your legacy in the most brutal of ways."

She stepped closer and lifted a cold hand to caress the flushed skin of my left cheek. "I know from where your tears spring. You suffer because once again you will not see your child in this life. Yet I must rejoice," she whispered, lifting the sword threateningly, "for I am convinced her last breath will see her in heaven, while yours will undoubtedly see you straight to hell. You will be separated even in death. That is perfect revenge. Don't you think?"

When she'd touched my cheek, my prayer had been answered. I couldn't let Juliana's evil extinguish the innocent lives of so many people. My lips curled back in a heated growl. "Then we will see the journey done together."

With a quickness that surprised even me, I grabbed her by the neck and snatched her into the air. She couldn't speak the evil incantations. She could only flail about in a desperate fight to be free. She brought the blade against my arm, my torso. I grunted as the blade hit me at odd angles, and bit into my flesh. I ignored the pain. I wasn't about to let her go. With the last of my strength, I allowed my tainted blood to quicken until my teeth grew long and sharp. Her face had grown nearly purple as I dug my fingers into her throat, cutting off her air. She could live without air, but not without a head.

She dropped the sword. Her hands latched onto mine. Her fingers sought to peel my grip loose. I let out a howl of rage, took her slender neck in my mouth and bit down. With a violent jerk, her head separated from her body and in the next moment, a cloud of dust swirled in the air. Ancient, bitter dust.

I hung limply with relief. Juliana was finally dead. "May you never rest in peace," I spat.

My chest still heaved with adrenaline. Released from her spell, I bent toward my captured foot, twisted the iron away and immediately fell to the ground. I lay there, bruised and humbled. My mind screamed at me to move, but my body would not obey. The beast had calmed within me; it longed to heal my wounds, but I couldn't lie there with the rain slapping my face and soaking into my clothes. Maya was in danger.

I stood, took up my sword and limped from the alleyway. It took me longer than I wished to find a street busy enough to warrant the sight of even one yellow taxi. Two buzzed by me, empty, without even slowing down. Anger rose, and when next I spotted one, I stepped in front of the oncoming cab. I braced myself, putting out my hands. It screeched to a stop, kicking up a spray of water. The driver cursed and shook his fist at me. I yanked the back door open only to find the cab already occupied. I wouldn't be dissuaded. Pointing my sword at the passenger, I forced him out. Finally ensconced alone in the backseat, I growled out my address. "And hurry."

The driver, eyes wide and hands shaking, punch the gas pedal, leaving his former customer sputtering in the rain. We made it to my building in less than forty minutes, time I used to heal my wounds. Looking up, I saw a blank wall of glass. Not one light shone from a window. All around the lights twinkled against the darkening sky, but my building stood eerily dark.

Evangeline was here.

My hands gripped the sword as I stalked up the steps to the front door. The doorman paused and suddenly stepped back as I approached. "See to the cabbie," I snarled.

He nodded, not bothering to open the door for me, and went to pay off the driver. I made a quick turn toward the stairs and vaulted up them. One floor at a time passed by me until I reached my floor. I forced the door open and plunged into the even darker hallway. My vision adjusted. The door to my apartment clearly hung ajar. A series of deep scratches marred the scarlet paint around the lock.

With the tip of my foot, I nudged it open and slipped inside. No one lingered in the front room. As I made my way inside, I distinctly heard the crashing of furniture. I raced toward the back of the apartment and skidded to a stop in front of my bedroom door.

Evangeline stood rock still, a look of horror on her face as she stared at Maya. Suddenly, she pointed a gun at Maya. I leapt forward, pushing her down and placing myself into the path of danger. One bullet after another ripped into my flesh. Grunting on impact, I stumbled back until I hit the wall.

I looked into the eyes of Evangeline. Her face had gone deathly pale. I felt blood bubble up from my lungs and trickle out of the corner of my mouth. Slowly, I slid down the wall, my feet jutting out in front of me as I crumbled to the floor.

Evangeline fell to her knees, dropping the gun as a scream of disbelief echoed within the room.

Maya

CHAPTER THIRTY FOUR

I lay sprawled on Alden's bedroom floor, my head burning from the impact, my gaze blurred. Deep silence entombed me. My vision slowly cleared and after a moment, I regained my hearing only to cringe at the loud, popping echos that wouldn't stop.

Gunshots.

Evangeline had tried to shoot me.

The gun's reverberating echo slowly gave way to Evangeline's screams. They slashed through my already sore head and were accompanied by a rhythmic shivering beneath my body. I refocused my eyes on Evangeline.

She sagged on the floor, the gun lying forgotten between us as she pounded her fists against the highly polished wood. Words filled with pain and disbelief slowly emerged from the incomprehensible outpouring of emotion. "Why? We have come so far. She doesn't deserve you."

I rolled my head to where her gaze pointed, enduring a bout of vertigo in the process. When my vision settled, a muffled cry escaped my lips. Alden sat bullet-riddled against the wall. Crimson seeped from his wounds to color the floor. He looked pale. Too pale. A grimace imprinted itself on his face as he concentrated on each and every breath. He looked close to death.

Evangeline stopped pounding the floor. Still sobbing, she scooted toward Alden, dragging herself through his blood. She gripped his shirt front and whimpered, "Why?"

His throat corded for a moment, and then he managed to say, "I love her."

The curled fingers loosened, and her head dropped forward. Muffled sobs wracked her body as she bent over Alden. "You love me. I know you do."

I slowly reached for the gun lying between us and pointed it at her, blinking back the pain and dizziness my movements caused.

Evangeline glanced back at me. Her doe-eyed look caused me to falter. She smiled sadly. "Go ahead. Shoot."

I hesitated. "I don't want to kill you." I felt pity for her. It was hard not to. She was a woman in love, a woman who desperately longed for Alden to return her affections.

Her smile turned scornful. "There's one bullet left. You would have to hit my heart to kill me. You'll miss."

At this close range? I didn't think so.

She turned toward me and the fullness of her beauty struck me again, yet something was wrong. I narrowed my eyes, and what I saw caused my heart to lurch. She was changing. Slowly, as if to prolong my torture, her wolf form emerged.

"Shoot me," she said on a deepening voice. Her eyes pierced mine. I froze.

Alden made a pathetic effort to grab her arm. She easily sloughed off his grip. Alden turned to me. His throat convulsing. "Aim to the right," he rasped.

Evangeline whipped her head toward him, her surprise apparent. I readjusted my aim and fired. The bullet ripped through her chest and she fell back, gasping.

Her form eased back fully human. Her chest rose and fell

on quick breaths. I crawled to Alden, though my eyes were on Evangeline. I didn't trust what I was seeing. Surely she would gain her feet and come after me again. Finding Alden's hand, I squeezed it.

"You hit her heart. She won't live long."

"How? I aimed for the right."

"Mirror twin," he managed to say.

Evangeline was the one with organs on the opposite side to her twin? I couldn't believe it. All of this seemed unreal. I shuddered and laid my head on his shoulder, gently, softly so as not to cause him any pain. I just needed to touch him; to feel the rise and fall of his breath.

Shouts from the front of the apartment rolled down the hall. I recognized Sundquist's voice. "In here," I cried.

A flash of light bounced down the hallway until Sundquist appeared. He wasn't alone. di Taro stood beside him. Their flashlights flickering over the area, quickly assessing the situation. I motioned them to pick Alden up. "Gently," I said as I rose with him. "He's been shot. We have to take him to a hospital."

di Taro eyes slanted over at Sundquist, then back at me. "There will be a lot of questions."

I stared him down, my jaw tightening against his prejudice. "I don't care. I can't lose him. Not now."

They carried him down the hall, but when they got to the living area, Alden motioned them to put him down. Without delay, they laid him on the couch. His blood instantly soaked into the expensive upholstery, creating an ugly stain. He pushed the men away and looked up at me.

Worried, I bent over him and cupped his face. "What's wrong?"

"I can't go to the hospital."

Tears swam before my eyes. "You are going. No arguments."

He shook his head.

Did he want to die? I knew so little about his kind. "You're life means more to me than any questions we'll face."

"A doctor can't help me."

I brought his palm to my mouth and pressed my lips against his usually warm skin. He felt cool. Too cool. I peered into his eyes, those gorgeous dark eyes, frustration making me mad. "Why did you leave?"

"Because I love you. I had to protect you."

He said it with such clarity, with such passion, I clung to his hand. "I love you, too."

I splayed his fingers against my cheek and his eyes darkened. "Juliana's dead. The coven is broken. You're safe. I…won't ask your forgiveness," he murmured, the effort of speech becoming more difficult for him.

I placed my finger against his lips and blinked rapidly to control my tears. "Hush. I don't care. I just want you to be okay."

"Listen," he pulled me closer, surprising me and worrying me with his strength. His lips brushed against my ear as he whispered for me alone. "You're stronger than you think. Be strong now."

I tried to pull away, afraid he was trying to make a death speech. "Don't say anything."

He wouldn't listen. "You're strong, but you're still too raw. You must learn all you can. Let di Taro teach you."

"Don't," I hissed, unwilling to hear anymore. "Save your energy to heal yourself."

But he wouldn't let up. "I'll agree to see a doctor if you do something for me. Tell Evangeline…there were two. A boy. A girl. Juliana took them both. I couldn't find our son, but our daughter..."

He pulled back and coughed. Blood foamed at his mouth.

I dabbed it away with my sleeve. My tears created a fog through which I viewed him. "Please, don't say anything else."

"Listen," he snapped, though it cost him. I bit my lip and nodded. He drew closer. "Our baby girl is alive. Evie needs to know before she dies. I owe her that much."

He lay back, visibly exhausted. I didn't want to leave him, but he was so insistent. I pressed my hand to his cheek, his skin cool beneath my fingers.

"Tell her," he pleaded on a ragged breath. "Please. Before it's too late." His breathing had grown labored, his face agitated.

"Maya," Sundquist said near my ear. "Do what he asks. I'll get something to stop the bleeding, and then we'll take him to the car."

He helped me to my feet, yet my eyes were fastened on Alden.

His gaze held a desperate edge to it, and he mouthed, "Thank you."

I didn't want to leave, but I couldn't deny him. "I'll be right back."

"I'll go with you," di Taro offered, though I knew I didn't have a choice.

Evangeline lay where she had fallen, her breathing even more ragged than Alden's. As di Taro's light fell on her, I noticed her skin had grown waxy, almost silvery.

"The bullets were silver." He grabbed my arm before I stepped toward Evangeline. "No matter what he said, you don't owe her anything. She tried to kill you."

I understood his point, but he saw the world through a lens blurred by hate. I gently pulled out of his grip. "I owe Alden."

We had left her in this dark room to die. Alone. Guilt scratched at my conscience. No one deserved to be treated like that.

di Taro stayed back, his hate for Evangeline's kind palpable. He had come to protect me from the beast. He'd like nothing better than to end her life now and walk away without a backward glance.

Cruelty isn't in my nature. I knelt down, slipped my hand beneath Evangeline's shoulders and gently, laid her head on my lap.

Her eyes had grown wild. I saw fear in them. Horror. "It's all right," I reassured her. "I won't hurt you."

Her golden blonde hair shimmered eerily against her graying face. I combed it back until it fanned out in angelic beauty. How did one begin to tell a dying woman a secret that may cause her more pain?

I took a deep breath and plunged ahead. "Alden wants you to know that Juliana tricked you. Your daughter is alive."

Evangeline grasped my hand. Doubt swam in her eyes.

"Alden wouldn't lie," I assured her. "Not about this."

"No." Her faith in Alden was deep. That he betrayed her in the end must have pained her as much as the bullet. She'd known him for centuries, had been his lover, his consort, his friend. Whatever had pulled them apart hadn't been strong enough to keep them enemies. Her love had been misplaced, but it was still love. I squeezed her fingers. "I'm sorry. I'm sorry for all you've had to go through."

I didn't know what else to say. Tears slipped from her eyes and into her hair, darkening the roots framing her face a dark gold. "Please. Don't leave." Her voice echoed in the room on a childish whisper. "I'm afraid."

A pang wrenched my heart. I desperately wanted to get back to Alden, but how could I deny her request? I glanced over at di Taro. "Get Alden to the car. I'll meet you there."

He stared at Evangeline, his flashlight piercing the blackness for a moment. He easily saw she posed no threat, gave me a quick nod and left.

The darkness swallowed all sound except Evangeline's sporadic breathing. The floor felt cold and sticky with her blood. She closed her eyes. Her chest fell on a harsh exhalation. I wondered for a moment if she were dead. Then her eyes popped open, startling me. "He'll find her," she rasped. "He'll find her and you'll help."

I didn't want to be here. I didn't want her death on my hands. Alden was hurt, maybe dying. If one bullet could do this kind of damage to Evangeline, what could half a dozen do to Alden? I wanted to be with him. My ears tuned to the sound of someone coming down the hallway. Running.

"Please," she begged. "Help him find her."

I stared into her startlingly blue eyes. They glowed from within, reflecting a lifetime of pain and suffering. Empathy welled within me. "I'll do what I can."

And I meant it. No sooner was my promise given than her breathing rattled out of her chest for the last time.

Sundquist skittered to a stop before the open door. He put his hand to his heart, his eyes wild, his breathing wilder.

I didn't want to hear what I saw in his eyes. Alden was dead. The irony of the moment wasn't lost on me. I had comforted Alden's attacker while he died not fifty feet away. I began to cry. I couldn't stop myself. I rocked back and forth, still holding Evangeline in a tender embrace.

"He's gone," Sundquist finally managed to say.

I shook my head. "No. I can't take this. He can't be gone."

"He is. I went to find a towel for all that blood, and when I got back, he…he was gone."

I bent over Evangeline, my tears washing her face in the harsh beam of the flashlight. How could Sundquist sound so callous? He acted as if Alden was a nobody.

"I'm sorry," he said, his voice sounding put out. "di Taro went to look for him, but now I'm having second thoughts. There's no love loss between those two. What do you want me to do?"

My rocking ceased. I blinked, unsure I heard him correctly. "What?"

"di Taro went to look for Alden. That man of yours is one tough guy. I found these by the couch." He opened his hand and lying in his palm were seven silver bullets. "How the hell he got these out should be quite a story."

I touched one of the bullets with my finger, the cold metal bit my skin. He'd dug the bullets out of his body? "Are you saying he left? That's he's not dead?" I pictured his lifeless form lying in the apartment stairwell between floors. "Are you sure?"

Sundquist nodded. "Yeah. He's long gone. Oh." His eyes widen when sudden understanding dawned. "You thought I meant he passed away."

Alden was alive and had left. I shook my head, trying to make sense out of what had just happened. "I can't believe this. He left me? Again?"

"What about her?"

I glanced down at Evangeline. I placed my hands over her sightless eyes and slowly closed them. "She's dead."

"Are you sure?"

I wasn't completely sure about anything right now. Alden had been shot I didn't know how many times, but he was alive, and he'd left. Gone. He hadn't waited for me. Again. I felt sick. I felt stupid. Why would he leave without me?

I glanced up at Sundquist. "She's not breathing, and I can't find a pulse."

"That sounds like dead, but…"

I gently eased myself away, and stood, my heart nearly tearing in two. "Take me home."

I couldn't stay here. If I did, I'd go mad.

Alden

CHAPTER THIRTY FIVE

A sliver of moon hung low in the sky casting just enough light to reveal my surroundings—a scarred metal trash bin, a broken light and a collection of beer caps kicked close to the building. I put a shaking hand to one of the bullet wounds that was dangerously close to my heart. There was luck and then there was miraculous, stupid luck.

I had to get up, get moving. I couldn't linger on the damp pavement all night, thinking only of myself. But the power to get up and move wouldn't come to me. I slouched against the building and slowly slipped to the pavement. God, every muscle in my body ached. I had to catch my breath. I had to accelerate the healing.

Faster, I told my body. It shuddered from weariness. I closed my eyes for a moment, and that was all it took. The old memory and my greatest folly swept over me.

The year was 1905. We had gone back to France to sample the delights of the impressionist movement, the bohemian lifestyle of opium, absinthe and the bourgeois behavior of the upper crust. It was a bawdy time. The Moulin Rouge—or as we affectionately called it, *The Haven of Hell*—was our playground where women painted their lips in vulgar shades of red and gyrated erotically amid a flurry of feathers and ruffled skirts sans underwear. Naked arms, and thighs and plump breasts were the norm and men took their pleasure whenever and wherever they pleased.

Juliana and her ilk thrived in the depraved atmosphere, becoming a favorite of the establishment. She was called the "Evening Star," a bright light in the dark of night. She truly glittered and overwhelmed her audience as her followers indulged their basest desires. It was there that Vilmos stretched his muscles and challenged the limits of society.

I remembered her still. The clear eyes and pink bowed mouth of a child. So young and innocent, she nearly took my breath away. Her hair fell in soft luscious brown curls down her back, swinging at her waist when she walked. The frozen cream in the crystal bowl held her complete interest. Vilmos had dressed her in a tight corset and pantaloons, draping only a thin silk shawl over her shoulders for modesty.

This was a game to him. Children were harder to manipulate, harder to deceive. They somehow saw through our disguise and saw us for what we really were.

He sat down opposite Juliana, a full bottle of absinthe before him, and pulled the girl onto his lap. "Look at what I found," he crowed like a silly rooster. He cared not who stared as he let his hands roam. In the end, the iced cream had melted, untouched. She begged to leave, to see her mother, to go home…those tears so large, they dripped like raindrops from God's eyes. He took her in the most callous way. Ripping into her neck. Her life, her soul…gone. Humiliated and then tossed away.

And I had stood by and watched: a prisoner created by a

long-ago choice. Shame and disgust coated my tongue. I couldn't speak, could barely breathe. Juliana somehow knew. She always did.

My punishment for caring? It was I and not Stovall who was ordered to dispose of the body. To destroy something so beautiful, so perfect, nearly killed me. But if I did not, the innocent she had been in life would change, and the selfish creature that would inhabit her body would enact untold misery on others.

Down into the pit of the Moulin Rouge I carried her, until I came to the room where the heat of fire blazed bright, but no warmth touched my defeated spirit. I did what I had done too many times before. I threw her empty body into the furnace and watched the fire cleanse her soul.

"Be at peace, little flower," I whispered.

"And a lovely rose she was," Vilmos chortled from behind me.

I closed my eyes and took a deep breath, calming the hate that raged through me. "Is there something you need?"

Vilmos stumbled forward, a bottle swinging awkwardly from his fingertips. For although it takes more than a few sips from a glass to affect a vampire, drinking a whole bottle of absinthe makes the demon all that more dangerous. "Such a pity you lot cannot conceive. Oh wait, you did manage to roll onto Evangeline one evening, didn't you? Too bad she didn't have a girl. With her good looks and your stubborn pride, I would have loved getting to know that little one." He leaned forward and whispered nastily, "Breaking her."

I clenched my hands into fists, rooted to the spot. I knew my place and the rules that governed our society. If I but touched him without permission, I would be executed. Although I hated the life I was forced to live, I still clung to a bizarre spark of hope that refused to die. Someday I would be free. I would be my own man before I died.

He leaned even closer, the smell of rot gut sickeningly sweet on his breath. "Maybe I should whisper to Juliana to let you try again. Evangeline should be willing. She usually is."

I cast a superior look at him. "If you don't need anything, Juliana is waiting for me."

He swung his hand holding the bottle toward the door. "By all means, my obedient little pup. Scurry on back." He took a long pull from the bottle and glanced back at the petite body engulfed in flames. "She was such an appealing thing. Uncommonly sweet."

I left, disgusted by his perversion, yet trapped in the circle of his influence. When I returned to Juliana, the night's revelry had grown in scope and noise. Her entourage was combing the crowd, gleaning the finest of flesh for her to dine on. She tilted her chin at just the right angle to catch the dim light and smiled up at me. "Did Vilmos find you?"

"Yes."

"Is he still alive?"

"Unfortunately."

She laughed, for my distress at Vilmos's cruelty usually raised her spirits. "Be patient. He won't live forever."

The muscle in my jaw twitched with a sudden jolt of anger. "I can assure you of that."

She swirled the liquid in her glass and cast a seductive eye at me. "Do I detect a threat? How delicious. But if you kill him, then you will die. What a shame to lose two of my favorites in one day."

Though I still longed for her approval, I found I could not play her game. Not tonight. "I'm sure you can bear the loss."

Her smile widened and she cut me with her words. "I'm sure I can."

Out of the corner of my eye, I saw Vilmos stumble into the night. Another innocent would soon disappear, and another mother would grieve, never knowing where her child had gone.

I blinked out of the stupor I had fallen into and forced the unpleasant memories away. Vilmos wasn't after just anyone's daughter. He was hunting mine. And by some blessed grace, I had broken that perverted bond that kept me tied to their demonic will. I had to leave. I had to track him—stop him.

From the entrance to the darkened street, a man appeared. I forced myself to my feet as he approached. After exerting the energy to get away, I was too weak to defend myself. Hopefully it was a beggar coming to bum a few bucks.

No such luck. It was di Taro, his bald pate shining softly in the dim light. His breathing was ragged. He stopped before me, bent over and placed his hands to his knees in an effort to catch his breath. "You gave me a hell of a chase."

"I didn't know you cared enough to follow."

"I don't, but Maya does."

Hearing her name made me cringe. "I can't have her following me. She's not ready. You know it, I know it, but she won't believe me. Everything she's been through lately has given her false confidence, and false confidence leads to—"

"Death." He straightened, the look in his eyes telling. "Yeah, I've seen that before."

"Tell her there isn't any other way. If she doesn't know where I am, then she can't follow me."

"Fine."

"Were you serious about training her?"

"Yes."

"Good. Do it right. Don't let her die."

He threw me a disgruntled look. "I know how to train."

I looked away, my heart breaking. When I looked back, di Taro had gone. "I love her," I said into the night sky. "Tell her that."

Only the wind answered, its message too muted to understand. But I didn't need to hear it to know what it said. Maya would be furious. She would never forgive me.

Maya

CHAPTER THIRTY SIX

I opened the door to my apartment and found a fine layer of dust covering every piece of furniture, as if I had been gone a year instead of a week. Mrs. Berrett had started flamenco lessons again. Her apartment was situated right above mine. When she danced—and she loved to dance—she pounded the floor with unbridled enthusiasm, shaking loose a century of embedded dust onto everything I owned.

Sundquist, who'd given me a ride home, went straight for the kitchen as I deposited my things on the table and wandered about aimlessly, touching familiar things, and breathing in the slightly stale air. A deep sigh rattled my chest. I suddenly felt ten years older, a hundred years wiser, yet everything was oddly the same, like my adventure had been an intense fabrication of an overactive imagination. I clasped my hand over my arms and rubbed away the sudden gooseflesh. I hadn't made it up. Demon vampires and werewolves and ghosts and all manner of nightmarish evil actually existed.

Sundquist cursed at my refrigerator's lack of content. "I could use a beer about now. Beau and I usually kick one back after a vampire hunt."

I yanked the curtains open and stared into the night. Hearing someone else speak the dreaded V word slipped everything into perspective. Though the world was the same, what I knew of it had drastically changed.

"Have some cranberry juice," I said over my shoulder. The juice was old and had probably fermented by now. Sundquist, I had learned, was a stereotypical male. He'd consume anything that had once been or would soon be a viable food source. He had a cast iron stomach and wasn't afraid to test its limits.

Affirmed that I hadn't made this all up, I entered the bedroom and sat on my bed, heartsick and confused.

Alden had disappeared. He'd gone to find his daughter and left me behind. No reason. No goodbye. He'd just disappeared like he'd never been. I reexamined everything that had happened, probed every word, and every gesture he'd made. Everything he had told me from our first meeting to the last had been true. He loved me, and I had felt that love to the center of my being. Yet just like Evangeline, my love hadn't been enough to hold him.

You didn't make him happy, a sour, little voice inside me whispered.

It was a disturbing thought, one I pushed away. *Happy* wasn't exactly the buzz word I would have used for our relationship. Intense. Heated. Passionate. Those were descriptors I'd choose. We matched. Perfectly.

I kicked off my shoes, pulled my knees to my chest, and dug my heels into the edge of the mattress. I hugged my legs tightly and placed my chin in the niche created between my knees. I'd long ago given up hope of finding real happiness with someone. That was why I'd buried myself in my work. I'd become disillusioned. And when I stopped looking, Alden appeared. We connected so completely, it scared me. I feared the intensity of our feelings wouldn't last. And it now looked like it hadn't.

With a groan, I fell back onto the duvet and wrapped the fuzzy throw around me as I scooted up toward the mound of pillows. I needed a hug. But just like always, the warm embrace of the fabric was the best I could hope for. I stayed there, huddled atop my bed, my eyes staring at my closet, not seeing, yet seeing everything. Where had it all gone wrong? Why didn't he want me to go with him?

"There you are," di Taro rumbled from the doorway.

I angled onto my elbow, "You didn't find even a trace of where he went?"

"Not even a trail of blood after he hit the street. Sorry."

I sagged back onto the bed. "He's begun to heal himself. I guess that's good."

Tears threatened to break free, and I furiously wiped at them under di Taro's narrowing glare.

He crossed his arms over his chest and growled, "So, is this what I can expect? Get your butt kicked around by a lovesick she-wolf, the guy you saved goes AWOL, and you turn all girlie on me?"

"I am a girl." One who'd been crushed to the core. The image of Evangeline laying on the floor, her eyes sightlessly staring up at me, caused my stomach to clench. "I've never killed anyone before."

di Taro's arrogance softened, and he took a hesitant step forward. "She wasn't going to stop. She gave you no choice."

"I didn't have a choice," I repeated.

It didn't help. I still felt sick. I still felt abandoned.

It was inconceivable that Alden would disappear without a word. I raised my gaze to di Taro. "Did he really leave without saying anything?"

He turned away for a moment, almost as if he were embarrassed. "Yeah, just like that."

I pressed my lips together, cutting off the sob that threatened to escape, self-conscious under his pity.

Then he turned back, his face reflecting the sharp angles and heavy dips of a fighter. "I could stand here all night and commiserate with you on your rotten choice in men, but I don't have the time. Neither do you. We have work to do. The nest is destroyed. Most of the pets are dead, and there are vamps running scared all over the city that're ripe for killing."

I slanted him a disgusted look. "Wow. That sounds *so* appealing right now. Thanks for the invite, but I'll pass."

His brows lowered over his dark eyes. "You'll pass? Don't you get it? I can teach you how to fight. We need you, Maya."

"You have the kids." How could he forget the killing machines he'd created? His own gun packing, sword fighting groupies.

"The kids." A pained expression crossed his usually expressionless face. "You were right. They need you…probably more than they do me. They have scars I can't even begin to understand." His gaze sliced into mine, enigmatic, like a street magician who charms you out of a dollar just to watch him pull a penny out of thin air. "You have to come back."

His plea jolted my heart. I couldn't deal with this. Not right now. I couldn't help him. I closed my eyes against his troubled look. If I didn't see him, I didn't have to care. Caring only caused me pain, and I wanted the pain to end. Swallowing hard, I shook my head, feeling the fuzzy fabric against my cheek like an encouraging caress. "No."

"Think on it."

I opened my eyes and stared at his suddenly vulnerable looking face. I strengthened my resolve, my chest growing tighter, harder. "I don't need to think about it. I won't do it."

He looked around the room, desperation chiseling away at his already tough features. He opened his mouth as if to say something further, but instead, he cursed softly and left. The room suddenly felt twice as large, and terribly empty. Good. I needed space to pull my heart back together.

"Well?" I heard Sundquist ask di Taro, tension scraping against the word.

"Come on," di Taro's deep, impatient tones boomed from my livingroom.

A moment later, the apartment door slammed shut and I

flinched. I was alone. It's what I'd wanted, to be forever alone and not feel the pain of a broken heart. So why did I feel worse?

I turned my cheek into the pillows, the tears burning against my closed eyelids as I began the lengthy process of reliving the past week. Where was Alden? And why, oh, why didn't he want me with him?

I searched out my shattered spirit, hugging each piece to me, and slowly fit them back together. Yet the mend was a jagged one, and I feared the scars would never heal.

I will not cry. I will not cry…

I did anyway.

At some point near dawn, I rolled onto my back and stared at the ceiling. My eyes hurt from the constant wash of tears, my throat had grown sore from holding back the sobs that wanted to be free.

For hours I'd waited, praying that Alden would walk in the door. He'd come back with the realization that he needed me. Minutes passed. Hour after hour. There were no eager footsteps in the hall. No knock on the door. I lay alone, one thought becoming perfectly clear. Alden wasn't coming back.

He didn't trust me.

I gave up on sleep. Somewhere within the last few days, I'd become an insomniac. My thoughts wouldn't grow still long enough to allow my mind sufficient rest. A thick fog surrounded my brain as I walked into the living room. I needed coffee. Maybe if I stimulated my brain with caffeine, when I came off the high, my body would crash. It wasn't the healthiest plan, but it was all I had at the moment.

As I made my way to the kitchen, I heard a strange noise coming from the hallway outside my apartment. It sounded like someone had bumped into my door. I instantly thought of Alden and the night he'd been attacked by Juliana's men. The bump turned into a weak knock. Desperate to believe he'd come for me, I rushed to the door and opened it.

Instead of Alden, a strangely handsome man, with pale skin, startlingly blue eyes and lush blond hair stood just beyond the threshold. The pulse in my throat jumped at the flood of memories, and his eyes lowered to the vulnerable spot on my neck. Vilmos grinned. "Hello, Maya. Remember me?"

Hadn't Alden said the coven was broken? Vilmos had killed my colleagues, had ripped up Alden's car as he tried to reach me. How could I forget him?

"I remember," I said, my eyes watching him warily.

"We're old friends. Good friends. That's what you remember." His smile widened showing the glimmer of sharpened canines barely hidden by his full lips. "Invite me in."

I stared at him, and even though I knew what he was, I still felt the pull of obedience. How easily it would be to do as he asked. My heart pounded against my ribs. I placed my hand on the door jam, opened the door wider and leaned forward.

"You've gotta be kidding me?"

With a sweep of my hand, I slammed the door closed, and leaned heavily against it.

A howl of rage rattled the walls and a string of profanity shattered the night. I suddenly began to shake. I slid down the door until I sat on the floor, my knees pulled close to my chest and willed the creature to go away.

Then I heard something familiar. Bone chilling. A scratching noise. I almost didn't believe it. I glanced over my shoulder at the door. It was poor protection from the evil that lay just beyond. I imagined him crouched in the hall, his face level with mine, his eyes glowing eerily. Somehow, he knew exactly where I sat, could hear my heart beat through the door.

"Hear me, Maya," the words purred like a whiff of perfume beneath the door. "Hear my words."

For reasons beyond me, I slowly turned and pressed my ear against the panel, my hands feeling the heat of his anger through the wood.

"That's right," his dulcet tones slipped into my ear, "your interest is piqued, as it should be."

"You can't come in," I said on a strained voice. At any moment, I expected to see his hand burst through the door and grab me.

He laughed, though no humor sounded. "You can't keep me at bay forever, sweet Maya. You are now the hunted. Every night I will wait for you. I will sit at your window. I will camp outside your door. Never will you know another night of peace."

My lungs pulled in a sharp breath. "Why? I just want to be left alone."

"Poor child," he said, and it sounded as if he meant it. "Did no one tell you? You've entered a never-ending nightmare. Once seen, you can never go back."

Horrified, I rubbed my forehead against the door, and fisted my right hand in frustration. This couldn't be happening. I couldn't live like this.

His sympathy permeated the door to stroke my bruised spirit. I could feel his palm pressed against mine. "It doesn't have to be like this. I've taken an interest in you. Immortality can be yours."

How many people searched for such a gift, and here it was being offered to me. My blood raced through my veins.

"With me, there will be nothing you can't have. You mustn't fear the change. You won't suffer. That I promise."

I squeezed my eyes shut and pushed the seductive voice from my mind. "Why me?"

"Why not you?"

The idea of never feeling pain again tempted me, and that shook me to the core. I pulled my ear away from the door. "Go away. Just go away."

It grew quiet. The wood under my hands grew cold. I shivered. I pressed my ear against the door again, harder, searching for evidence that he had gone. The night seemed to swallow the world, forcing time to slow. Each tick of the clock reverberated in my head.

For that brief moment, I thought he'd gone, but then he said, "I'm patient, Maya. I always get what I want in the end.

The coven will be mine soon. Yet I owe Juliana one last task." His seductive tones had turned cold. "Tell Alden, it will do him no good to look for her. I'll find his child before he even learns her name, and I'll destroy her as he destroyed Juliana—without a backward glance."

"Why do you care?"

"I don't. But Alden cares."

I jerked back, breaking contact with the door. Everything around me clicked back into motion. And then it hit me. I really couldn't go back. Sundquist had warned me. So had di Taro. Now Vilmos had just confirmed it. He was why Alden had gone. His kind of evil needed no rest. He would find the girl and kill her. And all I'd wanted to do was hide my head under the pillows and pretend this was all a dream.

No more. Knowing what lurked in the dark, how could I let the weak and disillusioned fall prey to evil? This was what Alden had meant. I had to be strong. I had to learn to survive, to fight my own battles.

I glanced out my window at the lightening sky. The sun was rising and with it a sense of safety. I called a cab, and while I waited, I grabbed a duffle bag and stuffed a few necessities into it.

By eight o'clock in the morning, I stood outside di Taro's warehouse. The sun glinted off the rain-washed building, making the dingy concrete and brick building look almost clean. I went inside and stepped into the elevator, taking in a deep breath. The smell of tobacco and garlic melded into the familiar smell. Still repugnant, yet somehow comforting.

I pulled the decorative cage closed and pushed the button. The thing rattled to life, groaning and shuddering like an old man on a cold day. When it threatened to stall, a few well placed kicks sent it climbing until the third floor came into view.

The kids were on the mat, taking their turn at fighting each other. di Taro stood back, his arms crossed over his chest as he watched his charges with a critical eye. He sought perfection and he got it more times than not. As I pushed the gate open, everyone stopped and looked my way.

Di Taro didn't say a word. He only stared at me, his eyes a volatile mix of excitement and impatience.

Wiggy took that moment to send a flying kick at Cade, who dodged the foot and sent the boy to the mat with a well-placed heel of his hand before his gaze returned to mine. Poison helped Wiggy up, though he did so without taking his eyes off me.

Baby, that wonderful mix of child and adult, stepped forward and swung her blade over her head, around her body and then let it fly across the room to land dead center of a painted bull's eye. Her gaze whipped back to mine as she planted her hands on her slender hips. "Well? What do you want?"

I threw my bag on the table and met each one of their inquisitive, impatient gazes. They were an intimidating lot. A far cry from the normal placid patients I usually dealt with, yet I'd never felt more sure of myself.

"I'm in."

A twitch pulled at Baby's mouth until it broke into a huge smile, her cherubic face dazzling me with its warmth. "I never doubted you for a second. Welcome to the world of weird, Maya."

di Taro grunted and turned back to the kids. "What are you looking at? It's just Maya. Come on. Let's show her how it's done."

Snap. Swish. Lunge. Twirl.

I kicked out at my opponent as he came near, but like a cat, he sprang out of my reach at the last moment. Sweat trickled between my shoulder blades. My shirt stuck to my skin as salt stung my eyes and coated my lips. I'd never worked this hard in my life. I would get stronger, but I had to learn to fight smart.

di Taro came at me again and instead of reacting to his charge, I engaged in one of my own. The force of the blow knocked him off his feet.

I stood over him, bouncing from one foot to another, expecting him to lunge forward. He didn't.

"I think that's enough for today, Maya." He lifted his hand to the back of his head and rubbed.

"Again," I demanded, swishing my blade in front of him.

He shook his head and got up. "I'm done for the day."

Done? He couldn't quit. I had too much to learn. "I don't want to quit. I want—"

di Taro sent me a frown. "I said—"

"It's glowing!" Baby yelled as she barreled into the room.

Both di Taro and I glared over at her.

"Th-the stone," she stammered, pointing in the direction in which she had come. "It's glowing!"

Without another word, I dropped the sword and ran toward one of the small back bedrooms.

Poison, along with everyone else, met us at the door, his body a tight whip of fear. "It's not time yet. He's got one more day."

I pushed past them to where di Taro had chained Snap to a bed. The room was only big enough for a bed, a side table, a closet and a mirror that hung on the wall opposite the window. As di Taro entered, he pointed to the kids. "Out. All of you!"

I stood by the bed and watched as the stone glowed brighter in Snap's hand, sending jolts of energy through his body and contorting his limbs. The chains rattled eerily in the confined space. As I watched, I realized I had seen this before. A dream.

Baby knelt beside me. "He's not alone."

di Taro pulled Baby to her feet. "Don't start, Baby." He shoved her at Cade. "Get her out of here."

She yanked her arm from his and glared up at di Taro, tossing her blonde curls defiantly. "I'm not playing. Someone else is near, and he's not good."

From what I knew about Baby, I was beginning to suspect she wasn't making it up. It sounded as if she could feel spirits. But I had to be sure.

I stepped between the two, my attention firmly on Baby. "What are you saying?"

Fear spiked her cheeks a pale pink even as it drained the rest of her face of all color. "Someone else is here," she whispered. With her big baby blue eyes grown wide, she stared at Snap. She looked like an old fashioned black and white photo retouched to highlight only her cheeks and irises.

"It's the demon," di Taro rumbled.

Cade stepped forward, panic filling his eyes. "It's using the stone on Snap, making him worse." Before anyone could stop him, he wrenched the rock from Snap's clenched fist. The amber pulsed heat, burning his fingers, and he dropped it to the floor with a curse.

"No," Baby and I both cried, but it was too late.

The room suddenly turned icy cold and dark. di Taro pushed Baby toward Cade and yelled at them to leave just as Snap's eyes popped opened. He sat up, a hiss of anger on his lips. His cold breath slipped past a pair of threatening fangs.

"Snap," Baby yelled as Cade struggled to get her out the door.

The boy's gaze raced around the room. Confusion and panic swarmed over his face, revealing every emotion he felt. I knew those feelings—to be dead and then miraculously alive. Yet Snap wasn't like me. He was more demon than human. Because of Cade, the stone hadn't healed him completely like it had me.

Finally, the boy's gaze stopped on the chains binding him. He lifted his arm to test the steel, and then looked up at di Taro with questioning eyes. "What's going on?"

The question was delivered with such obvious guilelessness, it took me aback.

di Taro took in a sharp breath. "Snap," he said with a sigh, his relief clearly visible. He took a step forward.

"No," Baby yelled. Her heart beat made the vein in her neck jump erratically. "Something isn't right."

The way she looked, the sound of her voice…I took a step back, but di Taro still wouldn't listen. "It's Snap. Even I can see that."

"No." The force in her voice finally broke through, causing di Taro to hesitate. On a whispered note of fear, she said, "It's Snap, but… it isn't."

di Taro's face grew pale. "Is it a demon?"

Horror filled Snap's eyes. His face grew taut. "I'm not a demon. I swear. I'm me."

Baby pushed out of Cade's hands and peered at Snap as if trying to look beyond the skin and into his soul. The intense scrutiny should have made him uncomfortable, it would've me, but he leaned forward. Anticipation transformed his face.

"Wait." Something in his look warned me, and I grabbed Baby's arm.

Snap growled. His chains suddenly broke apart as if they were made of string, and he vaulted off the bed. Baby screamed and Cade grabbed her and pulled her from the room. di Taro put himself in front of the door, and Snap knocked him into the wall. Hard. di Taro crumpled into an unconscious heap.

When Snap turned to follow Cade and Baby out of the room, I slammed the door closed and stepped before it.

A foolish action, but if I were to die, I'd at least give the kids a chance to get to the weapons and defend themselves.

Snap slapped me away from the door, but as he made to open it, I launched onto his back and yelled di Taro's name. He didn't even twitch. So much for the big save. I was on my own.

Snap peeled me off and tossed me onto the bed. I didn't have time to think, just react. We rolled along the mattress. His fist connected with my face and body too many times to count. My lip split. My cheek swelled. He pinned me against the headboard and slammed my head into the hard wood. Once. Twice. Three times.

Straddling me, he wrapped his hands around my throat. Blood pulsed thickly through my veins and thrummed against his fingers. A purple haze of anger flushed his face. His nostrils flared as his gaze lowered to the point just below my jaw.

Blood lust flared within his gaze, and his canines lengthened into lethal-looking fangs. Colors collided. My vision narrowed. I saw only Snap. I heard only his ragged breathing in my ears as he lowered his fangs toward my neck.

If di Taro didn't waken soon, I'd be another body dump in an abandoned building and a sad headline.

Under my disbelieving stare, Snap's anger melted and he yanked his hands away. His fangs retreated and a distraught look crossed his face. He looked from me to his hands and then to di Taro.

"Oh God, what's going on?"

Without another word, he sprang off me, ripped open the window and jumped. It was graceful in its execution, but startling to see. One moment he'd been there and the next he was gone.

I curled onto my side, clutching my middle and gasping for breath, my eyes fixed on the window. One overpowering thought entered my head. I was truly sick of being strangled by demons.

Baby and the boys rushed into the room, weapons raised, game faces on. di Taro moaned as he slowly came to, and I, still gasping for air through my bruised throat, eased myself into a sitting position against the pop and squeak of the bedsprings. Cade ran for the window and glanced out. Turning back, his eyes told me everything I needed to know. "He's gone."

"What happened?" Poison asked. "It wasn't Snap, huh? It couldn't have been."

"You think?" Cade said, his voice heavy with sarcasm. "Perceptive of you."

"Shut up," the younger boy snapped. "You're the one who screwed up."

Baby drew a shaking hand through her bouncy curls. "It was Snap. I saw him…but there was someone else."

Poison frowned and turned to Wiggy. "What's that mean?"

"He's got a squatter in there with him, doesn't he?" Wiggy said, his young face reflecting an adult understanding. "The stone nearly fixed him, but then…" he glanced at Cade, "dumbass here interrupted the process and left a gap big enough for a demon to get in."

Snap was possessed. I didn't even want to think of the torture he'd endure. Men did horrible, despicable things when possessed by evil. I didn't want to say it, but there was no way around it. "I think you're right."

"Well, shit! That can't be good," Poison offered, looking from one person to the next with a heart full of worry.

"We've got to find him," di Taro said as he finally stood, wobbly yet ready for action. With a steadying hand to the wall, his gaze encompassed us all. "Not only is Snap a danger to himself, but he's proven deceitful. We have to find him before he gives in to the demon inside him."

A hush fell over the kids. This was what they did—they hunted evil. "And if we do find him?" Cade asked.

di Taro didn't want to say it, but he gritted his teeth and forced the words out. "*When* we find him, we do what we have to do. What I should have done to begin with."

Baby shook her head, pure horror staring out from her eyes. "We can't *kill* him. Part of him is still Snap!"

di Taro rubbed the top of her head with an absent hand and muttered as he headed for the door, "You'd be surprised at what you can do when you have no choice.

Alden

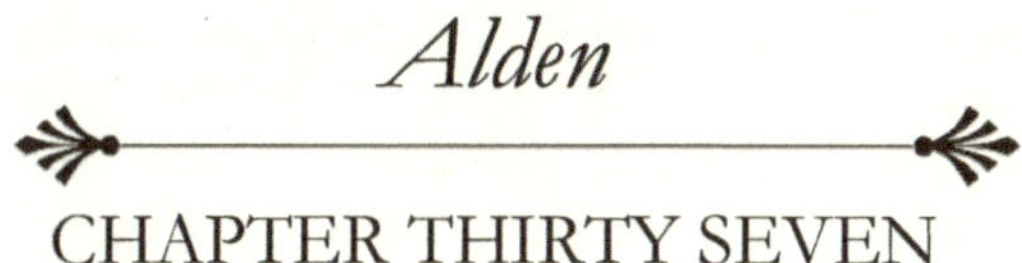

CHAPTER THIRTY SEVEN

With my hood pulled forward to shade my face like a delinquent thug, I slumped against the shadows of the abandoned warehouse, rampant mold and filth infecting every inch of its crumbling façade. I'd been in rougher neighborhoods, and in crueler times. I was used to fading into my surroundings, being an invisible spectator to an ever-changing world…but I'd never been so aware of the loneliness that now bit at my soul.

Barely a week had passed since I'd run out on Maya. How could I explain my actions? I couldn't expect her to listen, not now, not after she believed I'd abandoned her, something I promised I'd never do.

Truth be told, I couldn't have stayed.

God, how it hurt to deny myself what I wanted the most. Yet my love for my unknown child grew with every breath I took. The need to smell her scent, to hear her voice was overpowering. But above all else, I had to keep her safe. Odd how I could feel such a bond with a child I'd never seen. But it was there. Strong and insistent, an alpha male's need to protect and defend his own, much as Juliana predicted I would behave. Her cruelty lived beyond her death.

Juliana's demise had left a hole, but one not long for this world. Vilmos stood ready to capture Juliana's crown of power. I'd seen him search the streets for the remnant demons, the orphaned pets and the disillusioned humans, and they had crawled to him like the slaves they were, ready to obey a madman so long as he served their base needs. Never underestimate the perverse drive of evil infecting this world. It'll consume until it grows bloated and chokes on its own pleasures.

Vilmos would waste no time in gathering the coven under his dark wings. And I knew, without a doubt, he'd search out Maya. He'd be delighted to find her alone and vulnerable. My imagination worked overtime, envisioning her bitten and dumped in a dirty alley or a darkened corner of a forgotten street in Boston.

Though I feared the worse, I found her safely guarded in the loft with that odd group of dysfunctional humans. di Taro and I had made a deal. He'd keep Maya safe and hone her skills so I'd be free to search for my child. Though I knew he'd never hurt Maya, I had no doubt when he got the chance, he'd put a knife in my back. It was a demented sort of confidence, but one I trusted.

From deep within the shadows, I gazed up at the loft and prayed for one last glimpse.

At the point where darkness was nearly over and morning was but a sigh away, Boston sat in a suspended state of expectation. If one listened hard enough, one could hear it crying over the evil the night had brought. And the only hope of salvation came from a motley crew housed within an ugly warehouse on the edge of society. I could only pray that hope wasn't just an illusion.

The third floor windows showed a faint light. All night, I'd seen kids come and go, seen Sundquist enter and leave, but not Maya. She'd stayed inside.

But was di Taro strong enough to keep her there until she was ready? Soon she'd want to leave and face the demons. She'd kill. She'd get hurt. She'd see things no one should have to see. di Taro had won. He'd gotten the slayer he wanted. And what did I get?

Sleepless nights.

My worry had split, an even nightmare between Maya and my daughter. Doubt that the child existed nipped at my mind. Was I abandoning Maya for a pointless hunt? I couldn't believe that. Juliana's cruelty always had its feet in truth. That's what made it so sweet for her, knowing the end result would bring about real pain. I would hunt for my daughter. I'd search what was left of the covens scattering the world and tear them to shreds until I found her. I would hold back no mercy.

My lonely vigil would soon come to an end. I'd leave before the sun rose, but I waited a moment longer. I wanted just one glimpse. And then it happened. She stood at the window, her face pointed toward the sunrise.

"Maya," I whispered.

As if she heard me, she turned and peered toward the gloom where I stood. She raised her hand and pressed it to the window, her face tight with expectation.

In a heartbeat she disappeared. I pushed my hood back and strained to see where she'd gone, and then she reappeared across the street. For a split second, she stood there, barefoot in jeans and a t-shirt. A vision of purity. Of home. And then she ran toward me. I opened my arms, feeling their emptiness, and longed to full them. Her. Only her.

A breath of fresh air swirled around me as our bodies collided. Her arms wrapped around my neck. She buried her face in the hollow of my shoulder, and I pulled her close, breathing deeply of her scent.

"I love you," I whispered huskily in her ear. "I'm so sorry. I shouldn't have left like that, but…"

Tears sparkled against her cheeks as she pulled away. "Don't."

She kissed me. The touch a mere moment in my long life,

but it was the sweetest moment I'd ever experienced. She broke away, her hands caressing my face as if she were afraid I'd disappear again. "You're here now. That's all I care about. Come inside."

I brushed my thumb over the trail of her tears, my heart thumping madly in my chest. I had brought her so much pain, how could I bring her more? I stared into her eyes. "You know what I have to do."

Her hands stilled. I could smell her wariness, the tang of panic. "Let me come with you. di Taro has a brother who fell in love with a woman who was cursed by a witch. She took him with her to find a cure. Why can't you take me with you?"

She spoke what I feared the most. It was why I'd left. I touched a bruise on her cheek, one she had gotten from fighting, no doubt. A cut slanted along her bottom lip. "Look at you."

Her hand rose to her face. "It takes a lot to hurt me. di Taro thinks I'm indestructible."

"No one's indestructable."

"I know."

"You're not ready."

She stubbornly held on to her desire. "I don't care. I can't let you go."

"I *have* to go. I *have* to find her." How could I make her see I wasn't abandoning her? This was about righting a wrong. About saving a life. I brought her hands together and kissed her knuckles, staring into her eyes. "You did it. You freed my soul. I'm asking you to let me finish what I need to do."

I could so easily make her let go, but I wouldn't. I'd never force my will on her again. "Please, Maya. I need you to let me find her. I can't be at peace until I do."

She blinked back her tears even as misery seeped from her very being. It wrapped itself around me, and my heart broke within its grasp. I was asking too much. She would never forgive me now.

She brought her forehead to our clasped hands and her body shook with a deep breath. When she raised her head, the misery she felt was still there and something more. "How can I say no? She's your daughter. You have to go."

I almost didn't dare believe her, but the look of pure love shining from her eyes convinced me. I crushed her to my chest and pressed my lips against her temple. "I won't stay away. I'll come back and see you whenever I can, but until you're ready, I can't risk you coming with me."

Our lips met. I poured a longing of a lifetime into that kiss. I felt her tremble, and then she pushed me away, and said on a ragged gasp, "The next time you see me, I'll be ready. I swear it."

Before I lost my will to leave, I pulled away. Turning, I loped down the alley and away from the person I loved more than anyone else. She was safe. Tomorrow and every day after that, I would travel this street in my mind. I would remember the feel of her in my arms, and God willing, one day, the dream would turn real, and I would stay and never leave her again.

ACKNOWLEDGMENTS

A huge thank you goes to my critique partners, Tammy Baumann, Louise Bergin and Robin Perini. They aren't shy about telling me when I've hit the mark or not. Thanks for making sure I don't embarrass myself. But the biggest thank you I owe to my family. Year after year, they put up with me, humor me and tell me I'm not crazy. For such sweet lies, they deserve big hugs and tons of kisses.

ABOUT THE AUTHOR

Shea Berkley has a fondness for characters, whether in real life or those she makes up in her head while she's tending to a multitude of mundane tasks she's forced to do in order to survive. Writing gives her purpose (okay it keeps her out of trouble…mostly), and she can't imagine herself doing anything else.

AUTHOR'S NOTE

Thank you for reading *Stone Cold Dead.* I hope you enjoyed it!

If you'd like to know when my next book is available, you can sign up for my new release e-mail list at www.SheaBerkley.com. You can also like my Facebook page at www.facebook.com/SheaBerkley or follow me on Twitter at @SheaBerkley. I'm on Goodreads at www.goodreads.com/SheaBerkley, where you can see what I'm reading and post reviews.

P.S. If you enjoy reading this story, I would appreciate it if you would help others enjoy this book, too.

Lend it. Please share it with a friend.

Recommend it. Please help other readers find this book by recommending it to friends, readers' groups and discussion boards.

Review it. Please tell other readers why you liked this book by reviewing it.

www.ingramcontent.com/pod-product-compliance
Lightning Source LLC
LaVergne TN
LVHW041107080826
845145LV00007B/1715

* 9 7 8 1 9 4 2 3 7 3 0 2 5 *